crown

of

lies

CROWN
OF
LIES

BY

NEW YORK TIMES BESTSELLER
PEPPER WINTERS

CROWN OF LIES

PEPPER WINTERS

Crown of Lies
Copyright © 2017 Pepper Winters
Published by Pepper Winters

Published: Pepper Winters 2017: **pepperwinters@gmail.com**
Cover Design: by Cover it! Designs
Editing by: Editing-4-Indies (Jenny Sims)

DEDICATION

This book is dedicated to all those eagle-eye readers who will most likely notice I'm an English-born writer who uses words with pesky S's (tantalise), double L's (travelled), and the occasional extra U (favourite). I've done my best (and enlisted help) to catch the English in this American book, but to any New Yorkers who spy a few…all I can say is, I tried. I now have a love-hate relationship with Z's, learned a boot is a trunk and a lounge is a living room, and just how magical one language can be with two correct ways of writing.

Happy reading!

PROLOGUE

IN EVERY GIRL'S life, there is betrayal.

Betrayal from loved ones, unknown ones, and from the ones we choose to make our own. However, where there's deceit, there's trust, too. And sometimes, those two things camouflage themselves to mimic the other.

That was what he did.

The man who first stole my body and then stole my heart was the ultimate magician with lies.

I think a part of me always knew what he kept hidden. I always suspected and maybe that was why I fell for him despite his deceit.

But then his fibs fell apart.

And it was up to me to decide if I wanted to give him

trust

or

betrayal.

CHAPTER ONE

"YOU CAN'T BRING your daughter to work on a weekend, Joe."

"Says who?"

Steve crossed his arms, doing his best to come across as strict but failing. "Says you."

I hugged my frilly dress-covered chest, my head bouncing like a volley-ball between Dad and the man who helped run his company. My back tensed, waiting for their voices to climb and anger to emerge, but their elderly faces remained happy.

Ever since Mom died four years ago, I'd become susceptible to outbursts of emotion. I hated when Dad raised his voice or someone had a fight in public.

Dad looped his arm around my tiny shoulders, hugging my body to his. "When did I say I couldn't bring my darling daughter to work on a Saturday, Steve?"

Steve winked at me, his dark blond hair trim with his mustache bushy. "When you wrote the rule book for your company, *Joe*. There was fine print."

I knew they were joking—playing a game I couldn't figure out. I'd been to the office every day of the week, including Saturdays and Sundays. But because they expected me to buy into their little drama, I did.

I allowed myself to act younger than I felt, even though I was still a child and shouldn't grasp age and maturity just yet.

Mom's death and my induction into the workforce from a tender age had given me two ideals to follow: adulthood and adolescence. A lot of the time, I was treated and responded like an adult, but today, I didn't mind acting younger because I *wanted* to be younger for a change.

I wanted to be allowed to cry because today had become a massive disappointment and if I was a kid, I could let my hurt show. If I was an adult, I had to suck it up and pretend I was fine with it.

My sadness originated from something so stupid. I shouldn't care—especially seeing as I knew better. But Dad had let me down on a silly birthday tradition, and I didn't know how to tell him I was sad without coming across as a pouting kid who didn't value everything she already had.

"Rule book?" I piped up, glancing at Dad. "You wrote a rule book like school has? Is it as stuffy and strict on silly things like sock length and uniform?" I wrinkled my nose at Steve's crumpled shirt and creased trousers. "If you did, how come you're not dressed the same?"

Dad wore pressed slacks, gray vest, and a blazer with navy piping on the sleeves. Every cuff and pleat were military in perfection.

He looked nothing like the other suited men in his high-rise building, especially Steve in his shirt-wrinkled glory.

But that wasn't new.

Dad had been immaculate every day of his life since I could remember. Even in the photos of him holding me as a new-born at the hospital, he'd been in a three-piece suit with a chrysanthemum (Mom's favorite flower) in the lapel.

Steve chuckled. "Your school has a uniform, Elle?"

He knew this. He'd seen me here after school in my despised splendor.

I nodded. "I hate it. It's scratchy and gross."

"But you look so adorable in it, Bell Button." Dad hugged me closer. Secretly, I loved his cuddles (especially because we only had each other now) but outwardly, I had a twelve-year-old reputation to maintain.

Still playing their game, I sing-songed, "Daa-ad. You said

you wouldn't use that name."

He cringed dramatically. "Whoops. I forgot." He tapped his temple. "I'm an old man, Elle. I can't remember everything."

I nudged him with my shoulder. "Just like you forgot you wrote a rule book saying no daughters allowed on weekends."

"Exactly." He beamed.

"And how you forgot my birthday?"

Whoops.

I didn't mean to say that, but I'd bottled it up all morning. I did my best to joke, but my hurt refused to hide. He'd never forgotten before. He'd always woken me up with a silly gift and then done whatever I wanted for the afternoon.

Not the case today.

I'd turned twelve, and there'd been no cake or candles— not even a birthday hug.

Instead, he'd cooked me toast, told me to dress smart, then dragged me to work with him. He took me to the office often, but I'd hoped today would've been a trip to Central Park together, or at the very least, lunch at my favorite Thai restaurant.

Is fun no longer allowed?

Now I was older, did I have to earn an income like he'd kept telling me? That it was time to put the meager few years at school into practice?

I thought he was joking.

Then again, he was joking with this whole role-play. My heart skipped, doing its best to understand what was going on.

Steve gasped. "You forgot your own daughter's birthday?" He tutted, shaking his head. "Shame on you, Joe."

"Watch it. I can still fire you." Dad's face contorted as he struggled not to smile. He gave up, allowing a broad grin to spread. "That's the reason why I broke the rules and brought my daughter to work on Saturday."

I froze, unable to stop the happiness fizzing into being.

Wait…does that mean he didn't forget?

"What…to make her slave away?" Steve's eyes rounded. "Could've waited until she was thirteen, at least." He winked at me. "Let her see the world before shackling her to this place."

"She'll have plenty of time for that." He hugged me close, marching forward, pulling me with him. "Come along, Bell Button."

I rolled my eyes. "Again with the Bell Button."

"Deal with it." He chuckled, his graying hair catching the neon lights as we strolled down the wide hallway. The view of downtown Manhattan sparkled in the windows. Sitting regal on the forty-seventh floor, the offices of the CEO and top managers of Belle Elle never failed to impress and terrify me.

Dad owned this building along with a few others. He was loaded, according to the girls' gossip at school. However, only I knew how much time and energy he put into his company and was very proud of him. But also scared what he would expect from me now I was older.

For years, things had been changing. My childhood had ended two months after Mom died, revealing how different both our lives would be from then on. No more fairy-tale stories or bedtime read alongs.

No more *Aladdin* or *Beauty and the Beast*.

No more make-believe.

Instead, Dad read me ledgers and showed me catalogs of new season apparel for the company. He gave me homework on how to navigate our website and taught me how to decide if buying a dress at two dollars was good sense if we sold it for nineteen. To work out rent, taxes, employee salaries, and other overheads to see if that dress would make any profit (turned out it was only twenty cents after expenses and too low to make a sustainable profit).

I'd lived and breathed this place since I was so young. And now, it seemed it even controlled my birthday.

Dad stopped at his office and held the entry wide for me to scoot through. I continued to his desk while he closed the door. I loved his desk. It reminded me of an ancient tree that'd been outside our brownstone for years until it was cut down.

Throwing myself into his comfy leather chair, I spun around, kicking his drawers to increase my inertia on the second spin.

"Elle." Dad blurred as I spun again. He wasn't mad. His face split into a smile as he chuckled. "You'll make yourself sick."

I planted my hands on his desk, coming to an abrupt stop. "No, I won't. Those ballet lessons helped with my balance, remember?"

He nodded. "I do. You were a lovely swan in the Swan Princess."

I smiled, forgiving him for forgetting my birthday because really, spending time with him was all I needed. Here or there, it didn't matter as long as he and I were a we. "You need me to try some of the kid's clothes today?" I reclined in his chair. "Help design the window display from a girl's point of view?" I'd learned how to do all that, and I was good.

The company—Belle Elle—had been in my father's lineage for longer than I could comprehend. One of my great, great, too many great grandfathers had called his little shop Belle Elle after his wife, Elizabeth Eleanor, whose nickname was Belle Elle. I knew that because multiple case studies on my ancestry and newspaper articles existed. It was yet another element of my homework: to learn as much about our legacy as I could because in this world—where the US didn't have a royal family—we were classified in some circles as blue bloods.

Long standing citizens of an empire that'd been here since colonization. Slowly growing bigger and delivering more products from basic coats and hats for men and parasols and shawls for women, to full wardrobes, housewares, entertainment, and jewelry for any age.

Belle Elle was the largest retail chain in the US and Canada, and someday, it would be mine.

To a twelve-year-old girl who had fun playing dress-up with child-size mannequins once the customers had been kicked out, helped staff arrange new window displays, and could take costume jewelry home occasionally because her dad could write off a necklace or two, I was excited at the thought of this being mine. But to the woman slowly evolving—the one groomed on an hourly basis for such a future—was afraid.

Would I have what it took to control such a place?

Was it what I wanted to do with my life?

"I didn't forget your birthday." Dad linked his hands in front of his vest. "But you already knew that because you're my daughter and the brightest girl in the world."

I smiled, dropping my head in embarrassment. His praise never failed to warm and comfort me. I wouldn't tell him I'd worried to begin with.

I truly thought you forgot.

He continued, "Today is a very special day and not just because you were born." He plucked a piece of lint off his blazer, looking every inch a powerful CEO rather than the loving father I knew.

No matter where we were going, he always wore a suit. He made me adhere to the same strict wardrobe of pressed blouses, dresses, and smart trousers. I didn't, nor had I ever, owned a pair of jeans.

Perhaps today that would be my present.

I sat quietly, politely, waiting for him to continue.

"I brought you to work to give you two presents."

Phew, he truly didn't forget.

I tried to hide my eagerness. I knew how to camouflage my true feelings. I might be a child, but I was born an heiress and had been taught to act unaffected in every situation—good or bad.

"Look to your right."

I obeyed, reaching out to touch the black binder that always rested there. Dad would bring it home with important documents inside then take it back to the office with yet more vital paperwork. I was never allowed to touch it unless he was around—and only then to bring it to him.

I hesitated as my fingers ghosted over the soft leather.

He smiled. "Go on, you can open it."

I pulled it toward me and cracked it wide. There, like all the other times, were white, crisp pages scarred with multiple black lines of adult jargon.

"What does it say at the top?" He popped his middle blazer button and perched on the side of the desk. His long frame towered over me but not in a bad way; more like a willow tree where I liked to curl up and nap in Central Park on the rare days Dad did nothing.

"Last Will and Testament of Joseph Mark Charlston." My eyes raced to his. "Dad...you're not—"

He reached out and patted my hand. "No, Bell Button. Not yet. But one can never be too careful. Up until last week, my Will and Testament left the running of our family's company to Steve until you came of age. However, I never felt comfortable bequeathing such responsibility to someone outside the Charlston family."

I gnawed on my lip. "What do you mean?"

He pulled a pen from the small gold holder on his desk. "It means I've had it revised. I have no plans to leave this world early, so don't worry about that. And you, my dear, are beyond intelligent for your age, so I know you'll take all of this in your stride. Your education about our processes, factories, and employee structure will be accelerated, and when you're ready, you'll become CEO, and I'll step down."

My mouth fell open. That sounded hard. When would I have time to go to school and make friends other than the staff in the makeup department where I hung out when he worked late?

But how could I say no? I was all he had. He was all I had. We had to stick together.

My heart lurched, needing confirmation he wasn't going to leave me, despite his assurances. "You're not dying, though?"

He shook his head. "Never, if I had my way. This isn't meant to scare you, Elle, but to show you how proud I am of you. I won't deny that it will be so rewarding to hand over this legacy sooner rather than later, knowing with all my heart you will take it to even greater heights than I ever could." He passed me the pen. "Initial each page and sign."

I'd signed enough contracts even at my young age to know how to do it. Stocks that he'd put in my name; a house he'd purchased in some state I'd never heard of—even a limited edition painting that came from an auction house in England.

Bending over the paperwork, I curled my fingers tight around the pen, ignoring the sudden shakes. This was no different from all those other documents, yet it was so much more. This was my life. This was more than growing up and celebrating a birthday. This was every day, every moment, every final say that would manipulate me until I was Dad's age. I didn't have the luxury of figuring out if I wanted to be a doctor or an astronomer. I'd never go to the Olympics as a swimmer (even though my instructor said I was more rock than dolphin). I'd never be anything more than Noelle Charlston, heiress of Belle Elle.

My heart beat with a strange squeeze as I placed the pen on the paper.

"Oh, wait a sec." Dad pressed the intercom to connect him to his receptionist. "Margaret, can you come in, please?"

Immediately, a pretty, middle-aged redhead entered and came forward. Weekends were no different from weekdays in this company. "Yes, Mr. Charlston?"

"I need you to act as a witness."

"Sure." She smiled at me but didn't say anything as I flipped through the seventeen pages and initialed each, then took a deep breath and signed my name. The moment I'd finished, Dad grinned and spun the deed to Margaret. "Your turn. Sign in the witness box, please."

I passed her the pen.

She took it. "Thank you, Elle."

My nickname (not Bell Button—which remained a mystery on how it came about. Dad said it was something to do with how much I loved buttons when I was little, and bell rhymed with Elle) reminded me how I'd been named in a roundabout way for the first wife of our company. The woman who'd created an empire beside her husband until he'd died of pneumonia, and she ruled on her own for forty more years. Elizabeth Eleanor—the original Belle Elle.

Scrawling her signature, Margaret passed the contract back to my father.

He signed in the last box with utmost concentration and an air of relief.

"Is that all, Mr. Charlston?" Margaret asked.

"Yes, thank you." Dad nodded.

She gave me a small wave, before retreating to her adjoining office, leaving Dad and me alone once again.

He looked up from signing, his older eyes meeting mine. His face fell. "What is it? What's wrong?"

I shrugged, doing my best to seem carefree and not think about how big of a throne I had to fill. "Nothing's wrong."

He frowned. "You look…afraid."

I am.

I'm afraid of a world where you're gone, and I'm in charge.

I'm afraid of not being the daughter you think I am.

But he could never know that. This was my duty. My birthright. No matter my age or experience, I knew enough to know my existence was always destined for Belle Elle.

I smiled. "I'm not. This is just my face."

He chuckled. "All right, 'just your face.' Seeing as giving you our legacy for your birthday—ensuring you'll forever have wealth and stability—isn't a present to get excited about, look under my desk."

Happy butterflies replaced the fearful moths in my belly. "You mean…there's more?"

His eyes twinkled with fatherly love. "Of course, there's more. Now look."

I scooted the chair back and glanced between my dangling legs. Tucked against the back was a box tied with a big purple and silver ribbon.

The fear of responsibility and the weird obligation of having my life already mapped out for me vanished. I bounced in the chair. "You got me a present!"

He bent over and kissed the top of my head. "You're my entire world, Elle. I'd never forget the day you came into my life. And I would never dream of making you sign stuffy documents without giving you something fun for your birthday."

"Thank you so much!" I beamed, impatience to open my present stampeding through me.

"You don't know what it is yet."

"I don't care. I love it already." My eyes latched onto the box, desperate to see what it was.

He took pity on me. "Go on, open it."

I didn't need a second invitation.

Plopping off the chair, I crawled on all fours beneath his huge desk and tore eagerly at the ribbon. It fell away, pooling on the carpet. Cracking the lid, I peered inside.

The gloom beneath the desk made it hard to see, but then a tiny gray face appeared.

"Oh!" Full body shakes quaked through me as excitement and adoration exploded. "Oh! *Oh!*" I reached into the box and pulled out the cutest ball of fluff I'd ever seen. Falling onto my butt, I cuddled the kitten close. "You got me a cat?"

Dad appeared, pushing his chair away and ducking to my level. "I did."

"But you said I couldn't have any pets. That we were too busy."

"Well, I changed my mind." He turned serious. "I know the responsibility I'm putting on you, Elle. I know all of this is hard to figure out when you're barely starting life. And I'm sorry you don't have the freedom some of your friends do. I've been strict with you, but you're such a good girl. I thought I'd better give you something you actually wanted for a change."

I cuddled the kitten harder. It didn't squirm away or try to swat me like the cat in the pet store did when I snuck in on my own one day while Dad was distracted. This one purred and nudged its head beneath my chin.

Tears sprung to my eyes. Love billowed and overflowed. Somehow, I loved this little bundle as much as I loved my dad, and we'd only just met.

Gratefulness quickly overshadowed the love, and I placed the kitten on its feet, crawled as fast as I could toward Dad, and barreled into his arms.

"Thank you." I kissed his rough cheek. "Thank you!"

He laughed. Wrapping me in a tight embrace, he smelled so comfortingly of lavender soap. The same soap Mom used to make and stank up the house with while cooking a new batch.

"Thank you so much. I love him."

The kitten padded toward us and mountain climbed onto our joint lap.

Dad shook his head. "It's a girl. She's twelve weeks old just like you're twelve years old." He unwound his arms as I plucked the little kitten and buried my face in her sweet smelling gray fur.

"What are you going to call her?"

I frowned, taking the question seriously. "Silver?"

"Silver?"

I kissed her head. "Her fur looks like silver."

Dad chuckled. "Well, it's a perfect name."

"No, wait. Sage."

"Sage?"

"I want to call her Sage."

He didn't need to know I remembered most of the herbs and aromatherapy oils Mom used to make lotions and soaps. Sage was the last herb she'd given me a lesson on, and the leaves had a silver fuzz over them. Whenever I thought of that day, Mom felt closer and not so far away in Heaven.

I nodded firmly with my decision. "Yes, her name is Sage."

He gathered me close again, kissing the top of my head.

"Whatever you decide, I hope she looks after you, like you'll look after her."

I rubbed my nose against the kitten's cold, wet one, shivering against the weird sensation. "She will. She's going to come to work with me every day." I hunched, cradling my new best-friend. "Is that okay? Can she come to work with me?"

Dad's face fell again. What he said was true. He was strict with me, but he was strict with himself, too. He missed Mom just as much as I did. Did he think I wouldn't love him as much now I had a pet?

I reached up and touched his sandpaper cheek. "I love you."

Light returned to his gray eyes. He hugged me tight on his lap, our little trio squishing into one entity for a second. "I love you, too, Elle. And you don't have to ask if you can bring Sage to work. She's yours. As long as she's not on the shop floor, you can take her to the offices and do whatever you want."

I sighed in happiness as Sage navigated the cliff-top created by our legs. "You're the best dad ever."

His smile faded, the joy of the moment lost as he shook his head. "I'm not, Elle. I know I can never replace your mother and I know I'm asking so much of you to pick up the mantle of this company so young, but I love you more than anything, and I'm so grateful to have you in my life."

His words were heavy for a twelve-year-old. And they remained heavy even years later.

That birthday was ingrained into my memories for two big reasons.

One, I would never be lonely again thanks to Sage being in my world.

And two, Dad knew what he was sentencing me to and did it anyway.

I thought Belle Elle already owned me.

I was wrong.

CHAPTER TWO

<u>SEVEN YEARS LATER</u>

WHO KNEW TURNING nineteen would be such a sad day?

I sniffed back a stupid tear as I inputted end-of-the-month financial figures into the spread-sheet to prepare for the M.M.M.—also known as the Monday Morning Meeting.

I'd been at the office since seven thirty—just as I had every morning since I left high school at sixteen. I'd left because I'd learned all the generic life hacks the teachers had in their arsenals and didn't have the time, or the need, to go to university before my birthright gobbled me up entirely.

Belle Elle was my university, and I'd been attending nights and on weekends my entire life. As far as my knowledge and skills went, I was capable of running this company even before I hit twenty.

My father had made sure of it.

I was no longer a lonely little girl craving the freedom of her peers. But a resigned young woman who carried the livelihoods of thousands of staff upon her shoulders. It was up to me to ensure Belle Elle ran smoothly and made a profit to fill the pay packets and make sure employment continued.

My hard work and long hours were rewarded with positive yields and exciting business expansions. I earned satisfaction from new contracts and cheaper production costs. I'd never been to a party or acted out because work began too early to stay up late.

I lived and breathed merchandise and balance sheets.

And I'm fine with that.

I knew no other life. I had no right to feel so trapped. I had an amazing father, an incredible future, and everything I could ever want. I'd been given so much, but the price of such power and greatness was the removal of so many things I'd never enjoyed.

I'd never had friends because who wanted to hang around a geek who didn't know how to play? I'd never walked around the city on my own because the world was far too dangerous. I'd never gotten into trouble or done anything reckless. My days were surrounded by bodyguards, drivers, and managers.

The girls I knew from school only pretended to like me when I gave them discounts on dresses and shoes. In fact, the week before junior prom, I'd suddenly become the most popular girl in school, only to hear them whispering in the changing rooms at Belle Elle about how much they were saving thanks to lying to my face about friendship and the discount I'd given them.

And the boys were afraid of me because I spoke like an adult and crunched real-time spread-sheets in math rather than solved the basic algebra equation on the whiteboard.

I was never alone but forever lonely.

If it weren't for Sage, I'd probably have run away by now. But I couldn't leave her, and I *definitely* couldn't leave my father.

They needed me.

Everyone needed me.

Thinking of the little fluff ball made her appear. The sleek, pretty cat hopped up onto my desk, deliberately knocking over the old Tic-Tac holder full of paperclips. She swatted it again for good measure.

Instantly, the stress of the day and ache in my back from hunching over a desk for too long receded. "Hello to you, too."

She meowed, her cute gray face scrunching up as if she disapproved of me working past dark once again.

Ever since Dad gave her to me, she'd never left my side. The only time she wasn't with me was while I was at school, but seeing as that was over a few years ago, she was now my silent silver shadow. She traveled on my neck like a living scarf and trotted after me when I hosted meetings with men three times my age—who tried to trip me up and belittle me at the start of my reign. They soon learned I might be young, but I knew this company better than any of them.

Belle Elle was my mother, my best-friend, and boyfriend. It was my world.

Taking off the black framed reading glasses I'd taken to wearing after staring at a laptop for hours at a time, I scooped Sage up by her middle and dragged her onto my lap.

She purred loudly as she head-butted my chest. I kissed the back of her neck, nuzzling into her. Her fur was as soft as spun moonlight; her purr the only thing that made me shed the constant feeling of anxiety and despondency.

"You know how I feel, right?"

She purred louder.

"Am I a horrible person for feeling trapped?"

She pulled a face.

"I do everything that's asked of me. I take over more and more elements of the company with no refusal. I love my father with every bone in my body. I've dedicated my life to making him proud. I have self-worth, wealth, and the knowledge that I'll never have to ask for anything." I pressed my face deeper into her fur, doing my best to stem the unwanted self-pity. "So why do I feel so lost, Sage? Why can't I shed the idea so much more is out there besides work?"

She meowed, jumping from my arms to my desk and walking across my keyboard to scatter qwerty keystrokes in boxes where only numbers belonged. I tried to get mad, to yell at her because she'd just caused another ten minutes' worth of work to delete her tampering and ensure the numbers I'd inputted were still correct.

But I couldn't.

Because work was my life, and life was my work. I had nowhere to be, no one to see—nothing demanded anything of me but Belle Elle.

"Maybe that's my problem?"

Sage flicked her tail.

"Maybe I need to forget about work for a change and do something completely different." Standing, I moved toward the floor-to-ceiling glass windows and looked upon New York below. Twinkling lights, cars, and pedestrians appeared and disappeared beneath streetlights like different bugs—some large, some small—but all of them moving with purpose.

What would it be like to be down there with them? To wear jeans (gasp) and eat food from a street vendor (oh, no)? To be on my own, rather than watched by a driver and bodyguard.

Don't I deserve to know what else is out there before I give up everything?

Today, I'd turned nineteen.

I was old enough to have sex but not old enough to drink. I was old enough to run a billion-dollar company but not old enough to wander alone in a city promising such adventure.

My fingers flew to my neck, clutching the beautiful sapphire star necklace my father had presented me with this morning. We'd both been pressed for time but he'd sent the cook away, and together, we'd whisked up buttermilk batter and created a mismatch of blueberry pancakes before he gave me my gift.

It'd been a wonderful morning, and I'd treasured his company, the pancakes, and my necklace, but I couldn't help feeling like something was missing.

Mom was missing, of course.

But something else.

Someone else…a friend on two legs instead of four.

After an hour together, Dad and I had headed to work and lost ourselves in the cogs of such a demanding mistress.

I didn't know if he was still in his office working late, just like he would never know if I snuck out and pretended to be a girl from a different life for the night.

Wait…what?

The idea came out of nowhere. The betrayal and willingness to sneak behind my father's back was a horrid, terrible concept. Yet…so enticingly exciting.

You could do it…just for one night.

Do what?

The five points of the sapphire star bit into my fingers as I glanced at the congested street below again.

Be one of them.

Do what they do.

Go where they go.

Be free.

My heart bashed my ribs as the idea slowly manifested into potential.

Tomorrow was yet another day belonging to Belle Elle. But tonight? Tonight was my nineteenth birthday, and I'd yet to give myself a gift.

Could I do it?

Could I be brave enough to leave my world and everything I knew in order to sample what I could never have?

Could I seek something I didn't know how to find?

Sage wrapped herself around my ankle, head butting me with approval. Or at least, I'd take it as approval because suddenly, I couldn't imagine *not* doing it.

The prison gates I'd lived behind all my life creaked with rust and whined with disapproval, slowly hinging wide. I had a few short hours before the clock struck twelve and the enchantment of my birthday would vanish.

It's now or never.

Tonight, I would give into my urges and taste freedom for the first time.

And tomorrow, I would stop these childish regrets and fully embrace my crown as the Belle Elle empress.

CHAPTER THREE

MY FIRST STOP was the shop floor of Belle Elle.

Being our flagship location, the merchandise section took up multiple levels of the skyscraper. We sold everything from top-of-the-line technology to baby toys and everything in-between, and I knew every nook and cranny. I'd spent the majority of my life helping design displays and solving stock issues.

But not tonight.

Tonight, I wasn't there on business.

Taking the elevator down from the offices, I swiped my keycard and entered my passcode to prevent the alarms going off. The store had shut to the public an hour ago, and the hushed world of cotton and silk welcomed me.

I clipped in red high heels past pantsuits and high-fashion attire straight to the teenagers department. Ever since I'd signed Dad's Last Will and Testament—and even before that— I'd dressed like a woman. I'd never dressed in a garment with a popular quote or profanity like the kids at my school. I'd never worn anything valued at less than four hundred dollars.

That was about to change.

Browsing the racks of diamante encrusted jeans and off-the-shoulder tops, I found myself critiquing the display and position of the mannequins rather than shopping for an outfit.

Stop it.

You're a customer right now, not the boss.

Forcing myself to exhale and loosen my shoulders from

stress, I stopped beside a table with discounted denim. I grasped the pair neatly folded on top and shook it. The baby-blue washed jeans had a skinny leg and silver embroidery on the pockets.

I did my best not to recall the cost of bulk buying these from Taiwan. How I'd placed the order at the start of last year to be out for this season. How, even on sale, we were still making money because that was how businesses worked. Price high and then slowly discount until no more remained in stock, our margins slowly narrowing but still profitable.

Ugh, stop it.

You're not an heiress tonight. You're just Elle. A nineteen-year-old about to break all the rules and go out.

What would my driver, David, say when I didn't call him in a few hours to take me home? What would Dad say if I had so much fun tonight and I didn't return home until daybreak?

Does it matter?

You have to do this for yourself.

You're an adult.

Clutching those thoughts, I stole the pair of jeans, pilfered an off-the-shoulder cream and black top from the rack beside it, scooped up a black lace scarf from the new arrival podium, and traded the clothing department for the shoe emporium.

If I was going to walk around New York until midnight, I had to wear comfy shoes.

My blood-red heels would have to go.

Eyeing up a rack of recently ordered sneakers, I decided on a pair of white ones with rose gold piping—something I would never be allowed to wear as the figurehead of a billion-dollar company.

I'd worn heels every day of my life since I could remember. The only difference was they were lower when I was a child, and now, they were soaring, sharp stilettos.

Taking my new wardrobe into one of the changing rooms, I once again found myself assessing the locks on the doors and the wobble in the mirror from the second-rate glass. No flaws should exist in any aspect of our sales experience.

I made a note to have all the mirrors replaced next time we overhauled this department.

Slipping from my pencil skirt and black blouse, I rolled down my stockings and frowned at my underwear-clad form. The black bra offered support to my generous B-cups, but would the straps look hookerish peeking out from the off-the-shoulder top?

I had no experience dressing like this, even though I'd gone to countless runway shows and hand selected the latest fashions.

Suck it up and stop procrastinating.

Tugging the tight jeans on, I slipped the top over my head and secured the lacy scarf around my throat. I made sure it hung loosely so as not to cover the blue star glittering on my skin.

Ugh, no.

I yanked the scarf off again and draped it over the door. It wasn't needed.

I touched the sapphire star. This would kill my father if he knew how unhappy I was after he'd given me everything. I could never explain the emptiness inside when I was so blessed on the outside. And I could never admit that I'd heard him discussing my love life with Steve the other day. Wondering if now was the time to parade me in front of New York's finest bachelors in order to find a willing right-hand partner to run Belle Elle.

I shuddered as I traded my stilettos for the white sneakers. The thought of giving my life to a company that'd always been there was one thing. The idea of sharing my life with a man who would never understand me was appalling.

A meow sounded, followed by the streak of silver fur as Sage appeared under the changing room door.

I scowled. "What are you doing down here?"

I ought to regret teaching her to jump up and swat the buttons on the elevator. She was like Houdini with her ability to chase me down anywhere in the building, no matter if I'd kept her in my office or taken her to a meeting.

"You know you're not allowed on the shop floor."

She flicked her tail and leaped onto the small stool where I'd placed my pencil skirt. She meowed again then licked her paw.

"You also know you can't come with me tonight, right?"

Her head wrenched up as if I'd uttered some terrible curse.

She spread her claws and licked between them, daring me to say such blasphemy again.

I ignored her display of feline annoyance, pushing her off my uniform. "You heard me, Sage. Don't pretend otherwise." Bundling the clothes up, I took one last look in the mirror and decided I looked sufficiently teenagerish. I sure looked nothing like the head honcho of Belle Elle.

"Good." I nodded, fluffing up my blonde hair that cascaded down my back to my waist. Dad constantly moaned for me to have it cut, but it was my one rebellion. The length wasn't practical, and most of the time, I just let it air dry into messy waves. The only part of the perfect rule-abiding CEO that was wild.

Heading back to the shop floor, I grabbed a shopping bag from beneath one of the many cashier stations and tucked my expensive clothes inside. Once folded neatly, I tucked the glossy bag into the cupboard beneath the till where manila folders rested with daily tasks and checklists.

Two more things and then I would be ready to go.

I need a coat in case it gets cold and some cash.

I hadn't brought my handbag down from my office. Not that it would've made a difference if I had.

I had no cash. If I needed something, my assistant bought it for me. I only had a credit card for emergencies (not that I'd ever used it), and my I.D badge to access restricted parts of the building.

Sage joined me from the changing room and prowled down the aisle, dragging my attention to a small table with funky purses on display. Seeing as I'd stolen jeans, a top, and a pair of shoes already, I supposed taking a purse wouldn't matter.

And hell, while I was at it, I might as well take some spending money, seeing as there wouldn't be anyone to buy me anything tonight.

Using the universal key attached to my lanyard and badge, I unlocked the cash register and looked at the float. There were no big bills, only regimented change ready for a new day of transactions. The rest of the day's takings would already be counted, bound, and in our vault, ready for a bank run.

No matter.

Three hundred dollars in twenty-dollar bills would be fine.

Taking the wad, I wrote a quick note on a Post-it: *Noelle Charlston borrowed $300 in petty cash. Please contact her assistant, Fleur Hemmings, on extension #4456 to reimburse for morning business.*

I placed it where the bills had been (so no one would get into trouble for missing money), closed the till, and headed toward the purse display. Selecting one with a graffiti skull on a black background, I tucked the cash inside. The loneliness and strange lostness inside me slowly trickled away, blossoming into fear and excitement.

I flashed the skull wallet at Sage. "See, I can be a rebel if I want to."

She licked her lips, her whiskers quivering.

Stepping around her, I beelined for the final thing on my list.

I'd never worn anything less than thousand dollar cashmere coats. However, tonight I would wear…

I tapped my fingers, deliberating the jacket choice.

Tonight, I'll wear a patent leather black bomber with a price tag of $19.99.

Pulling it off the hanger, I fondled the cheap material. I'd always wanted to wear something like this. As I slipped it on, two emotions skittered: terror and the sudden desire to return all the clothes to where they belonged, and eager frustration to begin my exploration of the Big Apple.

I was afraid.

I was excited.

I was so sick of being sheltered and only being good at one thing.

It's time for that to change.

"Happy birthday to me." I tucked the wallet into my bomber jacket pocket, scooped Sage from the floor and rubbed her nose with mine. "I love you, but you can't come."

Her little face pouted.

"Don't look at me like that. I won't be gone long."

She meowed sadly.

My heart squeezed, but I steeled myself against her guilt trip and headed toward the elevators. Walking was so much easier and comfier in sneakers than heels. *No wonder people choose them over fashion.*

"I'm sorry, Sage, but it's only one night." Holding her firm with one hand, I pressed the button to summon two elevators.

One to go up and one to go down.

The up one came first, and I plopped her into it. Giving her a smile, I pressed my office level on the top floor. "Go back. Curl up in your basket. You won't even notice I'm gone."

She meowed again as the doors slowly closed.

I whispered, "Don't look at me like that. It hurts too much."

I hugged myself the moment she'd gone, feeling utterly alone and terrified.

Why am I doing this?

I should forget it and just go home.

But then the down elevator pinged and waited for me to be brave and commit to one night away from Belle Elle.

Hesitantly, fearfully, I stepped into it and prepared to become someone else.

Someone free.

CHAPTER FOUR

EVERYTHING seemed different.

Everything is different.

The air tasted richer. The traffic sounded louder. The temperature felt cooler. Even the sensation of cheap vinyl around my shoulders and cushy sneakers on my feet was different.

Nineteen years and this was the first time I'd been introduced to the world without finery or rules keeping me barricaded from living.

I inhaled deep, coughing a little as a taxi spewed exhaust. The burn in my throat was so foreign to the filtered air of the Belle Elle building that I grinned rather than grimaced.

The purse with its cash whispered to be spent, and my identification badge remained hidden in my pocket, reminding me who I was and how irresponsible I was being.

I had no phone for Dad to contact me. No method of communication or way of calling for help if I got lost or into trouble.

I was willing to put myself at risk just to live a little; to taste a different life to the one I'd been given.

I couldn't lie and say it wasn't exhilarating, but it was also absolutely *terrifying*.

Those first few steps away from Belle Elle physically hurt. The ache in my chest at disappointing my father hollowed me out until even my excitement at doing something new couldn't fill.

A few times, I second-guessed myself and almost turned around. I stopped, spun, and looked back at the huge hulking building where the shopping mega store was run.

But then I reminded myself if I didn't do this, I would never know what it was like to be normal. So I sucked it up, turned back around, and put one sneakered foot in front of the other, slowly entering the empire of downtown New York.

Strangers bumped into me, tourists asked me to take their photograph, and street vendors yelled about their wares directly into my face.

The sensory overload slowly eroded my shame for sneaking out and forced me to pay attention to every minor thing.

For hours, I walked.

I stared.

I breathed.

I let life take me wherever it wanted for a change. I had no idea where I was going or how to get back, but I let my feet get me lost because I had money to catch a taxi home. I knew my address—I wasn't that sheltered. I could afford to go wherever I wanted, and at the end of my adventures hop in a cab and return with a new depth to my existence. And a secret I would happily harbor forever.

At some point, I must've done a block and looped back on myself, so instead of turning left when I arrived at Times Square, I turned right and continued letting the city show me what I'd been missing.

Flashing billboards tried to convince me I needed the latest Jeep and Hummer. Hollywood stars and starlets glowed in LED wonder with snippets of upcoming movies. *Madame Tussauds* promised wonders forever encapsulated in wax, and *Ripley's Believe It or Not!* beckoned me to see things not common in everyday life.

Walking past a souvenir shop, a bunch of clocks held up by mini Statues of Liberty showed I'd wandered for a while.

Ten p.m.

By now, if I'd stuck to my routine, I would be at home, fresh from a quick treadmill-run and shower. I would answer a few last-minute emails and crawl into bed to read the latest romance before my eyes closed and the e-reader bopped me on the head.

Not tonight.

Tonight, strangers smiled or yelled—depending if they wanted me to do something for them or get out of the way. I either moved too fast or too slow, unable to fall into the rhythm of the mismatched crowd I'd adopted. My jacket overheated me from walking and being cramped into streets with sweaty people made me claustrophobic. My feet were flat, and my tummy was empty.

But nothing could detract from how freeing and awe-inspiring every experience was.

Turning another corner, I spotted a food truck promising the best Mexican this side of the border. Hadn't one of my bucket list items been to eat from a street vendor?

It might make you sick.

Yes, it might. But food poisoning would be yet another adventure I'd long been denied. Pulling the purse from my pocket, I joined the queue and waited my turn. As I shuffled to the front, I craned my neck to look at the guy leering down in a grease-spotted apron.

"What can I getcha?" He chewed a piece of gum, fingers twirling his pencil in impatience.

I narrowed my eyes at the menu behind him. "Um, what do you recommend?"

He scoffed. "Recommend? Lady, do I look like I have time to shoot the shit with you?" He pointed at the crowd behind me with his pencil. "Hurry up. I got paying people to feed."

I opened my wallet and pulled out a twenty. "I'll just have something chicken." I handed him the money. "Oh, and not hot. I don't like spice."

"Got it." He snorted. "Chicken and bland. Boring order

for a boring girl."

I tensed. "Excuse me?"

He looked me up and down. "Beat it, princess. Your order will be ready in five minutes. Pick-up is at the window down the truck." He tossed me a dirty ten-dollar bill. "Here's your change."

I curled my fingers around the money, annoyance and hurt making equal acid tracks inside me. I'd never been talked to that way. No one dared.

The fact he'd called me boring, when I completely agreed with him, pissed me off even more. I wadded up the money and threw it at him. "Know what? Add a beef something or other to that order, too. And make it extra spicy."

I walked off toward the collection window before he could insult me anymore.

CHAPTER FIVE

THE BEEF WAS a bad idea.

After collecting my dinner, I strolled toward Times Square where a few tables and chairs had been placed for milling pedestrians. The table was filthy, the chair rickety, but I'd never eaten with such vibrancy as my entertainment before.

The tinfoil wrapped burrito steamed with flavor as I opened it and inhaled. Determined to prove the greasy man wrong, I took a bite of the beef, chewed, and grinned.

It's not so bad.

Then the heat began.

My tongue shrivelled up.

The Mexican food kicked me hard. Quicker and hotter until my grin switched to a gasp, wheezing in spicy agony.

Water!

Oh, my God, I need water.

My eyes streamed with tears as I grabbed both burritos, left my commandeered table, and bolted toward the convenience store blinking with billboards of ice-cold water and cola bottles.

Charging inside, I yanked open a glass-fronted fridge, grabbed a water, and tore off the cap. I downed it in three seconds. And *still*, the fire burned my tongue and lips.

Gasping, I grabbed a chocolate milk.

Struggling with the cap, I finally got it open and took a few greedy sips. The full-fat milk helped temper some of the hateful rage. I exhaled a sigh of relief.

"I hope you're going to pay for that." A shop girl with pink hair raised an eyebrow.

Wiping my lips with the back of my hand (something I would never do in my real world), I nodded and collected another water bottle while somehow hugging my mostly-untouched burritos. "Yes, sorry. The spice caught me unaware."

She grinned. "Oh shit, did you piss off Pete?"

"Pete?" I placed the two water bottles (one full, one empty) and the half-drunk chocolate milk onto the conveyer belt.

The shopkeeper passed them over the scanner, ringing up the sale. "Yeah, the guy who owns the Mexican street meat." She giggled. "He makes a mean taco, but man, he's cruel on the hot sauce."

I ran my tongue over my still stinging lips. "I kind of asked for it." Shrugging, I smiled. "I don't get out much. I wasn't aware not to antagonize food sellers."

She bagged my purchases. "Yep, everyone knows that. Especially not to piss off the street kings."

I dug into my wallet and pulled out a twenty. She took it, opened the register, then passed me my change. The fact she spoke to me with no tension or concern made me relax.

I was so used to talking to women from a boss-employee relationship. No one joked in my presence or told me what to do in case I fired them. And those who did try to befriend me only did so for a promotion or raise.

I could taste fakery like a rotten apple.

We shared another smile before awkwardness crept in. I didn't know how to end a friendly conversation or even when to leave after buying something.

The girl saved me from standing there like an idiot. "Well, you have a good night. And don't piss off any more people, you hear?"

I nodded. "Got it. Thanks for your help."

"No sweat." She gave me a small wave before

disappearing from the till to finish stocking a shelf with chips.

Making sure I had both burritos and my valuable liquids to get me through the fire-breathing dragon of Pete's revenge, I left the shop and re-entered the manic world of shoppers and tourists.

I ducked and jived through the crowd, intending to sit back down and try the blander chicken burrito, only to find my table and chair had been nabbed by a family with three young children who blinked glassy-eyed with tiredness in the glow of the bright neon lights.

All the other tables were occupied.

Oh, well.

I don't mind. I can walk and eat.

Laughter caught my ears. I glanced at a table two down from where I stood, where four teenage girls sat. My lips twitched to share in their joke as I looked at what they were laughing at. Horror slammed into me instead.

They sneered and giggled at an elderly homeless man picking up aluminum cans in a trash bag.

I ached for him and the hopelessness of his situation. He was fully aware of the jokes and whispers, doing his best to ignore the girls as he chased a can caught in a puff of wind.

I'd been on the opposite end of homelessness all my life. I'd been born into a role that would ensure I'd never know the pain of cold and hunger. I'd been given so much, and what had I done? I'd run away for the night like an unappreciative teenager.

What was I thinking?

Embarrassment coated my insides. I couldn't look at the clothes I'd taken from Belle Elle or the food I'd bought with money grabbed from the till. Things I had every right to use but somehow felt like I'd stolen and broken my father's trust.

The girls continued to laugh as a can rolled out of the man's trash bag through a tear in the bottom.

I wanted to slap them for their immaturity and lack of empathy. I wanted to forget I'd ever thought I wanted to be a typical girl rather than who I truly was: a capable young woman who would never stand by while another was ridiculed.

Marching toward the homeless man who knocked on fifty (Dad's age) with a scruffy gray beard and holey beanie, I stopped and picked up the can. "Here you go."

He froze.

The way he watched with trepidation and suspicion lacerated my heart. His entire body waited for abuse, fearing what other misfortune I'd bring into his life.

"It's okay." I urged him to take the dinged-up can.

He did, reluctantly.

Once he'd tucked the can into his bag, I looked at the gauntness in his face and the way he licked his lips at my burritos.

My own hunger vanished.

"Here." I pushed the plastic bag containing the water and chocolate milk, followed by the burritos, into his arms. "You have them. I've only taken one bite. I'm not contagious, I promise."

His mouth fell open as he cradled the icy drinks and hot food.

Awkwardness fell and tears I didn't understand itched my spine. The look in his eyes was full of shock and utter gratefulness.

He quickly stuffed the food into the baggy pockets of his jacket and swigged the half-empty chocolate milk until it was gone. Wiping his lips with the back of his hand, he murmured, "Thank you."

I smiled. "You're welcome."

I knew it was time to leave. But I couldn't walk away—not yet.

Pulling my wallet out, I took the twenties, minus eighty dollars for me (as emergency funds to get home), and placed them into his hand. "Please, have this as well. Eat and have a night in a hotel somewhere."

He curled his fingers tightly around the money. "I don't

know what to say."

"Don't say anything." I stepped away. "Have a good night. And I'm sorry for those girls laughing at you. That's terribly rude. We're not all like that."

He blinked as if coming out of a fugue.

"Goodbye." I walked away feeling better and happier than I had in...well, forever.

CHAPTER SIX

ELEVEN P.M. AND the novelty of walking around a bustling city had begun to wear.

I didn't want to spend any more money on food—just in case a taxi cost over eighty. I had no idea how much transportation would be to get home.

My feet ached from all the miles I'd traveled. My back hurt from not being used to standing. And the crowd steadily became less polite and more disorderly as the night grew later.

The jostling of limbs and pushiness made me nervous, and thoughts of returning to a quiet bedroom where I knew who I was and how to play by the rules enticed me.

Stepping from the curb, I shot across the road (narrowly missing a speeding car), and stood on the corner where a pile of rubbish had gathered from passing pedestrians and shop-fronts ready for collection.

I looked up and down the road, hoping to see the yellow glint of a cab. I hated that only a few hours into my bid for freedom, I already wanted to go home. I truly was a boring girl like the food vendor had said.

But at least I'd explored on my own.

I know now I'm not missing anything.

I can put my childish whims behind me and agree the grass is not greener on the other side.

I stood for a few minutes, waiting for a ride but nothing came. Deciding to change my position, I joined the crowds again and carried on a little further. Once the congestion thinned out, I stood in front of a small alley and resumed my search.

Left, right, look and hope.

I stayed in place so I could raise my arm quickly the moment I spotted a cab.

The world faded around me as I focused on waiting for a ride. The allure of soft sheets and quiet rooms helped delete the chaos I'd been a part of for a few short hours.

I didn't notice the two men at first.

Perhaps I was too naïve or blind, but I didn't expect a hand to lash around my elbow on both sides—two men crowding me between them.

My heart leaped into my throat, gagging me from screaming.

My eyes popped with disbelief as they jerked me backward into the alley.

No!

I didn't comprehend what was happening.

Let me go!

I'd never been handled with such force before.

Their touch dug like five-finger traps into my arms.

Hurting.

Bruising.

"Help!" My heart stuck in my throat, preventing any more than a strangled beg. My uselessness gave them all the time they needed.

With a sinister chuckle, they dragged me deeper into the darkness, away from streetlights and people and taxis.

"Let me go!" I struggled, kicking and flailing. "Help! *Help!* Someone—"

But it was too late.

They pulled me further, laughing louder as my feet skidded uselessly on the grimy ground. In some strange recess of my mind, I noticed how dirty my shoes had become. How black now smeared the pristine white.

"No! *Stop!*" I lost my shock-stupor, giving into fighting

terror.

I bent and buckled.

I kicked and squirmed.

But they were too strong.

The street was too far away.

The world was too obsessed to care.

"Let. Me. *Go*!"

"Shut the fuck up." The harsh command was as sharp as a fishhook, digging into my mind with evil.

"What do you want?" I fought harder, winded and so, so worried. "I don't—"

"Told you. Shut the fuck up." They held me tighter, their fingers digging into my flesh like cleavers. "What we want is our business, not yours." One of them laughed.

Three-quarters down the alley, where the sounds of a busy metropolis were muted in favor of rankness from awful smelling trash, they shoved me forward, slamming me against the wall.

The air in my lungs vanished, leaving me empty.

I doubled over in pain as the nodules of my spine crunched against brick. I tried to suck in a breath, my long hair tangling in a mess over my shoulder.

I peered up through the blonde strands, doing my best to formulate an escape. To them, I was an inexperienced little girl who they could rob and hurt with no consequences. I had to prove to them otherwise.

Even if it's the truth.

The men chuckled, nudging each other with congratulations.

I didn't wait to see what would happen next. Pushing off from the wall, I sprinted through the small gap and dug for every bit of strength and courage I had. My mouth opened to scream—to scream as loud and as long as I could—but one man grabbed me, slamming me into his chest. The other plastered a metallic smelling palm over my lips, silencing me.

Sandwiched between the two, I understood my dire

situation.

The terribly, stupid *bad* situation.

"Where do you think you're going, little bitch?"

Hardness, where there should be no hardness, prodded me in the front and the back. They ground their cocks against me.

I shuddered, understanding right away that whatever they wanted from me wasn't just monetary but physical.

And I can't do a thing to stop it.

Tears sprang to my eyes, but I did my best to blink them away. I'd let shock get me into this mess. I wouldn't let pity make it worse.

Their breath turned heavy as they pressed harder into me. Not caring that their heads touched each other in their bid to consume me.

My bones turned to ash as my heart suffocated.

Please, please don't let them hurt me.

Being normal was suddenly the most idiotic concept in the world. I would gladly return to Belle Elle and never leave the crystal tower of business for the rest of my life. I would work every hour, of every day until I died if I could just walk away from this untouched.

Please!

I wriggled in their arms, trying to bare my teeth beneath the guy's palm to bite. He kept my lips firmly glued while his hips thrust against me from behind. His rocking knocked me off balance into his accomplice's sickly embrace. "Know what tonight is, pretty girl?"

My nineteenth birthday.

My stupid attempt at being normal.

I sucked in a breath, dragging in their scents of corruption and filth.

"It's the night you give us a good fuck then, if you're good, we let you go."

Horror flowed like ice water only to solidify into a glacier as his friend whispered, "We want your money and your jewelry as well as your cunt. Give them up willingly, and this will end much better for you."

He reached down, cupping me between the legs.

I moaned like a feral cat about to be butchered.

"Don't and things will get very, *very* bad." His fingers clenched around my core. "Fucking bad. Got it?"

When I didn't move apart from blinking yet more terrified tears from my vision, he pressed his groin into my belly. "Nod if you get it."

I didn't want to obey.

I wanted to tell them to *die*.

His friend snaked his arm around my middle, clutching me so hard my ribs bent, and the hardness in his pants bruised my spine. "Nod, bitch, then we'll let you go." He thrust again. "But if you scream, we'll beat you fucking bloody, and you'll wake up with nothing. Not even your clothes."

My lungs ached from lack of oxygen; caustic terror burned holes in my veins, drowning me in blood.

The man in front kissed my cheek. "Last time. Nod if you agree to our terms."

What else could I do?

I had no weapons, no experience. The most I could hope to do was delay by obeying until I spied an opportunity to run.

Please let that opportunity come sooner rather than later.

It hurt even more than stepping from Belle Elle in shame, but I nodded.

The moment I did, they stepped back. The one in front readjusted his trousers, fisting himself. "Fuck, it makes me hot when they obey."

They?

How many women had they done this to?

The world had been a vibrant adventure before. Now, it was a cesspool of criminals.

The man behind me came to my side, hemming me against the wall. They placed themselves strategically to block my exit. The shadows kept most of their features hidden, but one wore a baseball hat with a red logo, and the other dressed in a white jacket with the Adidas logo on the front pocket. They were the same height (about a foot taller than me) and both had dirty teeth as they smiled matching evil grins.

The one who'd been behind me in his Adidas jacket pointed at my neck. "First, let's focus on the jewelry, shall we? Give me that necklace."

I gulped. "What?"

The one in the baseball cap wagged his finger. "No talking. Do what we say, or you're fucked."

I flinched as he once again fisted the hard length visible in his pants. "First, we get what we want, and then you get what *you* want."

What I want?

My lips curled in disgust.

What I want is for you to drop dead in agony.

His accomplice chuckled. "What you want is a cock, stuck-up bitch. You can't deny it. Well, it's your lucky night. You'll get two soon enough. Now, hand over that fucking necklace."

"Please…" I clamped my hand over the sapphire star that I'd only had since breakfast but already meant so much. "Don't—"

"Breaking all the rules, aren't cha?" A fist came out of nowhere, crashing against my temple.

Bright pain detonated through my skull, forcing me back and sideways against the wall. I couldn't see past flashing lights. I couldn't hear through the ringing in my head. But it didn't stop one of them from grabbing the chain around my neck and yanking hard enough to break. The white-gold sliced into my nape before giving way, making me cry out in pain.

A hand landed on my breast, squeezing hard while a foot kicked my legs open and fingers grabbed between my thighs.

I moaned again, shaking my head to rid the receding punch. "No...stop."

A hand smashed over my mouth. "Shut the fuck up."

My vision slowly came back as Adidas dug his hands into my jacket and pulled out my purse. He counted the bills while

Baseball Cap kept me gagged and pressed half-standing, half-slouching against the wall. "Eighty bucks? Seriously, that's all you have?" His sneer was accompanied by gross breath. "We'll just have to get it out of you in other ways."

Digging his hand into my back jeans pocket, he pulled out my Belle Elle identification card. The flash of my portrait in a crisp black blazer and my blonde hair artfully coiled reminded me how far I'd fallen from my queendom.

If they killed me, my father would never know what happened. There would be no way to I.D my body or any explanation of how I ended up in an alley on my nineteenth birthday and not safe at home with him.

I hated how selfish I'd been.

How *stupid*.

If I survived this, I would never bemoan my life again. I would never take my company for granted. I would live an existence of utter gratefulness.

"Noelle Charlston. Looks like you have a cushy office job." Baseball Cap smirked. "Bet you use that nice ass just for sitting rather than anything else." He leaned into me, pressing his erection against my hip. "Ever been fucked over your desk, office girl? Ever given a boss a blowjob for a promotion?" He thrust hard. "I like the thought of you giving me a blowjob." He nodded at his friend. "Get her on her knees."

I scrunched up my face as I screamed internally.

I'd gone through school without boyfriends of any kind. I'd stolen a single kiss on the dance floor of my high school prom, but it hadn't included tongue. No boys had braved my father to ask me out. I was light years ahead in experience of managing and running a company, but so ill taught when it came to sex.

Blowjob?

No way did I want to do that. I had no idea how. And the idea of sucking on that part of a man made me want to vomit on my dirty sneakers.

But what I wanted no longer mattered.

My knees screamed as they pushed me to the ground.

I daren't look up.

Baseball Cap ducked with me.

Sitting on his haunches, he smirked. "Before we show you ours, you have to show us yours." Before I could argue or move, he ripped off my bomber jacket and tossed it into the darkness behind him. He tore at the off-the-shoulder t-shirt until it hung in tatters, revealing my black bra.

"Let's see what your tits are like."

Everything shut down as his hand moved forward to cup me.

I turned inward.

I tried to delete what was about to happen.

Only, he never connected.

A blur in the dark materialized like a phantom.

A man's grunting erupted.

Adidas fell backward, yanked by an unseen force. Baseball Cap whirled around, his fists up, ready to fight. "Who the fuck is there?"

Adidas groaned as a shadow connected with his stomach then with his jaw. I blinked in disbelief as the apparition stepped into the light, revealing another man with a black hoodie over his head.

He didn't introduce himself.

He twirled around and kicked Adidas in the chest, sending him careening to the dirty ground.

The new guy turned and locked eyes on me. Beneath the gloom of his hoodie, his intense gaze tangled me into knots. For a split second, my heart kick-started from fear to relief then sank back into terror.

First, there were two.

Now, there were three.

I wasn't safe.

Even if the newcomer seemed to fight on my side.

Scrambling to my feet, I pulled at the ruined pieces of my top.

The new guy followed my torn clothing, eyeing my bra. His jaw clenched and a low growl echoed in the alley. Whatever had sewn us together for those few seconds snapped.

He launched himself at Baseball Cap.

He tackled the wannabe rapist to the ground, punching him once, twice, three times in the stomach.

They rolled around, legs kicking, arms whirling until the hooded figure swung a well-aimed sucker-punch right into the nose of Baseball Cap.

The man dissolved from hooligan to helpless. His arms and hands came up to shield his face. His mouth bloody and breath ragged. "Fuck, we give, we give. Stop!"

Immediately, the hooded figure clambered to his feet. Wrenching a hand over his face, he grunted. "Second time I've caught you assholes. There won't be a third."

Adidas pushed off the concrete with both hands, climbing unsteadily to his feet. "Fuck you."

The hooded figure stepped forward and, with a quick jab, delivered another punch into Adidas's throat.

"Ah, fu—" He collapsed to his knees, his hands around his neck, gasping like a lunatic. "I—I can't—breathe—"

To my horror, I smiled a little. I had no sympathy for him, but I shouldn't take enjoyment from such violence.

Should I?

The hooded man pointed at Adidas squirming on the floor. "That was for being rude." His leg came out again, connecting with the white jacket covering Adidas's ribs. "That's for being a cunt." His face turned toward me, but I couldn't see his features in the dark. Never looking away from me, he threw another punch at Adidas's head. It wasn't at full power, merely a swat—a telling off. "And *that's* for her."

Stepping back, he crossed his arms. "Now, what do you have to say for yourself?"

Adidas still hadn't learned his lesson. He spat blood, glistening black in the night. "Fuck you twice, man. You can't scare us."

The hooded man took a menacing step closer.

Baseball Cap dodged forward, nursing a sore arm. He held up a hand in surrender, some sort of chivalry coming through to protect his asshole friend. "Look, we're done, okay?"

The hooded man glanced at Adidas—the asshole who'd been moments away from stealing my virginity. His voice lashed out like a dark whip, demanding obedience. "And you? Are you done?"

Adidas nodded profusely. "Fine. Sure."

"Good." The hooded man held out his hand. Blood marked his fingers, but I couldn't tell if it was from him or his victims. "Cough it up."

Baseball Cap scrambled backward, shaking his head. "Nah, no way." He patted his pocket with a sick gleam in his gaze. "Nah, man. You take the girl. We'll take the cash."

Hooded Man cocked his head. It was nothing more than an innocent move, but it dripped with threat. "Do you want to die tonight, Gio? Because I can arrange that."

Gio?

He knows their names?

How?

Adidas scoffed. "Do you know who you're fucking talking to?"

Hooded Man glowered. "I know *exactly* who I'm talking to and wouldn't your fucking father be glad to hear what I have to tell him?" He pulled his hoodie higher over his face, making himself featureless, a black void. "If you don't stop and call these fucking games quit, I'll do worse than beat you."

What the hell is going on?

I couldn't decide who was scarier: the two men who'd grabbed me or this savior wrapped in black.

The hooded man's voice was a menacing growl—a mix between gravel and velvet. His body was lithe beneath the oversized hoodie and holey jeans. He looked like a skater-rat—the poster child for rebellion and lawlessness.

He had the air of one of our in-store billboards with a

rough and ready skater in a half-pipe selling baggy jeans and chain belts with a spray can in his hand. When I'd approved the marketing, I'd feared it was a little 'rough' for our clean brand for teenagers. Turned out, that banner was tame compared to this man.

Baseball Cap stepped forward. "Hand over the money, Sean."

"Oh, for fuck's sake," Adidas grumbled, reluctantly pulling out my cash. I didn't care about the money, but if the faceless savior wanted to return my property, I wouldn't argue.

Hooded Man held out his hand.

Sean, the Adidas punk, angrily shoved the dollar bills into his grip. The second the cash changed hands, it vanished into the hooded man's jeans like a magic trick.

He turned to me, his face still a dark secret. "Did they steal anything else?" His gaze traveled down my front where I held my torn top together.

I flinched under his inspection, wishing my bra didn't peek out behind my hands, and my bare stomach wasn't so on display. My head pounded from the punch, and the pungent whiffs from the alley didn't help my swirl of nausea.

When I didn't reply, Hooded Man pointed at my destroyed top and discarded jacket on the floor. "Did they? Steal anything else, I mean? They tore your clothes. Do you want me to ruin theirs in return?"

My eyes widened. "Wh—what?"

His head tilted, hearing me speak for the first time. A low chuckle came from the blackness of his hood. "I can make them strip and run home naked if it would make you feel better." He waved at my tattered top. "You don't need to hide. I won't let them hurt you. You're safe with me."

The midnight rasp in his voice negated his promise. He was the safest of the three—for now. But he wasn't safe compared to my father or staff. He was the exact *opposite* of safe.

I swallowed, standing proudly despite my lack of modesty.

"I have no desire to see such vermin naked."

Adidas sneered. "You want to see my cock, bitch. Can't deny that shit."

I gave him a look I wished could melt his skin off his bones. "Believe me, I would rather go blind."

Baseball Cap bared his teeth. "That could be arranged."

Hooded Man took a step toward me, putting himself between them and me. "As entertaining as this is, I don't want to commit murder tonight." He glanced at me then at the two men who would've raped and hurt me if he hadn't shown up.

What am I doing?

Antagonizing criminals? All for what? A little dignity after having my self-worth threatened?

Holding my chin high, I said, "They stole my I.D card for work. I would like that back."

So they can't break into Belle Elle and I'll have yet more explaining to do.

Hooded Man turned to Adidas. "You heard her. Give her back the I.D."

Adidas cursed under his breath but pulled out the lanyard with my tag from his pocket. The second it switched hands, it once again joined my vanished cash in a blink.

Hooded Man closed the distance between us, turning to face them as he did. He protected me with his body while confronting them. "That's it. Run along."

Baseball Cap pointed a finger. "We'll get you back."

Hooded Man shrugged. "You keep being scum, and I won't be so nice next time."

"You keep thinking you're untouchable and we'll go out of our way to prove you fucking bleed like the rest of us."

Hooded Man stalked forward, his hands splaying before curling into fists. "We can prove you wrong, right now."

"Fuck you—"

"I prefer women but thanks for asking."

Baseball Cap charged. "I'm gonna kill—"

Adidas grabbed Baseball Cap's arm, stopping him midstride. "Come on, man. We've got better things to do."

Baseball Cap fought him, but then a slow smile spread his lips. "Yeah, you know what? We do." He smirked with evil. "*Much* better things." Blowing me a kiss, he said, "Pity we didn't get to have our fun, office girl. Bet you're torn up you didn't get to see what we wanted to give you, huh?"

Hooded Man crossed his arms. "Fuck off—"

He'd fought one battle for me. I wouldn't let him have the credit on this one.

Stepping around him, I let go of my tattered top and stood in my bra-naked glory. The fear. The adrenaline. The *pride*. "You're right that I'm an office girl who has no experience in fighting the likes of you. But you're wrong that I wanted to see your shrivelled-up jerky sticks."

Baseball Cap snarled. "You bitch."

"No, you don't get to call me that. *You're* the bastard. You're delusional and a disgrace, and if you think it makes you more of a man by trying to rape me, I'll do you a favor and cut off that jerky you call a cock and cook it for you." I smiled sweetly. "Along with office duties, I'm not bad in the kitchen, and you and your salami are only fit for frying and feeding to the dog." I held up my hand. "No wait, I wouldn't feed you to my dog, and I don't even *own* a dog."

"Ah, fuck." Hooded Man darted toward me just as Baseball Cap launched himself at my throat.

I stumbled back, only to slam into the arms of Hooded Man who spun me around, shielding me with his body. His fist came up, connecting once again with Baseball Cap's jaw.

"You can't even take shit from a girl without needing to be an asshole?" Hooded Man cracked his knuckles. "She's right. All you have in your pants is dried-up jerky." He swallowed a laugh. "Run along now, before I actually give this girl a knife and watch her fillet you for her frying pan."

Adidas grabbed Baseball Cap for the second or third time—I'd lost count. Together, they backed up. Their eyes black as the alley we stood in.

Baseball Cap raised his finger, pointing at both of us. "You'll fucking pay. Both of you."

Then they turned around and bolted toward the street.

CHAPTER SEVEN

FROM ONE DISASTROUS situation to another.
Silence fell in the alley.
They're gone.
But he's still here.
My skin prickled with intensity from the hooded figure, standing dangerously lethal and so damn close. I didn't look at him. I didn't want to make eye contact or give him any reason to become the villain after being the knight.

I looked at the ground. "Um, I owe you a thank you."

My naked stomach tingled as he scuffed a pebble and turned to face me. The darkness of his hood masked his features, but I felt his eyes lingering on my bra.

The reckless confidence I'd had when facing down Baseball Cap and Adidas vanished. I snatched the ends of my torn top, pulling them closed. The broken material hid a little but not enough of the black lace or swell of my flesh.

My heart bucked.

Had he chased them off because he was a Good Samaritan or because he wanted what they were about to take? Despite his assurances he wasn't like them…how could I be sure?

"Look, whoever you are. Thank you for saving me. But I must insist you let me go." I spotted the bomber jacket Adidas had torn off me and ducked to pick it up. Holding the black material in front of me like a shield, I said, "Step aside. Let me pass."

The glittering lights of civilization promised safety down the long tunnel of the alley. All I wanted to do was go home.

Home.

A taxi.

I need money.

Holding my hand out, I kept my eyes down. "Can I have my belongings, please?"

"Your belongings?"

His deep voice somehow avoided my ears and echoed deep in my belly instead. I shifted on the spot, a chill from him and the night sky painting me in goosebumps.

He came closer, tipping his chin up. Shadows slunk back as if afraid of him as I clutched bravery and looked up.

Everything about him was cloaked. "I won't bite."

I flinched, doing my best to drink in his face so I could remember it—just in case I had to file a police report.

Which I don't want to do as my father must never know about this.

His eyes and forehead remained hidden by his hood, but his lips were in full view. Firm and masculine with just the right amount of stubble that'd turned into a short beard. He was rugged, bordering unkempt.

One hand vanished into his jean's pocket. "Do you mean these?" He fanned the cash and my I.D badge.

I nodded. "Yes, those. Can I have them?"

He counted the bills. "Eighty bucks?"

I tilted my chin. "It's all I need."

Why did I feel like the biggest liar in history? I didn't know what it was like to have only eighty dollars. I had unlimited funds. Just because I didn't shop or had no one to lavish gifts with didn't mean I didn't appreciate the freedom of never having to look at a price tag.

"Need to do what?" He cocked his head, the hoodie still covering his gaze.

"If you must know. To taxi home."

"Ah." He said it like a full stop. As if it made perfect sense to this evening of nonsense.

I wriggled my fingers. "So…can I have it back?"

He ran my lanyard I.D through his fingers. "Let's talk about this first."

"What about it?"

"Your name is Noelle Charlston?"

"What of it?"

"You're named after Christmas."

I huffed. "I'm named after—" *One of the richest founders in retail.* I held my tongue. I didn't need this rescue to turn into a kidnapping for ransom.

"Named after what?" He danced the I.D over his knuckles with a dexterity that made my mouth go dry. A streak of blood marred the laminated photo.

I stepped toward him, despite every neuron wanting to run.

"My name is Elle. Just call me Elle, give me back my things, and let me go."

"I don't think so, Elle. Not yet."

I froze. "Excuse me?"

"You intrigue me."

"So?"

"So, it's not often someone intrigues me."

"Why?"

He moved closer. His body heat was noticeable in the chilly evening. "Because I don't normally take the time to actually talk to people. You're an exception."

I didn't know if I liked being an exception. Did that mean he might do other things that were an exception—like hurt me when he'd normally free me?

Nerves made me shiver. Clamping down on such weakness, my hand lashed out and snatched my I.D card. "There. I've taken back what's mine. You can't get mad. It never belonged to you." My eyes landed on the money. "Give that back, and we'll go our separate ways."

He smiled. His teeth were straight and white in the dark

scruff of his beard. "I don't think so, Noelle Charlston."

"Elle."

"Okay, Elle." He took another step, ungluing shadows from around him until only a foot separated us. I sucked in air as his black sneakers crunched on loose gravel and his hands came up.

I stiffened, waiting for him to take what his runaway buddies had tried. Only, his fingers didn't connect with me, they connected with the material of his black hood. Slowly, he pushed it away and let it fall, revealing his face.

My lungs forgot how to work as I drank him in.

Fierce eyebrows gave expression and authority to the intensity of his dark brown eyes. Dark hair bordering on black curled around his cheeks, forehead, and ears, speaking of wildness rather than tamed. His strong nose and refined cheekbones were perfect adornments to the beard bordering his lips.

Hell, those lips.

They were soft and damp and almost kind when everything else about him looked cruel.

I'd been around men in the office, but all of them were either overweight, older, or gay. I'd never been so close to an attractive male similar in age and completely ruthless in violence.

I stepped back, cursing the wobble in my knees. I wanted to put it down to fear, but my stupid heart said otherwise.

I was *attracted* to him.

Here of all places.

Him of all men.

My body found his utterly appealing for the first time in my life, and I had no idea how to deal with that.

What did that say about me?

I'd narrowly avoided being hurt and somehow indulged in an attraction for a man I'd met in the worst circumstances.

I'm not normal.

Whatever interest I felt could not be tolerated.

I narrowed my eyes. "What do you want from me?"

He smiled, his mouth once again bewitching me. "Not sure yet."

I pinched myself, trying to get my runaway hormones under control. I wasn't some horny teenager. I was a CEO who almost got molested. So what he was good looking?

That means nothing!

You need to go home.

Right now.

Steeling myself against him—grateful when my heart stayed in a normal *thud-thud* and not the desire-fueled flutter from before—I snapped, "What do you mean?"

He shifted, kicking one leg out for balance. It wasn't anything but an adjustment, but it drew my attention down his body. To how tall he was. How his thigh shaped the dirty denim. How he wore mystery like an expensive new fashion must-have. "I mean, there's something about you."

There's something about you, too.

Even the darkness of the alley couldn't detract from three things I noticed right away:

One, he was entirely too handsome (or I'd been far too sheltered to be alone with him).

Two, he had an aura about him that demanded respect that wasn't born but earned.

Three, he was filthy but didn't seem to care as I followed a stain in his hoodie then a scuff then a hole.

He just stood there, allowing my inspection as he repaid the favor. His eyes had fingers, trailing over my skin with gentle feathers, forcing me to catch my breath even though I remained still.

Oh, my God, get a grip, Elle.

Yes, he saved you.

Yes, he was brave enough to stop a crime.

But that's all there is to it, and all there'll ever be.

You are not a silly girl who gets crushes.

Time to go.

Whatever this was meant nothing.

It couldn't.

Things like this didn't happen in real life, and they certainly didn't happen in *my* life.

Just because Dad had stopped reading me fairy-tales long ago didn't mean I needed to fabricate such ridiculousness now.

I forced myself to look at his face. I'd almost forgotten what we discussed, which was idiotic, and crazy, and so unlike me, panic whizzed through my blood, making me curt.

"Money. I need it." I held out my hand, hating the wobble. "I want to leave."

"Leave?"

"Yes."

"You can't leave."

"What?" My eyebrows shot upright as my pulse thrummed in my punch-bruised temple. "Of course, I can leave. I *want* to leave. You said you wouldn't hurt me."

He held up his hand, oblivious to his dirty nails and dried blood on his knuckles. "Easy. You can go. I'm not holding you captive—I didn't mean that."

"What *did* you mean?"

He wafted the money, making the bills flop in his fist. "I mean…we need to talk about this money."

My hackles rose. "What about it?"

He ran his tongue over his bottom lip, distracting me. His gaze locked on mine, either aware of the reaction he caused or seeking answers to his own curiosity.

His voice lowered to a murmur. "I saved your life."

"You did." My voice slipped to a whisper, accepting the quietness almost with relief. Tension unwound from my shoulders only to spool tight again as he said, "I think the generous thing to do is offer me your cash."

Half of my brain knew why—he'd given me a service and nothing in life was free. But the other half was so befuddled, so drunk on his beard-covered jaw and kissable lips, I wrinkled my nose. "What for?"

He coughed with a thread of annoyance. "Payment, of course. For saving you. We just agreed that's what I did?"

Another injection of adrenaline flooded my veins. I nodded, wound up and jumpy with the way he watched me. "You're right. You did save me. It's only right you earn a reward." I wouldn't deny him payment—especially when it looked as though his clothes had seen better days. But I also couldn't fight the small terror of how I would get home.

You walked here.

You can walk back.

Technically, I could. I just couldn't envision walking through the city after what had just happened without jumping at shadows every step.

I'm not cut out for the outside world.

I should've stayed in my tower and played with my cat and ran my father's company like I'd been groomed to.

Hooded Man flicked the money with his spare hand. "Great. I accept. Thank you."

"Thank *you* for saving me."

He flashed his teeth. "You're welcome."

Something switched between us, removing the threat of violence, putting us at an impasse.

His shoulders sagged a little. Glancing at the money, his face darkened as if fighting an internal war. Suddenly, he held out the bills. "Here, take it."

"But I just gave it to you. You're right—"

His fingers latched around my wrist, while his other hand slammed the notes into my palm. "I don't want it."

I gasped at the heat of his touch. At the way my skin ignited beneath his. How the crackle of awareness increased a thousand-fold. And then it was gone as he yanked his hands away and backed up.

Dragging his fingers through his black-brown hair, he muttered, "I should go."

Here was my chance to return home without any more mishaps. I could nod and agree and walk out of the alley to summon a chariot to drive me back to my realm.

But his despondency made my fear switch to empathy. Just as I'd fed the homeless man in Times Square, I wanted to help this one, too.

If he is even homeless.

For all I knew, he was a masked crusader running around the city, getting dirty by helping women like me who had no right being out so late alone.

I broached the small space between us. "I truly am grateful."

"I know."

Steeling myself, I leaned forward and stuffed the bills into the front pocket of his hoodie.

Such a bad move.

Inside was warm with the faint grit of crumbs and life-dirt but against the soft material was a hard stomach, breathing fast.

"What the fuck are you doing?" His voice was a spur, kicking my heart into a frenzy.

I yanked my hand from his pocket, leaving the cash inside. "I want you to have the money. In return for a favor."

His face tightened. "I've already done you a favor, remember?"

"I remember." I glanced at his bloody knuckles where a few had swollen and bruised with injury. "Would you let me look at your hands or at least buy you some Tylenol?"

"No."

Okay...

"In that case, all I ask in exchange for the money is you to escort me home."

Home?

What the hell are you doing?

I couldn't afford to let this vagabond know where I lived. Dad would be mortified. Our furniture and belongings would probably be stolen once he figured out our daily schedule and knew when the house was vacant.

You're an awful person.

How could I think such things after he'd saved me?

Trust.

I had to trust him, despite outward appearances and circumstances.

Believe.

I had to believe in my gut when it said he wasn't to be feared.

I wanted him to have the money over a grouchy cab driver. All he had to do was walk me back.

"You want me to take you home?" His mouth parted. His face remained in shadow, visible but still a mystery. "Are you serious?"

"Yes."

"You want me to know where you live?"

"If you were going to hurt me, you would've done it by now." I opened my arm to incorporate the alley. "We're alone. You already know I'm terrible at escape. Yet you've been a perfect gentleman."

He barked a laugh. "Gentleman? Right." He scrubbed his face, highlighting the dirt on his neck as he looked at the sky. "How do you know I'm not just delaying my attack to put you at ease and make you pliable?"

"Pliable? Who uses the word pliable to discuss hurting women?"

He smirked, lips smiling, eyes not. "Me."

"And who is me?"

He frowned. "What do you mean?"

I put my hands on my hips. "You know my name. What's yours?"

He stumbled back. "You—you want to know my name?"

Was that a bad thing? Had he done something terrible and didn't want anyone to know? "Isn't it normal for strangers to share with another? That's how they stop being strangers."

He coughed, rubbing his nape. "Not where I'm from."

"Where are you from?"

His shock faded, smothered once again with a cocky

attitude. His shoulders came up, proud and standoffish. "You're nosy."

I bristled. "Only making conversation."

"Well, don't. Let's just go, shall we?" He looked around the alley. "I hate places like this."

I wanted to ask what sort of places were those, but I didn't dare. Instead, I focused on how I could get home. "Will you walk with me?"

"You think I'll protect you?"

Well, yes.

"You did before."

"That was because I don't agree with rape and robbery. Not because I have a hero complex. The minute you're out of this alley, you cease to be my concern."

"Oh." I didn't know why that hurt as much as it did. Straightening my back, I sucked up my fear, preparing to strike out on my own—like I always did. "Okay, then. Well…how much do taxis cost to get to Upper East Side?"

One eyebrow raised. "You live on the Upper East Side and have no idea how much taxis are?" He peered harder. "You don't just work in an office for minimum wage, do you?"

I didn't know why, but I wanted to maintain my identity as a low-income earner. I didn't want to come across as bragging, or worse, rubbing his nose in it. The longer we talked, the more I saw what his clothes hinted at.

He either lived rough or didn't have a home. He wasn't like the homeless man I gave my dinner to—this man didn't smell, and his clothes were cleanish (minus a few stains) even if they were a little holey. But he had that scrapper look about him—a glare in his eyes, speaking of mistrust and hardship.

"Let's agree to keep personal information secret, okay?" I asked. "You don't want to tell me your name. I don't want to tell you anything more." I held up my hand. "Agree to take me home, and we won't ask questions. Deal?"

It took a little while, but he finally slipped his hand into mine and shook.

It took everything I had not to react to the desire crackling from his palm.

He smiled. "Deal."

CHAPTER EIGHT

NEW YORK WAS an exciting city to explore on my own.

But exploring it with another person—someone intensely attractive and utterly unpredictable—was one of the most incredible things I'd ever done.

Ten minutes had passed since leaving the alley and in ten minutes, my pulse had skyrocketed then equalized to a steady thrum of awareness.

Walking beside him shouldn't be such an adventure. He was just a man. This was just a city. But every footfall felt different. Every breath and glance and heartbeat.

We navigated the crowds together, pulling apart and re-joining as the curb became congested then empty. Midnight struck the clock in Times Square, reminding me my birthday was officially over and a new day had begun.

I should be in bed.

I should call Dad to tell him I was okay, just in case he noticed I'd never come home.

Worries layered me, taking away the complex, not-entirely-understood joy of strolling through the city at night with a strange man at my side. I did my best to shove the thoughts away, but they remained like a constant toothache.

"This way." The man stepped off the sidewalk and crossed the road, keeping an eye out for oncoming traffic. "You sure you want to walk?"

"Yes, I'm sure."

"Okay." He stuffed his hands into his jeans pockets, his shoulders bunched around his ears. He couldn't be cold. The air temperature wasn't too bad. Although, I had shrugged into the bomber jacket and zipped it up to my throat to replace the ruined top, so perhaps it was colder than I gave credit for.

A fine layer of sweat decorated my spine from walking at his quick pace.

He didn't dawdle like I had. He moved ahead with long, leggy strides, expecting me to keep up. He didn't glance at me or ask questions. It gave me time to steal glances, whipping away memories of his height, mannerisms, and habits.

Not that I could read him.

His body language remained closed off; his arms tucked tight, jaw clenched firm. The beard hid the bottom half of his face, keeping him partially masked and perplexing.

Each step granted different thoughts: recollections of what'd happened with Adidas and Baseball Cap and what could've been the ruining of my body and mind if they'd succeeded in raping me. Followed by the relief that this cryptic wanderer had been there at the right time and saved me.

How could I ever repay that?

He hadn't just prevented a robbery. He'd stopped me from turning into a different person. He'd provided me with shelter from a crossroads that might've switched my existence from Belle Elle heiress to mentally broken dependant.

I wouldn't have let it break me.

But how could I know that? I believed in myself because of Dad's tutelage and support. But I was still young. Nineteen was nothing compared to the years ahead. The years this man had given back to me in a selfless act of protection.

The more we walked, the deeper the debt I had to pay. Shock gave way to realization of how close I'd come to being raped. I could still be in that alley, beaten, bloody, destroyed.

But I'm not.

He turned into more than just a stranger; he became my

shield. A shield I needed to repay by any means necessary because eighty dollars was *nothing* compared to what he'd done.

My thoughts kept me busy as we did another block, heading past closed stores and an occasional drunk pedestrian. I snuck glances at my companion, growing ever desperate to ask questions and learn pieces about him. To talk to the man who I'd only just met but who'd impacted my life more than anyone.

Did he know how grateful I was?

Did he understand what he'd done by saving me?

If he were homeless, I would help him.

If he were struggling, I would pay him.

A life for a life.

I wouldn't stop until I'd saved his as he'd done mine.

His dark gaze captured me. Turbulent and deep, the pools of ferocity and calculation hid softer emotions underneath. We weaved around thinning foot traffic, linked in some kismet way, moving close and apart, tethered with shared incident.

I hated that I'd already lied to him. That I hadn't told him my real profession and hidden who I was. But I liked him believing I was nothing more than an office worker with a shoe box for a home. I liked him thinking I was normal and not untouchable like all the boys from my school had.

I like the way he looks at me.

Like he felt something, too. Something he couldn't understand—something that wasn't sexual or chemical or named. But something tugging us to stay together, to chase whatever it was that bounced from him to me.

I smiled softly, dropping my head as his stare became too intense. The hot blush on my cheeks hinted at my inexperience but also my openness around him. If I didn't feel something, I wouldn't care how he looked at me. If my tummy hadn't turned into a trampoline, my heart double bouncing on my lungs, I wouldn't mind the taut silence slowly growing tighter every second.

My father would be happy I'd found a…friend?

Dad's firm but fair face appeared in my mind.

Oh, no!

My hand swooped to my throat to touch the sapphire star he'd given me—the star that made me feel so close to him. The one he'd bought me out of love.

It wasn't there.

My neck was empty.

They took it!

I forgot to tell him to get it back.

I slammed to a stop, looking over my shoulder as my fingers danced along my naked collarbone. Dad would kill me! He would know I'd been out and mugged because there was no other way I would've let that necklace go.

Shit.

"Is everything okay?" He slowed a little, his arms relaxing with hands stuffed in his front hoodie pocket.

"My necklace. They still have it."

He stopped. "What necklace?"

"My birthday present." I sighed heavily, the weight of tears already crushing. "I know a silly necklace won't mean much to you, but it was sentimental."

He spread his legs, once again drawing my attention to how lithe and fast he looked. "You didn't mention it when I asked if they'd taken anything else."

"I know!" I grabbed my hair, twisting it with nerves. "I forgot. It all happened so fast."

"If it meant so much to you, you should've remembered." His tone wasn't condescending or cruel, but his words bit into me like wasps.

I swallowed my sadness, embracing anger. "It was new. He gave it to me this morning."

"And you're sure they took it?"

"Of course, I'm sure." I spun around, yanking my hair off my nape to show the cut left behind from when they'd yanked the chain. "See?"

"I asked for your belongings to be returned." His face

hardened as if taking my loss personally. "They returned them."

"I know—"

"Be grateful you didn't have to give up something else other than a birthday trinket." He licked his lips, sullen annoyance bright in his gaze. "By the way, happy birthday." He turned and stalked forward, either expecting me to follow or doing his best to revoke his promise to escort me home.

He was right, of course. A silly gemstone in exchange for avoiding pain? It was a small price to pay. But my God, it hurt to think of my father's gift—my beautiful sapphire star—in the hands of those creeps. Being touched by them, sitting in their grimy pockets, destined to be sold to someone who would never know its origins.

Dad will hate me.

Guilt ate at me with sharp silver teeth. My father would understand if I told him the truth about what'd happened—if I was brave enough to admit I'd left without telling anyone. He would forgive me.

But what would this man think of me? He'd rescued me, and instead of being relieved, I'd almost burst into tears because a necklace that was worth a few thousand had been taken.

A life was worth more than a bauble. I wasn't a silly child anymore.

I'd never been a silly child.

I won't start now.

Breaking into a jog, I caught up to him and touched his forearm. "I'm sorry. I made it seem like I wasn't grateful. That I was blaming you for not getting it back." I licked my lips. "I'm not. I'm just sad I let them take it, but you're right. It's only a necklace."

He slammed to a stop, his eyes locked on where I touched him. He swallowed hard. "You don't have to explain to me."

"Yes, I do. I owe you. I don't want you to think I'm some sort of princess."

He shifted, his mouth pursing as he looked me up and

down. "What birthday?"

I blinked. "What?"

"How old did you turn?"

"Oh, um—" I struggled to tell him. Not because I wanted to keep my private life private but because he was older than I was. He looked mid-twenties with hardness only born from fighting every day of his life. I was soft where he was sharp. I knew how to fight but in boardrooms and on conference calls, not on the streets.

He sighed. "I get it. You don't have to tell me." Pushing away, he continued walking; his jeans scuffed by his dirty sneakers.

"No, wait." I trotted after him. "I want to tell you."

He paused as I returned to his side, comfortable beside him even though I didn't know him. "I turned nineteen."

He laughed, low and short. "Wow, I knew you were young but not *that* young."

"How young did you think?"

His eyes tightened. "Twenty, twenty-one."

"That's not a big difference."

He pushed off again, wedging his hands into his pockets, revealing a habit. "Still a teen."

I didn't let that irritate me. "How old are you?"

A slight chuckle sounded as he pulled his hood back up, hiding his shaggy black-brown hair, adding yet more shadows to his handsome face. "Older than you."

With the hood and the night sky, his face danced on my memory, already fading—as if my eyes hadn't captured his features enough to imprint long-term recollection.

I crossed my arms. "Tell me. I told you."

He glanced at me sideways. "Twenty-five."

"Six years. That's not much."

"It's enough to get some people thrown in jail."

"Some people?"

He tossed his head with a tight roll of his shoulders. "Forget it."

We walked in silence for a moment, my fingers trailing once again to my naked throat. I hated that I'd forgotten about my necklace. That I hadn't taken stock and asked for it back. Did that mean I wasn't worthy of such a gift—if I didn't appreciate it enough to remember?

In a rash decision, I said, "You know, if I had remembered to ask for my necklace, it wouldn't have been mine anymore."

He scowled, waiting for me to continue.

"It would've been yours."

Surprise flickered over his obscured face before finally settling into polite refusal. "No."

"No?"

"Just no."

Prickles raced down my spine. Half of me wanted to force him to accept the imaginary gift. A sapphire could've converted to showers and meals and a roof over his head rather than dangle around my silly little neck.

But he hunched his shoulders—not in a regretful way but more regal, more honorable than I'd ever seen. "I don't need your fucking charity."

His curse cut through our odd conversation.

I couldn't undermine his good deed by forcing him to hypothetically accept something he would never have. But he had to know how much I appreciated his help. "I'll give you more money when we get home, okay? I'll make sure you're compensated—"

"I'm not after your damn money," he snapped. "If I was, I could've done what they did and robbed you where there were no witnesses."

The busy city faded around me. "You wouldn't."

"You don't know me."

"You're right. I don't." I ignored my sudden shiver. "So tell me."

"Tell you what?"

"What do you want? Where are you from? How can I return the favor?"

He bared his teeth. "I want nothing. I'm from nowhere. And you can't return it."

I didn't let his fisted hands or taut body sway me. "Wanting nothing isn't true. And you're from somewhere...but I get if you want to keep it secret. Surely, there's something you need." I waved my arm at the congested pavement. "You're not walking for your health." I pointed at his bloody hands. "Talking about health, you should probably have those looked at." I moved closer, grabbing his wrist without thinking.

He stiffened.

Electricity sprang from him to me and me to him and every which way around us until we stood in a web of sparks from just the simplest touch.

His jaw clenched; his eyes narrowed and dark. Placing his hand over mine on his wrist, he ever so slowly pulled at my fingers until my grip was no more. Dropping my hand from him, he whispered, "There is something."

I shook my head, lost and confused and so scrambled I couldn't follow. He noticed the question in my eyes, answering for me. "There is something I want *from you*."

"What? What do you want?"

He glanced away as if he hadn't meant to say that. For a second, he looked like he'd bolt into the crowds and vanish. But then he cleared his throat. "Do you trust me?"

"What?"

His chocolate eyes locked on mine again. "Do you trust me?"

"I just met you."

"Doesn't matter. Yes or no."

What should I say? That yes, in some weird way, I *did* trust him. Or no, I wasn't stupid enough to trust someone who beat up two guys and then kept me longer than necessary in an alley.

He glowered, his intensity once again causing goosebumps. "Yes or no. It's not hard."

Slowly, I nodded. "Yes, I trust you."

"Good." He wrapped an arm around my waist and yanked

me off the footpath. Without a word, he herded me across the road. Reaching the other side, he let me go but didn't move far away.

Shared body heat hummed between us, growing thicker with things I didn't understand. Things all so new and foreign but desperately wanted. "Where are we going?"

"Central Park."

"What?" I slammed to a halt. "You can't be serious. No one goes in there at this time of night. For safety reasons and for security. It's not open."

He grinned; the streetlight above him painted him in a golden glow, looking part angel, part devil. "I know a way in."

I backed up. "I've changed my mind. Let's just go home."

His face darkened then solidified into determination. "You don't get to do that. You just agreed to trust me." He stepped forward, his chest brushing mine. The cheap material of the bomber jacket rubbed the lace of my bra, making me achingly sensitive. My neck bent to look up at him, drinking in the way his hair ran wild around his face, and his beard masked him, revealing only what he wanted to reveal.

"I'll take you home afterward." His hand came up, brushing aside a wayward blonde strand, his fingers kissing the side of my face.

I jolted but couldn't move away. The concrete had turned into super glue.

Before I could reply, he dropped his touch, grabbed my hand, and dragged me toward the wall of Central Park.

He looked over his shoulder as we patrolled the rock barricade. Hauling himself up, he swung his legs over and dropped into nothing.

I dashed to the wall and looked down.

In the darkness, I barely made out his shape a few feet below.

His head tilted toward me, once again cloaked in the shadows he seemed to rule over, only his hands and face visible as he reached up. "Jump. I'll catch you."

You'll catch me?

I wanted to yell, but the occasional late-night dog walker on the other side of the street kept me quiet. This was illegal. I didn't want to get caught. Imagine the publicity if this got out that I'd snuck out on my birthday, almost got molested, gave my dinner to a homeless guy, then gallivanted around the city doing bad things with a total stranger.

Who the hell am I?

I should turn around and find my own way home. I should hop in a cab and pay the driver when he dropped me off with the petty cash that was stored in the cloakroom upon arrival at Belle Elle.

I had so many options.

So I had no excuse when I deliberately chose none of them.

I slung my jean-clad legs over the wall, inhaled deep, and let go.

CHAPTER NINE

HIS ARMS WERE warm steel.

He caught me in my semi-slide as I plummeted down the rock wall. He didn't manage to catch my entire weight, and my legs jarred as they hit the ground, but he cradled my torso with infinitesimal gentleness.

We stayed like that for far longer than necessary, swaying in each other's embrace, somehow deleting the stranger danger and becoming acquainted instead.

He cleared his throat, moving back.

I shivered as his arms unraveled, leaving me to my own gravity, removing himself from my orbit.

He waited until I had my balance before striding into the gloom. "Now that we're in, keep an eye out for security guards."

Fear multiplied. "Guards? As in guards with guns?"

"Probably. Doesn't everyone in America own a gun?"

I hated that he was right. Even my father had one locked in a case at home. Not that he'd ever used it—that was why we had bodyguards.

The thought of how different our worlds were made me self-conscious. What would he say if I admitted that the building glowing the brightest on the horizon was mine? That I crunched numbers and paid bills on a daily basis valued at more than he'd probably seen in his entire life?

He didn't notice my sudden heavy steps as he slinked through the few bushes and disappeared into the dark.

Following him, I did my best not to imagine monsters in the swaying foliage and remain level-headed. I missed Sage. I missed her whiskers and long, silver tail. I missed normalcy and a place where *I* was in charge and not the universe taking me on a jeopardy-filled odyssey.

But even as homesickness filled part of my heart, freedom filled the other. The longer I was in his company, the more I found the confidence to be the girl who stood up to crooks in nothing but her bra. To speak my mind and chase after a man who did strange things to my stomach.

And above all, not to embarrass myself.

Whoever my guide was, he had an air of aloof confidence that made it vital he saw me as strong not weak if I wanted him to notice me and not just pity me.

We didn't speak as we navigated the bushes. A few lights here and there offered illumination, while the flashlight of a security guard patrolling in the distance made us hug the treeline.

"Where are we going?" I whispered.

"You'll see."

Our sneakers scuffed through brush and twigs, so loud to my ears but no doubt unnoticeable by whoever enforced the laws about breaking into this place.

Popping from the undergrowth, we dashed across a path and entered a grassy field with caged baseball courts under the half moon.

"Come on. Hurry." He held out his hand, guiding me toward the super high chain link fence. "Climb."

"What?" I peered into the star-lit sky. "Are you insane?"

He looked over his shoulder as a branch snapped. "Hurry." Pushing me upward, he didn't give me a choice. His hand landed on my ass, searing his fingerprints into my flesh. A comet somehow fell from the dark velvet above and lodged itself in my chest.

It took every ounce of concentration to climb when all I could think about was his fingers touching me where no other man had before.

He followed me, scaling so much faster with experience. Reaching the top, he slung his body over and just let go. His black-clad body fell with all the grace of a jungle cat.

I didn't have the balls.

I crawled over the top—thankful there was no barbwire—and climbed down a few rungs before finally dropping to the stable ground below. My fingers smarted from gripping the harsh metal.

He showed no sign of being affected at touching me in an intimate place so I didn't either—even though my ass cheek throbbed as if he'd spanked me.

"Won't they see us in here?" I glanced around for security cameras. I spied one aimed at the home diamond. "Wait." I hissed.

He turned around, his eyebrow arched in question.

"The camera." I cocked my chin at the lens glinting in the starlight.

"It doesn't work."

The way he said it made it sound as if he knew exactly why it didn't work. *So he's a vandal and a vigilante?*

Fighting my nerves, I paced after him until we stood in the center of the field. All around us (outside the chain link) were manicured lawns and sweeping trees to give watchers a spot of shade on hot days.

Once in the middle of the playing field, he fell into a cross-legged position and tugged my hand to join him.

I struggled against his weight for a second but finally gave in and joined him. The moment I was sitting, he pushed my shoulder.

My abs clenched against his pressure, trying to stay upright.

But it was no use.

His eyes locked on mine, adding more authority until I

gave up fighting and followed his command. Down and down, until my spine kissed the soft grass.

My heart chugged blood like it was starving.

Untangling his legs, he reclined, slowly slotting his body along mine, stealing my breath, making every cell spring into tiny knife-like blades of sensation.

His gaze landed on my lips, drawing awareness and concentration into overpowering levels. My head swam with the possibility of him kissing me. His gaze hooded, his own thoughts of kissing me coating his face.

I didn't know how I felt about him kissing me. Would I let him? Would I scream?

I hated to admit that I *would* let him. That I'd probably kiss him back. That despite my wariness, I trusted him, and if I was going to do something as reckless as kiss a total stranger under the moon in the middle of Central Park, it would be this nameless man.

Is this what he meant when he said he wanted something from me?

Did he think I was easy?

A sure thing?

Even with such awful thoughts in my head, my body didn't buy into the shame.

My chin arched. I licked my lips. The world stood still.

He swayed closer, propping himself up on an elbow to hover his face over mine.

Oh God, he's truly going to kiss me.

My first real kiss.

Something I would remember for the rest of my life, regardless if I remained a spinster to Belle Elle or married a man who would always be second best to my career.

But then…he stopped.

Pulling back, he shook his head and lay back down. "What the fuck am I doing?" Cradling his head in the palm of his hand, he looked up at the moon. For the shortest glimpse, a tortured need glimmered in his gaze then disappeared.

I sucked in a much-needed breath, trying to decide what

the hell just happened.

My mouth went dry. My chest full of feathered wings. Jitters took over my motor skills as I replayed the almost-kiss over and over.

A few minutes ticked past.

The grass rustled as he sat up, digging his hand into his hoodie pocket.

Pulling free a wrapped chocolate bar, he glanced at me with a faint glint of possession and indecision.

My stomach growled at the sight of food, reminding me I hadn't eaten since a mouthful of spicy beef burrito. He smirked at my noisy tummy then courteously but reluctantly offered me the chocolate. "Here. You sound hungrier than I am."

My hand came up, accepting his gift. Waiting to make sure I had hold of it, he dropped his arm. He sighed heavily, finding it hard to tear his gaze away from the chocolate and focus on the moon.

His own stomach gurgled quietly as he placed a splayed hand over his waist and pressed down.

Everything inside me hurt. The vulnerability of him in that moment. The generosity of giving up the only food he had, even though he was most likely starving. I worked with people on a daily basis who would rather throw out entire platters of food than donate it to those in need. The news on TV was full of greed and cruelty and rich assholes thinking only of themselves.

And then there was him.

A man I didn't know. A savior I'd only just met. But someone who had a profound effect on me in the hour we'd been together.

He sighed again, swallowing hard as he finally tore his gaze away and looked at the stars.

When was the last time he ate? Where did he get a candy bar? When was the last time he'd eaten anything more substantial than just chocolate?

My hunger turned to indigestion as I did my best to guess

his story. His body hunched as his stomach stopped growling. His sneaker-covered feet were thread bear and rubber-worn, speaking of so many miles traveled and no sanctuary found. The silver glint of the moon played on the black of his hoodie, making it seem as if he dressed in liquid mercury.

My hands shook as I opened the candy bar and slowly unwrapped it. His jaw clenched at the noise of the wrapper. The soft rustling of grass hinted he wasn't as relaxed as he appeared. The tension rippling off him was that of a starving wolf wanting to attack its prey but finding restraint...barely.

I couldn't stop staring at him. Couldn't stop my heart from pushing through my ribs to go to him. To demand his name, his background, to know how he had such a power over me.

What is this...magic...between us?

Was it like this between any boy and girl? Was the desire to cuddle close and listen as much as the need to curl close and kiss the basis of...*dare I say it*...attraction?

I scoffed.

Attraction?

What do you know about attraction, Elle?

You're a closet romantic who knows nothing but spread-sheets and merchandise.

I was an idiot to believe there was something going on between us—known or unknown, unique or mundane.

The chocolate bar melted a little in my fingers. My tummy churned; I did the only thing I could do. I had to accept his gift now; otherwise, he would know I suspected he was homeless and hungry and would never tolerate my pity.

But I couldn't eat it all because if he *was* homeless, what else would he have? How long would that eighty dollars last him in a city that was so expensive just to survive?

Tearing the chocolate in half, I sat up and placed his half on his knee. "Thank you."

His eyes found mine as his hand latched over the candy. His gaze danced over my face, lips, and hands. His fingers curled almost unconsciously around the chocolate with a feral gleam, just daring me to take it away.

Slowly, he nodded, accepting that I knew things he didn't want to say and agreed to eat because, if nothing else, there was trust between us.

I gave him some space by looking away.

Taking my time, I nibbled on the chocolate, nougat, and caramel, doing my best to focus on taste rather than my physical awareness of him.

It was impossible.

The entire evening—from the perfumed park, to the dewy grass, to the silent man inhaling half a chocolate bar—seared on my mind like an old-fashioned photograph, developing from blurred to sharp with hasty capture. A memory created by this man, this night, and this sugary confectionery. I would never again walk through Central Park without remembering him or how much he'd shaken up my innocent, boring world.

Taking tiny bites to make the treat last longer, I didn't expect conversation. So when a soft murmur interrupted the silence of the park, I jolted.

"Do you come here often?"

I wanted to giggle. It sounded like a cheesy pick-up line. He didn't crack a smile or soften. He was serious.

I looked at him through the waterfall of blonde hair that'd fallen over my shoulder. He'd already finished his dinner (or was that breakfast or lunch or a midnight snack?) Once again, the shadows of his beard and the silver-light made him seem mystical and not quite real. Too handsome to be real. Too *much* to be real.

I swallowed my nerves and chocolate. "Not as much as I would like."

"Why?"

"Because I work all hours of the day. I rarely get to leave the office."

He shifted his eyes from the open field to the tall buildings in the distance with their glowing windows and adult obligations. Belle Elle was the brightest jewel, mocking me, telling me to come home.

"Do you like it? Being cooped up all day with no freedom?"

I shrugged. "Who truly loves their work?"

He didn't reply.

"I get satisfaction from doing a job well done. I like knowing I've done something worthwhile." I looked down. "So yes, I guess I do enjoy it."

He kept his attention on the buildings, glaring at Belle Elle as if he already knew it owned my life and soul, and that whatever this was, it was nothing compared to contracts and lifetime legacies. "It must be nice to afford expensive things like birthday necklaces."

I licked my fingers free of my final bite of candy. "Do you know much about jewelry?"

He threw me a caustic look. "I'm not completely ignorant. Just because I'm—" He cut himself off, returning to stare at the cityscape. "I know enough."

"I'm not saying you didn't."

"Just drop it."

"For your information, I didn't buy that necklace. It was a gift. I did mention that."

He tensed. "From a boyfriend?"

"Would it bother you if I said yes?"

He laughed harshly. "Why would it bother me?"

I shook my head, my cheeks pinking in embarrassment. I had no idea why I'd asked or why it hurt so much that he'd found my question funny. "No reason."

I couldn't look up. The grass was suddenly incredibly interesting. I plucked a few blades, running them through my fingers.

Out the corner of my eye, I saw him twist slightly, his face hidden. Slowly, his hand came up, his fingers nudging my chin. I didn't want to look at him, but his pressure gave me no choice.

I let him raise my head. Our eyes locked and breathing became a task I could no longer perform.

"Do you trust me?"

I trembled as his fingers slowly unfurled from guiding my head up to linking around my nape.

I couldn't speak.

I managed the smallest nod.

His fingers tightened, pulling my face toward his. I sucked in a shallow breath as his gaze dove deeper into mine and his tongue wetted his lips. "I—I won't hurt you."

His whisper landed on my mouth just before he pulled me hard.

Our lips connected.

I froze.

The scent of grass and strange male hit my nostrils. The wildness of open skies and midnight made me uninhibited and free. My eyes grew heavy, closing of their own accord as he added pressure to the kiss, tilting my head with his grip behind my neck.

I gave up every control without a thought. My spine turned to water. My insides to steam.

He groaned a little, understanding my submission even when I didn't.

Scooting closer, his lips parted. The tip of his tongue darted out to test me. Test to see if I trusted him enough to let him kiss me in an empty park. Trust him enough not to go too far or hurt me.

I answered back in the only language I currently knew. My lips opened, my tongue hesitantly touching his with truth. The explosion of chocolate made me moan under my breath as he licked deep inside my mouth.

He didn't hesitate.

There was no sloppiness or confusion. His hand held me steady, his mouth worked mine, and every part of me flared with drowning, dark desire.

He shifted until his knees nudged mine, his arm wrapping

around my waist, deleting the space between us. The awkwardness of sitting on damp grass wrapped in a man I didn't know didn't stop the heat of the kiss from escalating.

Our tongues met and retreated.

Our lips slipped and connected.

With every heartbeat, we increased speed and depth until I lost control of the rest of my body and found my fingers in his long dark hair, tugging the lengths, learning the strands weren't soft like silk but thick and dreadlocked with neglect.

That I was kissing a potentially homeless man didn't stop me from wanting more. Grabbing a fistful of his hair, I pulled him demandingly into me.

He swayed closer then snapped. He pushed me backward, forcing me to lie down. The moment I was horizontal, he lay down beside me. One leg pressed over mine, his thigh deliberately going between my legs. His body weight pinned me down.

I tried to fight, doing my best to hold on to some resemblance of decency, but the moment he lay half on top of me, wedging our bodies together as if this was *exactly* what we were born to do—with his erection against my hip, and his arm around my waist, and his tongue in my mouth, and his touch on my neck…I gave in.

I wasn't afraid.

I wasn't lost.

Not like I was an hour ago when two men pressed their unwanted pieces of anatomy against me. This man…I *wanted* him to. This man I didn't know but shared an intoxicating connection with.

Lights flashed in my eyes as his tongue dove deeper, dragging another moan from every crevice left inside me. I looped my leg around his, arching my hips, pressing against his hardness, feeling myself swell and heat and melt and *yearn*.

He groaned long and low as our hips fought to get closer. Impatience I'd never felt before suddenly hated denim and zippers and rules.

Nineteen and never been kissed.

I would do it all over again if this was my first true sexual experience. If every firework going off in my eardrums and eyelids was because of him, I would gladly be celibate for the rest of my days to deserve more.

Because of him, I was unhinged and grinding with insanity, giving into madness I'd never understood.

How had my night ended like this?

Where had this spontaneity come from?

This recklessness?

My teeth caught his bottom lip, dragging a slip tide of violence and need from him. He growled into my mouth, nipping and licking exactly like the starving wolf I thought he was.

"Fuck, what—what are you doing to me?" His breathless grunt did things. Glorious, *delicious* things. His voice created knots and bows with my insides. It filled my stomach with whirlwinds; it affected my core until my panties grew as damp as the grass we lay upon.

I loved knowing I affected him the way he affected me. Adored that we were in this craziness together—tripping into whatever rabbit hole we'd found and deciding to kiss and kiss until we splatted against the bottom.

His hands roamed, skating over my sides, keeping to the boundaries of pleasure. I arched, twisting a little to intercept his fingers as they swooped up and found my breast.

We both gasped, stealing oxygen from each other's lungs and sharing a moan-filled shudder. My hands felt empty—I needed to touch something of his. Something I'd never touched before and didn't know how but I wanted to. So. Damn. Much.

Lights appeared again. I was delirious with need but with no experience or knowledge on how to relieve such desire.

I wanted him to do something. Touch something. Remove this tingling sparkling supernova deep in my belly. But he tore his lips from mine, his head flying upward in a rain of messy hair and smeared chocolate.

"Shit." He pulled away, leaving my body wanting and unsatisfied. "We've got to go. Now!"

The lights were brighter with my eyes open.

It wasn't him.

It was security.

"Hey, you!" A flashlight shone directly on us.

Kissing forgotten, he jumped to his feet and grabbed my hand. He hauled me effortlessly upright and yanked me into a run. "Go!"

I didn't hesitate.

My sneakers dug into the grass, propelling me as fast as I could.

"Stop!" The security guard gave chase, his flashlight bouncing erratically. He skirted the outside of the baseball field but most likely had keys as he jogged breathlessly toward the stands rather than try to out-run us as we bolted for the other side of the fence.

Reaching the chain link, the nameless man I'd just kissed grabbed my hips and boosted me a foot into the air. "Climb. Fast." His voice wasn't out of breath but throbbed with urgency. He rippled with the need to bolt.

I clutched the metal and scurried as fast as I could with my shoes barely fitting into the holes. The fence wobbled as he scaled it faster than I could, swinging over the top and dropping down.

"Come on!" he hissed.

I climbed faster, curling myself over the top.

He paced below, holding his arms out. "Jump. I'll catch you."

"What...*again*?" That he'd already demanded to catch me twice in our short relationship almost made me laugh. Had we formed habits already?

Hysteria at being chased made jumbled emotions run riot. Laughter became nervousness. Attraction became anxiety.

"Do it, Elle." His tone gave no argument.

The security guard had vanished, but it didn't mean he wouldn't pop up any second. Clinging to the other side, I looped my fingers tight.

"I'm here." He braced his legs, waiting.

Giving him one last glance, hoping to God he was a man of his word, I squeezed my eyes and let go.

The fall set my stomach tangling with my throat. I landed awkwardly like a bride who'd fallen from the altar into her groom's arms.

He grunted, pulling my horizontal form into his embrace. He stumbled but didn't drop me. Our eyes met; a half-smirk hijacked his lips. "Couldn't stay away from me, huh?"

I swatted his shoulder. "You're the one who told me to jump."

His face darkened. "I'm also the one who kissed you."

A flashlight appeared; a garbled shout was closer.

"Shit." He let my legs go, swinging me to vertical. The instant my feet touched the ground, he grabbed my hand and yanked me forward.

We ran.

Air and speed and night-sky.

More flashlights appeared from other ends of the park, dancing with rays of righteousness as back-up guards arrived, chasing us like hounds.

"Oh, my God!" I yelled. "What do we do?"

"Keep running." He pulled me forward, slipping into a faster gear.

I wasn't unfit (thanks to my regular gym sessions) but I couldn't keep up with his pace. My lungs burned. My mouth opened wide, gulping at unhelpful air.

A security guard appeared to our left, bursting from the night-shrouded bushes. Behind him ran four men in uniform.

Police.

Holy shit.

Why are the police involved?

We hadn't vandalized property or hurt anyone. We'd gone

for a stroll and kissed under the moon. What was so wrong with that?

"Fuck!" Nameless squeezed my hand, doing his best to drag me faster. "Come on!"

I shook my head, stumbling, dragging him back. "Ca— can't." Tugging on his grip, I did my best for him to release me. "My legs are cramping. Let me go."

"No." His fingers locked tighter. "I won't let you get arrested because of me."

Arrested?

That awful word and terrifying implications gave me a final shot of energy. I ran as fast as I could, for as long as I could. The flashlights slowly lost ground but then sped up to match us.

It's no use.

Lactic acid built up and up until I limped rather than ran. He had no choice but to either let me go or slow down. I didn't want him to leave, but I also didn't want him to face a situation he didn't need to.

"Go on." I gasped. "Run. I'll catch up."

He glowered at my lie. "You won't catch up. They'll take you into custody." He punched a sapling as we sprinted past. "Fuck! This is all fucked up!" Sweat glistened on his brow, his black hood streamed behind him. The soft slaps of our shoes on the pavement matched our ragged breathing.

He wasn't afraid of a reprimand. He was livid at being caught. I was sure we weren't the first to jump the wall and find some private time together. He was wrong to think we'd be arrested…surely?

But it was more than that to him. Whatever existence he lived was a dangerous one. I didn't know what he survived, yet here he was, pulling me forward on false energy granted from half a chocolate bar.

I had no right to get him caught. Not when I hindered him while he tried to do the right thing by keeping me safe. For the second time.

He doesn't even know me, yet he's claimed responsibility for me.

My heart lurched, doing its best to force out lactic acid and provide life-granting blood to my suffering legs. But I was done. There was nothing left to do but stop and accept the punishment.

"Listen!" I tugged again, planting my feet to create drag. "You go. I'm slowing you down."

"Shut up. Just trust me." He didn't look back or let go. "Run!"

I had money for lawyers if it came down to being arrested. He most likely didn't. I couldn't be responsible for taking his freedom away.

"No! Just let me go!"

Looking over his shoulder, he eyed the police slowly catching up. A decision flashed in his gaze just before his feet changed direction and he hurled me into the bushes off the path.

We crashed into branches and leaves. The world became an evergreen maze. But then he shoved my back against a trunk, wedged his body against mine, and kissed me so damn hard, so crazily thorough, I suffocated from running and kissing and every dangerous passion he poured down my throat.

My hands came up, clutching his hoodie as his tongue tangled with mine, knotting and licking, stealing every last breath I had.

Pulling away, he rested his forehead on mine, a roguish smile replacing his grimace. "I'm not letting you go. I've only just found you." A tenderness glowed in his brown eyes that I'd never seen from another other than family.

My knees trembled. "You don't even know me."

He placed a whisper-kiss on my mouth. "I don't have to know you. I *feel* you." His hand slowly threaded up my side, taking liberties I'd given him in a moment of insanity on a baseball field.

Never looking away, he cupped my breast, running his

thumb over my flesh.

I moaned a little, my jaw going slack as desire sprang thick.

He kissed me again, stealing my cry, pressing his hips against mine. "I feel you like this." He squeezed my breast softly. "And I feel you like this." He rocked erotically. "But I feel you most of all with this." His touch climbed from my breast to my heart, pressing down over the rapidly beating muscle. "I don't care that I don't know you. I know enough."

I didn't know what to say.

This couldn't be real.

How had my night gone from alley robbery to bush-filled kisses? How had I transcended from lonely workaholic to falling for a man I'd only just met? A man who lived on the opposite scale of me in every little thing. Wealth and poverty. Safety and danger.

"Come home with me." If I were older with my own apartment, that invitation would've reeked with sex. But I wasn't older and didn't live alone. My need for him to be with me wasn't just about me but him, too. I wanted to protect him, shelter him—to give him a better chance than the world had so far.

He chuckled, brushing his mouth over mine. Deliberately ignoring my demand, he murmured, "You asked me before if I would've been pissed if a boyfriend gave you that necklace."

I stiffened then melted as his tongue licked mine sweetly. "The answer is yes. I would've been fucking pissed."

My face burned. My lips tingled. I couldn't help my stupid grin. "It was my father."

His hand lashed out, dragging my face to his for another messy half-violent, half-tender kiss. I sucked in a breath as the same intoxicating arousal billowed. I bit his bottom lip. He groaned, nipping me back.

"This is crazy." I hugged him close.

"All things worth fighting for are crazy." He kissed my forehead.

"But I don't even know your name—"

And then we were flying.

Something heavy and brutal knocked us sideways, tackling us as a flashlight split through our sanctuary of bushes, showing the silhouette of a hulking security guard as he threw us to the ground.

Twigs sliced through my jacket, pebbles and dirt smeared my hands, and Nameless grunted in agony as another guard landed on top of him.

My shoulder screamed as I rolled incorrectly. The earlier punch to my temple pounded in sympathy, making the park swim.

Curse words and limbs flew as Nameless fought. "Get the fuck off us!"

"Easy, kid." Another guard appeared, grabbing a flailing foot. "It's over. Give it up."

The man who'd landed on me slowly stood up, towering with smug victory on his chubby face. "Can't run, girl. You're surrounded."

I glowered, scooting closer in the dirt to Nameless while he punched and fought.

"Let him go!" I clambered to my knees, whacking the back of some pudgy guy in a high-vis jacket. "Get off him!"

My arms were pinned behind my back.

"Give it a rest." Someone hauled me upright. "Don't assault a security guard, ma'am, unless you want to add that to your misdemeanors tonight?"

I tried to spin. But the man who held me gave no leeway. Yanking me backward, he said to Nameless, "Don't be a hero. You're outnumbered. Stop wasting time."

My eyes connected with the man I'd kissed. He ceased fighting, turning limp rather than scrapping with the security guard. We didn't look away as a police officer stepped forward and ducked to grab his wrists.

With a sharp smile, Nameless swung once, twice, then gave up. A last hoorah rather than an attempt at escape. His head didn't bow as his arms were yanked behind his back like mine, and the sharp click of handcuffs being fastened interrupted the night.

He breathed hard as the police officer jerked him to his feet, not caring half the garden came with him in a tumble of dried leaves and dirt.

The security guard who'd launched on him stood too, limping a little but with a cruel sneer on his face at winning.

We were marched out of the bushes and made to stand on the pathway where joggers and pram-strollers would walk in a few hours when the sun rose. For now, it was a processing place for illegal canoodling.

My heart thundered as I twisted my wrists in the cold metal imprisoning me. Tearing my gaze from Nameless, I glanced at the police officer lurking close to his captive. "Please, you don't have to arrest us."

Another police officer with graying hair and a heavy artillery belt rubbed his jaw. "See, that's where you're wrong. Trespassing is a serious offense. As is indecent exposure. Plenty of crimes committed tonight."

"Indecent exposure?" I scoffed. "When?"

"Making out in a public place."

"That's not illegal."

"I saw him feeling you up." A security guard with a sweaty face grunted. "Who knows how far you would've gone if I hadn't interrupted. Sex on a baseball field? That's a punishable offense."

My cheeks pinked. I didn't want to discuss anything to do with sex with these idiots. "That's your word against ours. We would never go that far. We're not savages."

"Speak for yourself." Nameless chuckled. "You can argue until you pass out, Elle, but you won't win." He narrowed his gaze with hate at the guards. "I know the law, and the law doesn't give a shit about the truth."

"Watch your mouth, son." The cop with the heavy belt pointed in Nameless's face. "You're already fucked, so I wouldn't be adding any more ammunition to your file if I were you."

File?

Wait, he has a file?

Shaking my head, determined not to let questions undermine me, I looked at the officer who seemed to be in charge. "Look, we're sorry. Can we just pay a fine?" I looked at Nameless, suffering such guilt that he'd saved me from being raped, given me one of the best experiences of my life, and now, he would be imprisoned all because I couldn't run fast enough. "Let us go. I promise we'll leave and never come back."

"No can do, little lady." The police officer with his heavy belt whispered to a colleague, nodding to something said on the radio clipped to his lapel.

He smirked at Nameless. "According to reports, you were seen beating up two men earlier tonight. They said they found you about to rob and rape a young woman, and they tried to stop you. For their troubles, you almost broke one of their cheekbones and cracked a rib or two."

"Bullshit." My kisser bared his teeth. "I was the one trying to prevent *them* from doing that." He cocked his chin at me. "That's the girl they were trying to hurt."

The officers and security guards all raised an eyebrow. "Is this true, ma'am?"

I shrunk a little but nodded. "Yes. He saved me."

"Saved you?" The officer coughed. "Saved you and then brought you to a closed park to do what?"

I swallowed. "I'm very aware of how this looks, but he's right. We met when he saved me. They—they were going to hurt me."

"And *he* would've hurt you if we hadn't appeared."

"No, that's not true."

"You don't know him like we do, miss."

A police officer came over to pat me down while another patted my savior's body. My heart stopped when they found the eighty dollars in his hoodie pocket.

95

"Didn't rob you, huh?"

"That's mine, fuck face." Nameless fought against the handcuffs.

"Of course, it is," the lead officer said. "How many times do we need to tell you, lying only makes it worse for you?"

I froze.

How many times?

How many times had he faced situations like this?

I tried to catch his eye. To apologize. But he kept his glare on the officer who pocketed the eighty dollars. The money that could've bought him a better meal and a roof for a night.

Another person arrived on the scene, his heavy footsteps familiar even before he appeared in the flashlight glow of the security guards. I should've known he would turn up. He had a police scanner and had most likely been looking for me ever since I didn't call for him to drive me home.

My shoulders rolled, wishing I could melt into the concrete and disappear.

He flashed his credentials I knew stated him as ex-marine and in the employ of myself and my father. David Santos, my driver, bodyguard, sometimes personal assistant.

Shit.

He threw me a quick glance then focused his intense black gaze on the lead officer. His barrel chest, large arms, and black suit that matched his ebony skin soaked up the night. "I'm here for Ms. Charlston. She's done nothing wrong."

The police officer standing beside me argued, "She's been caught trespassing—"

"Wait." The lead agent stepped forward, shining light onto my bodyguard's identification. He then beamed the flashlight at my face. "What did you say her name was?"

"Charlston. Noelle Charlston." David ground his teeth. "Ring any bells?"

I was grateful he was here, but I didn't want him to fight the battles I'd lost.

"David, it's fine—"

"Be quiet, Ms. Charlston. Let me handle this." He stood taller, his gloved hands clenching. "From Belle Elle?"

The lead officer stiffened. "Wait, Joe's daughter?"

"The one and the same."

The officer paused.

A second later, he ordered, "Release her."

Instantly, the handcuffs were unlocked, and I was pushed forward. I shot to the side of the man who'd saved me, kissed me, and given me the best birthday night out I could've asked for. "What about him?"

An officer laughed. "Oh, he's coming with us."

"But you—you can't. He saved me. He did a good thing. Don't punish him for jumping a fence and enjoying a park."

The officer smirked. "Oh, we're not arresting him because of that."

I couldn't look away from Nameless' face. My lips ached to kiss him again. His eyes roamed over me, full of the same tender affection and almost awestruck attraction from before. I had to be near him until I figured out what this meant. What this was between us.

They can't take him away.

"Then why?" I demanded, living in daydreams of taking him home, giving him the guestroom to shower and rest, cooking him blueberry pancakes, and introducing him to Dad in the morning. "He hasn't done anything."

The officer's laughed as if all in on a joke I hadn't heard. "He's done plenty."

"He has multiple outstanding warrants. Tonight is our lucky night." Jerking Nameless to his side, the lead officer added, "He's going away for a long time."

Nameless merely hung his head, his jaw working with a violent edge.

"You can't do that."

The cop's face drew with annoyance. "I think you'll find we can, Ms. Charlston. Now, if you know what's good for you, you'll go home with your guard here and forget all about this one."

He shook Nameless. "Say goodbye because I doubt you'll be seeing him again."

I moved forward—to do what I didn't know. To kiss him, run away with him—somehow fix this, so it didn't end this way.

He smiled sadly. "Do what he says, Elle. Go home."

"I can't go. Not without you."

"You know the way now. You don't need a guide to walk you."

I shook my head. "That isn't what I meant, and you know it."

He chuckled. "You said it yourself. It was too crazy to be true."

I ached to grab his hand, to hug him, but with so many pairs of judging eyes on us, I froze. That would be one of my biggest regrets in life. That I didn't reach out when he needed me the most. "Please...tell me your name. I'll get a lawyer. We'll fight these stupid claims."

"All right, time's up." An officer marched forward, grabbing Nameless around the elbow and dragging him away.

Tears sprang to my eyes. Uncertainty and fear spiraled at the thought of never seeing him again. "Please! What's your name?"

Nameless stumbled from another shove, his gaze never leaving mine. He looked sad and pissed and lost and resigned. So many emotions all at once. "It was fun while it lasted."

"Tell me!"

But he merely gave me a harsh smile, trying to mask the grief on his face. "I really enjoyed kissing you, Elle."

And then the officer turned him away and marched him into the darkness.

CHAPTER TEN

THE DRIVE HOME was one of the hardest things I'd ever lived through.

David didn't say a word; he merely drove with iron concentration and astute silence. He didn't ask questions. He didn't ask for a report from the police. He just escorted me from the park as if I'd come out of Belle Elle like a normal evening after work.

He didn't comment about how I'd been caught with a man. He didn't speak at all apart from to tell me to be careful climbing into the backseat of the Range Rover Sport.

Pulling up to the brownstone where I lived, he cut the engine and jumped out. A moment later, he pulled open the door for me and nodded in the darkness. "Have a good night, Ms. Charlston."

"Thank you, David. You too."

I didn't ask if he'd keep this to himself. My father would know. I wouldn't be able to keep my night-time wanderings a secret. But at least neither of them would know about the alley and how I'd met Nameless.

He nodded again and hopped back into the Range Rover.

I kept my chin high even though my heart sputtered at the thought of what would happen to Nameless. Was he in prison now? Would he go to trial? What sort of warrants did they have?

My questions would have to wait because the second I climbed the steps and entered the home I was raised in, my father grabbed me in a boa constrictor hug.

"Oh, holy hell, Elle. Where the bells have you been?"

I couldn't even rib him for his weird expressions tonight. I squeezed him back, drained and confused, lost and sad. "I'm okay, Dad."

"You ran away!" He pulled back, disappointment and hurt bright in his eyes. "Why would you do such a thing? And on your birthday, no less."

I shrugged out of his embrace. "I didn't run away." I kicked off my sneakers and padded into the living room where hints of my mother still existed everywhere. From the pristine cream linen couches to the white gauze draped around the window bay. A baby grand piano sat in the corner next to the ornate fireplace while knickknacks from my parents' travels littered side tables and coffee tables in a cluttered but designer way.

My piano lessons flittered into my head as my fingers played an imaginary chord, giving me something to focus on when all I wanted to do was burst into tears.

Dad followed, throwing himself into his overstuffed chair that'd long since compacted and wrinkled from his weight. "Where were you, Elle? You say you didn't run away, but you were found in Central Park. At one a.m! Do you know how dangerous that is?" His eyes cast over me. "And what the hell are you wearing?"

Damn, David had already told him.

I looked at the black bomber I couldn't unzip; otherwise, he'd see my torn top and bruises. My skinny jeans smeared with dirt and chocolate. I was so far removed from the daughter he knew. The daughter who lived in fashion catalogs and had nightmares of Christmas sale stocks being too low. I shouldn't be daydreaming about a man who tasted like candy or a kiss beneath the stars on a baseball field.

Had that really happened?

Was it real?

I sighed, knowing I had to grovel before I could ask what would happen to Nameless. "I'm sorry, Dad. I—I wanted to see what the world was like for someone who wasn't an heiress."

He sucked in a breath. "Why?"

"Because I'm nineteen and never explored the city on my own. Because I'm running a billion-dollar company and never been to a party or gossiped with girls or kissed a boy." I looked up, pleading with him to understand. "I wanted to be normal...just for a few hours."

He sighed.

Silence fell as he reclined heavily into his chair. Whatever anger he had blew itself out.

That was my dad.

He rarely exploded, and when he did, it didn't last long. Guilt sat even worse because now his anger had gone, his second-guessing and regret burrowed through me.

I inched to the edge of the couch, getting closer to him. "I was coming back. The man who was arrested was walking me home safely."

"Arrested?" His head snapped up.

"Yes. I think he's homeless and probably has a few crimes of stealing to eat. But tonight, he saved me." I wouldn't go into the details with my father—he didn't need those mental images of me trapped and scared to haunt him, or worse, use them against me if I ever tried to leave on my own again—but I did need to fight for the man who'd fought for me. "He was an utter gentleman, Dad. He was kind and a little rough but overall someone worthy of being given a chance."

I linked my fingers, squeezing tight to overcome my nerves and push ahead. It was a trick I used in the boardroom when firing a department head if they were found embezzling or not doing their job.

I could never show weakness.

Ever.

Tonight, I'd shown weakness, and it'd almost gotten me raped and a man locked up.

"We need to help him."

Dad frowned. "Help? How?"

"We need to hire a lawyer—get him good representation, so he isn't incarcerated."

He scowled. "If he committed the crime, it's only fair he suffers the consequences."

"Doesn't he deserve someone to fight on his side, though? I don't know his name but I doubt he has anyone. He saved me. The least I can do is try to do the same."

"You were gallivanting around the city with a man, and you didn't know his name?" He groaned, shaking his head. "What were you thinking?" He stood suddenly, rubbing his face as if in denial. "Elle, you've had a long night. I'm going to bed, and I suggest you do the same. Sage is in your room. I collected her from the office when I went to check on you and found you were gone."

His guilt trip worked. I slotted myself into his weary arms. "I'm so, *so* sorry. I should've told you."

"Yes, you should have." He hugged me, although reluctantly.

But if I had, you wouldn't have let me go.

He spoke into my hair, no doubt smelling spicy beef burritos and dangerous alleys.

I was glad my long hair covered the bruise on my temple and whatever other calling cards those thugs had left were hidden beneath my clothes.

"I know this is my fault, keeping you so sheltered and buried under work, but my God, Elle, I never expected you to go chasing after the first boy who showed interest in you. A boy who was *arrested*, for goodness' sake."

I smarted with shame. "It's not like that. He wasn't just any boy. He was—"

When I didn't continue, he sighed sadly. "He was what? A friend? A soul-mate? A teenage crush?" He pinched his nose.

"Elle, I will never stand in the way of you finding love. I *want* you to find love. Not a day goes by that I don't wish your mother was still alive to teach you how valuable love can be, but I won't permit you to throw away everything you have with a stupid infatuation over a criminal who doesn't deserve you."

"Dad...don't—"

His eyes dropped to my throat. Pain arrowed through him, followed by rage. "Where is your necklace?"

I jolted.

"Tell me, Elle. The sapphire star I bought you. The one I spent hours deliberating over. The one I bought because the blue matched your eyes and the star symbolized how much you mean to me?" His fists shook. "Where is it?"

I looked at the beige carpet. "I lost it."

The lie turned to paste on my tongue, but it was better than the truth. Better for him to blame me than to think of his gift in the possession of heartless thieves who meant me harm.

"For God's sake, Noelle." He shook his head, tiredness etching his eyes. "Not only were you irresponsible with yourself but with your gift, too. If you planned on using tonight as a demonstration that you were capable of spending some time alone away from the company, consider it a failure." His voice deepened with authority. "Until you can prove you are still the considerate daughter I raised, I don't want you leaving this house without David, do you hear me?"

My tears turned to anger. Heat smoked through me to argue back. To tell him just how suffocated I felt, how lonely, how lost. But I'd already hurt him tonight, and now, he'd hurt me.

We were even.

I smiled tight, hiding everything. We both had more to say but wouldn't verbalize. He was disappointed in me. I was frustrated by him.

It was best to go to bed before we uttered things we couldn't take back.

"Goodnight, Dad." I moved around him and left the

living room. "I'm sorry about the necklace."

As I climbed the sweeping staircase to my room on the third floor, my mind returned to the man who tasted like chocolate and had hands that could touch so sweetly but also cause such violence.

I would never forget him.

And tomorrow, I would do what I could to help him.

Because he'd helped me, and in some crazy way, he'd claimed my young, naïve heart.

I would get him free.

No matter how impossible that task would be.

CHAPTER ELEVEN

THREE YEARS LATER

"DON'T FORGET, YOU have that dinner meeting with your father, Mr. Robson, and his son tonight at the Weeping Willow." Fleur smiled, hoisting another armful of contracts and financial portfolios.

I removed my reading glasses and took the folders from her. The heavy thud as I placed them on my desk ricocheted through me. "Yes, I remember."

And I want nothing to do with it.

For the past year, my father had used every business meeting with his right-hand man, Steve Robson, to try to set me up with his son. He thought I couldn't see through his tricks, but the way he kept finding excuses for us to be around each other wasn't subtle.

"Anything else, Ms. Charlston?"

"No, thank you. Please don't put any calls through. I have too much work to finish."

"Of course." Turning in her pretty purple dress, Fleur left my office. Her wardrobe was smart but flirty, reminding me that outside the thick glass windows existed sun and heat and summer.

I hadn't been away from an air-conditioned building for more than a few minutes at a time for months. If I wasn't being driven from office to office, I was in store warehouses or shop-fronts or doing my best to catch up on sleep, that for some reason, had become elusive for the past three years.

Ever since my one night of freedom, sleep had evaded me. Dreams never came. Nightmares visited often. The damn guilt because I wasn't able to help him eroded me day by day.

You said you wouldn't think about him anymore.

I said that every morning.

And by every lunchtime, I failed.

The best I'd been able to do was realize how stupidly idealistic I'd been. My dad, bless his heart, had helped show me that it wasn't Nameless who I thought I'd fallen in love with that night but the *idea* of love.

No one could fall for a stranger in a few hours. Especially a girl who'd been attacked and molested and then corralled into breaking and entering a national treasure. My nerves and adrenaline would've heightened every experience, making it so much more than what it was.

I'd read into things. I'd imagined the heat behind the kisses and painted a perfect romance, when really, all there'd been was a dirty boy and a baseball field.

That's all.

I recognized myself for what I was.

I was young, fanciful, and Dad was entirely right that work took precedent over a silly infatuation.

He was nothing to me.

Just a man from my past who took my first kiss.

Got it, stupid heart?

I sank heavily into my chair. My elbows stabbed into the desk as I rested my head in my hands. Even now, with all my pep talks and conclusions, I still felt guilty for not doing more.

That's why I think about him.

Not because I still believed we were meant to be, or the craziness between us was serendipitous, but because I'd failed and left him alone in a prison that no doubt took whatever good was left in him and spat him out cold, cynical, and cruel.

I hadn't lived up to my oath.

A life for a life.

He'd saved me.

And I haven't saved him.

For months, I'd tried to track him down. I'd called the police stations, the county jails, even a few lawyers who worked pro bono to see if they'd been given his case.

But nothing.

I had no name and only a vague description—hampered by his beard, the night, and his hoodie.

The picture in my mind was of mystery and infatuation rather than a crystal image helpful for sketch artists or explanations.

It was as if he never existed.

But I knew he did because I still thought about the sapphire star necklace, and every time I snuck a piece of chocolate, Nameless exploded into my mind. I should get over it. It was one night. A nineteen-year-old's stupid crush.

I was more mature now.

Overworked and completely wrung out. Sage was getting older, but she still came with me to the office every day, still purred on my lap when sums and figures made my head spin, and still cuddled with me in bed when loneliness for a life I'd never have overtook me.

Two years ago, when my father had had a heart attack, I gave up my adolescent immaturity and no longer resented my role. The doctors said he would get better, but he should step down from being the boss.

The Last Will and Testament I'd signed came into full effect, and he placed me as the sole controller with the majority share of our stocks and the final say on all decisions.

To say I was scary to men of my own age when I was just an heiress was one thing, but to date now I was a conglomerate commander was utterly impossible.

Dad believed in love.

I didn't.

Not because I didn't want it but because my life's work had stolen that possibility from me. I had to accept that I had no time for romance, no patience for dating, and no prospects at partnership other than business expansion.

I was so lucky compared to most.

Love is a small price to pay.

I lived and breathed for my company, and on the rare evenings I had off, Dad was determined to play matchmaker with me and Greg—Steve's son.

It didn't matter that I had no interest in Greg.

I didn't care he was only three years older than I was and held a bachelor's in business from Yale. He was dry and humorless and the exact opposite of Steve, who'd been in my life from the start with his quirky nicknames and jokes when I started running Belle Elle.

He was my uncle in every way apart from blood.

Greg was the unwanted cousin who I wished was related to me so I had a legitimate reason for denying his advances.

Sage nudged my ankles, meowing softly beneath the desk where she hung out in her basket full of blankets and stuffed mice.

"Yeah, yeah. I know he's only looking out for me."

Dad wanted me to marry and find a partner to help run Belle Elle with. He'd met Mom when he was twenty, and it'd been love at first sight. He couldn't understand why I was still so very, very single at twenty-two.

It obviously didn't cross his mind that I was a powerful woman in a still sexist world where men—even if they didn't come out and admit it—were emasculated by a woman with a bigger salary than them.

My thoughts remained tangled as I diligently worked through the reports on our Hong Kong division before Fleur knocked on my office door, wrenching through my concentration.

"It's six p.m. You need to leave in thirty minutes."

"Wow, really? I thought it was two p.m. only five minutes

ago."

She giggled, her long brown braid jiggling over her shoulder. "Like you always do when you get in the zone—you lost time." She waltzed in with a dry-cleaners bag covering a black dress.

Placing it on the arm of my rolled leather couch, she said, "I don't know why you don't let me bring you something more fun and vibrant from the shop floor. I have a sneaking suspicion you'd look great in green." She held up her hands to make a frame around my face. "A rich emerald. Or perhaps a deep sapphire like that star you keep sketching when you're on the phone with suppliers."

I waved her away. "Black is fine."

"Black is all you ever wear."

"Black is business and no-nonsense."

"But life isn't." She smiled sadly. "Life is fun and chaos." Backing toward the exit, she added, "You should remember that sometime…." She left before I could fire her—not that I ever would because without her and Sage, I would have no one I could actually talk to who wasn't my father.

I glared at the black dress.

I wouldn't lie and say wearing another color wouldn't be fun, but I didn't have time for fun or shopping or fashion. I did the work so other people could do those things while leaving their money in our cash registers.

Sighing, I rubbed the back of my neck, saved my progress, and closed my laptop.

Sage slunk around my ankles, knowing the routine and that work was over for the day. "We're not going home, I'm afraid."

Her little face pouted, her whiskers drooping from her tiny nose. Picking the silver cat from the floor, I placed her on my desk as I stood to prepare for this sham of a date.

I kissed her soft head. "Don't look at me like that. At least you get to snooze in the car. I actually have to talk to the jerk."

She stuck her tongue out, coughing with a hairball.

"Yes, exactly. I feel like vomiting, too." Heading to the couch to collect the dreaded dress, I murmured, "The sooner this dinner is over, the sooner I can go home and forget."

And try to dream.

Of being nineteen again and kissing a man with no name.

CHAPTER TWELVE

THE RESTAURANT WAS packed as usual.

Friday night was the night every high-powered suit liked to be seen at the Weeping Willow. The eatery had opened four years ago, and in that time, it had created a name of fine dining, utmost decadence, and a gin bar with more selections than any other in New York. They prided themselves on expensive, exclusive liquors. And even had a bottle of gin valued at ten thousand dollars a shot.

Ridiculous.

"Ah, there you are!" Dad stood as I approached the reserved table at the back. The booth glittered in deep turquoise while a chandelier representing the branches of a willow tree wept over the circular table.

"Hi, Dad." I kissed his cheek, happy to see he had color on his face and a twinkle in his eye. Even though the doctors had told him he had to take it easy, he didn't. He still pulled long hours in his office across the hall from mine. And he stressed himself out by overthinking my future and lack of family if he suddenly died.

He was a lot of things my father but three words to describe him was a cuddly teddy bear. He had a habit of ignoring practicalities in order for happiness to rule.

"You look lovely." He grabbed my hand, forcing me to spin.

The black dress whirled around my kneecaps while the spaghetti straps clung for dear life to my shoulders. The bodice hugged nicely, but overall, it was a simple style in a simple color.

It was one of Belle Elle's biggest sellers—not because of how well it was made but because it was the perfect backdrop to show off accessories. Gauzy scarfs looked great with the spaghetti straps, necklaces earned prime real estate, and even big earrings polished it to runway class rather than high street clone.

Tonight, the only accessorizing I'd attempted was a dark blue shawl and a lick of eye shadow with thicker mascara. My blonde hair hung down to my tailbone. All my energy was spent on the company, not on myself, and I didn't particularly care if it showed.

I swallowed a groan as Greg stood up and kissed both my cheeks. His hand landed on my elbow, slightly clammy and annoyingly clingy. "You look gorgeous, Noelle."

I hate when he calls me that.

I hadn't been Noelle for decades.

I was Elle of Belle Elle.

The queen of retail.

I forced a smile. "Thank you. You don't look bad yourself." I nodded in approval at his black slacks and one size too big for him dinner jacket. The lapels were embossed with velvet. On any other man, it would probably look distinguished and sexy. But on him…*kill me now.*

Not that he was ugly—far from it. Greg had great dark blond hair, chiseled features, and a trim physique. What lurked beneath his looks was what turned me off. There was no…connection. No spitfire or chocolate smoke. And sometimes, just sometimes, I sensed a darkness in him that had nothing to do with me constantly turning down his requests for a date.

He had a coldness that made me wary even to be alone with him in public.

Most of the time, I chalked up my over imagination to the slight trauma from being dragged into the alley all those years ago.

I had to stop reading into things and imagining the worst.

I looked around Greg to his father, Steve. "Hiya."

Steve didn't bother unwinding from the booth but blew me an air kiss. His hair had turned white over the years, but his sense of humor never dried up. "You look as pretty as that Barbie doll you used to love before Sage came along."

I rolled my eyes. "Did you just call me a Barbie? In public?"

He shrugged. "Hey, it's not derogatory. Just saying you have a tiny waist, nice boobs, and blonde hair." He ran a hand over his casual gray blazer. "Look at me, I'm the perfect Ken— or at least, I was a few years ago."

I laughed, forcing myself to relax even though Greg still hadn't let go of my arm.

My father saved me by tugging me to his side and pushing me into the booth. I went willingly, trapped between Steve and Dad, facing Greg across the table.

Something rubbed my ankle.

My eyes shot to Greg's green ones. Turned out, I wasn't far enough away to prevent him playing footsies. I kept the same smile I used on assholes in the boardroom plastered to my face, even though I wanted to stab his face with the steak knife.

"So, Elle, you working hard tomorrow?" Greg grinned conspicuously as his foot stomped on my toes. "Want to go see a movie or something?"

The waiter brought our drinks—the joy of being known and regulars at this place. The server placed neat whiskey in front of my father and Steve, a gin and tonic for Greg, and a virgin daiquiri for me.

Just as I'd never been free since the night I met Nameless, I'd never been drunk. Not that liquor didn't appeal to me but the fact that each day I started work before the sun rolled out of its soft cloudy bed, I had no time for a hangover.

One day, a few pieces of the laces keeping me straight and narrow would snap, and then I'd derail and cause untold pain to my father by being stupidly irresponsible. I would drink to excess, sleep with a stranger, and call in sick for a solid week.

But that day was not today.

"I work hard all the time, Greg." I batted my eyelashes sweetly. "I'm afraid I never have time to do things like go to the movies."

"What about a walk?"

"That too."

"Carriage ride through Central Park?"

My smile faltered, remembering the arrest and subsequent disappearance of the man in Central Park. "Definitely too busy for that."

Dad coughed. "Now, Elle. You're making it sound like I'm a slave driver."

I laughed softly. "Not you, Dad. The company."

His face fell, trying to read my reluctance. I wouldn't tell him that most of the time, I used work as my alibi to avoid dates because the only man who asked me out was Greg, and that was only because he thought he knew me because our fathers were old friends.

Not to mention, if he married me, he would get the empire that he'd been raised with thanks to Steve's involvement. I couldn't begrudge his desire to control something that had been such a big part of his life.

But I could prevent it from happening.

Steve laughed, toasting me with his whiskey. "Here's to a workaholic who happens to be so damn good at her job."

I didn't know if I wanted to toast to that, but I did, clinking my glass with his.

The waiter appeared to take our meal order as the menu changed weekly. Before I could glance at the new specials, my father slid from the booth and mumbled he'd be right back. An itch started right in my heart. I rubbed my chest as love for the gray-haired man in his immaculate three-piece suit washed over me.

Where is he going?

I knew I'd hurt him with refusing Greg's advances, but I didn't mean to rib him with how much I worked.

That wasn't fair.

Greg interrupted my melancholy by ordering loudly. "I'll have the venison. Rare."

Steve pursed his lips before saying, "Make that two." He placed the heavy flocked menu onto the table, eyeing me expectantly. "You, Elle? I know your father will have the chicken or fish—on account of his heart—but you?"

I quickly scanned the list. I had no appetite, and my thoughts were across the room in the private gin bar to the side where my father had vanished. "I'll have…um, the salmon, please."

"No problem." The waiter took our order, tucked his electronic device that'd most likely already sent our order to the kitchen into his vest pocket, and collected our menus. The moment he left, awkwardness fell on the table.

Steve glanced at me then Greg. "So, you two, what's new in the world of twenty something's?"

I smiled for his sake, not Greg's. "Well, you know my world. You see me every day at the office."

"And you know mine because you see me every day at home." Greg rolled his eyes.

He was twenty-five and still lived at home.

Here, I could be smug and look down my nose. A few months ago, I'd moved out of the brownstone and into my own top-floor apartment only two buildings away from Belle Elle headquarters.

I'd cheated and bought it fully furnished, so some of the furniture wasn't to my taste, but I didn't have time to interior design or visit the stores or even browse our own shop for decorations. It had taken all my courage to move out, especially after Dad's heart attack, but I couldn't be there anymore.

Dad had understood.

He'd supported me and helped me pack and move the meager possessions in my bedroom and a few knickknacks from the living room.

For the first week, Sage had caterwauled at the view, telling me off for removing her from the brownstone where she could sneak into the garden late at night and do whatever it was that cats do. In the new place, she was glass and concrete bound, looking at the clouds rather than rodents.

"How are you enjoying your own place, Elle?" Steve followed my train of thought, surprising me.

I shrugged, smoothing out my napkin over my lap. "It's good. The building has great services with a gym and pool. It even has movie nights and neighbor parties once a month."

Not that I've been to any of them.

"That's fantastic." Steve grinned. "Perhaps Greg could come over one day, and you can show him how easy it is to live on your own. Get him out from under my feet."

"Yeah, good one, old man." Greg snickered, sipping his gin and tonic.

I shuddered, doing my best to hide the horror at the thought of having Greg in my apartment. With me. Alone. Of kissing Greg. Of letting him remove my dress and touch me. Of letting him see me naked and sticking his—

All right, stop right there.

I no longer lived at home and was one of the few women on the Forbes' richest list. I'd achieved so much, but in reality...in the three years since my first kiss, *nothing* had changed.

I hadn't been kissed since—unless a friendly peck on the cheek from doting father figures counted. I hadn't been naked around anyone, male or female. I still held the curse of not having enough time to lose my virginity.

Most days, I had no libido because I worked such long hours. But some nights, I remembered how it felt to be touched and have a man's tongue in my mouth and how I physically *ached* for something I hadn't understood that night on a baseball field.

And I delivered a release I'd become rather expert at.

"Yes, Elle. I could come over…say next week?" Greg rubbed his shoe against my leg, snagging my pantyhose and no doubt causing a ladder. "I could bring a bottle of wine. We could finally *get to know each other.*"

Steve scowled at the heavy reference to sex but didn't interfere. After all, we weren't children anymore. Yes, we had two meddling old men trying to influence our love lives, but I wouldn't give in to this.

Not after everything else.

Talking of my meddling old man.

Where is he?

The waiter arrived with four plates of delicious smelling food, all artistically arranged on turquoise plates with silver piping.

Inching from the booth, I ignored Greg's question and smiled at Steve. "Excuse me. I'd better go tell my father his dinner is on the table."

"Yes, good idea, Elle." Steve nodded, already picking up his knife and fork to dig in.

Greg narrowed his eyes, giving me a tight grin. "Fine. I'm not going anywhere."

Fighting my shudder, I slithered from the booth. My heels tap-tapped over gray-veined marble as I left the busy restaurant and entered the cozy gin bar. Teak wood hung in noise absorbing panels from the black ceiling. Stools with polished chrome and padded leather lined up neatly by the long bar while clusters of comfy chairs encouraged secrets to be shared and pacts to be made in the dark.

The whiff of alcohol and cigar smoke lingered on every air-eddy. I had no idea how the Weeping Willow got around the non-smoking rule, but small plumes of silver escaped men's lips as I made my way to the bar.

Specially positioned spotlights speared through the bottles

on offer. All twenty-two hundred of them—according to the owner who bragged when he'd first opened the place. Alcohol glittered like fireflies, tempting a drinker to keep testing until they found their soul-mate in liquor.

I expected to find Dad nursing another glass of whiskey, staring broodingly into the amber liquid as he sometimes did when I acted out or he couldn't shed the memory of Mom.

That wasn't the case tonight.

I slammed to a stop.

He's laughing with a complete stranger.

Dad sat on a bar stool with his feet tucked on the chrome foot-rest, a glass of whiskey (like I predicted) resting in his hands but forgotten. His face was alive, eyes unguarded and crinkled in mirth. I hadn't seen him so animated in years.

It warmed me and worried me in equal measure.

I looked at the man he was with. The guy had his back to me, but the cut of his suit was impeccable; his body toned and slim, his hair dark and thick with lighter highlights that could've been graced by a hairdresser or natural.

From where I stood, a couple shielded me like a living wall, but I was close enough to hear my father say, "Well, that sounds fantastic. You really should meet her."

Fantastic? What was fantastic?

I sucked in a breath as the stranger laughed. "It would be an honor to meet her. I'm sure she's as wonderful as you describe."

Are they talking about me?

The couple hiding me moved, leaving me exposed. I should walk forward and introduce myself. I should stop eavesdropping and act professionally. But something about the way my father and this stranger spoke sent my hackles bristling.

Staying behind milling people with an array of alcohol gripped in tight fingers, I slowly inched closer to the two men, straining with every step to hear.

"My daughter is very accomplished." Dad's tone billowed with pride. "But you sound rather successful yourself, so that shouldn't be a problem."

"Problem?" The man took a sip of his drink. "I assure you, I've never had a problem with women before."

Oh, the arrogance dripping from him.

Dad chuckled. "I wasn't saying *she'd* be a problem. More like you shouldn't find her power off-putting if you have success of your own."

Oh, my God, what is he talking about?

Where had my father gone? When had he turned into this hearts-and-flowers romantic, trying to match me off to any man who passed his screwed-up interview?

He's always been like that.

I hated that that was true.

The stranger nodded. "I can understand how a woman with a high corporate job and wealth can be terrifying to most." He leaned forward. "However, I can assure you, that won't be the case with me."

He spoke as if my father had handed me over to be bedded and wedded.

My teeth ground together as Dad said, "I must admit, I haven't heard of you before. Are you new to New York?"

The man swirled the liquid in his glass. "Yes. Arrived a few months ago. Unfortunately, my benefactor was not well, and we needed treatment that was only available here as a trial."

"Oh, I'm sorry."

My hands balled as my father gave this total stranger such sympathy. "And you're single then? You're planning on staying in town?"

Holy crap, the embarrassment level just erupted into volcanic proportions.

"I am. Customarily, I don't date. But now my benefactor is on the mend, I can indulge in playing the field."

Indulge? Play the field? My hands curled with indignation. Who *was* this man?

"My daughter isn't a conquest, Mr. Everett. If I do introduce you, you must give me your word you won't use her."

This had gone on long enough. I had to do something. Namely, throw my drink into Mr. Everett's face.

"Believe me. I have no doubt one look at your daughter, and I'll be quite happy to be monogamous until she gets to know me." The man raised his glass again, giving me a side profile glimpse of elegant cheekbones and handsome jaw.

I stiffened. He spoke as if I was a sure thing. That he could make me fall for him just by being alive.

I wanted to kill him.

But then I wanted to kill my father more as he smiled. "I'm sure you'll like Elle. She's beautiful and insanely intelligent."

Mr. Everett chuckled. "I'm fairly sure I can make your daughter like me in return. I have a knack, you see."

"A knack?" My father's face tightened, noting the cocky confidence of this man he was trying to marry his daughter to. "What sort of knack?"

"A knack for women who can't stand the opposite sex. A way of convincing them to give up control and relax for once."

Holy shit.

I rarely swore but *holy shit, shit, shit.*

This guy…there were no words for his arrogance.

Dad glanced at his untouched whiskey. "I admit Elle doesn't seem to like the prospects I put in front of her." His face fell. "I only want her to be happy. To have someone to shoulder the burden of her company with. To laugh occasionally with." His voice softened with sadness. "She hasn't laughed in so long. I'm worried about her."

If I weren't so angry, I would've suffocated under a fresh wave of guilt. I moved forward a step, breaking my cover, swirling with mixed emotions.

However, Mr. Everett ensured I'd never feel guilt again as he said, "Introduce me to your daughter, Mr. Charlston, and I promise you I'll make her—"

"Make me do what?" I stomped in my heels, crossing my

arms. My heart whirled wild while my breathing threatened to show how annoyed and hurt I was.

I glowered at both men.

My father shrunk, knowing he'd screwed up. But the stranger merely pinned me with piercing eyes and sent a chill down my spine.

He looked arctic and unreadable.

He smelled expensive and impenetrable.

He sounded powerful and untouchable.

My worst nightmare wrapped in perfection.

Tearing my gaze away, I hugged my anger and spat, "You sit here planning my future like you have control over me. What? You think you can make me fall in love with you? Get on my knees for you? Do whatever you tell me to, oh master?" I snorted. "The flat-out disgusting *nerve* of you!"

Mr. Everett rubbed his bottom lip where a droplet of liquor glistened. "If you give me time, I'll prove to you I can make you do all those things…and more."

I spluttered in outright shock. *"Excuse me?"*

My father stood up, putting himself between me and damn Mr. Everett. "I don't think that's quite appropriate conversation for the first introduction, sir."

"Seriously?" I eyed my father as if he was a stranger, too. "When is that sort of talk *ever* appropriate? When he's got me cuffed to a damn bed and making me cook him dinner? God, Dad." I threw up my hands, my skin flushing with indignation beneath my black dress. "Wow. Just wow. *Both* of you."

Backing away, I held up my finger when Dad tried to reason with me. "Nope, not going to hear it." I spun on my heel then looked over my shoulder, doing my best to ignore Mr. Everett and the way his gaze slipped over me, lingering on my breasts before latching onto my mouth. "Oh, and, Dad, once you've finished trying to be the world's worst matchmaker, your dinner is on the table."

I stormed off, unable to make the blazing exit I wanted as a crowd of people interrupted my flow, teetering slowly with their arms full of drinks, chatting about things I couldn't care less about.

I wanted out of there.

Something warm and firm tapped me on the shoulder, somehow finding bare flesh beneath the scarf wrapped around me. "Before you leave…"

My heart relocated into my mouth as I whirled around, coming face to face with Mr. Everett.

Up close he was even more stunning.

Damn him.

Curse him.

His dark eyes were calculating and intelligent, his lips perfectly formed with the barest hint of five o'clock shadow over his jaw and down his throat. His Adam's apple bobbed as he swallowed while the columns of muscle flowing from his neck to his chest, just visible beneath an open-necked silk gray shirt, upset me in ways I didn't understand.

He was pure, one-hundred percent male, and he watched me as if I was a woman who'd already sacrificed herself on his ego temple, and he was about to dine on her soul.

I crossed my arms to hold my insides together, trying to prevent the leaping gazelle my heart had morphed into from splattering at his feet. "What? What do you want?"

His eyes darkened to molasses. "I want—"

Dad sidled over, caution and worry etching his wrinkled kind face. "Now, Elle. Let me introduce you two properly."

"I think Mr. Everett has done all the introducing I need to hear." I tilted my head. "Isn't that right?"

Mr. Everett smiled ever so slightly, looking more sinner than gentleman. "I've only just started, Ms. Charlston."

Dad raised his arm, waving it a little in surrender as my heels ground into the marble, preparing to go to war. "Now, now." Coming to my side, he patted my forearm. "I apologize for talking about you. But you've got the wrong idea. This is—"

"Mr. Everett. I know." I glowered. "I just learned, thanks

to you, how he thinks he can turn me into a simpering idiot all because he's deemed me interesting enough to meet." I leaned toward Mr. Everett, not caring I gave him a shot down my cleavage or the way he sniffed at my orchid perfume. "For your information, asshole, I don't like men because of this exact reason. You're either a mamma's boy or think you rule the world." I pointed a finger in his face. "You'll never rule me, so you might as well stop whatever little game you're playing with my father and fuck off."

"Elle!" My father gasped. "What the hell, Bell Button?"

And he used Bell Button.

Of course, he did.

My life was officially over. Not only had he tried to set me up with this sexual deviant in the middle of a cigar-clouded gin bar, but now, he gave away childhood nicknames as if they meant nothing.

"Nice, Dad. Real nice," I muttered under my breath.

Mr. Everett noticed, a smug smirk twisting his lips. One look into his eyes and I knew he'd stored away my embarrassing title for ammunition in the future.

But there will be no future.

Because in ten seconds, I wanted to be gone and never see him again.

"I'm suddenly not hungry." I narrowed my eyes at my father. "Please give my apologies to Steve and Greg."

"Steve and Greg?" Mr. Everett repeated.

I sneered. "Two more men I refuse to have anything to do with so don't think yourself special."

Dad clutched my elbow. "Now, Elle, don't be hasty. You know how much you love the food here."

"*Loved.* Past tense." I gave a brittle smile. "This place doesn't hold the allure it once did, thanks to recent events." I looked Mr. Everett up and down icily, hoping he'd get frostbite.

Mr. Everett chuckled under his breath. "Are you always this dramatic or is it a product of being given everything you've ever wanted since you were born?"

The bar vanished.

The world quietened.

My heart stopped.

"*What* did you just say?" I leaned forward, swaying so close I had to take a step toward him, so I didn't tumble against his chest.

My father knew how inconsiderate that sentence had been. He moved from ceasefire to full-on battle negotiations. "Elle, before you start." He gulped. "I'm sure Mr. Everett didn't mean it like that."

"Oh, I did." Mr. Everett crossed his arms, somehow holding his glass of clear liquor upright, showing just how close we stood to each other when the sleeve of his shirt brushed the silk of my black dress.

Any higher and he would've touched my breasts.

Cocky bastard.

"I meant it exactly the way it sounded."

Red painted my vision. The endlessly long days. The pressure. The lost childhood and servitude. I couldn't let him get away with such a remark. I couldn't stand there and let him *smirk* as if I was a tantrumming adolescent who'd never worked and believed money came from fairy farts.

I inhaled hard to deliver my perfectly poised rebuttal.

Mr. Everett stood patiently, dripping with arrogance. "Well?"

I opened my mouth.

And then…I shut it again.

He's not worth it.

No man is.

They're all the same—believing I'm some bauble in my father's empire.

Some jewel they could commandeer for themselves and take over the company just like they'd take over me.

No.

Never going to happen.

I would forever be a virgin-bound husk before I ever wasted more breath and temper on a man who would always remain below me.

I moved my arm as Dad tried to squeeze my elbow, asking for discretion and quietness. He knew me. He knew I was borderline Hurricane Noelle. He'd seen me blow up only twice and both were at cocky men who believed their top salaries entitled them to cheat on their wives and not give a shit about their work.

One had cried as he left Belle Elle headquarters. The other had retired with a tarnished reputation.

Dad glanced nervously around the bar, waiting for Armageddon. Instead of giving him a second heart attack, I twisted my elbow, grabbed his wrist, and jerked him sideways. "Come along, Dad. I think this man has poisoned your mind enough."

"Elle, darling—"

"Don't you 'darling' me. Next time you think of setting me up, Dad, stop. I don't want another forced meeting with Greg just because you and Steve can see us playing house. I don't want some pity introduction with men who pass your critique. And I *definitely* don't want to see this one again. Ever." I sneered at Mr. Everett, doing my best to ignore the frustratingly erotic smile on his face.

He raised his glass of clear liquor, taking a sip. His gaze drifted over me with eyes as dark as goodbyes and a jaw so sharp it would slice my finger if I were ever stupid enough to touch it.

"He said you were head-strong. I didn't believe him." Mr. Everett chuckled in a deep rasp. "I've seen evidence for myself, and I have to admit..." He leaned closer in a cloud of expensive, heady aftershave. "I like it." Glancing at my cleavage quickly, his eyes flew back to mine. "Unhand your father, Ms. Charlston, and agree to a date with me."

My jaw fell open.

Did he just ask me out?

After all that?

I kept my face cool and uninterested. "Never in a million years."

"A million is a long time."

"It's also a lot of money if you want to be sued for sexual harassment."

He grinned. "I happen to have excellent legal counsel. You'd never win."

"I don't need to win to tell you to leave me the hell alone."

"Go on a date with me, and I might agree to your command."

"What part of 'leave me alone' didn't you hear? A date would defeat that wish to never see you again."

He smoothed his silky gray shirt. "I decide what to hear and what not to." His eyes narrowed with untold authority. "And I've decided your father is right. You are my type. And I'm yours. It's normal for us to find out what nature intends."

I couldn't.

I just couldn't deal with this insanity.

"We should find out what nature intends, huh?" I reached forward and plucked his still-filled glass from his stupidly perfect fingers. "*This* is what nature intends." I dumped the contents onto his ridiculously sexy swept back hair then leaned in until our noses brushed. "Come near me again, and I'll strike a match to see how well liquor and fire like each other."

Not caring about my father or Steve or Greg or even damn Mr. Everett, I straightened my shoulders and stormed from the restaurant.

Chapter Thirteen

MY COMPUTER EARNED the brunt of my anger.

The poor keyboard was bruised in places no technology should be bruised.

Ever since the Weeping Willow, I'd been strung so tight, my insides had transformed into something snarling and wild with big teeth. I felt like something lived inside me, ready to leap free.

Probably been reading too many shapeshifter romances again.

But still, all night I couldn't relax, and all day I revved with disbelief at Mr. Everett's gall.

Then again, was there anything to be truly upset about? He was an opportunist, and my father had been his victim. No harm done. I'd seen past the ruse and kept my father safe and far away from a scam artist.

So why can't I dampen the temper raging in my blood?

Because he's the only man to get a rise out of me?

The only one to show me a little of the truth hidden beneath the prim dresses and eloquent politeness of a workaholic?

That I had passion.

Depth.

Needs?

No, that can't be true.

Men were part of the population I didn't need. Even Belle

Elle could survive without the male counterparts. The sales figures for women's fashion were two-hundred times that of the men's department. In fact, I should propose at the next business meeting to cancel all male lines and just pretend the world had done itself a favor and deleted anyone with a penis.

You're talking gibberish.

Thank God that can't happen as you'd miss your father.

Thinking about my father and the word penis in the same context was disgusting.

But thinking of Mr. Everett in the same context...

Still disgusting.

My hands curled around my pen. This was Dad's fault—the same father dead set on marrying me off before my next birthday.

The clock on my desk said it was almost 5 p.m. I'd lasted the day and used my anger to wipe my to-do list clean. I'd never finished so early before, and I wished I had more tasks to do as there was no way I wanted to go home yet.

Poor Sage fed off my nervous energy, pacing around my office rather than napping in the twilight sunshine. And I was hungry again for the fifth time today—burning through calories faster than I could replace them.

Someone knocked on my door.

I looked up. "Yes?"

"Elle?" Fleur stuck her head in. "Your father wants a word before he retires for the night."

I froze. "Why?"

Another disastrous date set up?

Fleur frowned. "Um, not sure. He's family...I guess he just wanted to say goodbye?"

I dropped my pen, dragging a hand through my hair. "Of course, stupid of me. You're right. Send him in."

She gave me a sweet smile, sidestepping enough for my father to enter. His gaze, as always, went to the Chinese wallpaper to my left with cranes and rice paddies. The decoration line had been a trial we'd done in the houseware department four seasons ago, and it'd been a huge hit. I'd used some of the product myself to make sure it had longevity and style.

"How was your day?" he asked, coming around my desk to kiss the top of my head.

"Good." I sighed. "I got everything I needed to done."

"That's great." He grinned, but it didn't reach his eyes. His apology hovered in the space between us, big and marshmallow-like, and entirely obvious to both of us.

"Spit it out, Dad." I closed my laptop and shut my diary. "What's up?"

He blurted. "I'm so sorry about last night, Bell Button. I was wrong. You were right. He was a stuck-up jackass."

I smothered a laugh. "Jackass, I agree with."

His shoulders fell, his slim figure bowing while resting his hip against my glass desk. "I won't do it again, and I promise Steve and I will back down about forcing you and Greg together. I know you're not a fan, and it's wrong of me to interfere." He picked up my fountain pen with turquoise ink— the only frivolous thing I used when everything else was black and white with Belle Elle regulation. "I should let nature take its course and let you find your own true love."

I groaned under my breath. "Don't you start with what nature intends."

Splashing alcohol onto Mr. Everett's head filled my mind—payment for using that same line.

Had he thought about me in the shower while rinsing off? Had he cursed me when dropping his suit in for dry cleaning? *Serves him right.*

Dad's eyebrow rose, but he wisely didn't comment. The soft lamp on my desk highlighted the threads of silver in his hair like Christmas fairy-lights. "Is there anyone? Anyone at all?"

I stood, grabbing my handbag and swooping down to pluck Sage from her basket. She crawled up my arm and settled like a furry sausage around the back of my neck. "No. No one.

And you have to come to terms that there might never be." I patted his shoulder. "I'm happy. I don't need a man to validate my existence."

Besides, I'm so young still.

He acted as if I were already slipping down the side of the age-hill of no return.

His eyes grew sad. "If you knew what love felt like, you wouldn't be so sure about that statement, Elle."

"I *do* know what love feels like. From you and Mom and Sage." I moved toward the door, turning off floor lamps that I found gave a homely glow as I went. "Promise me you'll stop meddling, and I'll take you to dinner to make up for last night."

He strode forward, happiness replacing his regret. "On one condition."

I sighed dramatically, reaching up to scratch Sage beneath her chin. "What condition?"

He came forward and rested his hands on my shoulders, not caring when Sage swatted him with her paw. "Just promise me that when a man does come along who makes you fall in love, that you'll give him a chance. That you'll reserve judgment until he's proven he's worth holding on to, and then you'll never let him go."

My heart plummeted to my toes as I smiled brightly, hiding the internal agony he'd just caused. "I'll amend one piece of that promise and agree. *If* a man comes along. If that miracle happens, I'll give him a chance before I squish him."

What I didn't say was I'd already met that man. That significant person who got under my skin and made me dream.

Only thing was, I hadn't held on tight enough.

And I'd lost him.

CHAPTER FOURTEEN

THREE DAYS LATER, my life had returned to normal.

No more sleepless nights thanks to Mr. Everett—they were sleepless because of my guilt toward Nameless. Mundane mornings on the treadmill flowed into agonizing afternoons with board meetings.

Life was controllable once again.

Fleur continued to help me run the empire while Dad took a few days off at my insistence. His skin had lost some color, and I'd caught him coughing the other day with a rattle I didn't like. If it was the flu, I wanted him safe and warm at home while Marnie, the cook, made him healthy snacks. I didn't want opportunistic germs straining his already strained heart.

Steve helped me host a few conference calls from Beijing and Montreal about our new infant line releasing next month, and work once again tugged me deep into its clutches, erasing any memory of tipping alcohol onto some stranger's head.

Until the third day when I scooped Sage up and headed to the shop floor for a quick walk around. I did random inspections throughout the week—never announced or fore-planned, so employees weren't prepared.

If I had a spare fifteen minutes, I found no better place to stretch my legs than strolling around the racks of new-smelling merchandise, eyeing up displays, spying on staff, and scoring any areas that needed tweaking.

As the elevator carried me from the top floor to the bottom, the mirrored walls showed Sage as she lay over my shoulders, tapping my dangling crystal earring that matched the ivory dress with soft caramel lace. The lacy panel covered my chest and worked in a flower pattern to flare over my hips before reconvening at the hem.

Fleur had added it to my paperwork pile to take home with me last week. I'd thought it was too detailed and feminine for work attire, but when I'd tried it on this morning, I didn't want to take it off. The paleness of it should've washed out my blonde complexion; instead, it made me glow as if I'd just stepped off a plane from Tahiti.

Not that I knew what that was like. The only air travel I did was to factories around the world, and I ended up wearing ear protection and overalls while marching around in heavy boots with a clipboard.

The doors opened with a soft chime, and I strode forward in matching caramel heels, clipping quickly over the anti-slip driftwood-planked floor that our focus groups said calmed them with the gray tones and encouraged spending mentality.

Everything—from the warm beige on the walls, to the deep purple curtains in the changing rooms—was chosen by a color guru who convinced us purple made people believe they were rich because it was the color of royalty and wealth, and beige stole their worries and stress, allowing them to see the treasure trove of merchandise that could all be theirs for the small price ticket tucked demurely inside.

"What department should we investigate first, Sage?" I murmured so as not to attract attention from shoppers.

Not that I could avoid being noticed, seeing as I strode purposely through Belle Elle with a cat wrapped around my shoulders. Luckily, she was of the small variety and not tubby like some cats I'd seen.

I glanced toward the lingerie department where an equal number of awkward men bought gifts for their loves ones while bold women brazenly fingered G-strings and garter belts.

I knew the manager, Kim, would keep her staff in line; the displays were impeccable with its small scaffold of pantyhose, playful kink, and lace. I wouldn't waste my time on areas I didn't need to improve.

Narrowing my eyes, I searched for sloppily folded sale items or imbalanced banners or scruffy shop assistants.

The houseware section was a little messy with its figurines and lamp cords. The women's shoe department needed a memo to tell them to pick up empty boxes from customers pulling them from the shelves. And children's wear would definitely earn a slap on the wrist for a banner promising twenty percent off bibs when a high chair was bought.

That promotion ended two days ago.

However, the area that set my heart racing with chaos was the man's division where five-thousand dollar blazers were tossed over racks, obscuring pressed trousers and faultless shirts. Ties draped over mannequin arms like streamers, and the sock table was a rummaged disaster.

Sage meowed softly, most likely saying in kitty talk for me to calm down before I found the unsuspecting manager and fired him on the spot.

"Where the hell is he and his staff?" Striding forward, my hands curled as yet more disorder revealed itself. A shirt had fallen off its hanger and lay on the floor. The floor! Belts tangled in a viper-nest on the cash register.

What the hell is going on?

"Three warnings, my ass," I muttered. "This is grounds for instant dismissal."

I didn't care the men's department hardly ever covered the extravagance it cost to run with its cashmere imported material and on-site tailor from Savile Row. This was Belle Elle, and it had severely let my company down.

"What's the manager's name again?"

Sage snuffled into my neck.

"You're no help."

She meowed.

No matter how many racks I charged down, looking for a victim wearing a Belle Elle nametag and noticeable lavender work shirt, I couldn't find anyone. Not one.

Where on earth are they?

There should be at least three to four staff manning this section at all times.

My eyes fell on the brightly lit sign for the changing rooms.

I shouldn't.

Women weren't permitted in there. But surely, the boss was.

Tilting my chin with authority, I marched through the archway and slammed to a stop.

If I thought the shop floor was a disaster, the changing rooms were a catastrophe.

Clothes everywhere!

Thousands of dollars of merchandise on the floor and piles drowning the leather-studded ottomans.

"What is the meaning of this?" I placed my hands on my hips as four men—who I paid a decent hourly wage and should be on the shop floor enticing people to buy—all gathered around something of utter fascination.

Something I couldn't see.

The floor manager swiveled in place, his mouth falling open. "Oh, hello, Ms. Charlston. I'm sorry I didn't see you there."

"You didn't see me because clothes are *everywhere*. It looks like a World War Ten started in here." I motioned to the pyramids of expensive suits just crumbled on the floor as if they were five-dollar t-shirts. "Clean this mess up, immediately. And get your staff at front of house. There're no assistants out there."

"Of course, Ms. Charlston." The manager nodded; his identification tag showed his name was Markus. "Right away." Clicking his fingers, he snapped, "George, Luke, get back out there. Ryan and I can finish with Master Steel."

Instantly, the two younger staff members dropped the shirts looped over their arms onto the already overflowing ottoman and dashed past me with respectful, apologetic smiles.

I didn't watch them go. I couldn't. My gaze glued to the little human I hadn't seen thanks to staff and shirts surrounding him.

"Oh, I'm so sorry; I didn't know I'd interrupted something." I glanced at Markus. "Why didn't you say something?"

"Because you're right, ma'am. We don't need four attendants to dress one child."

I eyed the kid who stood in front of the floor-to-ceiling mirror, swimming in men's trousers and a blazer that came to his knees. I gave him a quick smile, moving closer to Markus. "Why is he in the men's department and not in children's wear? He'll never find anything to fit him."

The boy looked at me in the mirror, not bothering to turn around. "I'm not a kid."

I startled at the sharp staccato of his adolescent voice. The pinched look in his cheeks and wildness in his gaze spoke of a child running out of patience and either close to tears or temper. I hadn't been around many kids, but I guessed he was nine or ten.

"I want a suit. Penn said I could have a suit. Like him. I want to dress like him and Larry."

Sage squirmed on my shoulders, squinting at the boy. Just like me, she wasn't used to bossy children. Not equipped to reply to a sentence I had no way of understanding, I looked back at Markus. "Can you explain?"

Markus grinned at the boy. "Of course. This is Stewart. He prefers Stewie, though, don't you?"

The boy nodded. "Stewie." He poked a finger into his chest. "That's me."

"Okay…" I smiled as if it was a perfectly acceptable name and not a thick-type soup I found utterly unappetizing. "And Stewie wants a suit."

Stewie grinned, showing a gap in his front teeth where a baby tooth had fallen, and an adult one had yet to appear. "Yup. Penn is helping. He said all men have to have at least three suits. One for a wedding, a funeral, and business."

"A funeral?" My heart sank. "Is that where you're going?"

"No." Stewie brushed chestnut hair away from his face, eyeing his rosy cheeks in the mirror and ears that slightly protruded. "But it's better to be prepared. That's what he and Larry always say."

I moved forward, my hand sliding upward to scratch Sage as she hissed at the small creature. "And who are Larry and Penn? Your fathers?" The world was an open society these days. Larry and Penn could be married. Or they could be his uncles or teachers or just friends. Or brothers. Hell, Larry and Penn could be generous kidnappers for all I knew.

Stewie screwed up his nose. "Ha, that's funny." His mirth faded. "Wait...I kinda suppose they are. Now, I mean. I never had a dad before." His angular face brightened. He wasn't chubby like some children of his age were. He had a hard edge about him that couldn't be tamed, even in the ridiculously huge suit with cuffs hanging over his hands like penguin flippers.

I glanced over my shoulder to Markus. "Where are his fathers? Why are you and my staff playing babysitter?"

"Um, he's only here with one gentleman, Ms. Charlston. And he just popped out for a moment. Urgent phone call, I believe." He shuffled. "But he made the mess, not us. He and Stewie tried to find something smaller—smaller belts, socks, ties—an entire wardrobe, you understand. We settled on agreeing that Stewie would pick a suit he liked, and then we'd send it to be tailored to fit him."

My eyes widened. "But that will end up being an entirely new suit. There is no way a tailor can turn a man's thirty-eight into a boy's twelve."

"But isn't that what I'm paying for?" a cool, svelte voice murmured behind me. It throbbed with glamour while somehow bordered curt impatience. "Isn't that what Belle Elle prides itself on? Providing what other stores cannot? Because if it isn't...then my apologies; we'll go somewhere else."

I spun in place, my heart already leaping into a churning sea at his tone.

The moment my eyes locked onto the newcomer's dark brown ones, the past three sleepless nights and long hours caught up with me. Shaking hijacked my arms and not because I'd upset a customer and tarnished a little of what he rightfully said was our motto but because it was him.

Him!

"You."

"Yes, me." Mr. Everett smirked. "Nice to see you again."

"What are you doing here?"

He rolled his shoulders, his fingers tightening around his phone. "Same thing as everyone else, I suspect. Putting our money into your pockets."

I crossed my arms. "Yet you leave your son for my staff to babysit. That isn't part of their job description."

"I apologize. It was an urgent call and only lasted a few minutes." He looked past me to the boy swimming in wool and hand stitching. "You okay, Stew? Find something you like?"

Stewie turned and headed toward us, his feet dragging the trouser lengths like clown socks behind him. "Yep. I like this one."

Mr. Everett eyed the soft gray with navy blue pin striping. "Me too. Good choice."

Stewie shrugged out of the blazer and passed it to Markus who stood ever professional, minding his own business.

I couldn't decide if I wanted to run away or shove this miscreant out of my store. Son or no son.

Wait...he has a son.

He's married to a man named Larry and has a son.

Not only had my father got the story completely wrong at the bar, but Mr. Everett had also fibbed about being interested in me and having a 'knack' with women.

My temper steamed, and before I could censor, I said,

"Turns out you're full of lies, Mr. Everett."

His eyes narrowed as a dark cloud settled over his face. "Excuse me?" He opened his arm as Stewie slotted himself against his side, reaching for his phone and swiping in the passcode to pull up Angry Birds.

I stepped back as Sage sank her claws into my neck in warning.

Good call, kitty.

I let my arms fall, and tension disperse. It meant nothing that he'd lied or that he was gay. Why hadn't I seen it? Of course, he was gay. He was far too well dressed and manicured in every way—trim nails, groomed eyebrows, and thick sorrel hair with the occasional honey highlight. That couldn't be natural.

He wasn't natural.

He was fake.

And I was done.

"I apologize for interrupting your shopping experience. I hope you enjoy the rest of your visit to Belle Elle." Stepping forward, I did my best to avoid his bulk in the narrow hallway with changing rooms on either side.

He wasn't courteous and didn't step aside to let me pass. He just stood there, giving me the choice to squeeze past the small gap or wait and glare into his eyes.

The same eyes that had molten heat and a perpetually pissed expression. He was like sugar and salt, pollen and poison—someone dangerous. Prickles of self-preservation urged me to leave while frissons of curiosity whispered for me to stay.

I didn't like either.

I didn't like him.

Needing to gain control, I looked at Markus. "Please ensure this department is tidy as soon as possible. And ask the tailor to triple check Stewie's measurements so the alterations are perfect first time."

"Yes, Ms. Charlston."

"His name is Master Steel. Not Stewie," Mr. Everett clipped. "Just like I'm Mr. Everett to you and Penn to him and you're Ms. Charlston to everyone and never Noelle."

What the hell does that mean?

I stiffened. "Let me pass."

"No."

I sucked in a breath. "Don't ruin a nice afternoon out for your son, Mr. Everett. Your husband would be very sad to receive a phone call saying you'd been arrested for disrupting the peace in my department store."

His body shifted from tense to downright nasty. His hands opened and closed as if he'd like nothing more than to strangle me. His gaze flickered to Sage around my nape then back to my face. He didn't seem surprised I wore a silver cat as an accessory. "You'd like that, wouldn't you?" His lips quirked at the corners. "For your information, I'm not married. And I prefer my dates with tits rather than balls."

I flinched. "Hardly suitable conversation with a child present."

Stewie mumbled with his eyes glued to Angry Birds. "I've heard worse. Believe me."

"Worse?"

What sort of environment did Mr. Everett expose this kid to? Why was he so skinny? Should I get child services to do a 'random' house call?

"If you recall, Ms. Charlston, I asked you to go to dinner with me the other night. Why would I do that if I wasn't interested in women?"

I ignored his question. It didn't matter what his sexual orientation was or his reason for asking me out.

I wasn't interested in either answer. "I'm not sure why you had the need to inform an impartial stranger of your relationship preferences, Mr. Everett, but I can assure you, I don't care in the slightest."

I moved forward, nudging his shoulder with mine, letting Sage's tail flick his throat as I circumnavigated toward the exit.

"Now, if you don't mind. I have more pressing things to attend to."

I looked at the little boy. "Goodbye, Master Steel. I hope you like your new suit."

Without a backward glance, I marched as prim and proper as I could, yet some feminine part of me put an extra swagger in my hips. My own body irritated me, wanting to come across as aloof and sexy when really I shouldn't give a damn.

I *didn't* give a damn.

I'd dumped his drink on his head a few days ago, and now I'd told him off while he was spending *his* money in *my* store.

Oh, well.

That was all he was good for.

Adding to the bottom line and becoming nothing more than a nuisance on my day's agenda.

"Come on, Sage. Let's go back to the office." I made my way quickly through the racks, noticing the mess had been tamed to its usual regimented glory. The long sweeping walkway linking the departments beckoned; I increased my speed.

Something strong and unbreakable latched around my wrist, yanking me backward.

I tripped in my heels, falling.

I crashed against a very warm, very unmovable, very, *very* toned chest.

Sage meowed, leaping from my shoulders with feline grace and landing on her feet as whoever had the audacity to grab me spun me around and planted two possessive hands on my upper arms. "You don't get to do that again."

I focused on his mouth and how damn close it was. How his aftershave reeked of heavy notes and woodsy musk. How his fingers dug into me like talons.

How dare he touch me like that?

How dare he believe he had the right to leap over bounds of propriety and somehow trap me in the middle of an argument I wasn't even aware existed.

Snatching my arms from his grip, I glowered. "Don't get to do what?"

"Be rude and leave." His glare laced with dynamite. "At least, this time, you don't have access to liquids."

"If I did, I know where I'd pour them."

His temper crackled, igniting a magnetic field between us until invisible lines of energy lashed us together. Confused energy. Misplaced energy. Energy that couldn't possibly spark to the same frequency when I couldn't stand the sight of him.

"You'll never do that to me again."

"I agree." I nodded with a perfect snap. "Because I plan on never seeing you again. Glad we could agree on something for a change."

He rubbed his jaw, looking me up and down. "You said you never wanted to see me again at the restaurant, yet here we are." He looked around the store, noticing what I'd already seen—that we were alone amongst a lake of clothes, hidden by towers of suede jackets and designer jeans.

He stepped closer, backing me up into a rack of limited edition laptop bags for the hard working male. "Did you think about me, Ms. Charlston? Did you think about my offer?" He licked his bottom lip. "Did you think about what we could *do* together?"

The way he emphasized 'do' sent a ripple of frustration through my belly. Frustration born of annoyance and that dreaded awful concoction of lust. The same lust that'd swarmed without warning the night of my nineteenth birthday. The same lust that'd almost made me lose myself to a man I'd only just met.

I'd learned my lesson that night.

I wouldn't forget it now.

In this light, with the shop fluorescents blaring down and the patchwork of clothes around us, Mr. Everett looked nothing like that man in a black hoodie. It'd been dark that night with so many things happening. My memory struggled to cling to truth rather than embellish with myth. I remembered

Nameless had black hair matted into dreadlock-curls, a beard, and clothes that'd long since needed a wash. His eyes were a rich brown like devil's cake. His lips masculine and handsome, adding animation to an otherwise guarded face.

If he'd been my savior, then Mr. Everett was my nemesis in his perfected splendor and arrogant attitude.

My wits came back, pushing away the heat in my stomach and the fizz in my heart from confronting this man once again.

I slipped into CEO mode, shutting everything else off. The force-field hissing between us severed as I forced a laugh as brittle and bright as glass. "Wow, I knew you had an ego, but I didn't know it'd taken up residence of your entire body." I tapped my bottom lip with an ivory painted nail. "What question would you like me to answer first?"

He frowned. "What?"

I counted on my fingers. "One, no I didn't think about you because you barely factored on my radar of noticeable things. Two, no I didn't think about your offer because frankly, I forgot about you the moment I walked out of that restaurant. And three, I most certainly did not think about what we could *do* together because that would mean I noticed you, which I didn't. Which, I believe, I just clarified."

Sage wrapped her lithe silver-furred body around my ankles, creating static against my pantyhose. I bent down and scooped her up, careful to keep my eyes away from Mr. Everett's crotch. I wedged her like a teddy bear into my embrace rather than letting her resume her position like a parrot on a pirate's shoulder.

I needed her close. I needed to use her as support so I could get out of there and away from this man without either slapping him or kissing him.

I couldn't understand why my mind flashed with broken things—of violently attacking him, of giving into the unexplainable fury he invoked in me.

The way he watched me, with a languor simmering with bitterness, said if I gave into such stupidity and started something, he'd be the one to end it with me slammed against the wall and his hands up my skirt.

I didn't like him.

I most certainly didn't want him.

At all.

He chuckled softly. "Now who's the liar, Ms. Charlston?" He sniffed the air, almost as if he could drag my perfume and truth into his lungs. "You did think about me and you're thinking about what we could *do* right now." He lowered his chin, watching me from shadowed eyes. "Aren't you?"

I clenched my teeth and didn't reply. A haughty sniff would have to do because I didn't trust myself not to curse him to the underworld and call for security.

I never suffered passion as sick as this. Never wanted to cause physical harm to someone I'd only just met.

He was all wrong.

He made my good turn bad.

Leave.

Right now.

With a glare, I spun around and stalked toward the walkway and freedom.

Only, there he was again, darting around me and planting himself in my trajectory. Wedging his hands in his gray slack pockets, he smirked. "Want to know my answers to those three questions?"

His voice rippled over my mind but his posture turned a simple question into a labyrinth of disbelief. Something about the way he moved—the way his hands sought the sanctuary of his pockets.

It was familiar.

He tore apart my wondering by leaning close, plucking the energy lines still humming between us. "Do you want to know?"

"No."

"Too bad." He had the gall to walk forward, forcing me to either accept his closeness or step back.

I didn't want him touching me, so I backed up.

And then another step.

And another.

Back and back he forced me, all while our eyes never unlocked and no physical touch ensued. He did touch me, though. His gaze set fire to my skin with every second he stared. I cursed the way my stomach clenched as my spine pressed against a cabinet holding t-shirts in every color for any occasion.

He smiled coldly. "Seems you aren't opposed to doing what you're told, after all."

"What?" I squeezed Sage so hard, she sharpened her claws on my wrist.

"I wanted you against a flat hard surface and what do you know…you're against one."

My mouth went dry as his hand came up, looping around the silver pole of the cabinet stand. He didn't hem me in, but he did lean forward until most of his weight pivoted on his arm, his body hovering so damn close.

He made me prickly as a cactus, hot as a rainforest.

And wet.

I couldn't remember the last time someone had puppeteered my body in such a way.

Well, yes I can remember.

But at the same time, I didn't want to. Not while I was affected by a man so totally different to that chocolate kisser in my past. It was ridiculous but I felt like I cheated on him— trampling over my oath to help him, ripping up the debt I had to find and save him.

I hadn't lived up to my promise and every second I spent licking my lips, drunk on cheap chemistry, I cheapened what'd happened between us.

The same rush of pleasure I wanted Nameless to take now begged for a new master.

And I don't even like this man.

I didn't like myself.

But it didn't matter because my heart understood he was an egotistical asshole and my body deemed him acceptable enough to scratch my lust-itch regardless.

His gaze dropped to my mouth. His voice was soft, coaxing. "One, I did think about you. A lot more than I should probably admit. I thought about forcing you to accept my offer, so at least I could get you behind closed doors. And I most certainly thought about what we could *do* together."

His head erased the distance, his minty breath slipping past my lips and somehow taking up residence in my lungs, suffocating me. "I thought about it in the shower, in bed, fuck, even in my office." His head came down. His nose nuzzled the shell of my ear, disrupting the crystal earring so it tinkled softly.

His other hand came up, a single finger unfurling and tracing an electrical cord down my arm, slipping to my side and boldly pressing against my waist to my hipbone. "You're a stunning woman, Elle Charlston, and your father was right. Whatever man you end up with is a lucky fucking bastard, but I don't think anyone stands a chance."

He looked into my gaze with cold, pitying look. "You have a prison gate around yourself that you're too afraid to unlock and be free."

I *hated* that he understood me when he had no right.

I *despised* the way he'd used the word free when I myself thought that phrase far too often.

And I *loathed* that his body heat stung mine with sensation and my nipples tightened to pain.

I had no resolution to push him away.

His fingertip suddenly left my hipbone and landed on Sage's head. "It's funny that you're carrying your pussy around. Is that an invitation in some strange way?"

I spluttered. "Get your hand off my cat."

He immediately held it up in surrender before once again tracing a fingertip from my shoulder to my wrist.

It took every ounce of training and discipline not to shudder or puddle to the floor. How long had it been since someone had petted me? How long since I'd been touched other than a quick fatherly hug or pat well done?

Never.

That's how long.

Because even Nameless had never stroked me. He'd grabbed me, kissed me, fondled me, but never stroked.

I squeezed my eyes, doing my best to find normalcy. Grasping the frigidness inside that still remained like a never thawing glacier, I was glad my misplaced yearning couldn't melt it.

I was better than this.

Better than him.

Sidestepping where his arm wasn't latched to the cabinet, I ducked around a rack of hanging slacks and cloaked myself with government. "I think you over-estimate yourself, Mr. Everett. I don't care if you thought about me and I don't appreciate thinking about what you were doing to yourself in the shower."

I grew bolder as he stood there silently, a malevolent glare in his gaze.

Sage had enough of my embrace and crawled back to her spot on my shoulders. With my arms free, I let them hang proud and regal with my back tight and smile plastic. "If you thought you could overpower me, make me weak in the knees, and force me to go on a date with you, you failed yet again. Not only am I even more determined never to see you again, but you just gave away two very significant pieces of information that mean you're not nearly as mysterious as you think you are."

"Oh?" His eyebrow raised, the faintest sign of confusion lurking beneath the heated coal of his irises. "And what exactly is that?"

I grinned condescendingly. "Out of all the department stores in New York, you happen to choose Belle Elle. And out of the three chains we have in the city, you chose the head office. Why is that? Because you thought you might bump into me?" I shook my head. "Pity. I must admit you came at the right time and coincidence decided to shove us together but only to allow me to clarify that no matter what you say or do, my answer will forever remain no—"

"Seeing as you're taking way too much pride in thinking you figured out my shopping habits, let's move on. What's the second thing I've revealed?" His patent leather shoes squeaked as he moved, once again hinting he wasn't as comfortable as he implied.

His uncertainty fed my resolution. I held my chin high. "That you aren't just a man in a suit looking for a quick one-night stand in a bar."

"I'm not?" His face shut down. "How can you tell?"

"Because you have a son. Because you care enough to spend a fortune on something ridiculous because it's based on self-worth, not the wardrobe. And because you and this unknown Larry person obviously have some resemblance of a heart. Otherwise, that kid wouldn't want to have anything to do with you, yet he willingly curled into you to play Angry Birds."

His posture resembled a furious predator. "You're more observant than I gave you credit."

"No, I'm normally this observant." I clipped onto the walkway to freedom as if I was Dorothy on the yellow brick road to the wizard. "You just don't know me."

I strolled away before he could reply.

CHAPTER FIFTEEN

"THIS INVITATION JUST arrived for you." Fleur waltzed into my office the following day in a pink and yellow sundress that somehow flirted the line between work-appropriate and beachwear.

I glanced from my laptop to the flocked envelope she held, hating the way my mind took the interruption and ran swiftly from human resource issues to once again thinking about Mr. Everett.

I'd successfully pushed him away more times than I would admit. I did not need him in my brain anymore. I didn't even know *why* he was in my brain.

We had some weird form of connection, but I wouldn't buy into the bait and I definitely wouldn't be seduced by a man I couldn't stand.

"Who's it from?" I held out my hand as she approached my desk and placed the heavy invite into my awaiting fingers.

"It has a return address. Chloe Mathers, I believe."

"Chloe Mathers?"

Why do I know that name?

A memory tantalized me with some long ignored recollection, begging to be caught and tugged.

Chloe Mathers…

Fleur smiled and showed no intention of leaving as I spun the envelope in my hands and sliced it open with a letter knife.

I frowned, pulling free a single card with bronze accents on the corners and the standard description of being invited to a get-together.

My mind slammed into remembrance.

"Oh, no," I groaned. "*That* Chloe Mathers."

Fleur planted her hands on my desk, intrigue all over her face. "Who is she? It doesn't sound like you like her."

"It's not that I don't like her. More she doesn't like me." I flipped the invite upside down, trying to see something personal or hint that perhaps she'd sent this to the wrong person.

"She was the most popular girl in school. For a few months of the year, when it came time for school parties or proms, she befriended me. She and her little group of stuck-up witches would ply me with sleepovers—that I didn't want to go to, but my dad made me—and hold a seat for me in class— which I never sat in because they just cheated off my work—all to drag me to Belle Elle and get them discounts on dresses and shoes."

"Children can be such brats."

"Yep." I nodded distractedly, remembering how much I'd hated high school. How every hour I spent in the faculty classrooms and listened to teachers drone on was a waste because, unlike my peers, I didn't get to go home and play outside or hang with sweet boyfriends on the weekends.

Once the bell rang, David picked me up and drove me to Belle Elle where I'd work until well past most other students' bedtimes.

I looked up, nibbling with uncertainty and nerves I thought I'd deleted from being an outcast at school. "Do you think they sent it by mistake? Why would they invite me?"

"What is it?" Fleur plucked the invite from my hold, scanning the details. "It has your name on the top, so it isn't a mistake."

She read out loud, "You're cordially invited to spend the evening reminiscing and sharing life's progress with the girls from St. Hilga's Education this coming Friday at the Palm Politics. Yourself and plus one are invited." She wrinkled her nose. "Ugh, I can hear their contemptuous attitudes just from a generic invitation."

I hung my head, massaging the muscles in my neck. "It's short notice, isn't it? Do they mean this Friday or next?"

She glanced at the envelope, peering at the stamp. "Uh oh, it's tonight. It was sent a week ago. I guess it got lost in the mailroom. It is, after all, addressed to Elle the Ding Dong Belle."

I smothered my face in my hands. "Oh, God, don't remind me of that awful nickname."

"Man, kids are cruel," Fleur muttered.

I didn't untangle myself from my hands, pretending the pink light coming through my fingers could erase my childhood, and I could forget about pranks and nasty little girls.

Fleur straightened some paperwork on my desk, stacking a pile of folders, and placing a few stray pens into my stainless steel holder. When order had been granted, and my nerves had calmed somewhat—reminding me they couldn't hurt me anymore—that I was in my Belle Elle tower and they were down there in Manhattan somewhere, I looked up and breathed deep.

We were living our lives. Away from each other. It was perfect.

Only Fleur ruined my co-existence by saying, "You know you have to go, right?"

"What?" My mouth hung open. "No way in hell am I going."

"You have to. Not to prove to them how incredibly successful and powerful you are but to prove to yourself."

I scoffed, plucking a pen from the holder and tapping it wildly against my notepad. "I don't need to do anything of the sort."

She planted a hand on her hip, giving me a raised eyebrow and a look that said 'yeah, right.'

I ignored her. "No way. No how." I snatched the invite and stabbed my finger at the plus one. "Besides, I have no one to go with. If I had some drop-dead gorgeous man who could remind me to stand tall and not let them win, then *maybe*. But I don't, and they'll most likely have their man candy with a rug rat or two. And I'm still an outcast like I always was in high school with her cat."

Sage nudged my ankle, yawning with her cute little tongue shaped into a funnel.

"I love you, Sage, but you're hardly 'bring to a party' material."

I'd already unwittingly showed how sad and depressing my personal life was to Mr. Everett by wearing her on my shoulders yesterday.

No.

I'd had enough embarrassment in my life already without adding more to it.

Refreshing my laptop screen, I did my best to read forecast numbers and find them riveting.

Fleur shifted. "I really think—"

"No." I kept my eyes glued on the spread-sheet. "Now, if there isn't anything else, I'd appreciate some quiet, so I can get this done."

She sniffed but turned and plodded dramatically to the door. Reaching it, she turned with a spin so fast it kicked out her dress into a tulip flare. "You know what? I'm taking charge of this. You wore that ivory and caramel lace dress because I made it easy for you to do so. This is the same sort of thing. I know you don't like him, but he's handsome and will have your back."

My heart froze into a popsicle.

She'll call Mr. Everett?

How does she know about him?

He won't have my back.

He'll find some other surface to push me against and terrorize me more.

I stiffened. "No, Fleur. Whatever you're thinking. Stop it."

"You'll thank me once you've seen yourself in their eyes.

When you've felt their awe at how hard you work and their envy at your unlimited bank accounts. And you'll pretend you aren't, but you'll be happy when they flirt with your man and find out he only has eyes for you."

She's going to do it.

She'll call him.

She'll deliberately sabotage my desire never to see him again.

Before I could tell her I had no intention of being fulfilled by jealousy or had any desire to announce to the undeserving witches from high school what my bank account looked like, she was gone.

To ruin my life.

And I couldn't do a thing to stop it.

CHAPTER SIXTEEN

"I'M GOING TO kill my assistant tomorrow."

David raised an eyebrow as I climbed from the backseat of the Range Rover. "Nice of you to inform me. I'll ensure the appropriate lawyers are called."

I gave him a grim smile. "I do not want to be here, David. Do you think—"

He smothered a slight grin. "Ma'am, if you want, I'll drive you right home. But if you don't mind me saying, you look beautiful, and it seems a shame to waste such beauty without having one drink before you go."

I narrowed my eyes. "You're a meddler. Just like she is."

"I'm nothing of the sort. In fact, I'll help with the murder tomorrow if tonight is not a success." He closed the back door and headed toward the driver's seat, leaving me abandoned on the sidewalk about to enter the dragon's playground. "Consider me a willing accomplice. Now, go and have fun, and call me when you're ready to leave."

My emotions were full of poutiness and frustration. I could just tell him I was ready *now*. But I wasn't a four-year-old, and he was right. It would be a waste not to go in for a second—especially after Fleur's wardrobe ministrations.

Not that I approved.

The dress she'd chosen was the most daring, risqué thing I'd ever worn. For a cocktail get-together, she'd gone over the top with a russet-gold silk gown that slinked around my ankles and split up one leg to mid-thigh. The back was non-existent with just enough height to cover my ass but leave my spine exposed, while the front swooped up to my throat in a gathered cowl.

She'd even gone as far to do my hair for me. She'd fishtail braided it, so it sat over my left shoulder and kept my naked back on display.

The entire time she fussed with my hair and makeup, I'd muttered she was fired and to start looking for other employment.

But once she showed me the finished product, shoved me into the car, and told me my date would meet me there, I had to admit a smidgen (a teeny tiny smidgen) of excitement filled me to have a night out with people other than business associates or my father and Steve.

And to be honest, I looked forward to spending an evening looking the way I did while tormenting and verbally sparring with Mr. Everett. It was the thought of him being there to take the spotlight off me from the nasty school girls that moved my unwilling feet into the nightclub where a small section had been roped off for our reunion.

Palm Politics was a strange blend of tropical fronds and the décor of a court of law. One freedom and sunshine. The other prison and shadow. The bar was the podium where the judge would sit and the booths dotted around were a mini oasis in a boardroom of wood and strobe light sentencing.

Goosebumps covered my skin—partly from cold and partly from anxiety at facing these women again—especially in a place such as this. Why couldn't it be a simple bar with no theme or message?

I hated anything to do with law courts and police—it only layered my guilt with more rancid icing at the thought of Nameless.

I'd tried. I'd failed. I hadn't given up but even the weekly phone calls I made to police officers who were kind enough to answer my questions had no news.

If I was a lucky sleeper who enjoyed vibrant dreams, I might've concluded he was merely made up of fantasies and heroism, bound together by imagination magic, and made brilliant by adolescent devotion.

But he had to have been real.

I still had the faintest scar on my nape from where my sapphire star had been ripped away, and I still endured the faintest seduction of chocolate on my lips when I was blessed enough to doze in his dream-company.

Standing in the paddling pool of partiers, I doubled my promise to do more. To track him down, no matter the cost.

Starting tomorrow.

Or tonight if I can leave early.

My minor discomfort at being watched by leering judges and glinting prison bars switched to major annoyance as Greg appeared from the crowd, holding a glass of champagne and a gin and tonic.

My heart instantly tobogganed down a cliff and shot off the edge in denial.

Oh, God, I'm so stupid.

Of *course*, Fleur hadn't invited Mr. Everett.

No one knew I'd seen him again, and only my father knew what'd happened at the Weeping Willow.

She has no clue he exists, so how could I think she'd invite him as my date?

I'm an idiot.

She hadn't ruined my aloofness at refusing Mr. Everett's offer to take me out. But she had sentenced me to endure a terrible evening.

There would be no banter.

No sexy butterflies.

Nothing but obligation to ensure I remained professional—so I didn't hurt Greg, my father, or Steve, and could look everyone in the eye on Monday with no regrets or dismay.

It didn't matter my life would be so much simpler if I just gave into what everyone wanted. But my heart was stubborn and didn't find Greg romance material in the slightest.

"Hi, Elle." Greg passed me the champagne.

I didn't even like champagne. If he cared for me as much as he pretended to, he would've remembered that from all the forced dinners we'd endured with our fathers.

The night suddenly looked a thousand times worse.

I might be a bitch in the boardroom, but I wasn't mean, and Greg had dropped whatever plans he had to be here with me just because Fleur had called him.

I wouldn't be nasty.

But I wouldn't be overly gracious, either.

"Hello, Greg." I sipped the cold bubbles, hiding my grimace. "It's very nice of you to come with me. I hope Fleur didn't interrupt your evening."

He grinned, swiping a hand through his dark blond hair as his overly white teeth caught the strobe light glittering above. "Not at all. When she called, I couldn't believe my luck. Finally, a night out just the two of us." He leaned in with a wink. "Away from the chaperones."

I hid my distaste, forcing a smile. "Exactly."

He slotted himself beside me and, without asking permission, wrapped his arm around my waist. The warmth of his bare forearm tingled my spine and not in a good way. He'd come to this wearing a white t-shirt and black jeans. He looked handsome, of course—he was a good looking guy—but compared to the gown I wore and the finery Fleur had graced me with, I came across as ridiculously overdressed.

My heart plummeted even further off the cliff, splattering on the unforgiving terrain below.

Tonight had slipped from disaster to annihilation. Chloe would never let me live this down if they were all in semi-formal clothing and I appeared dressed like a prom queen.

Does it matter, though?

My brain tried to be mature and see the bigger picture. So

what Greg wasn't in a suit—it wasn't life or death. So what I might be over-dressed and Chloe might be the same cow I remembered—none of it made any difference to my tomorrow. I would still be me. I would still be as safe and as happy as I was yesterday.

Be brave, Elle.

And then leave with dignity.

Straightening my shoulders, I stepped out of Greg's embrace but immediately looped my arm through his before his face could fall.

Squeezing his bicep in thanks, I said, "Let's go mingle, shall we?"

* * * * *

Two hours I lasted.

Two hours where I was no longer me but a *better* version of me. Noelle was left behind, and Elle used the same techniques from dealing with men twice her age to wield mundane conversation with girls she'd long since forgotten about.

There was potty-training chats with Melanie and fake oohing and ahhing over her one-year-old Facebook pictures. There was biology class reminiscing with Frankie, pretending I felt the same way about our teacher Mr. Bruston, and how sexy his mustache had been.

Yeah, not at all.

There were snippets of cattiness from Maria and Sara about who ought to have gone out with Rollo Smith in summer camp, and the requisite fond recalling with Chloe about shopping late at night and running riot through Belle Elle when Dad let us sleep over in the lady's ware department.

She called me Elle the Ding Dong Bell only twice.

But each was like a knife in my side.

I didn't let it show.

I didn't hint at vulnerability or let my guard down.

Greg had no clue how hard this was for me. He merely guffawed at the nickname and plied me with more champagne I didn't want.

Every single conversation I put my all into. I smiled and nodded and listened. My cheeks hurt from fake grinning, my feet ached from standing, and my exposed back became extra sensitive to everything. My skin prickled with minor drafts as people moved behind me, warm patches as people stood close by, and even the tell-tale tingle of people staring at me, itching spots on my shoulder blades as their eyes became fingers and stroked me.

Out of the sixteen people here—eight women and eight men—Greg and I held our own. My dress had started the poshest of them all, but as more people arrived, I'd settled into an array of chiffon and lace, finally accepting that Fleur knew what she was doing.

The dress didn't take away my power. It *gave* me power. And for the first time, I believed in my own self-worth outside of Belle Elle. That I could hold my head high and not be afraid of judgment or wrongdoing. That I was my own person and not just a cog in the conglomerate my family had created. My world was just as good as any others—if not better.

The relief in that gave me a well of kindness to forget that Greg got on my nerves, and I didn't turn away from his touches of affection. I accepted three more glasses of champagne, even though the room grew warm and my skin glowed with bubbly heat.

By hour two, my bladder had done all the retaining of alcohol it could, and I excused myself to find the restroom.

Greg gave me a kiss on the cheek—which I didn't wipe away because the liquor made everything that much more acceptable—and left the roped-off area to make my way through the club.

I guessed the time was ten p.m. or so, but already, the place crawled with bodies and the aura of a good night ahead.

Finding the bathroom, I entered and slammed to a stop as I came face to face with my reflection in a full-length mirror.

Who the hell is that woman?

Her braid was a little disheveled with curls free and soft around her face. Her lips were puffy from licking droplets of champagne with remnants of pale pink lipstick. Her smoky eyes rimmed blue that looked far too sated and happy to be real.

I looked...loose.

My limbs moved with a relaxation I never had when sober. My movements less jerky and sedate.

Being tipsy suits you.

I rolled my eyes, listing a little to the left as the room swayed.

Being tipsy was a new experience and one I wouldn't often do. The false courage and intoxicating bravado could screw up my careful rules.

Greg suddenly didn't seem so annoying. Chloe wasn't such a bad girl. And the thought of going to work tomorrow was a task I had no intention of fulfilling as long as the beat of a bassy tune worked through my bones.

Wanting to return to the party, I quickly did what I was there to do and washed my hands. Drying my fingers on a paper towel, I ran the remaining dampness over my arms to cool my overheated skin.

I'd come to this club cold, and now, I was burning up.

Something else was burning up, too.

Something that normally only came alive around few very select males. My breasts were heavy, and a tugging sensation deep inside my belly demanded another drink—to let go for once. To stop fighting and let Greg kiss me because he was the only male around who knew what I was and who I had to be. He'd been raised in the same environment.

So what he annoyed me most of the time and didn't seem to truly care about me but only my legacy? He was a man. I was a woman. It was time to do something about my little problem and figure out how to be a sexual creature and not an untouched virgin any longer.

Striding from the bathroom, I walked with purpose, brushing against strangers and enjoying it for once rather than cringing at having no personal space. Up ahead, Greg laughed and touched Chloe's waist, bending to whisper something in her ear. The rest of the group mingled in twos and fours, chatting and drinking.

I knew those people.

I had a life.

I was invited to party with them.

I had freedom, after all.

Only, whatever freedom I thought I had jerked to a stop as a man's arm snaked around my waist, yanking me back. My languidness from champagne meant I folded neatly into his embrace, too slow to fight.

His lips landed on my ear. "If it was coincidence yesterday, it has to be fate today."

I froze.

Whatever tipsiness I suffered tripled as his hands roamed my ribcage, taking liberties he wasn't given, rubbing the soft silk into my skin in ways that should be illegal.

"Hello, Elle." His lips traced from my ear to my throat, nudging my braid to gain better access.

I shivered.

My body melted—not from him but the champagne. It *had* to be the champagne. I wouldn't allow it to be him.

Sucking in a breath, I tore myself from his embrace and swiveled to face him.

He was just as divine. Just as cocky. Just as dangerous.

"Are you stalking me?"

Mr. Everett grinned. "I wouldn't dare."

He stood in a gray suit with the cuffs of his blazer and white shirt pushed half-way up his forearms. How he managed to get the material that high over how muscular his arms were, I didn't know. The strobe light decorated his hair, making it seem light then dark, light then dark. The yin and yang of right and wrong—the glimpse of imperfections that made him eternally frustrating.

"After all, why waste my time when the universe keeps

putting you in my path?"

My mouth watered as his gaze locked onto my lips. A black ravenousness filled his eyes that any hot-blooded female understood—virgin or promiscuous.

"I don't believe it's the universe." I blinked, forcing myself to cling broken-nail tight to sanity. "I think it's some sort of game you're playing."

He lowered his jaw, stepping closer until our chests brushed. My nipples tightened embarrassingly hard. Not wearing a bra meant my reaction was noticeable through the burnished gold dress.

He licked his bottom lip, his gaze dropping to my breasts then back to my mouth. "If I *was* playing something, are you intrigued enough to learn the rules?"

"Never."

His lips smiled but his face was toxic. "Little liar."

His hand came up, tucking a wayward curl behind my ear. His fingers captured the diamante chandelier earrings I wore, tugging gently. "I think you are ready to play with me, you just don't want to admit it." He bent his head, breathing into my ear. "I've been patient, but I meant what I said to your father. I can make you do things, Elle. Things you want to do. Things *I* want to do. I particularly liked when you said you'd get on your knees and call me, what was it? Oh, master?"

I jerked back, but with his fingers holding my earring, I daren't move quickly or far.

He bent forward. His tongue licked my lobe just once.

A lightning bolt arched from his tongue to my belly. A crack. A fissure. A deep cavernous ache I needed, *needed* to fill.

"One date," he murmured. "That's all I'm asking."

The champagne switched to more potent alcohol. Had I truly had four glasses? It felt like twelve.

I swam in air. I wobbled in heat. I swayed as his hands locked around my hips, dragging me into him. Surrounded by people yet all alone in our little cosmos, he rocked his erection into my stomach, grinding his teeth with the same angry desire rampaging in my blood.

The room spun. I did my best to keep control. "I don't—I don't even like you."

"I don't like you."

"Then—" He shocked me mute as he kissed my cheek, then rewarded such sweetness with a nasty nip.

"Then what?" he taunted. "Finish, Elle."

My head weighed more than the galaxy. "Then…let me go."

"Can't." The tip of his tongue soothed the pinch of pain from his teeth.

Can't?

My mind doggy paddled through syrup.

Why can't you? Isn't mutual affection the first key to unlocking passions padlock?

His fingers looped around my throat, full of threat, robust with peril. "Liking each other doesn't matter." His fingers dug tighter into my skin. "What matters is how you feel about this." He glanced around, assessing how public we were, before his hand swooped between us and cupped between my legs.

The world shot to a standstill.

There was no more music. No more club.

I stood in mud so thick, I couldn't move. My only way free was this bastard and he was the one drowning me.

Everything inside me clenched then stretched then multiplied with a thousand screaming *'mores.'*

"Tell me to stop, and I'll stop. Tell me to remove my hand, and I'll remove my hand." His fingers feathered over me, rocking his palm against my clit; his fingers pressing over the tight lace protecting me. "But if you tell me you're all right with this, if you tell me to keep going, then you play by *my* rules. You become mine in every fucking sense."

I shivered as his fingers probed harder. I'd never been touched that way—let alone in a crowded bar.

"I—I don't know." Words were the hardest thing in the world to form. "I don't know what to say."

"I'll help you." His hand vanished. His body separated from mine as he grabbed my wrist and dragged me into the dark hallway of the bathrooms. Marching past the men's and women's, he tucked me against the wall and pressed me hard against it.

The moment I was trapped, he put his full weight on me, grabbed my leg, and hoisted it over his hip.

I gasped as he rocked his erection again, pressing directly where his hand had been only seconds before. "Oh—"

"That's one word." His face flashed with raven desire. "Say a few more. Agree to play with me."

My head wanted to roll back and break away as his mouth fastened against my throat—kissing, biting, sucking. I wanted no more thoughts, no more dos and don'ts. No more reasons why this was wrong and I needed to end it before I forgot everything.

My hands automatically flew to his hair, yanking on the softness, twining my fingers through his thick, healthy strands. The exquisite feel of him jerked me from the moment. For a second, I'd expected dreadlocked curls and chocolate. Of soft beards and urgent moonlight.

My body swelled but my heart shriveled.

Mr. Everett was not Nameless. Yet he was the second man to ever kiss and touch me in such a way—an accolade I didn't know if he deserved.

"Wait—I don't know what you want."

He chuckled into my neck. "I thought it was fucking obvious." He thrust up, his shoes squeaking a little on the hardwood floor as he slammed me into the wall with his pressure. "I want to fuck you, Elle."

My insides puddled at the crudeness. My ears rang for more even while my lips curled in disgust.

"I want to take you, own you, control you." His voice bordered on feral. "I'm not going to lie. I could say I wanted to date and pretend to fall for you. But I won't."

Conversation helped remind me I was human not an

animal. I latched onto words. "So...you just want sex?"

"What I want is to kiss you." His head came up, his lips glistening from sucking my throat. "Let me do that, then decide on the rest."

He hypnotized me. He corrupted me.

I breathed fast.

He saw a split-second answer—an answer I wished I could retract—and his mouth descended on mine.

His lips were soft but commanding, tearing through my chastity, spearing his tongue past my teeth.

I moaned as he took a kiss and turned it into something else. He switched it into water and fire and heat and chill. He hoisted me up the wall until the floor no longer existed, just air. Holding me up with his hips jammed against mine, he seared our bodies together.

And then, it was over.

Sharp, sweet, sudden...entirely soul-destroying.

"Say yes."

"Yes?"

"Yes to letting me have you." His voice blistered. "Say yes and you're mine and whatever comes next is my choice, not yours. You'll answer to me. I'll do whatever the hell I want. Sometimes, you'll hate me. Other times, you'll be grateful for my interference. Most of the time, you'll probably want to kill me."

He kissed me again. "But I can promise you if you say yes, fuck I'll make you feel good. I'll give you what you've been looking for. I'll make you free."

The stream of eloquence matched his hard-edged charm. He was pretty. Too pretty. So pretty it masked the ugliness hidden inside. It made me forget that there were more things to seek than just beauty—deeper things. Things he didn't possess.

In that hallway, in his arms, I didn't care.

I hated that I didn't care.

But that was the truth.

He made me shallow.

"Elle?" A voice interrupted our rapid breathing and aching bodies.

Instantly, Mr. Everett let me fall to my heels, backing away and subtly arranging his blazer over the obvious erection in his slacks. His eyes never left mine, full of promises and menacing intimidation.

I gulped, looking over his shoulder at the man who'd interrupted whatever the hell had happened.

Greg.

Smoothing my hair, I stepped forward.

Mr. Everett fell into rhythm with me, crossing his arms like a silent protector and aggressor all in one.

Greg glowered at him. "Who the hell are you?"

Mr. Everett glanced at me with a wicked smirk. That smirk held every sentence he'd uttered. Every command and description. He wanted me. I wanted him. He didn't like me. I didn't like him.

Hatred turned to frenzy.

A perfect drug for danger.

Everett's lips moved; his voice worse than the champagne with intoxication. "Who am I, Elle?"

My blood quivered to finish what he'd started. My brain short-circuited to bypass the fact I wanted him while hating him. If he could knock me so off balance with just a kiss, what could he do to me in bed?

He'd made me selfish as well as shallow.

But I can't sleep with him.

Could I?

I didn't like him. I didn't trust him. I definitely didn't believe I could ever fall for him.

So what?

You're old enough to have sex with no strings.

He's proven to have a heart somewhere. He has a son.

He. Has. A. Son.

He could have a wife and baggage and so many other mysteries I couldn't hope to solve. Carnal greed could never trump such laws.

Curling my hands, I shook away the fervour he'd dazed me with.

It didn't matter I wanted, needed, craved. It would never happen…if he was with another.

But he might not be.

Are you saying you'd ignore everything else and use him if he's single?

My nerves returned a thousand fold.

When I didn't reply, Mr. Everett prompted me. "Answer your friend. Tell him who I am to you." He narrowed his eyes. "Are we playing or shall I walk away?"

Such an innocent question loaded with sexual mist and unsatisfied misery.

My fingers fell to my dress, stroking the material, seeking comfort and answers.

"What the fuck is going on, Elle?" Greg marched forward.

I couldn't believe the champagne had made me think I could tolerate him. After being kissed by Mr. Everett and then even remotely entertaining the idea of doing the same with Greg, I couldn't imagine it. It would be like seeing the most spectacular sunset only to be told I had to live in fog the rest of my life.

"One second, Greg." I held up my hand, testing the locks and chains around my sexuality as they quaked under pressure. "Answer one question, Mr. Everett. Then I'll give you an answer."

"Fine." A sly grin decorated his handsome face. "But rest assured if your answer is yes, that's the last time you'll call me Mr. Everett."

"Oh?"

He looked triumphantly at Greg as he bent to whisper in my ear. "You'll be screaming my name as I stick my tongue inside you. You'll be sobbing my name as I make you come over and fucking over."

I stumbled.

His hand grabbed my elbow, a low chuckle on his breath.

"That name is Penn. You might as well get used to it if, of course, your answer is what I hope."

"Elle, are you sick?" Greg came forward, his eyes trying to murder Mr. Everett...*I mean Penn.*

I waved him away, flushed and nauseous, entirely too skittish to be hemmed in by another man after flashes of nakedness and dirty sex swarmed my mind.

"Yes, I'm fine." Ignoring Greg and giving all my attention to Penn, I asked, "My question is, are you with the mother of your child?"

Penn didn't reply.

"What?" Greg's eyes widened. "Not only are you cheating on me with this scumbag in a nightclub hallway but he's cheating on a family?" He threw his hands up. "For fuck's sake, Elle, I thought you were better than that. Your father believes you're better than that. *My* father believes you're better than that."

I snarled, hating the disgust in his voice even though I hadn't done anything wrong. Not yet, at least. If that was how those who knew me would look at me, I wanted nothing to do with whatever kinky pleasure Penn offered.

But it was as if Penn knew that.

He brought me close, whispering in my ear again as I kept my eyes locked on Greg. "I'll answer your question, but I'll also answer the other you just thought. First, I'm not married nor have I ever been. I'm as single as you are. I'm as confined as you are. That's all you need to know. Second, you're right to think people will judge you. The moment I've been inside you, people will know. You'll be different. You won't be able to help it. Rumors will start. Friends will change. Future love interests will hate you."

I stiffened, but he pulled me closer. "But I won't let you be subject to those rumors alone. Tell me yes, and I take control. You won't have to make any decisions or take responsibility for what we do. It'll all be on me." His tongue traced the shell of my ear, hidden from Greg thanks to my fishtail braid. "Give me that word, Elle, and I'll show you exactly what I mean."

I stood at the crossroads, staring at Greg and the future my father wanted—the one where I stood side by side with a man who knew Belle Elle the way I did and would help run the business—while a stranger held me and pressed his cock against my hip, blatantly claiming what wasn't his to claim.

One was a long-term choice. The other a short-term adventure.

I'd had enough long-term commitments in my life. I wanted to be different. I wanted a rumor or two because that would mean I was interesting and not predictable.

Greg made my decision ridiculously easy.

He came forward and grabbed my other elbow, pulling me away from Penn. "Elle, I'm willing to overlook whatever you just did with this bastard. You're drunk. I know I should never have given you that champagne. Let me take you home where you belong."

Home.

I no longer wanted to be at home.

I wanted to be lost and crazy and wild.

I yanked my arm from his hold. "I'm sorry, Greg. But I should've told you."

"Tell me what?"

Locking my eyes on Penn's, I whispered, "Yes. My answer is yes." A little louder, I added, "But it doesn't mean I like you."

"Doesn't mean I like you, either." Penn smiled full of cream and sharpness and calmly wrapped his arm around my shoulders, tucking me close.

Together, we faced Greg.

I didn't know what I expected Penn to do, but it was his turn to be in charge. I was in charge on a minute basis in every aspect of my world. If he wanted to share that control in a few areas, then fine…*be my guest*.

"I must apologize, too." Penn smiled coldly. "We weren't

ready to tell people, but I guess now is as good a time as any."

"Tell people what?" Greg's eyes filled with panic, not at knowing he'd lost me but that he'd lost any chance at owning Belle Elle. His true colors revealed.

Relief siphoned through me to be free of whatever takeover he'd planned. To finally see what I'd suspected all along—that I was right to be wary of him, smart to listen to the faint warning bells whenever he was around.

"Tell them that Elle and I…we're together."

I flinched a little as Penn kissed my cheek. Still uncomfortable and aroused and so confused I had no idea if this was what I wanted or not.

Too late now.

"Elle is mine. In fact, I'm taking her home right now. My home." He pushed me forward, deliberately forcing Greg to the side so we could pass. "We'll just say our goodbyes to the others."

Greg spluttered something I didn't hear.

I turned to Penn. "What do you mean the others?"

"The reunion you're here with."

How does he know that?

It added to all the other questions I had about him. All the ponderings and wonderings and itchy uncertainties he invoked.

Was it coincidence at Belle Elle or manipulation that he'd been there when I'd done my rounds?

Was it luck he was here tonight or careful planning?

Would answers to those questions change what I was about to do with him?

That was one question I didn't want an answer to.

My heart raced, already out of breath with what I'd agreed to participate in. "Let's just go. I'll call them tomorrow with my apologies."

"Oh, silly girl." He laughed. "The moment you said yes all your choices became void. This is my game now."

CHAPTER SEVENTEEN

"YOU MUST BE Chloe."

"I am." The girl who tormented me in high school simpered, tossing her red hair like a high-strung model. Her green dress complemented the tan she said she'd earned from the Caribbean last week. Her gaze sank into Penn as if he were some prize to be won. A prize she'd very much like to taste.

Penn pulled me to his side, feathering his hand up and down my arm. Such a simple touch, but it bruised with claiming and domination.

"I believe you know my partner, Elle." The mastery of his voice and damning sentence locked my spine and made Chloe jolt.

"Wait, partner?" She blinked. "I thought she was with Greg." She glowered at the way Penn found subtle ways of touching me. Her eyes found mine, hot with jealousy.

I'd never seen that grisly emotion on her face before. She believed I was beneath her to ever covert what I had.

Not tonight, it seems.

She sniffed. "You got two men now, Ding Dong Bell? A little greedy, don't you think?" Her giggle was forced and fake.

For a moment, I'd been proud to earn her cattiness. Penn was the type of man any woman could appreciate and desire with his crisp suit, unreadable eyes, and aloof handsomeness.

But that damn nickname stole everything, hurtling me

back to the school hallways as if I'd never left. I wanted to sink into the ground and never reappear.

I waited for Penn to mock me, just as Greg had. I tensed for him to snicker and roll his eyes at my misfortune. But he stood cold and primitive, a velvet purr falling from his mouth. "That's an unimaginative slur to call a friend, don't you think?"

Chloe fluffed her hair. "Oh, Elle knows it's in affection. Don't you, Bellie?"

I didn't respond.

Penn did, though. "Unoriginal nicknames are a sign of low intelligence." His snark cut through her tartness with an axe. "And in answer to your condescending question...Elle only has one partner. Me. And believe me, I'm all she'll ever need." His eyes smouldered with decadent chocolate. "I'll make sure of that."

His caresses turned heavy with guarantee. He danced the line of appropriate and wicked, deliberately stepping over it to antagonize those I had no wish to antagonize.

I wasn't petty or prideful.

I wanted to leave.

I opened my mouth to reply, but Penn squeezed me, keeping me silent. His touch was a hot poker controlling me and making me wet in equal measure.

The other girls from school slowly looked up from their conversations, paying attention to the tense standoff while trying to appear uninterested.

They didn't fool Penn or me as he smiled his signature sexy smirk and grabbed my chin. His lips planted on mine in a brutal kiss, marking me, consuming me as his tongue stole my arguments and his power pinched my remaining breath.

He stupefied me.

He bewitched me.

The instant I released the tension in my spine, he let me go—as if he'd deliberately kissed me to keep me out of my head and in my body with him.

"Are you going to tell them the good news, or shall I?"

His authoritative tone blended with a dark flirt.

I blinked. "Tell them what?"

I was one step behind.

I couldn't catch up.

I'd never been that way before. I'd always been the boss—always leading. I didn't know if I liked being a follower.

"Tell them you've decided to let me own you."

"Wait, what?" Chloe's mouth hung open. "What does that mean?"

I shook my head, rubbing the sudden goosebumps on my arms. Penn said we were playing a game. Yet I didn't know the rules or what was expected. To verbalize it in such crude terms in front of the bitches from my past wasn't appropriate.

My forehead furrowed.

He answered Chloe before I could. "We met a few days ago, and it was love at first sight." He dragged me close. "It took some convincing but Elle has agreed to give me a chance." He glanced at Chloe, filling his pretty face with ardent satisfaction. "She said yes."

"Yes to what?" Frankie appeared, eyeing Penn from his black shoes to his five o'clock shadow.

"Yes to marrying me."

The world screeched to a halt.

Wait...what?

"No, I—" I flinched, trying to tear myself from Penn's embrace.

He held me tighter, his fingers sinking like keys into my arms, turning a lock, keeping me bound to him and useless.

Chloe's mouth hung wider. "Wow, Elle, I never knew—"

"Never knew she was the sexiest woman alive?" Penn snarled with sudden viciousness. "Never knew she was one of the richest women alive? Never knew that she was ten times the fucking woman you'll ever be?"

I stood gobsmacked.

Why did he fight for me?

This was too much. Too fast. Too scary. Too far out of

my comfort zone.

Yes to marrying him?

I *never* agreed to that.

I'd agreed to sex.

Stupid, silly, sensual sex.

And now, it's time to say no.

I tore myself from his embrace, my body shaking. "Stop. That's not true. Don't spread such lies." I stared helplessly at Chloe whose face had turned snow white. "I'm so sorry. Ignore him. I don't know what's gotten into him. We've only just got together. We're not engaged. He's not—"

"What my fiancée here is trying to say—" Penn interrupted. "Is she's too kind-hearted to rub her success in your face even though you do the same to her. I don't need to hear stories of what it was like to grow up with you. I see her, and I see you, and I understand the shadow you made her exist in. But not anymore."

His teeth flashed as he snarled. "I'm stealing her from you now. From all of you. She's mine. And it's a sad loss that you never figured out what an incredible creature you had under your noses the entire time."

Greg sidled up, hate stares fired at Penn. "You don't know jack, dipshit. Elle and I were raised together. I know her a fuck load better than you ever will."

"You're the blindest of them all." Penn pointed at him. "I don't care how long you've known each other. You fucked up." He laughed low. "You'll never get her back because she'll never be the same once I've had her."

My cheeks turned into flames of hell. I ducked my chin, doing my best to hide. I wanted the club to vanish and Penn to disintegrate into dust.

Words and curses tangled to spew at him, but he pulled me from the crowd, away from cringe-worthy declarations, away from high school trolls and wannabe boyfriends, and through the nightclub to the fresh air outside.

I managed a few gulps of oxygen before he yanked me

down the alley between the nightclub and a restaurant and slammed me against the brick wall.

Quicksilver memories of another alley and another man tried to twist my present with my past. Garbled commands, ripped clothing, fists flying in the dark.

Nameless shot bright into my thoughts.

His black hoodie, his closed-off answers, his mind-melting kiss.

And then history had no power as Penn's lips crashed over mine and he replaced my remembered kiss with a savage one.

He kissed me and then he *kissed* me.

Each swipe of his tongue blasted through my decorum, dragging alive the sexual being who'd never been allowed to evolve.

His right hand bunched my dress up my leg. My brain tried to split—to focus on the foot traffic only a few feet away and not on the blistering heat of his fingertips on my inner thigh.

And then nothing else mattered as his touch found my core, pushing against my underwear.

He didn't ask permission.

He didn't pull back to see if I was okay with this.

He merely kissed me and fingered me over the lace.

All I wanted to do was to let go. To trust in the magic he created in my blood and allow him to be as arrogant as he wanted. To take charge.

But I couldn't.

I couldn't let him get away with what he'd said. His lies. His verbal bashing to people I had to converse with.

He was far too brash and daredevil for my world.

His mouth kept working mine, dragging a moan deep from my lungs.

I had a second before I drowned under his powerful wave and lost myself. A second and then I would be gone, and I couldn't blame anyone but myself.

So I bit him.

My teeth sank into his lip, not holding back as I did the only thing I could to slow things down and *breathe*.

He stumbled backward, holding his bottom lip where a bead of blood welled. "Fuck."

My ribcage rose and fell. I sucked in gasps, giving in to the slight hysteria he'd caused. I held up a shaky finger. "Don't touch me."

"Touch you? Fuck, I own you."

My braid caught like Velcro on the bricks behind me as I shook my head. "No. You don't."

His eyes etched with black. "You said yes, remember?"

"Yes to a beneficial sexual relationship. Not to damn marriage!"

"That's what's got you afraid? Marriage?" He chuckled "I have no intention of marrying you."

I frowned. "Then why lie about it?"

"Why not?" He shrugged. "Why do other people have to know exactly what we do and who we are? Why do they have to hear our truth when they're so fucking fake themselves?"

I hated that he had a point.

He placed a hand on the brick wall by my head, his body swaying into mine. If he touched me again, I doubted I'd have the willpower to stop him for a second time. My clit still throbbed from his touch, the echoing bands of release a phantom cry in my veins.

"Stay back."

He lowered his head, a tight smile on his lips. "Fine." Holding his hands up in surrender, he kept his distance but didn't move away. "What will it take for you to let me touch you again?" His voice dropped to sand and sleet. "Because I *really* want to touch you again."

I shivered, doing my best to keep my thoughts focused and not on the molten heat inside. Having him so close didn't help. He'd been gorgeous in the club—dappled in strobes and painted in shadows—but out here; out here where the vague lights of apartments and streetlights didn't dare enter the sanctity of the alley, he was camouflaged in darkness.

His shoulders strained against the stitches of his suit. His forearms ropey and tanned with his cuffs pushed up. His entire body flexed as he waved a hand with feline grace, hiding the throbbing tension between us, pretending he hadn't just fired my libido to the point of excruciation.

"I'm not answering any more of your questions," I hissed. "Who the hell are you? What do you want from me?"

Sighing heavily, his lips pouted, blood smeared a little to make him seem part vampire. "You already know what I want."

"But who *are* you?"

"I'm someone you can be free with."

"I don't know what that means."

"It means you don't need to be afraid of me."

I clasped my hands together, seeking comfort from myself. Fighting with a strange man—even one who'd touched and kissed me—in a deserted alley wasn't exactly encouraged. Once again, Nameless came to mind and I couldn't stop comparing the two men.

Nameless had been the hero.

Penn was the anti-Christ.

One saving, one damning.

I knew which one I preferred.

I stood firm in my heels, locking my limbs from betraying my lie. "I'm not afraid of you."

He cocked his head. "Are you sure about that?"

"I'm not sure about anything anymore."

He ran a hand through his hair, disrupting the strands into a mess. "Isn't that the point?"

"Stop answering everything with a question."

"Fine." He stood tall, his legs spread with dominion. "You said yes to me. I won't let you take that back. But I will try to ease your mind." His face tightened as if this game had higher stakes for him than he let on. "I'll only say this once, so listen carefully. I will lie to others about us. I will paint a picture that isn't true. I will curse and hurt and do whatever I damn well want, but you have my word on one thing."

My voice carried on a hesitant whisper. "What word?"

"That I won't lie to you. What you see from me will be the honest fucking truth. I'll only hurt you if you want me to hurt you, and I'll protect you even while I do it. Give me yourself, let me take control, and I promise you, you'll enjoy it."

My heart only heard the word hurt and envisioned images of him abusing me. "Why would I enjoy you hurting me?"

"The answer to that question will come later. It's a matter of showing not telling."

I paused, sucking in another breath. My world had vanished, and I had no way of returning. Once again I stood at a fork, hidden in a dirty alley. Unlike last time, where I'd had to beg Nameless to help me, Penn had to do all the convincing.

He shifted in the darkness, dragging my attention back to his height, body, and undeniable command. "Tell me your objections."

"My objections?"

"Your objections to letting me fuck you."

My mouth watered but I didn't swallow. I wouldn't show any signs of weakness. "I have too many to list."

"Try me." He crossed his arms.

My eyes wanted to drop to the ground. My fingers wanted to stroke my dress with nerves.

I did neither of those things. I treated him as I would any bossy manager, negotiating our terms for a successful business deal. "I find you arrogant and rude."

Which makes me wet.

My nose turned up. "I don't like liars, and I don't like men who think they can use me."

Even though I'm contemplating giving my virginity to you.

He rubbed his jaw, his gaze dragging over me as if he could hear my silent answers and focused only on those. "I'm arrogant because I've earned my success the hard way. I'm rude because I have no time for idiots." Stepping forward, he hovered over me, pressing me against the wall with sheer will.

"You already know I won't lie to you."

His head crept over my personal boundary, his nose nuzzling my ear. "And I promise you, I'll use you. I'll use you every morning and night. I'll use you on your knees. I'll use you strapped to my bed. But with every use, you'll beg for another. You'll *beg* me, Elle." He bit my earring, tugging it until a sharp bolt of pain appeared. "That's what you should be afraid of. Nothing else."

I pushed him away, taking a greedy step toward the sidewalk.

I wasn't equipped for this. I needed to ease into sex, not be thrown headfirst into debauchery. "I've changed my mind. My answer is no."

Strong fingers wrapped around my wrist, yanking me back. "Like fuck it is." He pressed me against the wall face first. His hands clamped on my hips, pulling me back to meet his as he thrust up.

I moaned, long and low. A noise I'd never made before and had no idea where it'd come from.

"Oh, Elle, you're a little liar yourself." He tightened his hold, grinding into me. "Is that what you want? Seduction? Do you need to be seduced to let me inside you?" He bent over me, his lips landing on my shoulder blade. "Because I can do that. I can coax you, or I can force you. I can give you any fucking fantasy you want."

His voice darkened to nightmares. "You don't have to hide with me. You want it rough—" He looped his hand around my nape, crushing my cheek into the brick as his other hand slid down my body and scooped up my dress, up and up until his fingers found my inner thigh and aggressively cupped my core.

My heart exploded through my ears as intensity I never thought existed came alive beneath his fingers.

But then he switched.

The violent hunger in his touch melted into gentle petting. He pulled me away from the brick, hugging me, supporting me while his tongue licked my neck and his fingers feathered so lightly over my clit. "Or do you want it soft?"

I shuddered in his arms, confused when my body reacted more to anger rather than sweet.

"I'm attracted to you, Elle. I have been since I saw you. I know you want me too because right now, my hands are on your pussy, and you're so fucking wet." With a harsh breath, he pushed aside my panties, running his finger along my bareness.

He hissed in my ear as my hips rocked involuntarily. "There you go. Stop lying to yourself. That's the worst crime. Tell me what you want."

"I still don't like you enough to tell you."

He was utter temptation.

Beyond reasoning and comprehension. But he pissed me off as he chuckled low in my ear, taking pleasure in my undoing as he pressed his finger into me.

I lost the ability to stand. The delicious throaty echo of his laugh sent a coil of desire shooting right into my soul.

I clenched around his finger as he sank deeper.

"Your body likes me enough for your mind and heart."

My nerves heightened to a magnitude I couldn't withstand. His touch. His control. His manipulation—it made him more than human.

I didn't stand a chance.

"Just sex…" I panted as he fingered me.

"If that's what you want."

"Just lust."

"So much fucking lust." His touch seemed to double in size, dragging heat and sharp, sharp need.

A single finger.

It was too much.

It wasn't enough.

But my body, after years of neglect and build-up of countless nights imagining such a thing, surrendered entirely.

Penn sucked in a breath as I allowed my head to fall back over his shoulder, giving him utter control. He held me against his body, his finger never ceasing.

"Is that another yes?" He kissed my throat, biting it as his finger thrust upward. "Tell me it's a fucking yes before I lose my goddamn mind."

I nodded.

And that was it.

Penn Everett vanished, replaced by a hunter. Spinning me around and shoving me against the wall, he kicked my feet open and drove his finger higher.

My mind panicked that he would take me here like this. My first time would be against a dirty wall outside a nightclub, but he proved I was right to trust him. That I could give him power even though I'd never like him. That I would always hate him, purely because he wasn't Nameless and I'd clung to the ridiculous delusion that I'd find him, save him, and find a happily-ever-after.

Penn was the harbinger of truth in that respect.

I'd failed Nameless. I would never find him. It was time to accept that and move on.

Starting with sex.

"I'm going to make you come." Penn breathed into my skin. "And then…you're going home. We'll save my place for another night."

The bands of muscles in my core clenched around his finger as he pressed my clit with his thumb. His free hand grabbed my jaw, holding me prisoner while he kissed me so damn deep.

With his tongue inside my mouth and his finger matching the same pulse, I let it happen.

I didn't hold on.

He didn't drag it out.

I'd always been sensitive—always had a naughty ability to seek pleasure in banal situations. I'd stopped blushing years ago when I crossed my legs in a meeting filled with stuffy businessmen and enjoyed the tingle of desire just from the seam of my underwear. I'd accepted my body and how hotly it ran, simmering sweetly, ready to overflow into climax whenever I wanted.

Penn didn't know that.

He knew nothing about me.

But somehow, my body spoke to his and his touch sought those triggers inside.

His finger arched up, hooking hard.

Holy...

My mouth popped wide, shuddering in yeses.

He grinned in triumph, knowing he'd found one button to punish me with but there were countless more.

His kisses turned reckless. His fingers thrusting *right there.*

The recipe turned tentative sparks into fireworks and fireworks into detonations and detonations into a mushroom cloud of pure bliss. The orgasm scurried up my legs, down my spine, and convened in my core to explode in an avalanche of pleasure.

"Oh...*God.*" I sucked in air as I drowned, but he didn't give me time to breathe. He kissed me, sucked on my tongue, and let me ride his hand until the final wave of my release abated.

Slowly, his body peeled away from mine. "Well, that was interesting."

His lips disengaged, leaving me bruised and stinging while he repositioned my underwear and removed his touch, letting my dress slither over my thighs.

Without another word, he pulled me away from the shadows toward the busy pavement, caught the eye of David, my driver, who'd miraculously appeared, and placed me reverently into the Range Rover.

CHAPTER EIGHTEEN

THE NEXT DAY, I went to work as if nothing had happened.

As if everything at the Palm Politics was a figment of my imagination.

As if I hadn't come or given Penn any part of myself.

I still hated him.

But my body...*it wants more.*

Fleur handed me my meeting minutes, and I performed my duty in two conference calls like normal.

But *nothing* was normal.

I couldn't stop replaying what had happened. Where the hell did Penn go after he'd taken what he wanted...or was that given? He'd given me an orgasm without expecting one in return. He'd sent me home rather than kidnapped me to his place.

Had he gone home?

Had he found some other stupid woman to fall for his corrupted charm?

I hated that I wondered.

He was nothing more than sex. We'd agreed to that. *I'd* been the one to stipulate it.

So why does it leave a sour taste in my mouth?

As the day wore on, I itched to research him. To find out who he was, who Stewie was to him, who the mysterious Larry was. What did he do for work? Where did he live? What had he told my father in the gin bar?

He left me with more questions than Nameless did.

I didn't know how to contact him. I didn't know how to tell anyone what had happened. He'd done exactly what he said and controlled me without trying.

By the time the afternoon rolled around, my heart was ragged from fretting and my insides tight and jumpy. I couldn't stop imagining how I'd next bump into him and what he would make me do.

Would I say yes?

Would I say no?

Would he even give me a choice?

Those two daydreams caused twitchy anxiety to infiltrate my blood.

I stared blankly at my computer screen, dying for a distraction from both work and Penn when Fleur stuck her head into my office. "Um, there's someone here to see you."

Instantly, my body screamed yes. All while my mind bellowed no.

Then rationale took over.

It can't be.

How could he gain access to my building? Why didn't he call to tell me he was coming? Security wouldn't just let him up unless I'd cleared his name, which I hadn't.

My libido leaped at the thought of him, but self-preservation flipped into CEO mode. Last night had been terrifying in both good and terrible ways. He had a habit of making me forget myself and spinning lies I couldn't unscramble.

I couldn't have him on my turf. "Tell him I'm too busy. Either take his phone number, and I'll call him when it's convenient, or he'll have to make an appointment off site."

Take that, Penn.

"Do you know who it is?" Fleur asked, suspicion bright on her adorable, pixy face. "Why are you acting weird?"

"Weird? I'm not weird."

"I didn't say *you* were weird. I said you're *acting* weird." She fiddled with an orange button on her burnt sunshine dress. "What's his name?"

"Who?"

"The man you're avoiding."

"Who said—"

"Spit it out, Elle."

I chewed a smile. "Penn Everett."

Fleur inched closer, her eyes wide. "Did you meet him last night at the party? Oh, I knew you should've gone." She swooned dramatically. "Did he ask you out? Wait, I thought Greg was your date?"

I pretended to enter a few numbers into my laptop. "I met him a few days before the party, but yes, we confirmed an arrangement last night."

Fleur jumped up and down like a child. "An arrangement. What sort? A sexual sort? Look at you, you sexy minx. I demand you tell me everything."

"Not until you tell him to leave." I pointed at my door, laughing a little at her antics. "In fact, tell him I'm far too busy for the next four years, and even though my answer is yes, he'd better have the patience of a saint if he wants to see me again."

Let's see how he gets around that.

He wanted to play games. Well, I could make up a few rules as we went.

She giggled. "Whatever he did to you last night has done wonders for your sense of humor." Moving toward the door, she grinned. "Finally, you're learning how to have some fun." She saluted me before vanishing out the door. "Leave it to me. Consider instigation with a new love interest in progress."

I groaned under my breath as snippets of male voices sounded in the hallway then were cut off as Fleur closed the door, preventing more eavesdropping.

I probably shouldn't have ordered her to tell Penn to wait four years. What if he took it seriously and left? As much as his personality appalled me, the thought of him leaving before delivering on his promises made me mildly sick.

Hating myself, I pushed away from my desk and tiptoed to the door. Pressing against it, I struggled to follow the conversation on the other side.

"You must be Steve Hobson?"

That voice…it was already so familiar—hardwired to my belly and gasoline for every hidden desire. The sly smoothness; the cocky deepness. It wasn't fair he was handsome and spoke like a rascally poet. He might not be marriage material, but he definitely delivered on fantasy.

Penn wasn't my future, but he could do very well for my present.

Steve's voice flowed through my door. "Yes, I am. I'm Mr. Charlston's oldest friend and colleague. You are?"

Without any hesitation and a lot of smugness, Penn said, "I'm Elle's fiancé."

My knees gave out.

What?!

I thought that lie was just for the girls at Palm Politics. He couldn't go spreading such untruth around. My father would hear.

Oh God, Dad.

He'd be elated.

And then he'd be crushed when I called it off.

"Ah, yes. My son, Greg, mentioned something about an incident last night," Steve said. "I thought he was exaggerating." The disappointment in his tone crushed me like a little girl.

"I figured he'd mention it." Penn's voice dropped to deadly seriousness. "I'm aware your son has feelings for my wife-to-be, sir, and I only have respect and regret that he didn't deserve her affection. But rest assured, if he gets in my way, I won't tolerate it."

"What does that mean?" Steve snapped.

"It means Elle belongs to you in business. But she belongs

to me in everything else." His tone lowered possessively. "We're together now, and no one will interfere. In fact, I'm here to collect her. It's time for her to come home. We have lots of things to *do* tonight."

Even behind the door, the sexual innuendos reeked with promise.

Steve cleared his throat, no doubt wondering when I had the time to hook up with a complete stranger and why Greg wasn't the one taking me home. "I see."

My tummy clenched at how forlorn he sounded.

I liked to think it was purely for wanting me to be happy and believing his son was the right candidate for the job, but some part believed he had ulterior motives. He'd been nothing but loyal to this company, my father, and me, but running a business for so long that wasn't yours must take a toll. Possession was a fundamental human flaw.

"You must excuse me; I'm late for our date." Penn chuckled. "As you know, Elle is strict on time-lines."

Fleur's voice piped up. "I'm afraid, Mr. Everett, Ms. Charlston has said she's busy for the next four years, and you'll have to make an appointment."

"What?" His tone snapped through the door.

A nervous giggle percolated in my chest. Why did I want to piss him off? I'd pay for it later, no doubt.

Shit, this was a bad idea.

"Why is Ms. Charlston telling you to make an appointment when you're telling me you're her fiancé?" Steve asked suspiciously.

"No disrespect, sir, but it's none of your business."

Steve replied, "I think you'll find it is. Elle means a great deal to her father and me. She's really stepped into his shoes and taken the company to even greater heights. She's far too successful for her own good, and that means pariahs are out there who see her as an easy target to her vast empire."

Damn you, Steve.

Everyone made it sound as if I were some elusive unicorn

to be hunted and snared. I wasn't special or unique. I was bland and boring. A workaholic imprisoned since birth.

"I'm not one of those pariahs, believe me," Penn muttered. "However, I can't say the same for your son."

Oh, my God. Did he truly just say that?

"Excuse me?" Steve blurted. "My son and Elle are extremely close. It's only a matter of time before they progress from friends to something more. Whatever you think you have with her is at best a silly fling and at worst a future heartbreak. But mark my words, Greg will be there to pick up the pieces and make sure Elle is happy and protected. I don't for a second believe in this marriage bullshit."

I hated the optimism in his voice along with the vaguely concealed threat for Penn to back away. That somehow Steve, even though he'd watched me turn from child to woman, still believed he controlled me enough to decide who I should share my body and life with.

I'm surrounded by manipulators.

"That will never happen," Penn snapped. "After the interesting conversations I've had with Ms. Charlston, I can safely say she isn't remotely interested in your son."

Oh, no. Please someone stop him.

"In fact, she distinctly said she didn't want to have a thing to do with him. She wants me. And she has me. Just like I have her. We're engaged."

Steve mumbled something I couldn't hear.

Penn said, "That may be, but perhaps Ms. Charlston should be given the space to decide who she wants in her bed. Currently, that's me, asshole."

Okay, that's it.

Wrenching my door open, I barreled into the waiting room. The soft furnishings and potted trees couldn't distract me from my blistering anger toward the two men.

"Once again, I'm shocked stupid." I clamped both hands on my hips. "Steve, I expected better of you."

Steve had the decency to look down with his face flushed.

"Sorry, Elle. I wasn't saying that you and Greg were together but trying to protect your right to decide."

"No, you weren't. You were trying to keep Belle Elle in the family. You and Dad are everything to me, and that's why I won't hold a grudge, but if you try to push me together with Greg again, I'll refuse to speak to you. Do you understand?"

"But Greg really likes you."

"Don't care. Not interested."

Wow, the relief in finally speaking the truth and not worrying about other people's feelings was immense.

"Hello again, Elle. Does this mean you're available for our second date now and not in four years' time?" Penn planted his feet and smirked. "After all, you just admitted you're more interested in me than anyone else."

I turned burning blue eyes on him. "I'm only interested in watching you fall off one of our buildings, Mr. Everett."

He chuckled. "Oh, now. Don't be like that. I just did you a favor. One of many, I might add. You no longer have to deal with Greg." He fiddled with a cufflink. "That was because of me. You owe me."

"I don't owe you anything. I revoke my yes." My nose tipped upward. "It's been amended to a resounding no. Now, go away."

I spun around and marched back into my office, slamming the door in his face. The second I was away from him, I kicked off my heels and bolted into the bathroom. Grabbing the sink, I stared at myself in the mirror. Hot points danced on my cheeks, and wild insanity replaced my calm capableness.

What was I thinking by saying yes to that man?

I hated the way he made my blood boil. I couldn't stand the way he spread rumors and none-truths on my behalf. No man since Nameless had earned a reaction from me—either in like or hate. I wasn't ready to fight. I didn't have time to welcome attraction.

"God, this is all a mess."

He was a mistake, and one I had to fix right away before

he railroaded my life and ruined everything. If he didn't take my no as gospel, I would call the police to instate a restraining order.

Perhaps, I should become a nun? Then I'd never have to worry about sex or marriage.

I could just focus on what I was good at.

Business.

Splashing water on my face, I rubbed at the smudge of mascara and tamed some of the flyaways. Feeling mildly normal, I nodded at my reflection. Agreeing that my work was done for the day and I'd go home, take a bath, and try to forget about Steve, my father, and most of all, damn Penn.

Opening the bathroom door, I jolted as the man I wanted to throw out my window sat smugly on the couch facing my bookshelves of magazines listing our clothes, houseware awards, and charity plaques for our work with selected organizations.

"You again!"

"Me." He looked me up and down. "You got your shirt wet."

I glanced at the sheer white fabric that was now see-through to the dusky pink bra I wore beneath it. I slapped a hand over my chest and stalked toward my desk. My stomp didn't have the same effect in stockinged feet as it would've in heels, but at least I was able to shrug on a cream and black piping jacket and hide a bit of my damp cleavage.

Sage ventured out from under my desk, baring her little fangs at the interloper.

"I thought I told you to leave." Doing my best to get back in control, I snapped, "Besides, it's not a shirt. It's a blouse. If you weren't such a Neanderthal, you'd know that."

"Why would I know that? I'm a guy who wears guy's clothing. I have no interest in women's unless it's on the floor after I've taken them off her."

I glowered. "Fascinating insight into your true character, Mr. Everett." I pointed at my door. "As you weren't invited into my office, I'll kindly ask you to go. For the second time. And while you're at it, retract your lie about our upcoming nuptials."

"You lost the power to tell me to leave the moment you said yes." He never took his eyes off me. "It's too late to change it to a no. However, if you're so incensed, then hear me out and I'll go…for now."

I moved around my desk to stand in front of it and crossed my arms. "Hear what? I'm sure I heard all I needed to. You're an egotistical maniac who I have no interest in doing anything else with."

"Your body told me a different story last night." He chuckled. "And just to clarify, if I wasn't an 'egotistical maniac' as you put it, then you'd consider letting me fuck you…like our original agreement?"

I frowned. "What?"

He stood up, breaching the space between us until he stood only a foot away. My skin prickled as goosebumps erupted under my wet blouse.

Sage hissed, swatting the air with her claws in warning.

Penn took no notice of her. "I'm sorry." His face darkened with sincerity. "I know I didn't have a right to talk about you like a trophy to be won from your father. And I'm sorry for warning Mr. Hobson to keep his son away from you." He smiled tightly. "I would say I did that for your benefit, but really, I did it for me." His eyes fell on my chest. "I don't do well with competition."

"Well, your rules and jealousy are pointless because I have no intention of going to bed with you."

"Lies, Elle. I thought you'd agreed we'd only have truth between us."

His deep, heady aftershave stole up my nose, tying my thoughts into a sinful knot.

I didn't reply as he deleted the remaining space between us.

I leaned back, my butt hitting the edge of my desk and my

tummy locking into place.

"You know…I work in an office, too. I know how lonely these job spaces can be." He licked his lips. "I also know how fantasies can spring from nothing." His hand crept forward.

I flinched, expecting him to touch me. However, he placed his palm on the glass table, hemming me in on both sides. "Tell me, Ms. Charlston. Have you ever had sex in here?"

I froze. "Excuse me?"

His gaze hooded. "Has anyone bent you over your desk and fucked you? Stolen your power and used it against you?"

I shivered uncontrollably. My mouth urged to scream for Fleur to help. Was he threatening to take me? Here in my office?

I shoved him.

He stumbled backward, a black look dripping over his features. He shook his head, dispelling the clouds, once again settling into cocky. "I take that as a no."

For a split second, I remembered the words from the assholes who hurt me in the alley. *'Have you ever been fucked over your desk, office girl? Ever given a boss a blowjob for a promotion?'*

It wasn't an unusual concept.

I was sure many people had done just that and had lots of fun doing it. But I never had. And I wouldn't today—not with Penn or anyone else who threatened my safety and position. *Especially* when chilly ice replaced my blood, struggling to separate that night in the alley and today with Penn.

The way he watched me was too close to the guy in the Baseball Cap—too intense, too focused on something he couldn't have but would happily take anyway.

"Leave, Mr. Everett."

"I told you to call me Penn."

I cocked my chin. "Fine. Leave, Penn."

"Not until you agree to dinner with me."

"Never."

"Never is too long to wait." He glowered. "And besides, we've already agreed on the ground rules. You want to fuck me.

I want to fuck you. Playing hard to get is only making me want to do that sooner rather than later."

"No."

"No what?

"No to everything. I told you, I changed my mind."

"Why?"

"Because I said so."

He licked his lips. "Yes, but why? Why change your mind after what happened last night? From what your father said, you work too much, you have no friends, and you severely lack fun in your life."

My heart sank. "He said that?"

"I read between the lines."

"Well read between my lines. N-O. Spells no. I'm too busy to play with you."

"I said I was sorry."

I stiffened, trying to sniff his new game. "Go on."

He shrugged. Even that was sexy, dammit. "I shouldn't have put words into your mouth. It's up to you to decide if you want people to know about us." He looked up beneath his brow. "And the only way you can decide that is if you go on a date with me."

I opened my mouth to argue, but he interrupted—another habit he seemed to have. "Don't answer for yourself right now. Answer for yourself in five years' time. Where do you see yourself? Here in this office doing the exact same thing with the exact same unhappiness?"

God, I hope not.

"Or do you want to see if you could have this and more? Work and play? Love and obligation?"

My eyes shot daggers. "You think I could love you?"

"I think you could have fun with me."

"I think otherwise."

He grinned. "That's what this is about. To see if our opinions line up."

"Are you going to leave if I say no again?"

"Nope." He came closer. "I'll just keep showing up at really inconvenient times until you say yes." His aftershave drugged me again. "Choose the easier option, Ms. Charlston. Let me have you. It's the only way forward."

"What will you do to me?"

Instantly, my office thickened with sexual tension.

My breath hitched as his eyes drifted to my mouth.

His voice lowered to scorching charcoal. "Anything I damn well want." His hand cupped my cheek, holding me tight. "I'll strip you, taste you, devour you. I'll eat, lick, and bite you. And only once you're begging will I fuck you."

My body flushed as hot as the sun, as bright as Venus, as untouched as Pluto.

I shoved him away and stalked to the exit. All I wanted to do was dare him to try it. To fight and claw and let him subdue me because, *holy hell*, he made it sound delicious. But the other part—the vanishing part—was afraid of losing herself.

Sex was too powerful.

Sex should be done between two people who liked each other and not a couple with nothing in common.

I cleared my throat and my mind. I clung to common sense. "I suggest you leave before I knee you in places a lady should never knee a man."

He hunted me, bringing with him cyclones full of lust. "If you want to touch that part of me, I would prefer it was with something softer than your knee." He chased me, once again corralling me against a hard surface.

This time the door.

"Your hand would work." He cupped my wrist, slipping his fingers through mine. "Your hand is welcome." His eyes turned jet black with need. "I could come from your hand alone."

I fought my shiver but couldn't stop the goosebumps darting up my arms. His touch was possessive but soft. Strong but coaxing.

His fingers squeezed mine as he swayed closer. "Or if you

didn't want to use that part of your anatomy, your mouth would do equally well." He licked his bottom lip. "In fact, I want both."

"Never."

"Never?" He smiled. "Don't lie." His hand crept up my arm to my shoulder, adding pressure until my knees threatened to buckle. "Let's see how soon never is, shall we?" He kissed me sweetly. "I fingered you until you came last night. The least you can do is blow me."

I like the thought of you giving me a blowjob. Get her on her knees.

The rapists and alley stole the present, hurtling me back before Nameless had found me. Before he hurt them for hurting me. Before he prevented my life from tumbling into ruin.

Why did Penn cause flashbacks that I'd successfully put behind me?

Why did he awake sharp instincts?

And why were those instincts scrambled between trust and mistrust, unable to see the truth hiding in his lies?

My office returned. The alley disappeared. Penn was still there. His pressure on my shoulder stronger, pestering me to fall into servitude before him.

I breathed hard. "You expect me to wrap my lips around your cock? Here? Now? In my office?"

He nodded. "Absolutely." He fisted my hair without warning, tilting my head to attack my throat with his mouth and teeth. "Here, you're god. Here, you're in charge. It turns me the fuck on knowing you're the one with all the power, yet you're considering getting on your knees to serve me."

It took every ounce of willpower, every brave denial, but I managed to untangle my fingers from his and tear my neck from his kisses. "Too bad for you, you'll have to remain turned on. I have no intention of doing such a thing."

"What are you afraid of?" His eyes narrowed. "You know this is a game. You understand the rules."

"I don't understand any of this."

"The rules are sex. Mutually enjoyed sex. Despite what you think, you like being told what to do." He gathered me close, inhaling my perfume. "Give me two minutes. Two minutes to command you, and if you don't like it, I'll walk away."

My heart beat crazy. "Two minutes?"

He bit his lip, nodding. "You have my word."

"If you break it, I'm turning you into a eunuch with a sharp kick."

He chuckled, stepping back and spreading his thighs. "There are worst things I can imagine than your leg between mine." His eyes were dark as nightmares. "But for now, get on your fucking knees."

Get her on her knees.

A similar command had torn me apart. The thought of sucking strange men in an alley grotesque. However, this command turned my chest into a furnace, charring my heart to dust.

I didn't know what happened to my brain.

I didn't understand how hate could be such an aphrodisiac.

But he circumnavigated the CEO. He spoke to some primitive part of me.

I wanted to tell him to leave.

I wanted to prove I had more respect than that.

Yet I sank down the door to my knees.

Sage watched me as if all her respect for me as her human evaporated.

Damn cat.

Penn shuddered, looking part monster, part angel. "Shit, you make me hard when you obey." His gaze fell on my breasts. "Now that you're playing, we're going to do a little show and tell."

Before we show you ours, you have to show us yours.

The alley.

I was back there again.

Huddled in pain, grasping at dignity.

I stayed silent, doing my best to stay alive while my heart tried to slam through my ribs.

The past and future were merely two dimensions separated from each other by the present. Yet I lived in neither. I existed in the glue bridging them together, somehow allowing three years ago to affect today.

I wanted Nameless to barge into my world and rescue me for the second time.

Penn's hands fell to his belt, pushing aside the tails of his midnight blazer, and undoing the leather slowly. "I'm going to show you what you do to me, Elle. But in return, I want to see you."

Let's see what your tits are like.

I gulped.

He morphed into one of those bastards, flickering with Adidas symbols and expensive suits. He never looked away as he pulled the belt, unthreading it and letting it hang in the loops. "Unbutton your shirt."

Forcing myself to shed the memories and focus entirely on him, I latched onto the most idiotic thing I'd ever uttered. "It's a blouse."

"I don't care." His growl echoed through my core. "Unbutton it."

My hands shook but slowly connected with the pearl buttons and hesitantly undid one.

This was now. Penn was now. Nameless was yesterday.

It took more effort than I could afford, but I shut the door on the past and slotted firmly back into the present.

"The next." Penn trembled as he locked his hands on the button of his waistband. The crisp cream shirt and dark jeans he wore made him untouchable yet so normal.

I popped the next button, breathing hard and quick.

He followed, undoing his and pulling on his zipper.

Without waiting for his command, I undid buttons three then four; my eyes locked on his hands as he pulled his zipper down and down.

When my blouse hung undone, and his zipper had nowhere else to go, our eyes met.

Our lips parted; mirrored images of desire.

"Open it." His voice had lost the playful kink from before, slipping straight into serious smut. "Let me see you."

With bravery I didn't know I had, I pushed my blouse away from my breasts, revealing the dusky pink bra.

He groaned, his hand disappearing into his jeans.

My stomach clenched so hard, so deep, I bent over a little in surprise.

His lips twisted. "Do you like that?" He squeezed himself, his thighs tightening beneath the denim. "Do you like knowing I'm this hard all because of you? That I haven't been this hard in years. That all I can think about is sticking this in every place you'll let me."

Oh. My. *God.*

I swam in heat. I drowned in liquid. I was so wet my panties were soaked.

"Pull your bra down, and I'll show you more."

My fingers hooked on the front cups of my bra as his latched around his jeans and levered them a little off his hips. Never looking away, objectifying both of us by only watching our bodies and not our souls, he reached into his tight black boxer-briefs and pulled out his cock.

My core spasmed as I swallowed hard and pulled my bra down, revealing my pebbled nipples and heavy globes of flesh that had long since been neglected.

"Fuck, Elle." His hand grasped his long length. The head glowed with darker flesh, a droplet glistening on top. Veins ran down the sides, bulging with desire—the same desire throbbing in my clit.

All I could see…all I could think about…was sex.

My legs parted a little as my hips became loose and wanting. An emptiness echoed inside me, becoming more and more cavernous the longer I stared at him.

"Do you want this?" he murmured, his face black with

lust.

There was no banter or connection. Whatever respect we had for each other was tarnished by the way I stared up with him standing over me with his cock in his hand. It ought to be degrading, but I found a different sort of power on my knees. The way he panted. The way his hips rocked with a subtle sway even he wasn't aware of.

We no longer lived in the real world but sex, sex, sex.

I nodded just once, licking my lips.

"Jesus, Elle." His head fell forward as he squeezed the tip. "Say it out loud. Do you want my cock?"

I didn't care if anyone was outside my door eavesdropping. I didn't care that I should stop this and throw him from my office.

I embraced the river flowing inside me and whispered, "Yes."

"Where? Where do you want it?"

So many places.

So many foreign, wonderful ready-to-be explored places.

But first, the one he wanted. The one he'd hinted at, and the reason I was on my knees. "My mouth."

He groan-growled as he stepped forward. His shoes hit my knees, his height towering over me with his cock speared from his angry fist. "Suck it then."

My breasts ached with pain I'd never experienced.

I sat taller on my knees.

I reached forward.

My fingers so close to claiming him.

But then he stepped back, tucking his erection away, shaking with need and discipline. He didn't do up his belt or zipper, but he flashed a silver watch on his wrist. "Your two minutes are up."

The sexual trance he'd put me into shattered.

I shivered with sudden cold and yanked up my bra in disgrace. Grabbing the sides of my blouse, I huddled before shooting upright with rage so bright, so brilliant, I wanted to rip him into pieces.

"That's it?" I snarled. "Was that all a stupid game to you? A ploy to show me that you can make me do what you want, after all?" A heavy gathering sat between my legs, throbbing to be touched. Desperate for a release.

"I wanted to be sure there were no lies. You saw how much I want you. I saw how much you want me." He kept his distance, refusing to touch me. "Next time, I won't accept your bullshit."

"Next time?! You think there'll be a next time? This was the only time, and you just humiliated me."

"Yes, well, you almost made me come just by licking your fucking lips."

I opened my mouth to retort, but angry tears crept up my spine. The lust in my blood eroded my self-control. Spinning around, I grabbed the doorknob and yanked. I didn't care his trousers were undone. I didn't care my blouse was open. I wanted him gone. I wanted it now.

His hand slammed against the wood, shoving it back into the frame with a loud smack. His body heat pressed against me, the teeth of his open zipper digging into my pinstripe skirt.

"You think you can leave? I didn't say you could."

"Let me go."

His hands pressed flat against the door, caging me.

Sage meowed loudly, attempting to join my battle to make him leave.

I couldn't think with him so close. I could only feel. And by God, I could feel. *Everything*. His breath on my nape, his chest rising and falling against my spine. And his cock twitching against my ass.

The domination and power of his will were tangible things, suffocating me under his command. Everything outside of him and me ceased to exist. My entire body begged for whatever he would do next even while my mind bellowed at me to scream.

Whatever existed between us was visceral, indescribable,

completely imprisoning.

"I'll never let you go. Not until I'm through with you." His lips landed on the top of my shoulder. "Turn around, Elle."

My body shuddered in an overwhelming wave of arousal. I wasn't supposed to like this. I wasn't supposed to get wet under his cruel, commanding tone. His body heated with hunger and demand, dragging urges from deep inside me. Urges I could no longer deny.

I wanted him.

And I didn't know how to handle that.

I refused to turn. Sadness interfered with my desire, scrambling me up inside. "I can't do this with you. I'm not equipped."

His lips caressed my hair. "You can. You're doing it right now."

"But I don't know what comes next. I—I—"

"You do. You know exactly what comes next." His hand splayed over my stomach, pulling me back into his hips. His cock was big, hard, and so hot. "This goes inside you. It makes all that confusion and emptiness vanish."

I spun in his arms.

"How? Nothing has that power."

"Trust me." His fingers latched around my throat, pinning me against the door. He fell forward, wedging his entire length along mine. Aligning his cock to my clit, he thrust.

The action was so crude, so basic in mating, I moaned.

"Wrap your legs around my hips."

Shifting my skirt high so I could spread my legs, I jumped and did exactly what he told me, my body taking control.

He grunted as he caught my weight before crushing me against the door again. "We're both going to come. We're going to do it together. And we're not going to overthink it or ruin it by refusing what our bodies so fucking desperately need, got it?"

I had no other choice.

I nodded.

I didn't know if he meant he planned to take me against my door or if he'd use his fingers or expected my mouth but all questions died like flightless birds the moment he thrust again.

Reaching between us, he pulled down his trousers, freeing himself and wedging his naked cock against my panty-covered pussy.

With my legs around his waist, his hardness lined up perfectly against every inch of me.

"Christ, you're soaked." He looked down. "Soon, I'm going to see every inch of you, Elle, but for now, you owe me an orgasm."

Confusion hit me. So he meant to keep the tiny piece of cotton and lace between us? That we would grind and come but not consummate?

His jaw clenched, his messy hair tumbling over his forehead. His biceps bulged from holding me as he curved into me. "Kiss me." His voice was hoarse.

I gave up my questions and denial and tipped my head up.

He groaned, capturing my mouth with his. His lips were firm and warm. His pressure the perfect accompaniment. His tongue dived inside, tasting me, fighting me with deep licks.

And then, he moved.

Slow and deep, thrusting his long length against my wet panties, grinding into me at exactly the right spot. His hands dropped to my ass, tightening and pinching with each rock, driving me insane.

He didn't attempt to enter me. He remained on the outskirts, keeping cotton as our prison guard, letting temptation be our mistress.

I lost track of everything as his kisses swept me away and his hips kept me anchored to him and only him. I distantly noticed my hands swooped up to capture his face and hair. Tugging and yanking, I directed him to kiss me harder, thrust faster—deepening the connection between us.

He growled into the kiss, his tongue turning into a lashing whip as his body moved faster over mine, igniting electricity and chemistry and fire. The pounding of his heartbeat echoed into me as we clawed and clung, climbing and climbing, desperately seeking the pleasure just out of reach.

"Fuck, I want you." He thrust harder. "I can't stop." Cupping my ass, he angled me in just the right way. My clit spindled with the beginnings of an orgasm.

I pressed tight against him, aware of every hard intoxicating piece of his body.

His face contorted. "Jesus, I'm going to come."

My skin misted with sweat, blistering with sensitivity. Penn's hand slid up my thigh, grabbing me so hard I shivered with a mixture of fear and abandon.

A low rumble vibrated in his chest as his pace increased and I clutched him tight. Our teeth clacked together as our kiss turned sloppy, our bodies turned manic, and the orgasm teasing us erupted into being.

I split in two.

I melted into a puddle.

Wave after wave, I shuddered in his arms, cringing and crying as his cock kept me flying far too high. I was vaguely aware of his head falling back, his fingernails breaking my skin and the shot of stickiness on my inner thigh.

Even sated, my body still strained to get closer, to increase our contact until he was inside me, not just touching me.

I didn't know who shook more—him or me.

Lowering his head, his face blank and eyes dazed from his release, he claimed my mouth again with a thread of violence I hungered for. He drank me as I drank him. We groaned together as he rocked slower this time, highlighting sore extremities, encouraging final tingles to remain.

Then someone knocked on the door.

Shattering our moment.

Reminding us we weren't alone.

CHAPTER NINETEEN

"ELLE, ARE YOU free for a quick chat?"

I froze in Penn's arms as Dad's voice deleted any sexual heat, slamming me back into a girl who had no right, *none*, to act the way I just did.

"Shit," I hissed under my breath.

The knob turned beside my hip where Penn still wedged me against the door. His eyes narrowed as he grabbed it, preventing it from unlatching.

"Answer him," he growled low. "Tell him to leave."

"Elle? Are you in there?" The knock came again.

My racing heart made it hard to speak. "Yeah, Dad, I am. Just—it's a bad time. Can you come back later?"

A slight pause followed by a huffed, "This is important. I'd rather we have a quick talk now."

Every nightmare had come true.

"Uh, okay. Just—"

Penn stepped back, letting my legs slide from his hips to place me on the floor. The moment I was standing, he let me go, hastily tucking his cock into his jeans and yanking up his belt. He gave me a look so villainous he stole my breath.

"Just give me a minute!" My hands flew to my hips to pull my skirt down, but Penn stopped me with a slight curve in his lips.

His finger smeared something sticky and cool on my inner thigh. His voice didn't break a murmur. "You're about to have a conversation with your father while my cum is drying on your skin." He smiled ruthlessly. "I think it's safe to say you're mine now."

I couldn't talk to him about cum or sex. Not with my father only a few feet away. Shoving him back, I wrenched my skirt down, hastily did up my blouse, and dragged my hands through my wild hair.

Eyeing Penn, who'd tucked in his shirt and buttoned his blazer, I didn't ask if he was ready before jerking the door wide and smiling so fake and big, I was sure I had sex written all over my face. "Dad! How nice to see you."

He flinched, looking me up and down in surprise. "That's quite a welcome, Elle." His gaze slid past me to Penn standing in the middle of my office, a respectful distance away from me. "Ah, so Steve wasn't lying."

Strolling into my office, my father sniffed. "Can someone please explain to me what is going on? I've heard rumors of an engagement?" He turned to me, hurt blazing in his eyes. "Elle?"

Oh, no.

I fired harpoons at Penn before striding forward to sit on the couch, needing to get off my feet before my knees gave way. Sage immediately hopped onto my lap, reprimanding me with her beady little gaze. "It's not what you think."

"Not what I think?" Dad strode forward, never taking his attention off Penn. "Wait a minute. I know you."

Penn cleared his throat, holding his hand out in introduction. "We've already met. At the Weeping—"

"Willow, yes. I'm old, but I'm not senile," Dad grumbled, shaking Penn's grip before letting go and marching to my desk where he leaned against the edge with his arms crossed.

Just like that, he stole the position of authority, doing his best to manipulate me even though he probably wasn't aware he'd slipped into parental mode.

All my life, he'd done this. A subtle posture, a minor head tilt. I loved him, and he loved me—and I knew he'd never do anything to hurt me—but he did control me as much with disappointment as he did with affection.

"I wasn't saying you were." Penn straightened his shoulders, his gaze landing on my thigh where beneath my skirt the remnants of his orgasm slicked and coated my legs.

The urge to cringe was strong. I wasn't used to having such things left on my body after doing something not exactly permitted in an office. But there was another urge too…slightly bolder than the first. The urge to demand Penn got on *his* knees for a change and wipe it off.

The image of him bowed before me knotted my insides, even though I knew it would never happen. He was too in control to ever let me boss him.

"Well, someone had better start talking before I call security." Dad narrowed his eyes at me. "You hated this guy a few nights ago, Elle. You threw your drink in his face. What the hell did I miss that he's not only permitted into our building, but I hear from Greg and Steve that you're engaged." He rubbed at his chest. "I'm hurt that I found out that way. I'm even more hurt that my own daughter misled me."

Panic gathered as I worried about his heart. Why was he rubbing his chest? Should I call a doctor? I wanted to mollycoddle him but worried that if I changed the subject to health rather than clarify this massive misunderstanding, I'd be in a lot more trouble.

I gathered my hair over my shoulder, twisting it into a rope. "You don't have any reason to be hurt, Dad. It's all a big mistake."

"What do you mean?"

I stroked Sage's warm fur. "I mean we're not engag—"

"She means we were going to ask your permission, but unfortunately, sir, my possessive nature came out last night when Greg implied I wasn't good enough for your daughter." Penn strode toward me and took the spot beside me on the couch.

Sage stiffened but didn't try to kill him for being so close.

Smoothly, like he'd rehearsed this very moment, he captured my hand, brought it to his lips, and kissed my knuckles. "I'm aware Elle and Mr. Robson's son have been raised together with the understanding of one day marrying, but that is no longer an option."

Dad's mouth hung open. "It isn't? Why?"

Penn gave me a sly smile, dripping with intrigue and falsehoods. "Because, with your blessing, of course, I wish to marry Noelle."

I groaned, hanging my head. "He doesn't mean that, Dad. It's a game—"

Penn silenced me with a quick pinch to my hand. "She isn't fully aware how I feel about her yet. She believes I'm ridiculous to want to marry her when we've only just met, but she isn't an old romantic like we are, is she, sir?" He grinned at my father, baiting him with the tasty hook guaranteed to spark his interest.

Dad snapped it up, bait and sinker. "You believe in love at first sight?"

Penn leaned back into the couch, dragging me with him, imprisoning me with his arm over my shoulders. The move was relaxed, but his body hummed with tension I couldn't decipher. "Absolutely. The moment you mentioned her at the bar, she sounded like my type of woman." He turned piercing truthless eyes to me. "And the instant I saw her, the moment she gave me a vodka shower, I knew." His free hand nudged my chin with sharp knuckles, guiding my lips to his.

Sage leaped off my lap and tore under my desk.

I tried to pull away.

I had no intention of kissing him with Dad present. But just like all the other times, he gave me no choice. His mouth caressed mine with chaste affection—the perfect recipe of truth and besotted affection to hoodwink my father.

I hated him for that.

I despised the way he lied to my last remaining flesh and blood.

Tearing my lips from his, I tried to stand, to go to my father and explain this was all a big misunderstanding and not to listen to him.

But it was too late.

My father had lost the suspicious glint, his body no longer tight with protection. His heart had flown back to a happier time when he met my mother and fell ass over head at first sight.

His face glowed. "You mean this is real?" He glanced between Penn and me. "This isn't a prank? All that animosity at the start, Elle, you were just overly passionate?" He chuckled. "I remember your mother had that tenacious streak. She'd swat me for no reason on lots of occasions." His voice grew wistful. "I miss that."

"You've got it all wrong. It's not tru—" I started.

"It's very real," Penn murmured. "I've fallen for her, and I've already claimed her. I hope you don't mind."

"Mind?" My father leaped upright, smacking his hands together. "I'm ecstatic. To think Elle finally has a partner to lean on. A man who comes with his own success to ensure hers isn't taken advantage of."

Temper percolated. He spoke as if I were some damsel who needed protection from big bad ogres rather than a very capable businesswoman.

But I couldn't fault him for being so enamored with the idea that I would be as happy as he was with Mom. I just wished it were true. Dad and I very similar but in matters of sensibility versus dream-world, I had no tolerance for make-believe anymore.

I'd trusted that crazy spark with Nameless. I'd begged my father to help me turn the city upside down and turf out the truth. I'd cried myself to sleep more times than I could remember wishing Dad would be more helpful in finding the one man who made me feel so alive, so myself, so true in every sense.

But he'd refused.

Sure, he'd helped at the start. He'd gone with me to the local prisons and stood beside me while I garbled about hoodies and beards and alley-rescue. But his patience, that normally had no bounds, was tight and short lived.

I'd finally gotten him to admit his reluctance one night when I'd threatened to sell my shares in Belle Elle and step down if he kept road-blocking me to find Nameless.

All it had taken was two sentences to see how stubborn he was. I still remembered it clear as crystal: *"I've indulged you for long enough, Elle. It's time you forgot about that boy and moved on." His face had lost its jovial love, slipping into sternness. "He's a criminal. If you think I'd let my company be co-run by someone with a record, you don't know our code of ethics very well."*

And that…well, that had been the end of my quest and the moment of me switching childhood for adulthood. I'd seen something pure in Nameless but my father only saw what society called him.

Even if I had found him, I would never have been allowed to bake him blueberry pancakes or let him sleep safe in the guest room. My father, for all his kindness, actually had a flaw. And it hurt me more than I could ever say.

Sadness crushed me as Dad rushed over and pumped Penn's hand. "Congratulations. I'm so happy for both of you." Tears glistened in his eyes as he dragged me from the couch and bear hugged me. "Bell Button, I'm so—I'm—words can't describe how much this means to me. To know you'll be cherished and adored and no longer be alone when I'm gone."

His arms banded so damn tight, my lungs had no space to expand.

I patted his back, torn in pieces about doing the right thing and telling him right away or letting the lie snowball and end up killing him when the truth came out. I also nursed the three-year hurt that he'd approved Penn just because he came from wealth and success (which I had yet to find out about) and didn't have a record. He was acceptable. Nameless was not.

As much as it would kill me to destroy his sudden elation, I couldn't do it. I couldn't let him believe I'd chosen the dream he had for me. This was Penn's fault, not mine. My father's pain would come from the asshole who thought he could lie to my father and not be reprimanded.

"Dad, can I talk to you. In private?" I shot a glare over my shoulder. "The engagement isn't what you think. Penn and I aren't truly getting married."

"What?" He pulled away, his face falling into ruin. "But I thought—"

"She's being cautious, sir." Penn stood and joined our huddle. "She doesn't believe in love at first sight. She thinks I'm trying to hurt you with lies." He grinned coldly. "What she doesn't understand is a man like me needs assurances before I fully invest myself. I need her agreement on marriage in order to fully open myself and reveal everything I have to offer." He shook his head sadly, completely ignoring me, and continued talking to the hopeless romantic of my father. "I'm sure you understand. After all, you look like a man who has lived with a broken heart for many years." His tone softened, but beneath it lurked glittering steel. "Your daughter has the power to break, not just my heart, but my world. Is it so wrong of me to want her hand in marriage now, so I can be brave enough to show her everything I can?"

I rolled my eyes. "That is a load of utter bull—"

"It makes perfect sense." My father hugged me close. "Elle, I'm so proud of you and how mature you're being about all this. I'm aware you're more cynical than I am when it comes to love but seeing you with him—it makes me so, so happy."

Only because you believe he's good for Belle Elle. That he's unsullied with gossip or misdoings—unlike another.

I'd had enough. My temper snapped. "I'm not going to marry him, Dad. Both of you stop this charade right now."

Penn glowered, hiding his glare as my dad laughed. "You say that now." He tapped my cheek like a child. "I know when there is connection and chemistry. And you two have it in spades."

He backed toward the door. "In fact, I'm going to leave you in peace, but you have my blessing. Both of you." He glanced at Penn. "I'm glad we had that chat at the bar. I know a bit about you, Mr. Everett, so you're not a total stranger. However, when you get a chance, how about a round of golf or a beer to patch up any remaining holes in my knowledge? Eventually, I'd love to meet your benefactor and any other family you might have."

"Of course." Penn bowed his head with old-fashioned respect. "At the soonest opportunity." He grabbed my hand, holding me tight. "And please, call me Penn."

What would Dad say when he found out Penn had a son?

What would *I* say when I found out what Penn did for a living and why my father valued his success so highly?

What would any of us say when the truth came out, and this was over?

My father opened my office door, beaming so bright I thought he'd swallowed a star. "All right then, Penn." He chuckled. "Well, Penn, play your cards right, and soon, I'll be calling you son-in-law." Blowing me a kiss, he added, "Welcome to the family, son."

I waved like a robot as he disappeared and closed the door.

He left.

I lost it.

Whirling on Penn, I hissed, "Get out. *Right now*."

He grabbed my cheeks, yanking my face to his. His lips collided hard and brutal, his tongue lashing mine into submission.

I didn't fall for his seduction this time. Shoving him, I darted around my desk and pressed the intercom to Fleur.

She answered right away as Penn stalked me, coming closer with a shadowed look in his gaze.

"Anything I can get you?" Fleur's voice helped remind me

the world hadn't stepped into the twilight zone, and I was still the queen of this establishment.

Sage stood proudly on my desk, giving Penn an evil cat-smile, knowing he was in trouble.

Straightening my shoulders and drawing up every ounce of courage, I snipped. "Yes, call security. My *fiancé* needs help leaving the building."

CHAPTER TWENTY

I MANAGED TO avoid my husband-to-be for three days.

He called the office.

He somehow got my cellphone number.

He already had my father on his side.

And he'd corrupted my body against me.

But he hadn't succeeded in controlling my mind, and he *definitely* hadn't mastered my heart.

I was weak where he was concerned, I would admit that. And he'd drawn me into his untruths to the point I couldn't look my father in the eye and tell him it was all a big fabrication.

He was too happy. His skin was rosier, his walk bouncier, and his outlook on life chirpier. Fears about his heart and another attack kept me from shattering his happiness.

For now, I'd let him believe Penn and I were together. But once I'd earned what I wanted from him and was no longer a virgin with commitment issues, I would break it off, end the fake engagement, and go on with my life.

Who knew, perhaps I would surprise everyone and accept Greg as my future partner because at least he was normal and predictable. I could have my fling with danger and then appreciate Greg all the more.

Everyone used everyone else. I didn't let guilt eat at me for using Penn—especially when he was the one using me just as much.

"We're here, Ms. Charlston. Would you like me to wait, or do you believe the meeting will last a while?" David twisted in the driver's seat to face me sitting in the back.

My hair hung neatly over my shoulder, my black skirt with cream lace belt and Chinese blossom jacket painted me as the leader of the largest retail chain in the USA.

I clutched the folder on my lap. "The last time I met with this supplier, I didn't leave for four hours."

"I remember." David grinned. "I also recall you texting me apologetically saying you wouldn't be much longer."

I nodded. I was younger then and less adept at offsite meetings and the guilt at leaving David waiting in a car for so long. That was his job—along with other tasks, but I didn't expect him to be bored or uncomfortable.

"If you have errands you'd like to run, feel free. I'll call thirty minutes before it's due to end to give you time to return."

"Are you sure?" His large bulk twisted further in the seat. "If you think it's only going to be a short meeting, I'll wait."

I shook my head. "I'd rather know you were busy than bored."

His ebony skin bounced the streetlight off his forehead as he laughed. "Sure. Well, I'll have my phone, and I'll keep an eye on the time. If I haven't heard from you by ten p.m., I'll head back anyway."

"Okay." Hoisting the files into my arm and grabbing my handbag, I let myself out of the Range Rover and smiled at the doormen who bid me welcome to the Blue Rabbit.

I'd eaten here before. The tapas menu served second-to-none delicacies with delectable samplers. Not that I'd been able to eat very much because last time had been a business meeting, just like tonight.

Most of my social engagements, minus the last-minute high school get-togethers, were with bigwigs from other companies, improving our relationships or building on already established trade agreements.

Stuffing my face with salmon crostini or risotto balls wasn't exactly correct etiquette.

Striding in cream heels, I approached the maître-d. "Hello, I'm looking for the Loveline party?"

"Ah, yes. Right this way." The headwaiter nodded and guided me into the restaurant, around quaint tables and big tables to a large one at the back of the room where it was quieter. Blue velvet drapes hung on the walls while the salt and pepper shakers were in the shape of cute bunnies.

Nearing the table, Jennifer Stark stood up and waited with her hand outstretched. "Hello again, Ms. Charlston."

I shook her hand warmly. "Please, call me Elle."

"Elle then." Letting me go, she sat back down while motioning to the three other diners around the table. "This is Bai, Andrew, and Yumaeko from the merchandising and production departments in Shenzhen."

"Hello." I nodded politely.

Settling into the last remaining seat, I glanced once around the restaurant, afraid that just like the other times I'd been in public, Penn might show up. He seemed to have a knack for finding me.

Jennifer leaped straight into it while two waiters brought water and an array of starters to the table. "As you know, Loveline is an up-and-coming label we're hoping will find a niche market at Belle Elle."

I opened my folder and pulled out my voice recorder. I'd long since stopped trying to take notes. This way Fleur could type up the important points when I headed into the office tomorrow.

"Can you tell me a bit about what Loveline will consist of?"

Jennifer smiled shyly at her co-workers before reaching into her bag and pulling out a pamphlet. She kept it face-down, passing it over the white tablecloth. "The world is much more open about sexuality these days, and we believe capitalizing on this openness is a prime opportunity, especially with more erotic literature and movies in the mainstream market."

I turned the leaflet over and promptly slapped it against my chest, so the young waitress didn't see the giant glittery dildo on the front. "You're proposing sex toys? In a major department store?"

"We're proposing toys for adults in a private room located within the lingerie department, yes."

My cheeks burned.

Up until Penn came into my life, I hadn't had to deal with sex at all. Now, my dreams were saturated in skin and panting. My days consumed with kissing and thrusting. And now, I had to talk about dildos being sold under our brand.

"I'm not so sure that's appropriate."

Jennifer grinned, her red hair tied in a neat bun on the top of her head. "I thought you'd say that, so I brought the latest numbers from Mark Sacs in Australia, who recently introduced the Loveline to their department stores with record-breaking success." She slid another pamphlet toward me, only this time, the numbers and graphs weren't so risqué.

My eyes widened as I glanced at the figures. "Wow, that's impressive."

"The entire stock of two hundred Seahorses and three hundred Hummingbirds were sold in the first week alone. They've had to reorder three times since introducing, along with a massive bump in sales on lingerie just from add-on purchases." She grinned. "The bottom line talks, Elle."

I looked up. "What exactly is a Seahorse and a Hummingbird?"

Her business partners chuckled as she slid over a small black bag with pink crepe paper sticking from the top. "I thought you might ask. Included are samples from our top sellers including the Tiger Tail, Rattlesnake, and Panda kiss."

"All named after animals?" I tugged the bag and placed it securely in my lap, leaning over the top to keep the contents hidden while I peeked inside.

There in neat, classy see-through teal boxes were an array of dildos, vibrators, and bejeweled plugs.

I closed it, swallowing hard as my fantasies imagined Penn wielding one of those as he fisted his cock in his hand. Jennifer was right. Men and women still played. I was in a long-running game myself and had no doubt others dabbled with toys and apparatus.

Why not capitalize on such an emerging and now acceptable market?

Dad will have a fit.

But I was the boss.

And I was curious.

Placing the bag by my ankle, I linked my hands on the table and smiled. "Let's talk."

* * * * *

Penn (8:45p.m.): *Three days is too long. I've allowed you to avoid me out of respect. But tonight, you're mine.*

Penn (9:15 p.m.): *I have methods to find you, Elle. I gave you my word I wouldn't lie to you, so believe me when I say I'm tasting you tonight and you'll fucking beg for more.*

Penn (9:35 p.m.): *Seeing as you didn't text back, I've used the GPS on your phone to find your location.*

Penn (9:55 p.m.): *Fuck, you look sexy while you talk business.*

My head shot up, glancing around the restaurant.

I'd felt my phone vibrate a few times during the business meeting but hadn't checked it. I didn't want to be rude and interrupt the flow of figures and forecasts. I'd only taken it out to text David and tell him I was almost done and to bring the car around.

That was until I found multiple texts from Penn.

My heart mimicked the rabbit salt and pepper shakers, hopping around my chest as I searched the last remaining diners. Being a Tuesday meant few people lingered over their meals, needing to head home for another early start tomorrow.

"Everything okay?" Jennifer asked, signing off her credit card bill for the tapas we'd nibbled on throughout the presentation. I'd offered to pay, but she hadn't let me. Not that she would mind, seeing as I'd placed a significant order to be delivered in two months to test the market.

It was sinful buying sex toys to put into a mainstream retail chain, but with a bit of rejigging in the lingerie department, a grotto for adults could be built rather easily with strict rules about entry and all the necessary precautions of unlabeled opaque shopping bags and codes on receipts rather than in-depth details of their purchase.

If I was honest, it was rather exciting.

Just like the complex feelings I had at the thought of Penn watching me.

But after scanning all the tables, there was no sign of him.

"Yes, I'm fine." I looked back at her, slouching in relief and fizzing with disappointment.

He's not here.

I didn't know why he caused two polar extremes. I wanted him here. I didn't want him here. Neither was a lie. I literally felt both things at once.

Jennifer pushed her chair in, gathering her materials and smiling as her colleagues stood. "It was a pleasure to meet you again, Elle."

We shook hands. "Likewise."

I closed my folder and ensured I had my little black bag of samplers and my handbag.

Together, we all left the table.

I turned toward the exit.

And there he was.

His elbow leaned on the bar while his ankles crossed elegantly. He held a tumbler to his mouth, his eyes glued to me as if he hadn't been looking anywhere else. As if he *couldn't* look anywhere else.

Half of me wanted to slap him while the other half wanted to kiss him until we were kicked from the restaurant for obscene public displays of affection.

I swallowed hard as my feet remembered what to do and followed Jennifer and her partners toward fresh air and my awaiting car ride.

Tipping the rest of his drink down his throat, Penn pushed away from the bar and strolled ever so causally but not casually at all toward the same door I did. He wasn't in a suit this time, but in a black long-sleeve sweater pushed up to his elbows and faded denim jeans. The material wrapping his chest clung to every ridge and muscle, reminding me I'd seen what he hid in his jeans but hadn't seen anything else.

My fingers itched to tear it off him.

To find out if he was as perfect naked as he was dressed.

My heart mangled itself into sexually frustrated pieces as I exited and lost sight of him. Jennifer and her partners said their goodbyes before hopping into a Town Car to return to their hotel.

David jumped out of the awaiting Range Rover and grabbed my belongings. "All good? Ready to go?"

I should say yes. I should leap in the 4WD and demand he peel away like a racecar driver to keep me out of the clutches of Penn Everett. But I dawdled deliberately, raking a hand through my hair and pretending to soak up the balmy night sky.

"I'll take her home."

The smooth, sensual voice wrapped around me from behind as Penn stepped to my side and placed his hand on my lower back.

Three days deleted in a poof of desire.

My anger with him for lying.

My rage at being manipulated...all gone.

He'd made this itch inside me intolerable.

He would have to be the one to fix it.

Penn smiled, leaning forward to capture the little black bag from David's fingers. "We'll take that, too."

My eyes widened as I gulped. "How do you—"

Know what's in there?

I stopped midway because the question was useless.

Judging by his texts, he'd been watching me for a while. He would've seen flashes of the product as I fondled a few under the table, testing the rubber dildos and doing what Jennifer suggested to see how lifelike they were.

My cheeks burned as Penn captured my hand. "Elle, please tell your driver that you're happy to let me take you home and that I'm not kidnapping you or holding you under duress."

I blinked, noticing David's tense shoulders and the way he'd pushed aside his blazer to reveal the hidden holster and handle of his weapon. "It's okay, David. I know him."

"Ma'am?" He didn't take his eyes off Penn. He looked him up and down. "He does look familiar, now that you mention it."

Familiar? Why would he look familiar?

Penn was anything but ordinary and I was fairly sure I'd never bumped into him before. Besides, he himself had told my father he'd only recently returned to New York after being away for a time.

I said politely, "His name is Penn Everett."

Penn amended. "Ms. Charlston's fiancé."

I cringed. Words dangled on my tongue to deny it, but what would be the point? My father already believed, Steve, Greg…what was one more in the scheme of this storybook?

David shifted in place. "I see." He didn't relax, though, which I found mildly disconcerting.

He turned his attention to me.

Years ago, when my father had hired him to protect me, we'd worked on a series of codes I could say if I felt threatened or couldn't speak honestly. If I was being held at gunpoint or being robbed, a simple phrase would send David into military mode.

"Any other orders for the night, ma'am?" He waited, giving me time to speak one of the codes.

I'm tired and believe I'll take a bubble bath tonight: code for a kidnapping.

I'm not feeling well; I might walk instead: code for a robbery or gun in my side.

I said neither.

The silence dragged on a second too long before Penn tugged on my fingers.

Without hesitation, I moved with him. "No, not tonight, David."

David didn't try to save me again.

CHAPTER TWENTY-ONE

TEN MINUTES INTO the walk, my nerves got the better of me.

Squeezing Penn's fingers, I asked, "Where are you taking me?"

"My place."

"Why?"

He chuckled, his face shrouded in darkness. "Why do you think?"

My tummy clenched as his voice lost its decorum and slipped into sin.

"To fuck you, of course." His teeth flashed as he added, "I've waited for as long as I can. You haven't told your father I was lying about our engagement, and you haven't run back to your bodyguard. Therefore, I know you're up for whatever I have planned, and you will not argue." His jaw lowered. "Will you, Bell Button?"

My mouth watered with how wrong but how right that sounded. Fantasies of what could happen tonight unraveled with lightning desire—

Wait.

He called me Bell Button.

Anger took precedent. "That isn't your nickname to use."

"No?" He raised an eyebrow. "Yet you let—what was her name? Chloe—call you Ding Dong Bell. Do you prefer that?"

My teeth locked together. "I prefer neither. Elle is perfectly acceptable. So use it."

He laughed in a soft sigh. "So defensive."

"Not defensive. Protective."

His head shot up, his eyes sinking into me like barbs. "You feel the need to protect yourself around me?"

"Constantly."

His shadow swallowed me. "Why?"

"Why what?"

"You know what. Answer the question and stop dancing around it." The way he pushed for an answer hinted he had ulterior motives to know why I barricaded myself from him. Why I would never let myself feel more for him than just physical desire.

We'd known each other a week or so. I was woman enough to admit I found him immensely attractive. I was girl enough to admit I liked the idea of instant true love. But I was realistic enough to know that would never happen for a business owner like me.

Besides, he was ruthless in his own success. Webbed in lies and hidden in half-truths, he was not a man to trust with anything breakable—especially my heart.

My body would bruise.

But it would heal.

It didn't stop the fact that Penn wanted something from me.

If it was just sex, then our motives were in line.

But the more I spent in his company, the more I sensed that wasn't his end game.

I narrowed my eyes, trying to see past his arrogant shields and read what he truly meant. But all he revealed was a man supreme in his ability and self-worth. A man as proud and as pompous as a peacock.

Yet…he has a son.

How could someone so cold and emotionally unavailable have a child dependent on him? Where was Stewie's mother?

Who was Larry? What the hell would happen between us once we'd slept together?

The questions built on top of his in an unstable Jenga tower. One wrong answer and the entire foundation of our so-called relationship would crumble.

Tonight was not the night to let it fall.

Tomorrow it could.

Because by tomorrow, I would've got what I wanted, he would've got what he wanted, and things would go back to the way they were. Penn and his lies would fade from my life before he caused any more damage.

"You ask why, yet I could ask you the same question." I pushed ahead, leaving the glow of a streetlight and stepping into a pool of night. "Why do *you* protect yourself from *me*?"

He slammed to a stop. "I don't."

"You do."

His jaw worked, his hands opening and closing by his sides. "I'm guarded; there's a difference."

"Is there?" I cocked my head. "Funny, I would say protective and guarded were the same thing."

He stormed toward me, grabbing me by the throat and marching me backward until I hit the façade of an apartment building. The brick was hard. He was harder. I was the soft middle that didn't stand a chance. "If you ever try to psychoanalyze me again, you'll be sorry."

I swallowed, forcing fear past the cage of his hand around my neck. Even now, my body hummed beneath his grip. It seemed my cells had embraced the sensation of eroticism and found any grasp appropriate.

"Why would I be sorry?" My voice barely registered audible. "What would you do? Kill me?"

I meant it flippantly, casually. A phrase tossed around far too often and never meant. But instead of either ignoring the cliché dare or admitting he ran much darker than I thought, he smiled with all the sharpness of a butcher's arsenal. "Perhaps."

My heart leaped out of my body, racing to borrow a

telephone to call the police. But my insides burned with a different flavor than before. If lust was a color, I'd been bathed in reds and pinks for days. Now I swam in blacks and deep, deep purples, wanting nothing more than to let go and forget who I was and become who I dared never be.

Straining against his fingers, I deliberately strangled myself in his hold. "What are you going to do to me if I accept I'll never know you and admit I don't want to? What will you do when I admit I'm using you like you're using me? Fuck me?"

He never looked away; never reduced the pressure on my throat. "I told you that was my intention."

He constantly had me at a disadvantage. I was sick of it. If I wanted to hold my ground, I had to start acting more myself and not a timid little girl. Gathering my courage, I murmured, "Stop threatening, and get it over with then."

His fingers spasmed. His body weight landed on mine. "Get it over with?"

"Yes. I want you to fuck me then leave me alone."

A slight groan fell from his lips. "You can't say things like that on an empty street."

"Why not? I would've thought empty would be preferable to busy. No one is here to watch."

He shook his head, dark hair dancing over his forehead. "Busy means I'm forced to keep my hands to myself." He yanked me close, dropping his fingers from my neck to my breast while his left arm looped around my waist.

The soft thud of the bag holding the sex toy samples landed on the sidewalk as his hand massaged my flesh, his thumb and finger pinching my nipple. "An empty street means I could turn you around, hoist up your skirt, and sink inside you without being seen."

I shivered.

It sounded so wrong.

It sounded so *good*.

Forcing myself to remain sane, I looked up at the buildings all around us. The faint glow of families and the shadows of activities moved subtly above. "We'd be seen, regardless if we saw them or not."

He followed my gaze, his throat exposed as his head tipped up. His fingers twitched on my breast. "You're right."

His touch fell away as he took a step back. "Pity."

Collecting the bag again, he slipped back into a prowl, dragging me with him.

* * * * *

"You live here?"

He nodded as he pulled a key from his pocket.

"As in the whole building?" I looked up at the mini skyscraper with its high sash windows and faded duck-egg blue exterior.

"It needs work, but that's why I bought it." He unlocked the ancient doorknob and pulled me into a foyer with art deco tiles, a square chandelier, and peeling wallpaper. The ceiling soared at least four stories above us with a double width staircase curling up in a spiral to multiple floors.

"Wow."

He let me go, moving toward the wall where the flick of a bronze light switch magically graced the place with illumination. The soft click woke up countless light bulbs, glittering with dust and weathered with time.

"Like I said, a work in progress." Once again, he captured my wrist, carting me up the stairs. He didn't give me a chance to marvel at the original craftsmanship or question how long he'd been the owner.

It was as if the building didn't exist to him. As if the only thing that mattered to him was me.

I didn't speak as we made our way up and up. He didn't stop on floor two or three or four. He kept tugging me higher until we entered floor ten or eleven and unlocked yet another door in the dingy moth-nibbled hallway.

It was like stepping into a different world.

We'd headed through a time capsule and entered a resplendent suite of art deco charm, 1930's decoration, and immaculate presentation.

My mouth fell open as I drifted forward. "This—this is incredible."

"Of course, it is. It's mine." He locked the door behind him then strode through the space. "Just like you." His jaw tightened beneath his five o'clock shadow. "I only own incredible things."

My heart lurched rather than my body.

Was that an odd compliment? A nod that he did care for me beyond physical gratification?

Don't be absurd. Your heart is wrong. It's on a sabbatical, researching myths on love and finding no solid proof it exists.

Penn was everything poems and fables promised. If it wasn't for the brooding anger or taut protection he sheltered behind, of course.

If only I could make him swallow a truth serum and tear out answers—reveal just how shallow or deep he ran.

I couldn't take my eyes off him. I expected him to fit in with this space, to feel at home and move freely, yet something didn't sit right. He kicked off his shoes and padded barefoot over polished mosaic wood floors, but something was missing. He wasn't at ease. He moved as if this was as foreign and new to him as it was to me.

Why is that?

"How long ago did you move in?" I kicked off my heels, placing them by the kitchen island.

Penn smiled. "You're asking questions?"

"Is that against the rules?"

He paused; something flickered over his face that I couldn't decipher. "Some aren't. Others are."

The crypticness gave me a headache. "So you can't tell me how long you've lived here?"

"You overheard part of what I told your father at the Weeping Willow. I've moved back to town recently. So if you believe that, then you'll believe that this is a new purchase."

"Why do I need to believe something if it's true?"

He didn't reply.

I pushed with another question. "You said your benefactor was sick. That you returned for him. Is he okay?"

A softness flowed over him—something so unexpected and endearing to see. Whoever his benefactor was, he cared for him a lot more than he would admit. "He's fine now. It was a rare form of blood cancer. They have it under control."

"That's good."

"It is."

The conversation stalled. Awkwardness settled like a third wheel. I felt responsible. Before, our silence had been potent with desire. Now, it hung heavy with confusion.

Why did I care about him, this building, and whoever his mystery benefactor was?

I'm here for one thing only.

Same thing as he was.

Taking a deep breath, I marched across the room. His arms opened wide, knowing what I did—that the only way to delete the sudden weirdness between us was to return to the basics.

The place where hate and like didn't matter.

His lips stopped my thoughts. His arms ceased my worry. He let whatever restraint he had left fray and stalked me backward, his mouth never leaving mine, his sheer power corralling me against a sideboard.

His fingers grabbed my jaw as he kissed me hard.

His taste of mint and darkness flooded my senses.

I trembled in his hold.

As quickly as the kiss began, it ended. His fingers stung my oversensitive skin as he tugged me forward, moving stealthily toward a door past the open plan kitchen, living room, and dining. All around, large picture windows allowed the city to entertain us with its electric vibrancies and pedestrians below.

Opening a door, Penn let me go, allowing me to drift forward into his bedroom while he tossed the black bag onto his bed.

I followed it as the silver glitter dildo called the Seahorse bounced out and lay accusingly on the dark gray coverlet.

Penn didn't notice. Or if he did, he didn't glance at it. I doubted he'd notice anything else now I was in his lair. I was his conquest, his trophy. I didn't know why I got the feeling this was more about him than it was about me, but in an odd way, I was glad.

I could take what I wanted without having to worry about emotions getting in the way. I could keep myself protected all while giving him every intimate part of myself.

I shivered as he stalked toward me, crowding me against the wall. He seemed to prefer me locked in place, unable to go anywhere.

He hadn't offered me a drink or something to eat.

He'd brought me here to fuck me.

That was all.

I knew I might be hurt by that later. That for all my bravado and belief I could keep this about sex, I might still over-analyze and read into every moment. But right now…right now all I wanted was him. All I needed was him, and I was prepared to be cold-hearted to do that.

"You're so fucking beautiful, Elle," he murmured, planting one hand on the wall by my head, imprisoning me. The pulse in his neck was visible as his gaze slipped from warm sable to brutal black. His other hand landed on my cheek, his thumb grazing my jaw to the corner of my mouth.

He paused, holding his thumb there. "You don't have a clue what you're doing to me, do you?" He pressed his erection against my belly. "And I'm not going to tell you."

What? What am I doing to you?

The way he said it ached with tenderness. For the briefest second, he wasn't some rich tycoon about to strip and devour me but a sweet seducer drowning beneath his own untruths.

That was the problem with being guarded.

People with lies could never make friends. But people with trust could never make enemies.

Both were weak.

I sucked in a breath, parting my lips, allowing him to insert his thumb into my mouth.

The intrusion was sexy and hot, and his skin tasted of salt.

I wanted to ask why he wouldn't tell me. That I wanted to know what crazy power I had over him when I felt so helpless in his presence. But he leaned forward, licking my bottom lip as he held my mouth open with his thumb. "I'm not going to tell you because I'm going to show you."

He leaned against me, chest to chest, hips to hips. He trapped me just as he had in my office and the alley and the street and my department store.

He trapped me, and it dredged up yet more memories of three years ago when a hooded man freed me from robbers and awoke my teenage soul. The differences were startling. One man had unlocked my world. This one did his best to imprison me.

Neither would be successful.

Only I held that power, and it was my prerogative to lend it to another or deny it.

A faint hint of anger and untapped desire siphoned from him to me, yet beneath that, there was something else. Something I hadn't felt from him before.

Softness wrapped in barbwire.

It didn't diminish the intensity of how he watched me, touched me, controlled me with the multiple facets within him. His facial scruff scraped my cheek as he bent his neck and kissed my throat. My eyes slammed closed as his teeth bit my collarbone. His aftershave shot up my nose as his hands landed on my sides, swooping up to rub my nipples with his thumbs.

His lips traced up my neck, kissing but not gently. Nothing about Penn was gentle. It all came from a place of violence mixed with pleasure. The slipperiness of his teeth added a thrilling dimension to his warm mouth, and I moaned as he once again captured my face in his strong, cool fingers and tipped me just the right way.

His lips sealed over mine, sweet to start then vicious. My body slammed against the wall, harder and harder as he tried to consume me, his lips causing bruises that would never heal.

I had no choice but to let go. To give up standing and breathing and thinking.

If I didn't, I'd scream with his possession.

Giving in was the easiest and only option.

Because then I could stop thinking and just *be*. Be a woman, desire...me.

He controlled every minute thing.

He was right when he said he wouldn't lie to me.

The kiss told me things he no doubt wanted to keep hidden. Things like 'this is me, this is who I am. I won't apologize'. And beneath that...beneath those sexy messages of wanting to fuck me was a deeper, darker thread.

A thread that dared me to argue, to probe deeper into who he was, to switch him from passionate stranger to someone I could perhaps call...not a friend, but at least an acquaintance.

His other hand looped around my spine, jerking me from the wall, shoving his fingers down the back of my skirt. He fingered the lace of my G-string and the top of my ass, rocking his erection into my belly.

I need air. I need sanity.

But he scooped me into his arms, letting my legs dangle between his as he stalked toward his bed and threw me down, tossing the black bag onto the floor.

His face contorted with lust. "We'll use toys another time. Tonight, I just need you." Grabbing my jacket, he forced me to wriggle free as he removed my arms from the sleeves.

The minute I lay there in my blouse and skirt, he smirked. "I hope you're not too attached to these."

With a furious yank, he ripped my blouse apart. The tiny seashell buttons pinged into all corners of his room while cool air kissed my naked belly, revealing my black lace bra.

He groaned, bending over me to press a kiss on the swell of my breast.

Without thinking, I held his head to my chest, breathing hard, panting quick, running my hands through his hair with affection I didn't necessarily feel.

He reared back, his gaze narrowed and full of rage.

We stared at each other, silently waging, trying to figure out how lines had blurred already. Pulling back to stand by the edge of the bed, Penn left me speechless, breathless, wondering what the hell was happening, and just who he was beneath the surface.

His hands landed on his belt, yanking the leather free and ripping it from the loops.

My skin was needy and demanding. I wanted him close. I wanted him on me. Screw the tiny voice of fear that my first time would hurt.

"Take off your clothes," he growled thickly, his voice no longer entirely human as he shoved his jeans down his legs and stepped out of them.

Sitting up on the bed, I obeyed, shrugging out of my damaged top and reaching behind to unhook and unzip my skirt. The moment it unfastened, I lay back down, shimmying from the material until he grabbed the ends and yanked it the rest of the way.

My garter belt glittered in the low lamps by the window and door. My pantyhose reminded me everyone else knew me as the queen of Belle Elle, yet Penn was the only one to tear me down until I was naked and begging for a single touch.

His gaze latched between my legs where my black G-string matched my bra. He bit his lip, then grabbed my ankles, yanked me down the bed, and pressed himself on top of me. His fist slammed into the mattress with all the frustration and rage he wouldn't admit, making my heart hammer and blood race.

"Fuck, I want to be inside you."

I surrendered to his feral kiss, letting him direct and guide me. His fingers plucked at my garters, undoing my pantyhose until they hung undone around my thighs. He rocked his cock against me—the only things separating us were two pieces of cotton.

Terror tried to interrupt my pleasure—things like birth control and protection and the fact I should tell him it was my first time.

But embarrassment kept my lips shut.

Penn was experienced. He couldn't hide that fact with the way he attacked my mouth and body with confidence born of expertise.

If he'd noticed I was a follower in this and no longer the leader I'd been groomed to be, he didn't care or mention it. I just hoped he'd take charge of the protection issue, and if he entered me too fast, then I would say something but not before.

I clutched at his black top, needing it off. Needing skin on skin.

He listened, tearing his mouth away to reach over his head and pull the second to last piece of clothing off.

My hands flew up of their own accord. I traced his abs and up to his chest. He didn't try to stop me and the luxury, the *privilege* of touching him filled my blood with heated desire.

Staying braced on one arm over me, his fingers looped around my panties and pulled them down. My hand latched onto the other side, keeping it high, protecting my modesty. I didn't know why, but sudden shyness attacked me.

He gritted his teeth. "Let go."

I bit my lip, refusing silently.

"Elle." His growl sliced through my unwillingness.

Closing my eyes briefly, I let go and allowed him to drag the lace down my legs. He slipped them off my ankles and tossed them over his shoulder. Clamping a powerful hand on my inner thigh, he spread my legs. "So fucking beautiful."

I trembled as his stroked upward, running his fingertips along my wetness. "Christ, Elle."

My mouth opened as he pressed a finger slowly inside me.

My breasts ached, and I reached behind me to undo the confines of my bra. He grimaced with agonizing need as I revealed the final part of me. He swallowed hard as my body welcomed his finger, my hips rocking upward to meet him.

"Touch me," he commanded. His finger hooked inside me, dragging a gasp through my lungs. I reached forward blindly, unsure what to do and how hard to grasp.

He tipped forward, giving me access to his boxer-briefs.

With an out of control heartbeat, I pulled aside the tight cotton and inserted my hand into the warm depths.

He shuddered as my fingers latched around him.

"Jesus." He bowed as I squeezed hard, unsure if soft or violent was his undoing.

I copied the pressure he used on me—not being gentle, not giving him time to adjust to being touched.

His finger speared upward, pressing against the sensitive spot inside that turned everything into liquid gold. Grunting a little as I fisted him deeper, he inserted another finger.

The stretch. The burn. His fingernail scraped a little as he didn't give me time to adjust.

I matched his punishment with my own, digging my nails into his shaft, pumping him in the same way he thrust into me.

"Goddammit." His head bowed, his lips wide. "Fuck, that feels good."

His greedy cock leaped in my hands, demanding more. Something hot and sticky coated my fingers as I swooped over the crown and back down again.

He hooked his finger deeper, causing me to writhe on the bed. My voice erupted on a gasp. "Oh, God."

"Finally, you speak."

I shivered, sinking back into myself as he stroked and teased. Words seemed a million miles away in the realm of conversation and humanness. I was somewhere deep inside where only feeling and sensation were permitted. "I wasn't aware you wanted me to."

"I want to know how this is for you." His eyes blazed. "How?"

His thumb landed on my clit. "Do you like this? Do you

need more? Less? Tell me."

I answered back with a squeeze of his cock. "Do *you* like this?"

He groaned. "Do you really need to ask?" His hips thrust into my palm. "I'm practically coming all over your goddamn fingers."

The confession sent lust and desire and giddy, giddy happiness fizzing like fireworks.

My body slowly melted, becoming more inviting, wetter, hotter.

He noticed.

A dark gleam entered his gaze. "I have no intention of fingering you all night, Elle. Just like I don't expect you to jerk me off." His fingers stroked me ruthlessly. "I want to fuck you. I need to be inside this." He hooked his grip, pressing something intimately hardwired to an exquisite button inside my belly.

Another press and I could've climbed up whatever pleasure hill I currently trampled, striding closer toward the summit. But each time he pushed me, he pulled me back a little—making me out of breath and desperate for the top where I could finally rest and be rewarded.

He pulled away, removing his touch, making me empty. "Tell me now if that's going to be a problem." He fisted himself, looking between my legs. "Tell me if you're having second thoughts because once I'm inside you, I won't be able to stop."

Now was my final chance to admit I wasn't ready. That this was too soon. Too fast. Not done by rational women.

But the words weren't there.

The only ones I knew were: "I want this. I want you to fuck me."

His eyes snapped closed as his stomach tightened. "Your wish is my command." Shoving my thighs wider, he pushed his boxer-briefs down his legs and threw them to the floor. Reaching for his discarded jeans on the bed, he pulled out a condom packet and passed it to me.

"I take you're not on the pill."

I took the slippery foil. "No."

"Fine." His jaw gritted as his gaze locked on my shaking hands. "Put it on me then."

I had no intention of telling him I'd never done this before. Ripping the packet, I carefully pulled out the odd smelling latex and pinched the top like I'd been shown in sex education at school.

He didn't say a word as I positioned it over his crown and rolled it down his very impressive length.

He shuddered as my fingers went further than necessary and cupped his balls. His eyes flared wide before I pulled away, unsure if I was allowed to do that or not.

Wedging his hips between mine, he snarled, "Answer me one question."

I was obsessed with the sight of his sheathed erection only inches away from my core.

He grabbed my chin, forcing me to meet his eyes. "Are you a virgin?"

I stiffened. "How—how would you know that?"

"I don't know that. That's why I'm asking."

I licked my lips. "I'm—"

He waited with angry eyes, the tip of his cock nudging against my entrance. "Tell me, Elle. Otherwise, this will be very painful for you." Pushing forward, he entered me just a little.

The discomfort burned, but in a good way; but he had so much more to go. So many ways to rip me apart if I wasn't honest with him.

I dropped my eyes. "This is the first time I've been with a man."

His forehead furrowed. His face replayed a memory I couldn't see. His hips pushed forward again, inch by lazy inch. "I'll go slow."

I tensed. "Okay."

We breathed in the same ragged rhythm as he slipped ever

so slowly into my body. When he hit an unbreakable barrier, I clenched with trepidation and pain.

He stopped.

A few dazzling drumbeats of my heart, and I forced myself to relax a little.

He pressed deeper.

His dominion was collected but incomplete. There was nowhere I could look without him being there. No scent I could breathe without it being him.

I couldn't do a thing but allow him to penetrate me in every sense of the word.

Another inch and a sting began—an awful burn that brought tears to my eyes. I turned my head, doing my best to bury my face or bite down on freshly laundered sheets.

"Hurts?"

I nodded, unable to look at him. I was a failure at this.

"I told you I'd protect you even when I was hurting you, remember?" He grunted, dragging my eyes to him. He loomed over me like a demon with muscles etched in shadow, a face chiseled from granite.

I nodded.

"Well, then, this is going to hurt." The flash of lust on his face distracted me then all I knew was pain and pleasure and pain and pleasure and pain, pain, *pain*.

He impaled me swiftly, sharply. No more creeping softly. No more adjusting or seduction.

He fucked me.

He took me.

He consumed me.

CHAPTER TWENTY-TWO

"OPEN YOUR EYES, Elle."

I couldn't, not with the tears trickling down my cheeks. Tears I didn't even understand. I wasn't crying because it hurt—the pain had already faded a little. I wasn't even crying because I'd given this man who I didn't know the final piece of me that no one else had earned.

I cried because in his strange arms, with his delicious body inside mine, I found a smidgen of that freedom I'd tried so long to find.

"Open your eyes," he ordered again, rocking into me.

I obeyed, drinking him in, noticing the small beads of sweat on his brow and the wildness on his face.

I shifted beneath him, my hips adjusting to fit his. My tears dried like salt tracks. "You're huge."

"You're tight."

"It feels...nice, though."

"Nice?" He half-smiled, fighting back the quick flashes of darkness he kept hidden. "Just nice?" He pressed into me. "No other description? No better word for me fucking you?"

"Sore?"

He scowled. "I was thinking of another."

"Hard? Full? Desperate?"

His face eclipsed with shadows. "Desperate?" His voice switched to ragged breath. "Desperate for what? This?" He arched into me, his back bowing, his hips driving into mine with power and precision.

My neck tensed, my skull digging into the bed as my shoulder blades came off the mattress. A wave of pain and a crash of pleasure. It seemed I couldn't enjoy one without enduring the other.

But I'd never experienced anything like it.

I wanted more.

So much more.

But I'd have to wait because bliss like this meant he must've come, and I'd read men couldn't have multiple orgasms like women.

You haven't come yet.

It didn't bother me. Tonight had been a simple task to lose my innocence. It rid me of that minor complication, and the next time (if there were a next time), there would be no pain, only pleasure.

My hips moved, kissing the top of my mound to his lower belly. A thank you. A request. A bit of both.

He licked his lips, self-control etching his face. "You want to continue?"

"There's more?" My lips parted as eagerness washed through me. "You didn't…finish?"

He chuckled; it shook his body inside mine. "I won't take offense to that. But if you honestly think I'd just enter you and be satisfied, you need some serious lessons on how I fuck."

He looked down at where we joined, encouraging me to watch, too. He pulled back a little before pushing forward. The pain morphed to pleasure, warming and melting with a fine veil of sharpness.

Embracing the fire feeding on the lust inside me, I placed my hands on the top of his ass where his back clenched beneath my fingers. "More."

He planted his fists into the sheets by my head. "Fine." He slipped from slow to serious, driving into me.

My core clenched around him. A twinge of discomfort

tried to steal me away.

Screw the pain.

I wanted this.

All of it.

He groaned long and low, his hips thrust upward, hitting some part of me that shattered into stardust. His hips jack-knifed into mine, as deep and as close as he could go. He let go. He drove again.

Thrust. Thrust. *Thrust.*

Whatever place orgasms lived suddenly swarmed alive like a hive with its ferocious queen. The buzzing flew from my toes to my knees to my spine, from my fingers to my arms to my tongue.

Everything ignited, and I jumped.

I jumped from the tower of Belle Elle. I forgot about my career, my rules, my boundaries.

I deleted myself.

I met Penn in the black debasement and spoke crude consonants and tasted dirty vowels. "I want you to fuck me. I want you to make me scream." I dug my fingernails into his ass, jerking him to me. "Give me what I want." I bowed off the bed, capturing his mouth with mine, taking control all while submitting the remaining power I had. "Fuck me...please."

I should've prepared for the unleashing.

I should've expected what would happen with such an invitation.

But it still took me by surprise. Still thrilled and terrified and teased.

"You fucking asked for it." His smile was pure criminal as his stomach tightened, and he drove into me so hard, so fast, his hips bruised my inner thighs. His mouth latched onto mine, our teeth clacking, our tongues knotting, every last masquerade at being civilized...gone.

He didn't just take me up on my offer.

He doubled my stakes and went for everything he could claim.

He fucked me.

No, that was woefully unjust.

He broke me, fixed me, split me.

His body slammed again and again and *again* into me. His cock sliding in heat and wetness, dragging more from me. The orgasm buzz increased, consuming everything.

His stamina made my legs jelly. Every feminine atom burst with bliss. My hips tried to meet his, but his pace kept me pinned to the bed. With a ragged breath, he slapped a hand over my heart, pressing my lungs, preventing me from gasping, counting my charging heartbeats.

My skin burned with sweat, turning his grip slippery. His fingers slid off me, slamming into the mattress. His arm buckled, wedging his entire weight on me. His hips thrust as if he had no power over his body anymore. As if all he was, all he was meant to do, was possess me until I possessed him in some karmic twist of fate.

I gasped and panted and gulped as sex turned to the most basic of coupling.

He buried his face into the sheets, his back suddenly going ramrod straight, his cock pulsing inside me.

I froze, not knowing what to do.

I knew exactly what I wanted to do.

My fingers turned gentle, caressing his spine. The moment I touched his sweat-misted back, he reared up, baring his teeth. "Don't. I'm just—" His jaw worked. "I'm so fucking close."

"Don't stop."

His face scrunched up with sexual agony. "I don't want to finish yet. I haven't had enough of you."

My cheeks pinked even as triumph blew trumpets in my belly. "Oh."

He bent and kissed me, unapologetic with lust and his desire to come. His eyes remained closed, barring me from reading him or trying to guess if this physical act meant more to him than mutual release.

I couldn't figure him out, and I desperately needed to if I

was going to survive whatever he'd done to me.

Because he *had* done something to me.

He'd awakened me, and I could never go back to sleep.

"Fuck, you feel too good." With a feral grunt, he pulled away, withdrawing, and leaving me empty. Sliding down my body, his legs fell off the bed, his knees thudding against the floor.

Before I could ask what was wrong, his hands landed on my inner thighs and pushed my legs apart. His mouth—the same one that'd been kissing me—landed on my core, his tongue pulsing inside me with a different kind of wetness, a more intimate kind of heat.

I bowed off the bed, clutching the sheets in shock. "Oh, my *God.*"

He bit my clit with careful teeth. "You're sore, and I need to fuck you hard. I doubt you'll find a release with me. So…you're going to have one now."

The sheets didn't provide enough traction to grip onto. I grabbed his hair instead.

He cursed something deep and dark. His voice twisted my stomach into bowties. His tongue entered me again. It wasn't enough after the deep penetration of his cock; the shallow claiming left me straining for more.

But then his hands joined in too, pinching my clit as his fingers ran beneath his tongue to press inside me, granting girth and dexterity, pushing me up the cliff of an orgasm I'd bathed in since he turned me from pure to deviant.

Just like in my office, he didn't mess around.

He wanted me to come.

I would come.

My legs tried to close around his head, but he slammed a hand onto my thigh, spreading his saliva and my arousal. Grabbing my wrists, he kept then pinned on my belly while his tongue worked me harder.

The orgasm had colors like a dark rainbow—all blacks and grays and reds and oranges. I felt it gather. I saw it swirl. And when it descended from my bones and ligaments to gather in my womb, it glittered like some magical malicious force.

His tongue was the wand that spent that magic, dragging it from me, forcing it to explode in body-crippling waves.

"Oh, God. Oh, God. Oh, *God*." I climbed the bed, him, the world. I went blind, deaf, mute.

I drowned in every crest.

I hadn't finished coming when he climbed my body, hooked my leg over his hip, and slammed back inside me.

"Yes!" It was a scream. I had no shame. I screamed again as he drove brutally fast and deep. "Yes. Oh, God, *yes*."

The pain...was no more.

The pleasure...was too much.

Thick, hot, welcome and an undeniable primitive need to feel him all the way, deeper, deeper, harder, harder.

His tongue slid over my neck, his teeth settling over my artery like a wolf mounting its mate.

I kissed his shoulder, reveling in the saltiness, the rawness of how two naked people could be.

My fingernails landed on either side of his spine, digging hard.

"Harder," he ordered with a commanding bite. His tone kissed the dregs of my orgasm, rekindling it, fanning it, transforming embers into flames.

The soreness turned to a luscious pulling as he drove faster.

"Fuck, take it. Fucking take it." He reared over me, his elbows locked, his fingers tangled in my hair, keeping my head imprisoned and eyes pinned on his.

The bed creaked as he worked both of us into a slick mess of sweat and pleasure.

I couldn't look away, and in his brown gaze, I found something unbearably carnal, so unfiltered and truthful that my core tightened, begging for another release.

His lips smashed against mine, cutting me off from his thoughts. I lost my mind and gave into the time-honored instinct to rock with him, to accept his control, and allow him to feed and deny me every hunger he summoned.

"Fuck, you feel good. I knew you would." He hit me at an angle that sent the world fracturing with black spots. His expert claiming sent another spindle of need to join those hungry flames.

I was sore and loose and wet and delirious, and I didn't think I could come again. But he had a power over me I couldn't ignore.

A smaller more tentative release found me, ecstasy radiating into my fingertips as I trembled and gathered beneath him.

My eyes remained open as the bands of muscle contracted almost secretly, tiptoeing through my body as if unpermitted.

I came softly, deliciously, wantonly.

His eyes widened. "You came?"

I swallowed as a final clench left me boneless, lost, and entirely drugged with endorphins.

"Fuck, you came. You fucking came with me inside you." His gaze possessed me, and he lost it. Positioning himself higher over me, he grabbed my wrists and slammed them over my head.

And then, he *fucked* me.

"Shit, shit...*shit*." His voice scrambled with breath. Inside me, he grew thicker, heavier, harder, hitting the top of me with every pound.

He was wild, unleashed; his control and lies undone.

His face, normally so handsome and regal, splintered into a broken veneer as he let go.

"*Fuck!*" An animalistic roar fell from his lips, his orgasm tearing up his back and into me.

I let him do what he needed.

I drank in his vulnerability and relished in the fact he let me see him the way not many people would.

He shattered.

He shivered.

He shuddered as the last wave wrung him dry.

Only once long moments had disappeared, and we'd returned from whatever stratosphere he'd catapulted us to, did his fingers unlock from my wrists and trail down my arm to cup my cheek.

With eyes soft and no longer angry about things I couldn't understand, he kissed me.

This kiss was different.

It wasn't a claiming or a thank you.

It was a stripping back; a peeling of the masks we wore.

An acknowledgment that we'd started something that, unfortunately, wouldn't have a happy ending.

CHAPTER TWENTY-THREE

THE LARGE CLOCK hanging in Penn's kitchen said I'd only been at his place one hour and thirty-two minutes, yet the whole world had changed.

Either time sped up without me, or we shot into the future where everything was different.

Where I was different. My body was different. My entire outlook altered.

I ran my hands down my buttoned blazer for the tenth time, smoothing my skirt. I tried to ignore my tangled hair that needed a deep condition and an hour with a brush, and pretended I wasn't bare beneath my clothing.

Once we'd finished and Penn withdrew from me, we'd dressed silently and reconvened in the kitchen. I stuffed my lingerie into the black bag full of sex toys, intending to take both home. However, Penn grabbed the handles and placed the parcel on a cupboard on the way out of his bedroom.

He didn't say a thing.

His body language alone said all of those items were staying here—whether I liked it or not.

He moved barefoot while I clipped in heels. He ducked around the large island and grabbed two glasses from a frosted-glass cupboard. Filling them both with water from a carafe in the fridge, he passed one to me, watching me over the rim as he drank.

He'd slipped into light colored jeans and a black t-shirt, looking every bit the bad boy I should never introduce to my father, let alone go along with his lies that we were engaged.

Nerves multiplied with tiny legs, racing over my shoulders the longer we stared in silence and drank. I wanted to call David to collect me. The longer I stood in Penn's presence, the more he withdrew to the point that any warmth that'd existed between us howled with frost.

I shifted on the spot, placing my half-drunk glass of water on the counter. "I guess—I guess I'll go home now."

He raised an eyebrow and finished his water. Wiping his lips with the back of his hand, he nodded. "Good idea."

I tried to hide my wince, but I wasn't successful. I didn't know why he'd shut me out—then again, he hadn't let me in. He'd invaded my body, but that didn't give me a return pass to rummage around in his soul.

The idea of calling David and waiting for him inside Penn's apartment wasn't appealing. The sooner I was away from the harsh intensity where splinters of whatever we weren't saying stabbed me, the better.

Hugging myself—making sure my broken blouse was tucked tightly into my skirt to prevent gaping open and my blazer was buttoned tight—I nodded as if we'd concluded business and the meeting was over.

Realistically, this was a business contract. He didn't like me. I didn't like him. But the sex had been incredible. I had nothing to compare it to, but if I had to do it all over again and let Penn relieve me of my virginity, I would.

Moving toward the door highlighted how sore I was. The tenderness of my inner thighs, the achiness of my core. The heavy pulling made me want to sit down, not walk down flights of stairs and wait on a cold street for my driver.

But I wasn't welcome anymore.

Penn's glare said as much.

He lied about us being engaged, yet couldn't lie about how much he needed me gone.

I stopped by the exit, keeping my back stiff. "Well, goodnight."

"Goodnight." He'd escorted me to the door as if not trusting me to leave on my own. Reaching around me, he unlocked the door and opened it. He pursed his lips as I stepped over the threshold. He didn't smile or offer a word of kindness or even condolences.

It felt like a break-up even though we were never together.

I shrugged, fighting the urge to fidget. "Um, thank you. I...enjoyed that."

A slight smile warred with an impenetrable glare. "Me too."

Nothing else.

No hug. Or promise to do it again soon. Just two little words that put a full stop—no, an entire page break—between what'd happened in his bedroom and now.

Questions whispered in my ear. *Do you want to see me again? Why did you keep my lingerie and sex toys? Did I feel as good to you as you did to me?*

I silenced each and every one.

Turning my spine to steel, I raised my chin and walked away.

* * * * *

My phone was dead.

Of course, it was.

Tonight had gone from blissful to full of heartache, and I only had myself to blame. Standing outside Penn's building, I took note of how far my apartment was. I figured it was walking distance but didn't know how long it would take. And in heels, after an incredibly long day, and extremely passionate sex, my body was not in the mood to hike through the city.

Another night slipped over this one. A night where I'd willingly stepped from the confines of my company and explored without a phone or back-up plan. Nameless had found me, saved me, and relieved me of some small part of my innocence. Tonight, Penn had claimed me, corrupted me, and stolen the rest.

Both nights had left me with sadness and unease.

I shivered as a gust blew down the street, encouraging me to walk and ponder rather than stand like an idiot kicked out of Penn's home.

Putting one foot in front of the other, I didn't let the tickle of rejection climb up my spine and squat on my shoulders. I kept focused and cool—nothing more than a CEO out for a midnight stroll with a torn blouse and soreness between her legs.

Rather than tramp all the way home (and get lost in the process), I'd walk toward the busier side of town and hail a cab. I would've given away a small fortune for my phone to work so I could call David. A few years ago, I hated being surrounded by staff and not having any freedom. Now, I appreciated having people I trusted. It made my life stream-line, not this messy unknown I currently lived in.

Catching a cab hadn't worked well for me last time. I had an awful feeling something terrible would happen again. Mainly because the similarities about that night with Nameless and tonight with Penn couldn't be ignored.

I let myself think freely about Nameless—without frustration toward my father or guilt. To recall the ease in his company even though we had just met. The trust he demanded even though I knew nothing about him. I felt safe with Nameless, despite the overwhelming teenage attraction scrambling my insides. With Penn, I was terrified for my well-being and personal relationships as he bowled through them with falsehoods.

My father didn't understand that, in some awful way, I'd doomed myself that night. I'd taken an adventure full of danger and kisses and made it far too idealistic. I put Nameless on a pedestal and figured if I couldn't have him, I didn't want anyone—effectively blinding myself to other prospects—other men who I had no doubt would be just as special and probably much better suited for me.

Just because I don't like Greg doesn't mean I won't like every male in the world.

And besides, I was still so young. Dad forgot my age most of the time. He saw me as the pillar of his company and his happiness. Because I didn't have a family of my own yet, he believed he'd failed.

Marrying me off wasn't about me but him.

Why didn't I see it before?

I slammed to a stop.

Dad was a good parent, but when it came to having everything neat and organized, he overlooked my age, wants, and who I was as an individual. So what if he wanted me to be partnered off?

I didn't. Not yet, at least.

It was time to tell him not to meddle in my life anymore and for me to stop using his heart attack as an excuse to bow to his every command.

Nodding in resolution, I strode off again with renewed vigor. The ache between my legs throbbed, making it hard to concentrate, but for the first time in years, I felt calmer. Like I'd taken control of my future in some small way.

I'd slept with Penn on my own terms. It hadn't ended as nicely as I'd hoped, but I'd used him and enjoyed it. I'd expanded Belle Elle with a line of adult toys. It was risky and tantalizing, but I'd made that decision.

I was in charge of all things.

I can do this.

I can be honest with myself and him.

Stepping off the sidewalk, I crossed the deserted street, heading toward the glow of the business district ahead.

Unfortunately, New York was bipolar when it came to a woman walking on her own. One moment, it could be the most welcoming host with its tidy streets and beckoning streetlights, and the next, it could switch into a two-faced joker with piles of rubbish and a lone hooded man patrolling toward me beneath a burned streetlight, letting darkness swallow it whole.

I slammed to a stop. My heart left its normal home in my ribs to split into two and drop into my legs.

In an ordinary situation, on a bright sunny day, having a faceless stranger prowl toward me wouldn't be an issue—mainly because I'd have David there. But in this situation? It bothered me. A lot.

Looking behind me, my brain came up with and discounted ideas as quickly as they came.

Run.

Hide.

Walk forward.

Return to Penn's.

He's probably harmless.

You're reading into things.

Regardless of the truth, none of my scattered thoughts were options because the hooded figure looked up, revealing the black void where his face should be. The distance between us vanished step by step. I crossed the street again, hoping I was just in his way and not his target.

The moment my feet touched the other side, the man copied me.

Shit.

The crunch of his dirty sneakers echoed in my ears as he came to a standstill a few feet ahead. His fists hung by his side, his long legs encased in black jeans while the dark gray hoodie was covered in red stains that I hoped were from ketchup and not other sinister goo.

I stopped breathing.

Was this the world's cruel joke? That I couldn't be safe on my own at all? That the two times I'd been without my dad, David, or another man, I was victim to anyone who wanted to prey on me?

Was the earth sexist and teaching me I needed a man to survive?

Anger scalded away my fear. "What do you want?"

The man chuckled. "Money."

"I don't have any. I left my purse with my driver."

Shit, shouldn't have said driver.

He licked his lips—the only thing visible beneath the cape of the hoodie. "Ah, you're one of those."

"One of what?"

"Rich bitches." He came closer, reeking of unwashed body and dirt. "Gimme your money, and no one gets hurt."

Three years ago, I would've screamed for help and bolted.

Now, I was handicapped in heels and aching from sex. I was older. I'd battled more wars with men in the corporate world. If he wanted money, fine. I would argue that he should go and earn some rather than steal from innocent pedestrians.

"Go away. I'm not interested."

"Not interested?" He cocked his head. "What part of 'gimme your money' sounds like a negotiation?"

I crossed my arms, hoping he wouldn't see my torn blouse beneath. "Doesn't matter. I'm not giving you any."

"Yes, you fucking are." His fists clenched. "Now."

"I'm not lying. I have no money."

He took another step, forcing me to take one back.

His lips turned up in a vindictive smirk. "Jewelry then." Trailing his eyes over me, he noticed my crystal earrings. "Those. Gimme."

Without hesitation, I pulled them from my lobes and handed them over. I wore nothing else. No bracelets or rings. The only necklace I'd loved was my sapphire star that'd been stolen from me in such similar circumstances.

"And the fucking rest." He palmed my thirty-dollar earrings I'd sampled from the Belle Elle costume jewelry rack as if they were the Hope diamond.

I splayed my hands, cursing my shaking. "I told you. I don't have anything else."

"Bullshit."

"I'm telling the truth."

He advanced again. This time, I held my ground even though my heart once again grabbed its rape whistle ready to blow.

"How about I search you? Make sure you're not lying?"

I gritted my teeth. "Touch me, and you die."

He laughed; it bounced off the buildings standing as witnesses to our standoff. "Sure, bitch. What you gonna do? Stab me with your shoe?"

I looked down at my patent silver pumps—the flash of bling to match my earrings. "Thanks for the idea."

Kicking one off, I quickly scooped it up and brandished the metallic spiky heel. "You've taken what I have. Now, get lost."

Pushing back his hood, he bared his teeth. He wasn't ugly, and he wasn't handsome. He was just a thief, hungry and doing bad things. "I don't think so, rich bitch."

Nothing about him was familiar, but he was a lonely man in a hoodie late at night.

My curiosity wouldn't forgive me if I didn't confirm for sure.

My tummy clenched as I went against survival and leaned in. I searched his face. I gave in to the consuming question that'd popped into my head the moment he'd appeared.

Is it him?

Was it Nameless?

But hope turned to dust.

It isn't him.

This man was older—pushing past thirty. His teeth were black, his skin sallow, his hair lank and thinning. He was skinny and about Nameless's height, but unless he was a really rough-looking older brother, my homeless savior wasn't here.

He charged forward, grabbing my breast with rancid fingers. "Can't pay me, then I might as well hurt you."

"Get your fucking hands off me!" I stumbled back, swinging my shoe, doing my best to connect.

He ducked, grabbing me.

I struck.

Vicious victory warmed me as the sharp heel grazed his

temple.

"Fuck!" He reared back, holding the side of his face.

That was all I needed.

Kicking off my other shoe, I turned and transformed into something that could flee. A rabbit, a gazelle, a horse, a bird.

I pushed every ounce of power into my legs and struck off barefoot.

I didn't focus on the pebbles hurting my soles. I didn't scream as I stood on a piece of broken beer bottle. I didn't cry as my insides howled from being used and now forced to gallop.

I just focused on freedom. Like every day of my life.

"Come back here, you bitch. You owe me!" The footfalls of my assailant gave chase, driving me to grab every air molecule, transform every dreg of energy, and turn it into rocket fuel as propulsion.

I careened around the corner, spying Penn's building.

So far.

I'll make it.

I skidded on an old newspaper but didn't slow down.

The thief cursed and grumbled, keeping pace with me, slowly catching up.

Headlights appeared in the distance, bright and glowing, warm and welcoming.

I flew off the sidewalk, directly into the car's path.

Instead of slowing down to help, the vehicle sped up as if to run me over and deliver my corpse to the man currently wanting to hurt me.

I waved my arms. "Stop. Help!"

The darkness in the car showed a single driver, their hands clenching the wheel. He drove directly for me. I had a split second to decide what to do—where to run before he struck.

But the collision never happened.

The driver wrenched the steering and drove over the curb, slamming to a stop.

The engine screamed as the front door flung open and a

man leaped from the interior. "Get in the fucking car." He pointed at me. "Now!"

It took a second to register.

My ears knew that voice.

My body knew that body.

I'd never been so thankful to see someone. Even if he'd thrown me from his house. Even if he hurt me in ways I wouldn't admit.

Penn threw himself over the hood as the man chasing me skidded to a standstill only an arm's length from grabbing me.

I pressed against the car, my mouth gulping air. My feet burning from sprinting on concrete and debris.

Then my pain was no more as Penn launched himself at the man. "You motherfucker."

Together, they went down.

Penn landed on top of him and didn't give gravity the joy of crunching him into the pavement before his fists rained on his face.

He didn't speak. Just beat him.

The robber did his best to cover his face with his arms, curling up, trying to push Penn off. But he didn't stand a chance.

I counted one, two, three, four, five fists to the jaw before Penn effortlessly pushed off from the man's chest and stood over him.

He cracked his knuckles as if he'd just washed his hands not doused them in some criminal's blood. "Rob again. Try to rape again. And you're fucking dead." With a black shoe, he kicked the man in the ribcage. "Got it?"

The guy looked up, blinking through a rivulet of blood. For a second, his eyes were blank, full of hate and rebellion. Then they focused on Penn's face. On the way he stood so regal and calm, demanding utmost obedience. Recognition popped in vibrant color, and the robber swayed to his feet, wrapping an arm around his kicked chest, and holding his head with the other. "Shit, it's you."

What?

I froze, desperate to know what he meant.

Penn stiffened. "Leave. Tonight is your lucky night."

The man nodded, dropping his eyes, forgetting I even existed. Turning in his filthy sneakers, he took off at a stumbling jog.

He ran away with my earrings, just like the men in the alley ran away with my sapphire star.

I'd been saved again, but this time…all I felt was terror not desire.

CHAPTER TWENTY-FOUR

"GET IN THE fucking car, Elle." Penn's voice remained low and hushed but rang with steely authority.

He knew him.

He knew Penn.

How? Why? What does it mean?

I blindly grabbed the door handle and cracked it open. Numb, I slid into the passenger seat as he strolled nonchalantly to the driver's side and climbed in.

A few seconds passed after the doors slammed shut, cocooning us in heavy, oppressive silence. His bloody knuckles clenched the steering wheel as if he could throttle it.

My throat had permanently closed with fear and questions. So, so many questions.

How did that man know Penn?

Who *was* Penn?

And why…just why…did he beat up that man with the same effortless grace as the man in the alley that fateful night?

Penn reached across the gear stick, placing his hand on my thigh.

I flinched, yanking my legs to the side.

His fingers dug into my muscle, keeping with me. He breathed hard, squeezed me, and then let me go. Pressing the clutch, he slid the still rumbling engine into gear and drove off the curb and back onto the road.

The bump jostled us, but we didn't speak.

I daren't.

I didn't know what to think.

Part of me wanted to over-analyze everything; to replay the way he disciplined that guy and try to connect dots that weren't there. My imagination worked over-time, doing its best to believe that perhaps I knew Nameless' identity all along. That maybe, just maybe, he'd been the one to find me after all these years and not me failing to find him.

But one awful flaw sat like a toad in that perfect fantasy. Penn didn't have a gentle bone in his body like Nameless. Nameless was cool and prickly but beneath that armor had been kindness—sweet wrapped up in daggers.

Penn was just the blade, shiny and impenetrable, one dimensional with refracting surfaces to distort my true perception.

The only problem was I couldn't distinguish one punch from another. I was seeing things—making things up—trying to link two very separate incidents into one.

To do what?

Find meaning in why I slept with Penn?

Validation that I wasn't some romance-broken girl, after all?

"I owe you an apology." His voice barely registered over the hum of the tires on the road.

I tensed, staring out the window. "I owe you thanks."

His head snapped left and right in denial. "No. I kicked you out. I thought your driver would collect you, but then you walked off."

"You were watching me?"

He didn't reply. "You almost got hurt."

"But I didn't."

"If you had...fuck!" He punched the steering wheel, making the horn blare, shattering the sleep in many apartments. "I would've fucking killed him."

"I wouldn't have asked you to."

He glowered. "I wouldn't have done it for you."

"So you would've taken a life purely because you wanted

to and not to somehow avenge me?"

"I would've killed him because he touched what wasn't his to touch."

My heart beat wild. "So you protected me, not because I shared your bed and gave up a significant part of me, but because in your twisted ideals, I'm a possession that only you can touch?"

His jaw worked as he drove fast through residential streets. "Yes."

"Not because you feel anything for me?"

"No."

"Anything at all."

"Nothing."

"But the sex was good."

"Yes."

"Do you want to see me again?" I hated that I had to ask; that I cared about the answer. He'd turned into a bastard who terrified me. He'd hurt that thief with such ease.

But with him emotionally withdrawn and icy, it helped remind me what we had was purely physical. I didn't like him. Not in the slightest. I didn't even feel some resemblance of gratitude-induced affection from him rescuing me. He turned everything that could be good and exciting into bad and unwanted.

But I'd tasted what sex could be like. And I wanted more. I wanted to be selfish for *me*. So, for now, I'd accept his asshole persona and ignore my questions.

"I don't know." His confession wasn't what I expected.

"You don't know if you want to sleep with me again?"

He half-smirked. "We didn't sleep together, Elle. We fucked."

"Thanks for the clarification." I huffed, crossing my arms. "Forgive me; do you want to fuck me again?"

His fingers latched tighter around the wheel, the leather creaking. For a moment, his head shook with a silent no. Then a cocky smirk stole the truth with yet another lie. "Yes, I want to fuck you again."

Why the hesitation?

Why say we are engaged if he only intended to sleep with me once?

Why the cold shoulder and strict boundaries?

Why, why, why?

"Good." I sat prim, reveling how the ache in my womb turned liquid again. "Me too." Testing my innocent mouth with erotic commands, I added, "I liked fucking you. I want more."

His gaze shot from the road to mine. "More?"

I swallowed, fighting back my embarrassment. "I want your uh…cock. I want you inside me again."

He groaned and focused on the road, the speed we traveled far too fast. "Fuck you for saying that."

"*Excuse* me?"

"You heard me."

I had no come-back for being cursed at.

How rude.

What an ass!

I sat silent, stewing as the neighborhood switched to one I knew and my penthouse on top of the white sparkling building up ahead beckoned me home.

Home.

Where Sage would be waiting and Penn could fuck off with his secrets, curses, and lies.

Pulling to a stop, he turned off the car and climbed out.

I didn't wait for him to get my door. Cracking it open, I jumped out only to wince and hobble as the cuts from running tormented me.

"Fuck, look at your feet." Before I could reply, he scooped me into his arms and carried me toward my building.

The doorman nodded and opened the large entryway without showing any signs of shock. Penn left his black Mercedes coupe parked haphazardly on the street and marched me through the foyer of my building.

"Everything okay, Ms. Charlston?" Danny, the night manager, called. His lined face worried beneath the navy cap of his uniform. He eyed Penn with wariness.

Preventing me from yelling for help or for Danny to call security, Penn growled, "I'm taking my fiancée to her apartment. She's fine."

I squirmed in his arms. "You are not my fiancé. Stop telling everyone that." Waving at Danny, doing my best to keep up appearances rather than panic the neighborhood, I said, "Everything's fine. Sorry for the odd entry."

Danny waved back, frowning and unsure but polite enough not to intrude.

The moment we left the foyer and entered the bank of elevators, I hissed, "Put me down." I pushed at Penn's chest. "I can walk."

"Your feet are bleeding."

"I don't care. I want you gone."

He looked down, his brown eyes bordering oak-black. "That wasn't what you said a few moments ago."

"That was before you told me to fuck off."

"I didn't tell you to fuck off. I said fuck you. There's a difference."

"There's no difference."

He punched the elevator button and strode into it as the doors opened instantly. "Press your floor."

I did so then froze as the doors whispered shut, imprisoning us. "Wait, how the hell do you know where I live?"

"I researched."

"You stalked, you mean."

Once again, he didn't reply. The ride upward was awkward and strange and loaded with every foreign sensation imaginable. I hated him holding me, but I liked his protection at the same time. I hated the way he took control but liked his need to make sure I was safe.

Ugh, I just hate him.

I don't like any of the other stuff.

The elevator stopped, and Penn stepped off, pausing in the middle of the fancy wide hallway. Two doors—left and right. Two penthouses taking up one-half of the entire floor each.

He glanced at me. "Which one?"

I crossed my arms—or the best I could while reclining in his embrace. "Don't you already know?"

His gaze tangled with mine, deliberating to show me a truth or lie.

He chose the truth.

Striding toward the left door—the correct door—he waited while I inputted the nine-digit code rather than a simple key then leaned on the door handle to enter.

I made a mental note to change the sequence tomorrow, seeing as his eagle eyes had watched the nine digits with quick intelligence.

His attention swooped over my foyer where a chandelier hung from the ceiling in crystal glitter before pooling onto the floor with a glass table imprisoning it. For a statement piece, it had oodles of wow factor.

A loud meow sounded just before a silver streak charged from the white couch facing the floor-to-ceiling windows directly for Penn. Sage latched onto his leg, no doubt sinking her claws into his calf.

I laughed softly. "Seems I'm not the only one who doesn't like you."

"The feeling is mutual, I assure you." Wincing, he stalked forward—with Sage still clinging to his leg—entering my sleek kitchen, where every cupboard looked like a high gloss wall with no handles or appliances in sight—all hidden or magically designed to keep such necessities of life a mystery.

Placing me on the white bench top, he grabbed Sage, ripped her off his jeans, and plonked her down beside me. She swatted him, hissing, but immediately leaped into my lap and purred, stretching to lick my chin with her sandpaper tongue.

"You did well." I scratched her neck. "Thanks for protecting me."

Penn snorted, turning to locate the sink. He wouldn't find

it. It was hidden beneath a large slab of bench top that revealed the tap and bowl with a press of a button by my orchid plant.

He searched for two seconds then stalked off, leaving me gaping after him.

Where the hell is he going?

A few moments later, he returned with a white towel from the guest powder room and a bowl that had contained blue marbles for decoration now filled with tepid water.

Without a word, he dropped to his knees and grabbed my foot.

I froze, gobsmacked as he wet the towel then slowly, carefully, with all the tenderness in the world washed my feet, running the towel so, so gently over the lacerations from the beer bottle I'd run over.

I sucked in a gasp, my breath wobbly as he cleaned the towel and the water turned pink with my blood.

There was nothing else in that moment.

No questions. No lies. No lust.

Just him giving himself in ways I never imagined he would.

My heart stopped thudding, settling for the slightest tiptoe as if afraid one wrong move or noise would shatter this strange new existence.

His hands were swift but sure, soft but serious. He didn't tickle me while he felt my instep to make sure no debris remained, and he didn't take advantage when my legs spread with instinct as he rubbed my ankle with his thumb.

He tended to me, and once I was tended to, he stood, placed the bowl onto the counter, then grabbed my face in his warm hands.

He stared into my eyes, barriers in place, curtains protecting his true thoughts. He didn't speak, but he leaned forward and his lips claimed mine in the most sensual kiss I'd ever been given.

His tongue was velvet. His mouth cashmere.

I swooned into him, utterly seduced and unbound.

There was magic in this kiss, a spell promising secrets, a connection to sever all other connections.

And then, it was over.

As silently as he'd washed my feet, he turned around and walked out of my apartment.

Just like that.

CHAPTER TWENTY-FIVE

A FEW DAYS passed.

I didn't contact him.

He didn't contact me.

It was as if he never existed.

If it weren't for the fading cuts and bruises on my feet, I would've struggled to believe the night at his place even happened.

My mind was a broken record—even work couldn't distract me.

All I could think about was Penn washing my feet, Penn hitting that guy, Penn sliding inside me.

He'd shown two totally different sides of himself, and I couldn't unscramble what it meant. I'd hoped having some time to myself would deliver decisions on what to do. To make up my mind to forget about him or chase the answers slowly turning me hollow.

Spread-sheets and conferences calls didn't help, and the lack of contact did the opposite of what I wanted. My heart grew fonder (just like that stupid saying). My idiotic mind sketched him in a kinder light than the one he'd shown. I second-guessed his pretension and conceit, making up stories that would explain his sudden switch to guardian and medic all in one.

Just like my unpaid debt to Nameless, I had one toward

Penn now. I owed him thanks at the very least for ensuring I returned home safe and my injuries were disinfected.

When he finally *did* text me, I no longer wanted him to fall off the face of the planet but was grateful to hear from him.

Penn (08:47a.m.): *How are your feet?*
Elle (08:52 a.m.): *Fine. I never said thanks for taking care of me.*
Penn (09:00 a.m.): *Are you saying it now?*
Elle (09:03 a.m.): *Maybe.*
Penn (09:06 a.m.): *Are you sore?*
Elle (09:08 a.m.): *My feet?*
Penn (09:08 a.m.): *No. The other part I touched that night.*

Sex between us exploded into my senses: sight, sound, taste, feel—I wasn't in my office but back in his bed. I had no intention of letting him know how much I wanted a second round.

Elle (09:09 a.m.): *Oh yes, that's right. I'd forgotten about that.*
Pen (09:10 a.m.): *Do you want me to refresh your memory?*
Elle (09:11 a.m.): *Perhaps you should.*
Penn (09:12 a.m.): *I want to fuck you again.*
Elle (09:14 a.m.): *So do it.*
Penn (09:17 a.m.): *Fair warning, I won't go so easy on you next time.*

I choked a little.

I'd played fairly easy to catch, and the thought of tangling in bed together sounded far too tempting. But if I let him into my body again, I might not be able to keep my feelings out of it. Damn him for washing my feet and showing me he could care. How could I keep my heart frosty if he'd thawed a little?

The answer was I couldn't.

We'd slept together. We'd had three days apart. It was a good time to end this charade before everyone he'd lied to got hurt. I'd thanked him. I could move on.

Elle (09:20 a.m.): *I've changed my mind.*

Penn (09:23 a.m.): *What the fuck does that mean?*

Elle (09:27 a.m.): *It means the sex was amazing, but it doesn't change the fact you lied to my father. You made him think he can relax knowing I'm going to be taken care of—his words, not mine. I can't let him believe we're truly together. He has heart issues. I enjoyed the other night but don't expect anything more. Let's end this now before it gets complicated.*

No text came back.

My phone vibrated alive in my hand.

Penn calling…

"Oh, shit." Huddling over my desk, I deliberated whether I should ignore the call. Problem was he knew I was around because I'd responded to his texts.

Sucking in a breath, I pressed accept. "Hello."

"Don't hello me, Elle."

"Okay…"

"Don't okay me, either. Especially in that tone." His voice dripped with sex, pooling directly into my core.

"Well, if you're not going to let me speak, why the hell did you call me?"

"I'll tell you why. Because I found your last message ridiculous."

I held my tongue, waiting for him to continue.

"It so happens I've spoken to your father."

"What?"

"And he approves of us."

"He'll approve of anyone with a penis and a pulse."

As long as it's not Nameless or someone with a criminal record.

"Thanks for that stab at my self-worth," he purred. "Nevertheless, I have a lunch date with him today. If you say you're sorry and admit you want me to make you come again, I might let you join us."

I couldn't do this.

"Hold up. You *might* let me come on a date with my *own* father?" I rolled my eyes, glowering at Sage as she pranced over my desk. "I can't hear you because your ego is so inflated."

"I think you mean my cock. My cock is inflated thinking about fucking you again." His voice dropped from crude to cool. "I'm meeting your father at the Tropics in three hours. Come or don't. Your choice."

He hung up.

I had a good mind to call him back and screech that I wasn't some possession to be played or a toy to be tormented. But someone knocked on my door. "Elle?"

Oh no, this day just keeps getting worse.

"Yes, Greg, you can come in."

He strode in with all the arrogant airs of a playboy dressed in a baby blue polo and pressed jeans. His dark blond hair was tussled in just the right way to hint he was always this good looking with no effort, when I happened to know—from many childhood get-togethers—that he took *hours* in the bathroom manscaping.

Yet another reason why I could never be with Greg. He valued his appearance more than any other thing in his life…including whatever woman he ended up with as his wife.

"Hi, Elle." He perched on the edge of my desk, his butt nudging aside paperclips and scattering pens. "Whatcha doing today?"

Sage gave him a kitty-glower and leaped off the glass to return to her nest of blankets by my feet.

I forced myself not to roll my eyes. "The usual. Running my family's company. You?"

"Just had the weekly brief with my old man. Logistics is boring compared to all the number-juggling you guys get to do up here."

When Greg left school, Steve and my father had worked out a position for him to fill. A position that wouldn't affect Belle Elle's reputation or bottom line if he lost interest or screwed up. Being the head of the logistics department ought to be a full-time, full-on occupation, but his executive assistant was far too good at her job, and Greg took that as an opportunity to play retired.

"It's not fun." I smiled huge and bright. "Believe me."

And you're not allowed to fiddle with things you know nothing about and don't give two craps over.

He plucked my turquoise ink fountain pen and spun it in his fingers. "Want to go to dinner with me tonight? Hanging at the Palm Politics with those girls from your school was fun." He flashed me a grin. "I enjoyed it. And I know our fathers did. They're so happy we got together on our own accord and not at a family dinner."

Unable to help myself, I grabbed the pen from his fingers and placed it back on the desk. "Sorry, Greg, I'm busy. Maybe next time."

"Next time what?" His eyes narrowed, that edge of darkness revealing itself. "Next week, you mean? Next month? When, Elle? I'm not going to wait around for you forever, you know."

The faintest clanging of warning bells began. His smile remained, but the harsh malice he managed to hide so well glimmered.

I sat taller. My will to be cordial faded under the need to kick him in the balls and show him that he might've seen me in tutus and crying over bullies, but he didn't know me now. I wouldn't put up with his passive-aggressive behavior—certainly not in my office.

"I never asked you to wait, Greg. In fact, I distinctly remember telling you I only want to be friends."

He scoffed, once again snatching my pen, daring me to steal it back as he clenched it hard in his fist. "See, that's the thing with you, Elle. You send mixed messages."

I rubbed the anger prickling my arms. "Don't confuse your own meddling for my approval."

He leaned forward, bringing spite and jealousy whiffing into my nose. "I don't meddle. You want me. Everyone fucking knows that."

I pursed my lips, hating the way my heart scampered when I wanted to remain angry.

It would be so easy to do what Penn did and lie. To say I was with him now. Engaged. But I wouldn't do that because I didn't need Penn to fight my battles for me. Besides, Penn had told him point blank that I was his now, yet Greg tried to claim me anyway.

I went with a roundabout lie. A dressed-up little fib. "You're mistaken. I'm with someone."

"Bullshit. Go out with me. One date. What's so bad about me that you won't even *eat* with me?" His annoyance shimmered like a bloodthirsty guillotine ready to fall. "Stop being such a bitch."

The gentle clanging of bells turned into an orchestra of caution. I *hated* him looming over me, perched on my desk. I stood, pushing my chair back, and crossing my arms. "Call me a bitch again, and I'll have you fired."

He slapped his thigh. "God, you're adorable when you act all CEO."

I ignored that.

Reaching for the only thing—the only person—who popped into my head, I snapped, "Are you expecting me to cheat on, Penn?"

He guffawed. "Cheat? Come on, Elle. I know it's all a scam. You've known the guy two minutes. I've known you for twenty-two years. He doesn't stand a chance." He leaned forward, smelling clean and soap-like compared to Penn's mysterious deep aftershave. "You're having a fling. Shit, I've had them too. You think I mind if you fuck him?"

I bared my teeth, holding my ground. "You should if you're as in love with me as you claim."

His smile was toxic. "Love? Who said anything about love? I said we're meant to be together. We're compatible. Our families own Belle Elle, and we work side by side. I'm not afraid of some bullshit asshole who thinks he can steal what's mine by sticking his dick in you."

Every nerve ending wanted to bolt out the door. My eyes shot to the intercom button where Fleur could bring reinforcements. Alone with him in my office was worse than alone on a street with a thief.

I can't let him get away with this idiocy. Such treason.

Rebuttals came swift, forming fast on the typewriter of my mind, slipping into orderly fashion to school him. I'd had enough practice with bastards like him.

You don't intimidate me, asshole.

Greg continued, loving the sound of his own threat. "You've had your fling, Elle. But I'm the one you're meant to be with. I'm the one who has our fathers' blessings, and I'm the one who deserves Belle Elle, not him or some other schmuck who thinks they can steal what's mine—"

My patience snapped.

I left prim and proper and embraced fire and ferocity.

Grabbing his baby blue polo in my fist, I yanked him off my desk. He stumbled to his feet, shock making him pliable.

"Listen to me, Greg, and listen good." My voice was a hiss. "You will never and have never owned Belle Elle. Belle Elle is *mine*. You work here. You. Are. My. Employee. If you think I would *ever* marry someone like you—someone pompous and self-centered and nasty—then all the years together haven't taught you a thing. I *rule* you, Greg, so get the fuck out of my office, get back to logistics, do your goddamn job, and if you ever try to threaten me again, I'll call the police." I shoved him away from me. "Am I perfectly clear?"

For a second, the world teetered. Two scenarios lived side by side.

One, me bleeding on the floor from Greg's punch, my skirt ripped, and his hands where they should never be.

And two, him backing down and finally conceding defeat.

I was stupid not to recognize the war brewing between us. To let Steve and my father make it seem like a harmless flirtation while Greg had already kicked me from my office and plastered his name over the plaque on the door.

He'd been counting my money and power since he left diapers.

"This is the end of whatever this is, got it?" I held my head high and pointed at the door. Sage meowed loudly in support. "Leave. Now. I won't ask again."

Slowly, a sly smile slithered over his lips. He no longer looked preppy but provoked and already planning retaliation. "I see you're not a little girl any longer, Elle." He swayed forward. "I like it."

"Get out!"

He chuckled and strode to the door, leaving me gobsmacked that he'd obeyed.

Opening it, he turned and blew me a kiss. "Just so you know, your little speech was cute, but I know you don't mean it. You're as much a liar as that asshole you're fucking." He wiggled his fingers condescendingly in goodbye. "I'll visit you next week, Elle—give you some time to cool down."

His eyes turned to ice. "However, the next time I come for you; next time I ask politely for you to join me on a date, you're going to say yes, Noelle. Just watch."

CHAPTER TWENTY-SIX

"ELLE! WHAT A pleasant surprise." My father stood from the neatly dressed table with a toucan bird arrangement and multi-colored water glasses stark against the white table-cloth. Even the cutlery had splashes of color in the form of engraved parrot feathers on the handles. The restaurant wasn't called the Tropics for nothing.

"Hi, Dad." I accepted his cheek-kiss, smoothing down my light gray dress with black and pink panels on the sides. The skirt was tight, just like the bodice, making self-consciousness tangle with the anxious residue of dealing with Greg.

He wouldn't back down—I saw that now.

I'd done my best to be productive after he'd left, but my instincts wouldn't stop ringing those damn awful alarm bells, and my mind ran in a panic trying to find a solution.

I'd told Greg I would fire him, but without cause, he could sue. Not to mention the mess it would cause between Dad and Steve.

They were best-friends. Such good friends, I honestly didn't know whose side Dad would pick if I told him I wanted Greg dealt with and gone.

I sucked in a breath, trying to calm down. The stupid couture dress restricted my ribs from expanding. Once again, I'd been dressed in something against my will.

When I'd told Fleur to hold my afternoon meetings

because I had to go monitor a lunch between my father and Penn, she shot down to the retail floor and returned with this dress, a lace scarf made from bohemian wool (whatever that was), and single stud diamond earrings.

My hair she left loose but added a few curls while the rest she straightened. It hung even longer than normal down my back.

"What are you doing here?" My father smiled, pulling out a chair and inviting me to sit. "Not that I don't want you here, of course."

I knew Dad would arrive fifteen minutes before Penn. He was forever punctual—to meetings or lunch dates, even the theater productions my school forced me to participate in when I was a child.

Penn would be on time, I had no doubt. But I would use these few precious minutes alone with Dad to my advantage. First, I would deal with Penn, and then I would deal with Greg.

Not wasting any time, I grabbed the yellow and green napkin and spread it over my lap. "We need to talk, Dad. Quickly before Penn shows up."

His eyebrow rose. "How did you know he's my lunch companion?"

"Because he told me. He mentioned I could join, so I'm not gate crashing without an invitation."

His face melted with romance. "Ah, young love. He can't stand to spend even a few hours away from you."

Yes, that's why he's avoided me for three days.

I avoided telling him that, along with all the other secrets I suddenly seemed to have from my father.

Is that what lust and love do? Does it segment off a person's life from shareable to private?

I'd been so open about my entire world before Penn came along. Now, I struggled for subjects that were appropriate.

Taking a sip of the water already sparkling in rainbow glasses, I blurted, "Penn and I aren't really engaged—just like I've been telling you from the beginning."

Dad froze. "What?"

"He lied to you. I have no idea what he intends to do or say today, but I wanted to tell you…none of it is true. If he starts telling you I'm pregnant or that we're eloping to Cuba or I'm moving in with him…don't believe a word of it. Okay?"

His face turned white. He reached for his water.

Fear for his heart tried to gag me, to steal back what I'd said and tell him it was all a misunderstanding; that I was the one lying. Only, he shocked me by asking, "*Could* you be pregnant?" His eyes filled with wisdom he didn't often let me see. For a man so successful in business, he embraced his kooky nature and whimsical fancy so much, he made me forget how intelligent he was—how no deal—good or bad—went through without his scrutiny. "Why would he lie about you being pregnant if there is no truth to you being together?"

My lips glued tight. I had no answer to that.

He lowered his voice, glancing at the other diners in the quaint restaurant that served healthy salads and light lunches. The ceiling had been painted with a rainforest canopy. The windows adorned with artwork of dangling spider monkeys while the occasional python dripped from a light fixture. "Be honest now, Bell Button."

I shook my head. "I'm—no. We're not together."

"But you have been."

"We're not engaged. That's all you need to know."

"Not yet, anyway. I admit it was a bit quick, and I was going to address his intentions today and get to know him a little better, but you can't deny you're interested in him and he's interested in you. It's all over you, Elle."

I didn't like the sound of that.

What's all over me?

The tension from dealing with Greg, or the apprehension from dealing with Penn?

I missed uncomplicated. I missed being alone without males messing things up.

Brushing aside that nasty revelation, I leaned forward. "If I ask you to do something for me…would you?"

He answered with no hesitation. "Anything. You know that." He placed his hand over mine on my napkin. "Name it."

"Hire a private investigator."

"What?"

"Research Penn Everett."

"Why?" His eyes narrowed. "Has he hurt you? Did something happen?" He looked me up and down as if he could see bruises and misdoings and was ready to shoot the guy in a wild west duel.

"No, but something doesn't sit right. Something happened the other night. It made me think about the man I mentioned when I was arrested in Central Park."

His body language shut down.

He removed his touch, sitting taller in his chair. "I thought we agreed that that nonsense was over. You did your best to find that boy. I shuttled you around law courts and police stations with nothing more than a vague description. I was patient, Elle. I went along with your desire to track him down, but we didn't find him. I thought you'd let that go."

I only let you think that. I'm still looking. Still hoping.

"I had—I mean, I have. But I would like someone to look into Penn's background. Where he's from, who his parents are, what does he do? Does he have a criminal record, for goodness' sake? Is that too much to ask?"

"It's not too much to ask." That sexy, silky commanding tone slipped down the back of my neck. "In fact, if you do exactly that—ask—I'll gladly fill in those blanks without hiring someone to tell you."

"Ah, Mr. Everett. I mean, Penn." My father stood, extending his hand in welcome. "Pleasure to see you again."

I remained straight-backed in my chair, not apologizing for what Penn had overheard even when I wanted nothing more than to huddle in shame.

Penn shook Dad's hand then turned his endless dark gaze on me. "Go ahead, Elle. I invited you here so you could ask questions. That we might have a conversation rather than base our connection on purely physical."

I blanched, glancing at Dad. Penn just admitted we had a sexual relationship.

My father crinkled his nose a little before clearing his throat and offering Penn to take the seat next to me. "Yes, conversation can be very worthwhile. I think it's a great idea." He glared in my direction. His stare said it all: *you want to know something? Now is the time...so ask.*

CHAPTER TWENTY-SEVEN

MY QUESTIONS SAT heavier and heavier with every second that ticked past.

This sham of a lunch date had been going on for forty minutes in which time a waitress in a bright orange uniform had taken our orders: Dad had a Vietnamese pork salad, Penn had a Thai beef noodle, and I had a mango fish salsa.

The artfully presented meals had been delivered, and as we ate, Penn and my father shared tidbits of golfing handicaps, best courses around America, what Penn planned to do with his benefactor now he was feeling better, and every other boring nonsense non-important topic they could cover.

Not once did he mention Stewart—his son.

Not a peep about Larry—his friend/brother/father/secret lover.

Not a whisper on the past he refused to share.

By the time I'd finished eating, my stomach churned, and anger simmered so hot, I couldn't damper it no matter how much water I drank.

Greg had ignited my temper. Penn just added rocket fuel.

Dad noticed I was strung up. He didn't make it easier on me by trying to link me into conversations with open-ended suggestions like, "Elle used to come with me on the odd time I went fishing. Do you like to fish, Penn? Perhaps you two could spend some time together away from the city?"

Penn pushed away his empty plate, cradling a glass of water. He hadn't ordered any alcohol as if he didn't want his mind to be affected in any way. "I don't like to fish. But I'm open to spending time with Elle in other ways." He licked his bottom lip free from a water droplet. "In fact, we could go away next weekend, if you'd like? I have to visit a friend out of the city."

I crossed my utensils, pushing away the rest of my lunch. It was now or never. "What friend?"

Dad glanced at me, hearing my sharp tone. He didn't reprimand, though. Settling into his chair, he gave Penn and me the space to discuss everything we'd left unsaid.

Penn placed his glass on the table, narrowing his eyes.

This was the start of the battle.

Bring it on.

"Do you really want to know the truth, Elle?"

"Yes."

"Sometimes lies are easier."

"Truth is the only thing I want."

"Fine." He ran a hand through his hair, disrupting the dark shine, encouraging wayward highlights to glimmer. "My friend is in Fishkill Correctional Facility. I visit him when time permits."

"Prison?" I frowned. "Wait, isn't that a place for mentally disturbed?"

"Insane people?" Penn shook his head. "It used to be. Not anymore. Now it's a medium security."

Dad leaned forward, finishing off his pork salad with a grimace. The glow of Penn's company and rosy hope for a happy future was marred by the mention of a prison.

I chewed a smile.

Dad asked, "What did your friend do?"

Penn cleared his throat—not in an embarrassed way but more of a 'how much to reveal' pause. "He's a thief."

A thief.

The punches from the other night.

The way Penn didn't hesitate to cause bodily harm.

There'd been two in that alley three years ago. Two men who'd tried to rob and rape me. Was it possible Penn was one of them? Or was he Nameless? A cold-hearted version of the hero with no remaining empathy? Or was he someone completely different and I'd made all the clues up in my head?

I needed to focus, but after dealing with Greg, I struggled to see Penn as much as a threat as I did before. He was a nuisance with his story-telling, but he wasn't malicious like Greg had revealed.

I couldn't decide what question to ask, so I skipped to another just as important. "Does your son live with you?"

Penn scowled, his body tensing against the subject change. "Why do you think he's my son?"

I scrunched my napkin. Was he about to lie again? "I saw you at Belle Elle. He spoke about you and Larry as father figures."

"Father figures," he repeated noncommittally.

"What does that even mean?" My temper spiked. "You are, or you're not."

"I am, and I'm not."

I crossed my arms, doing my best not to overflow with annoyance. "That isn't even an answer."

Dad jumped in. "What you're saying is he's adopted?"

Penn smiled, granting him respect but not me. "On the way to being adopted, yes."

"On the way?" I sniped.

"Yes, the paperwork has been filed. We're awaiting the good news."

"We?"

"Larry and I."

"So you *are* gay?"

Penn looked at me condescendingly as if I just didn't get it. "No, Elle. I'm not gay." Taking another sip of water, his eyes darkened over the rim. "I thought we clarified that the other night when you came to my home asking me to help you with a small matter."

Dad locked his gaze on me. "A small matter? Is everything okay, Elle?"

I fought the heat blooming on my cheeks. "Yes." My teeth locked together, making it hard to reply. "Fine. Penn is just being troublesome."

"*I'm* being troublesome?" He pointed at himself, shaking his head. "I think you'll find I'm being nothing but cooperative."

"If you were being cooperative, you would tell me who you truly are, where you came from, who Larry is, who Stewie belongs to, and what the hell your friend is doing in Fishkill." I breathed hard, not caring my father watched me as if I was about to snap. I'd already snapped once today, and I bounced on the tightrope to break again. "Tell me the truth, Penn—if that is even your name. Then perhaps we'll see how cooperative I can be."

Silence cloaked the table. My outburst rang in my ears.

Penn didn't move.

Dad shifted in his seat, but I remained locked in a vision battle with the man who'd taken my virginity, kicked me out, then rescued me.

I didn't want to admit it, but beneath my hate and dislike and mistrust and wariness was the fluttering of feelings. When he'd washed my feet…I'd softened. When he'd pressed inside me, I'd caved. I didn't want to acknowledge it, but he'd affected me more than just physically.

And I hated that more than anything.

This isn't worth it.

I had a business to run. Greg to deal with. Distractions such as this were a waste of my time.

Standing, I threw my napkin on my dirty plate and sniffed. "You know what? I no longer care. It was a pleasure getting to know you, Mr. Everett, but I don't want to see you again."

Turning to my father, I added, "We're not engaged, Dad, nor have we ever been, trust me. I slept with him—you might as well know that, seeing as he's implied it in every innuendo he could. Do I feel good about that? No. Do I regret it? Yes. Am I pissed he lied to you about our engagement? More than anything. Now, if you'll excuse me, I'm returning to the office where I'm in control and don't have to put up with men like him—" I pointed a finger at Penn's carefully schooled expression.

I didn't wait for my father's reply. Or for Penn's rebuttal.

As I stalked past tables full of laughing diners, I crushed my heart for flying so fast. I'd done nothing but run away from that man since we'd met.

I disguised it with bluster and bravery, but really, I was terrified of him.

Petrified of the way he made me feel beneath my dislike.

Scared of the way my instincts nudged me harder and harder to look past the man and see someone I thought I'd never find.

But most of all, I was disappointed in myself.

Because for the first time, I'd been the one to lie.

Everything I'd said to my father, every word I'd growled about Penn—wasn't true.

I felt good about sleeping with him.

I didn't regret a thing.

And yes, I was annoyed about his lies, but I was more interested in the snippets of truth behind them.

It didn't matter now.

I had other fights to win.

It's over.

CHAPTER TWENTY-EIGHT

CENTRAL PARK HAD two faces.

The sinful one it showed in silver moonlight with hooded nameless men, and the innocent one where sunshine dappled green grass and children squealed in the distance.

It'd been so long since I'd strolled through the lush greenery.

Three years too long.

Nameless...

He was in the trees and the breeze.

He was all around me but never there.

My heels clipped on the sidewalk, keeping me locked in the fury vortex of the restaurant. Needing to calm my heart rate, I slipped off the pretty pink (but crippling) shoes and switched pavement for turf.

The springy softness gave simplicity to the complication my life had become over the past few weeks.

The Tropics restaurant was nestled in a prime position on the border of the park. I had intended to call David immediately to collect me, but then the sunshine promised to calm me before book-keeping and running staff added a different kind of stress.

I would walk for a bit, soak up some vitamin D, and then call David to return to Belle Elle and deal with the pile of worry I'd left there. I'd cuddle Sage, work until my eyes were too sore, then return home and lock every single door against the world.

I hadn't gone far—a few minutes at most when footsteps sounded behind me. Firm and faultless, masculine and moving fast.

My back tingled as I strode into a faster pace.

If it was who I thought it was, I didn't want to talk to him. Pacing quicker didn't help.

Angry fingers looped around my elbow, yanking me backward. "You don't get to leave, Elle. Not like that." His eyes were brighter in the sun—more aged port than oak whiskey. A few lines etched around his mouth as if he struggled just as much as I did.

Which didn't make any sense, as he'd been the one messing me around since the beginning. He was the one who'd caused Greg to explode with jealousy and threaten me. He was at fault in all of this.

I jerked my arm back, breaking his hold. He only let me go because a woman with a stroller narrowed her eyes as she went past. "Stop following me." I fell into another barefoot stride, cursing him when he matched my rhythm, joining me on the grass, his black shoes glinting in the sun.

I hated that in his graphite suit with ice blue shirt, he came across as priceless and sharp as a diamond. There were no mistakes in his veneer. No hesitation—as if he held all the clues.

Which he does.

"You ask questions, yet didn't stick around to hear the answers."

I snorted. "As if you'd tell me the truth."

His fingers looped with mine, pulling me back gently this time.

I gasped as he ran his thumb over my knuckles. His face softened. His shoulders fell. Somehow, he switched the fight between us into a white flag. The urge to push and push—to crack his façade—paused, willing to accept him in that moment. Mask and all.

He half-smiled, a mixture of reluctance and tolerance. "Try me. Ask again."

I blinked as the sun blinded me, dancing off his hair, hiding his face for a second, so he stood there with no features or belonging to a name.

He could've been anyone.

He could've been Nameless.

He could've been one of the men who mugged me.

He's a stranger I let inside me.

I shuddered at a how irresponsible I'd been. How I'd let myself be glamoured by his fancy games and pretty face. How I'd let lust take ordinary brain cells and transform them into flirtatious floozies.

I don't like him.

I don't like him.

I don't.

The sun sparkled, burning my lies even as I forced them to be true.

Tiredness suddenly blanketed me, heavy and thick, stifling and oppressive. There was only one answer I needed to make all the other questions obsolete. Just one. The biggest one of all. "You want me to ask? Fine, I'll ask." I inhaled deep and jumped in. "Where you were on the 19th of June three years ago?"

Nothing happened.

No trumpets, no choir, no streamers at winning the magical prize for asking the right question.

There was no flinch or shock or outright denial.

The date when I'd met Nameless, when I'd kissed him in this very park, meant absolutely nothing to Penn.

His body remained relaxed, his head cocked curiously to the side. "What?"

I wanted to tell him to forget it.

That all my silly sleuthing and ponderings were wrong.

I had my answer.

But now I'd ripped off that particular bandage, I couldn't

stop. I had to let it out before it crippled me. "It was my nineteenth birthday. I ran away from Belle Elle for one night alone. I walked, I explored, I was hurt by two men. A third saved me." I sucked in a breath as emotions that should've subdued and faded by now swelled. "He brought me here. To Central Park. We kissed." I moved closer.

He stepped back, his face hardening with things I couldn't decipher.

"We ate chocolate. We *felt* something—"

"Penn, there you are. You're sooner than I expected."

A man appeared from the passing crowd, holding a remote control airplane with Stewie by his side. The kid clutched a controller as if dying to activate the plane and send it soaring rather than leave it trapped in the older man's grip.

Penn exhaled hard, his face etched with things I desperately wanted to understand. His posture had somehow lost its sedate softness, mimicking a granite statue. His mouth a tight line. His fists curled rocks.

Tearing his gaze away from mine, he visibly struggled to smile. He shoved his hands into his pockets in a mixture of defiance and self-protection—just like another I'd known once upon a time. "Hi, Larry."

I jolted.

Larry.

So this is Larry.

My habit of studying people who were either in business or in some way advantageous to me came back. I guessed Larry was in his mid-sixties with salt and pepper hair, stocky build, and intelligence brimming behind black framed glasses. He looked at Penn with utmost fondness and pride.

Penn took a step back from me.

Invisible ropes snapped, untethering us with painful ricochets.

My previous confession vanished as if it'd never been, destined never to be clarified or denied.

Clearing his throat, Penn regrouped and performed social

niceties. "Larry, this is Noelle Charlston. Elle, this is Larry Barns. My benefactor."

Two answers in one.

Larry and I nodded, extending hands to shake. His grip was warm from holding the airplane, his fingers gruff but kind. "Pleasure. I've heard a lot about you."

My eyes widened as I flicked a quick glance to Penn. When, how, and why would Penn discuss this sorry excuse of a relationship? Why would he talk to another yet never talk to me?

Because you're just a girl in his bed. This man shares his life and secrets.

I'd never been a jealous person, but I suddenly understood the green acrimony knowing Penn would never let me in like Larry. That I was wasting my time—time I'd stupidly spent when I'd promised myself my heart was impartial to whatever Penn conjured.

Jumping in before Penn could, I said, "Happy to meet you, too. I've heard your name in passing." A small part of me wanted to hurt Penn; to ruin whatever tales he'd told this man about me. "I must clarify a few things upfront. I'm not engaged to Penn and have no intention of ever doing so."

Larry chuckled. "Oh, I know you're not engaged."

I took a step back. "Ah, well, I'm glad. I wasn't aware what rendition of lies Penn had told you."

Penn had the decency to flinch. "I might not have ethics as pure as you, but I don't lie to Larry. Ever."

They shared a look that weighed with countless years, trials, and confidentiality.

The intimacy made me uncomfortable. Not because they were lovers, like I'd thought, but because they were father and son in every sense of the word. It didn't matter they had different last names and most likely blood—family was created not born.

My eyes fell to the boy still hankering after his remote control airplane. His hair tousled in the wind, his eyes bright and happy.

Stewie was part of that family. Soon—according to Penn—he'd be legally part of it if it were true about an adoption. But that didn't help unscramble my other questions. If Penn was adopting Stewie, did that mean he knew Stewie's mother and felt obligated? Perhaps, Larry was the one adopting and not Penn? Would that make Stewie his brother?

What titles did each have in this weird family dynamic? My head hurt trying to figure it out.

Stewie tucked the controller under his arm, reaching for the airplane in Larry's hold. "If you guys are gonna stand around talking, I'm gonna fly Bumble Bee." In typical boy fashion, he hadn't acknowledged me or noticed the heavy tension between the adults.

I took a deep breath, ignoring the men and focusing on the boy. "Your plane is called Bumble Bee?"

Stewie nodded. "Yup." He pointed at the tail where a hand painted bee in its black and yellow glory glowed.

"Wow, very cool. Bet it hovers really well."

"Nah, it soars." Stewie grinned. Today, he wasn't in the suit Penn had had tailored for him. Instead, he wore jeans and a green t-shirt with the slogan, *I don't think outside the box. I never got in it.*

His innocence tugged at a piece of me. I envied him a little. Envied him for being a part of Penn's life—knowing him in a way I didn't and probably never would. Even if we did give our connection a chance, how could I ever be sure what he told me was the truth?

Larry asked, "Did you have a good lunch together?"

I raised an eyebrow at Penn, letting him answer that. He muttered, "It ended sooner than it should've."

I nodded at his reply. "It did. But for valid reasons."

Larry rubbed his jaw, brushing gray bristles from not shaving this morning. "Ah, I see." He smiled. "Well, I have no doubt Penn will make up for it, Elle. You don't mind if I call you Elle, do you?"

I shook my head. "No, it's fine."

"Come on…can I fly?" Stewie shuffled on the spot, eyeing the open grass just down the path.

Larry chuckled. "Yes, yes, impatient one. Let's go."

Stewie whooped and shot off, carrying the massive plane like he would an oversize puppy with his arms wrapped tight.

"You're welcome to come and watch," Larry invited, motioning for me to join him.

My first instinct was to shake my head and back away. "Oh, no, that's all right."

But Penn stepped closer, his eyes dazzling in the sun. "Come."

He blinded me. Dumbfounded me. Did he always look so resplendent, so persuading? Or was it the warmth of the sunshine and the fact my body heated with now familiar need? I no longer had skin but a map of desire that needed to be touched. "I don't know—"

"You want answers, but you're too afraid to chase them." He stepped back, withdrawing his overpowering intensity for me to go with them. "I thought you knew how to fight harder than that."

His voice deepened on the word fight.

My ears twitched.

Was he admitting to something?

Or was it me merely reading into things again?

"Come on, Elle. Ten minutes. What's the harm?" Larry grinned. "I'd be honored to enjoy your company a little longer."

My willpower fizzled.

I found myself nodding. "Okay."

CHAPTER TWENTY-NINE

STEWIE WAS RIGHT.

Bumble Bee did soar, climbing past the treeline into the cerulean blue horizon.

"He's done that a few times." I squinted upward, my hand shielding my eyes from the glare.

"He has. It was his birthday present a few months ago. Every chance he gets, he practices." Larry clapped as Stewie executed a perfect swan dive and recovery. "He's obsessive about things he wants. Doesn't let it go until he's perfected whatever it is he's chasing."

Penn stood on the other side of Larry, closed off to me, using the excuse to watch Stewie's aerobatics to avoid looking at me.

Stewie ran forward as the plane caught a gust of air and wobbled mid-flight. He didn't look where he was going and tripped over a twig in the middle of the field.

"Oh, no!" I slapped a hand to my mouth as Stewie toppled forward.

Penn charged.

With speed not quite human, he scooped Stewie mid-fall and swept him around in a circle using his inertia before placing him on his feet.

Stewie laughed, high-fived him, and continued flying his plane as if nothing had happened.

Yet *everything* had happened.

To me, at least.

In that microsecond when Penn caught Stewie, all shields were down. He was younger, older, kinder, crueler, innocent, and guilty all at once. I saw hints of what I daren't believe was possible. My heart took over and hammered with hope.

Each thud was a question.

What if?

What if?

What if?

What if Penn was Nameless?

What if Larry had somehow found him, saved him from prison, and done what I'd failed to do?

What if he'd come back for me?

But if that was true, why was he so mean? Why so closed off and impenetrable? We'd felt something that night. Something real if only so fleeting. Why punish me?

Would you listen to yourself?

You're making up stories that have no earthly way of being true.

You're worse than Disney with your ideals of true love against any odds.

This is reality, Elle!

Larry interrupted my inner scalding. "Penn said you have questions that he hasn't answered yet."

I startled. "He admitted to that?"

"Of course. We're open about most things."

"That's an honorable thing." I knitted my fingers together. "He told me you'd come to New York for treatment. Judging by how well you look, I think it worked."

Larry ran a hand over his bristle-covered jaw. "I hate that I had to lean on him so much." His smile was sad. "Nothing has more power than seeing someone you care about sick or grieving." He shrugged the sudden dysphoria away. "But you're right. The treatment worked. Thank goodness. I wasn't prepared to leave just yet. I have too many things to do before I go."

"Things?"

"People and things." He smiled secretively. "My work, and now Penn's, is never done."

My brain dried up. I had no reply. I didn't know what he meant or how to ask for clarification.

"Penn mentioned he'd taken you to the new building he just bought. What did you think?" Larry prompted with a new but just as aggravating subject.

"What did I think?"

"All that space. It's exciting, isn't it?"

"Space to do what?"

Larry winked. "He'll tell you. It's not my secret to ruin." He looked at me pointedly. "I see you struggling. If my suggestion means anything—which I know is asking a lot, seeing as you don't know me—but if you want to know him, give him a chance. It isn't what you think. And you'll need an open mind to accept. But we're all a little corrupt, doing our best to fit into a world that's broken but still demands perfection."

"What—what do you mean by that?"

"I mean thieves can become saints. Saints can become thieves. Most of us deserve a second chance."

Penn looked up at that moment, his dark gaze targeting mine. He half-smiled, his hands loose by his sides, his body straight but not as stiff as before. Without thinking, he placed his palm on Stewie's shoulder as he bumped into him, racing below Bumble Bee not looking where his feet were going.

That simple caress—so expected and wanted was enough to crack my already fractured shell.

Penn's hair was no longer shiny with sunlight but covered with a black baseball cap. Either Stewie had given it to him, or he'd had it hidden in a pocket. Either way, it shielded his eyes, and I saw another scenario I didn't want to see.

Penn could easily be no one. He could be someone. He could be pain or happiness or heartbreak.

That was the problem.

How was I supposed to fall for a liar?

Blindly?

Trustingly?

Not at all?

I needed time.

I needed space.

I need to think.

"It was lovely to meet you, Larry." I tore my gaze from Penn's and smiled at the older gentleman. "I've got to go."

I left before Penn could change my mind for the second time.

CHAPTER THIRTY

SAGE CURLED UP on my lap as I sipped a glass of sparkling apple juice and stared at some TV program I hadn't paid attention to for the past two hours.

Ever since leaving Central Park, I'd been in a fog I couldn't shake.

I'd returned to work but had been absolutely hopeless. Steve had found me heading into my office and asked how Greg and I were. He acted as if he didn't know his son had threatened me, and I didn't want to flippantly tell him in a Belle Elle hallway. I scheduled a meeting with him next time he was free to discuss a leash for his wild heathen of a son.

Dad hadn't returned to the office after the restaurant, Fleur answered my urgent emails on my behalf, and for the first time since I had my appendix out two and half years ago, I claimed health reasons and headed home to do my best to get my head on straight.

Greg worried me.

Dad concerned me.

Steve annoyed me.

And Penn…Penn claimed my thoughts in my home as much as he had in the park or at my office.

My heart had a box with three different puzzles mixed up inside. The pieces were tangled, their edges able to fit together to form an incorrect Frankenstein of three scenes, but unless the three puzzles were separated, none of them were true.

Puzzle one: Penn was nobody but a successful businessman who was bored and liked to lie.

Puzzle two: Penn was Nameless and treating me with contempt because…?

Puzzle three: *I have no idea what's puzzle three.*

"What am I doing, Sage?" I cuddled her close, drawing comfort from her warmth and familiarity. "I've slept with the guy once, and I suddenly can't stop thinking about him? Is that normal behavior? No wonder love is frowned upon. It's a workaholic's nightmare."

She purred, not even bothering to open her eyes and answer me.

A knock reverberated through my apartment. For a second, I thought it was the TV, but then it came again from behind me.

The door.

Someone is at my front door.

The only people who ever visited (make that person) was Dad.

No one else.

Don't let it be him. Please.

The knock came again.

And again a few seconds later.

"This isn't fair," I breathed into Sage's fur as I scooped her into my arms and climbed off the couch. Every step I took toward the front door sent my heart chugging a proverbial wine bottle until I wobbled with fake intoxication.

Looking through the peephole, Penn stood smart in different clothes than this afternoon's lunch date. He'd put on light-colored jeans and a white long sleeve t-shirt that sent my libido melting.

"I don't have anything to say to you." I hoped he could hear me through the door. "Please, go away."

"I'm not leaving. Open up." He held up a brown paper bag with a gold embossed logo on the side. "I've brought dessert."

Dessert?

It was ten p.m. on a week-day. Most normal people had finished eating by now and were winding down for bed.

Shifting Sage into one arm, I reluctantly opened the door. "Bribing me with sugar won't work."

"Are you sure about that?" He smirked. "You opened the door, didn't you?"

I scowled as he stepped over the threshold uninvited. "Only to tell you face to face to go away."

"Tell me after we've had a sugar fix."

I grumbled under my breath and shut the door. Following him into my kitchen, I took pity on him this time and motioned toward the sheer wall where a simple push opened the cupboard holding the cutlery.

He found the utensils, grabbed two spoons, then skirted around me and headed toward the couch. Dropping his weight into the comfy white leather, he placed the brown paper bag on the glass coffee table and pulled out two containers of chocolate mousse.

The emblem of the bakery was from the Gilded Cocoa. A high market delicatessen that served the best pastries and confectionery in New York.

Fine, I would admit. He had good taste.

Sage decided she'd had enough attention and leaped from my arms. Landing on four dainty feet, she took off into my bedroom where no doubt she would claim my pillow like she did every night, telling me in no uncertain terms that my bed was actually hers.

"Are you going to have one of these, or are you going to make me a diabetic?" Penn glanced over his shoulder, eyeing my black maxi dress.

I'd made the mistake of showering when I got home—hoping it would relax me—then dressing in my comfiest piece of clothing.

With no underwear.

I didn't want to eat mousse with Penn in my apartment with no underwear on.

"Sit, Elle. For fuck's sake."

"Don't swear." I shuffled around the couch and took a stiff seat beside him.

"Don't tell me what to do."

"Don't turn up uninvited to my apartment."

"Don't fucking ask questions you're not prepared to hear the answers to."

We breathed hard, fists clenched, fire glowing in our veins.

Reaching for the chocolate, Penn shoved a glass container into my hand and jabbed a spoon into the other. "Eat. Then if my company is so goddamn repulsive, I'll leave."

"I don't even want dessert."

"Christ, you test me." Shifting closer, he stole the spoon he'd only just given me, scooped up a decadent sized mouthful of chocolate, and pressed it against my lips. "Take it."

I pressed my mouth together. The scent of rich cocoa and cream made my taste buds tingle, but I wasn't refusing the sweet—I was refusing him for reasons I could no longer truly remember.

He smeared the chocolate over my lips, painting me with edible lipstick. "Open, Elle." He couldn't tear his eyes away, his chest rising and falling the more he teased me with the dessert. "Open, just once."

His voice throbbed with sudden need.

I reacted to his lust, inhaling quickly, opening just enough for him to slip the spoon into my mouth. The moment the cold metal hit my tongue, and the richness of chocolate mousse sang on my taste buds, I moaned a little.

His jaw clenched as he withdrew the utensil, leaving the morsel behind for me to suck. I didn't chew. I let it dissolve and infiltrate my blood with a rush of sweet, sweet sugar.

"Again." His voice no longer resembled a man but a beast aching for sex. My nipples hardened beneath my dress as I obeyed without question this time.

The heat in the living room increased by a thousand degrees. He scorched me with every move, stare, and command.

Lust wasn't just a word; it was an axe that cut all chains of propriety. It was the gun that shot common-sense dead. Lust was a kidnapper and killer all in one.

Gathering more chocolate, he sucked the spoon clean, his tongue flashing out to make sure he caught every last drop. The fact he shared my spoon, *licked* my spoon did crazy things to my tummy.

Another scoop of chocolate.

This time, he inched closer, placing the container on the coffee table and grabbing my nape with his free hand. Holding me steady, he pressed the mousse to my mouth, breathing hard.

I opened for him.

He placed the dessert on my tongue.

I sucked the sweetness off.

He withdrew the spoon.

He didn't give me a chance to swallow.

His fingers tightened around my neck, jerking me forward. I tumbled into him, my mouth opening in surprise, his lips smashing against mine with violence.

His tongue met mine, the chocolate thick and cloying and rife with memories of another chocolate kiss.

Nameless.

I'd been fighting for so long. Too long. I carried guilt too heavy. I wallowed in shame too great. Kissing Penn while my heart remained in the past with another chocolate kisser unraveled me.

The long day.

The angst, the worry, the unknown.

I snapped.

Throwing myself into his arms, I intensified the kiss until our teeth smashed and violence was the theme not desire.

He fought back, letting himself go.

His hands tore at my dress, finding the straps on my

shoulders and shoving them down to imprison my arms while freeing my breasts.

Shoving me backward, he instantly smothered me with his body. "You want this? You want to fucking do this?"

I nodded, unhinged. "Yes, fuck me. Don't hold back."

"Jesus, I can't. I can't hold back anymore."

It was messy, sugar riddled, and full of things we needed to say, but we had no time or rationality left to talk.

Shoving my dress up, he found I wasn't wearing underwear.

He lost the last shred of decency. "Fuck, Elle. Just—fuck." He crushed me, his mouth suffocating mine, his taste becoming that of chocolate and sin. His fingers found my wetness. His body convulsed as he jammed his erection into my thigh.

I didn't wait for instructions.

Grabbing his belt, I undid the loops, unzipped his fly, and sank my hand into his tight boxer-briefs to grasp his hot length.

His back turned rigid as he pressed into my palm.

Two fingers speared into me, filling me fast and hard.

I cried out.

He silenced me with yet another dangerous kiss.

His thumb landed on my clit, rubbing me in circles while his fingers rocked against my G-spot.

Everything locked tight. The quivering need built and built. The desire to snap my legs closed made me squirm beneath him.

"Condom. Back pocket," he snarled, working me hard.

Somehow, I managed to slip my hand into his jeans and find the condom. I shattered between living in the brewing orgasm and forcing myself to remain sane enough to wrap him in latex so he could fuck me.

The thought of him replacing his fingers and just how incredibly good it would feel was the only thing that kept me coherent enough to rip open the packet, roll down the slippery protection, and sheath him.

He nipped my neck, shoving my hand away and wedging

himself between my legs.

"You don't get to run from this. Not again." He thrust.

He didn't line up or take me gently.

One moment, we were two people.

The next, we were one.

My body screamed as he split me in half.

Then sobbed as the orgasm he'd conjured turned into something with serrated blades for teeth and sharp, sharp bliss.

"Look at me." He drove into me again. "Look at me if you're going to come."

The tightening hurried inside me. His hips pumped into mine, our clothing forgotten in our rush to join.

My gaze locked with his, imprisoned for eternity by the fierce triumph, the epic guilt, the tangled lies he webbed.

I was no longer a shy virgin. I was no longer a meek woman. I was past any shame I might endure by letting go and living entirely in this moment. "Fuck me. *Please*."

"Come. Then I will."

How had he completely possessed me? How was it he'd claimed me so I would do anything he asked, be anything he wanted?"

Pleasure built into a supernova, roaring, pulsing, demanding to pulverize into stars.

He thrust again, anger painting his face. "Give in, Elle. You're mine." His hips kept punishing, adding punctuation to his eroticism. "You know it. I fucking know it. So let me fucking claim you."

I closed my eyes. I couldn't look at him. I couldn't let him see that I wanted to let go. That all my life of business wheeling and dealing was nothing compared to what this felt like. But I didn't trust him. And trust was too big a problem to ignore.

I could never just listen and not question. I'd never be able to fully let go, open up, and stop searching for his secrets.

But that conclusion could be shared after.

Right now, I would obey because it meant we'd both find mutual happiness if only for a few orgasmic seconds.

Then…I would show him the door.

For good.

His hips drove into me. "Stop thinking. Let me inside you."

I took it figuratively, opening my legs wider.

His primal growl echoed in my chest as I gave into him. I went supple, submitting entirely. He angled himself higher, somehow swooping upright, hoisting me into his arms while still filling me deep.

Sitting on his knees on the couch, he cradled me in his arms while my legs draped either side of him. His fingers became white-knuckled as they locked around my hips, keeping me wedged as far down his cock as he could.

His head fell forward as he watched us fucking. Slowing, his cock pulsed inside me, dragging out the pleasure to agonizing joy.

"Oh, God, yes…like that." My body turned limp as I focused completely inward. He supported me as he did it again, slowly learning me as I learned him, trading our dictionaries, our thesauruses, making sense of this new language we'd developed.

"Please, Penn," I whimpered as the billowing orgasm became a physical entity. It was part human, part wind, part ocean. It needed somewhere to go, someone to explode for.

"Fuck, I love it when you beg." His lips latched onto mine. We kissed hungrily. We kissed savagely. "Do it again."

I didn't hesitate. "Please. Please make me come. I *need* to come."

His grip bruised me as he thrust up, sending my breasts bouncing.

My thoughts scattered, my nerve endings trembled, my entire body clenched. "I'm so close. God, please…"

"Come, Elle. Fucking come."

My breathing stopped.

The world turned sparkly and gray.

I couldn't hold off anymore.

My brain turned to sounds rather than words.

My body turned to liquid rather than bones.

I came.

I came and came as Penn fucked me as ruthlessly and as thoroughly as any hot-blooded lover.

The moment I finished, he looked down, shoving aside the bunched material of my dress, hypnotized by his cock driving into me. "Fuck, yes. This—this is truth right here, Elle."

His hand roamed to my breast, clutching my flesh with passion bordering on pain.

Grabbing my hair, he drove into me harder, harder. His roar added gasoline, and I plummeted stronger and faster than ever before. My back bowed as he pulled my hair with a vicious yank.

"Shit, take it. Take me. Take everything." His words scrambled with grunts as he chased me off the cliff.

His orgasm quaked his body, his forehead smashing against my shoulder as he emptied himself.

He didn't look up for a long moment. His breathing ragged and lost.

I stroked his hair, calming him even though I needed calming myself.

Time lost all meaning as we slowly returned to earth and disengaged.

I couldn't look him in the eye as he pulled off the used condom and placed it in the brown paper bag the mousse had come from.

Standing, he tucked himself away and did up his trousers, followed by fastening his belt. Once presentable, he raked a hand through his hair.

"Tomorrow night."

I looked up, smoothing my dress, still shivering from orgasm aftershocks. "What?"

"If you have any plans, cancel them." He strode around the couch, pausing in the middle of my apartment. "You're coming with me. Dress in silver. I'll pick you up at Belle Elle at seven."

He left me alone with the chocolate mousse and my crazy conclusions.

CHAPTER THIRTY-ONE

ALL DAY I'D struggled between working and reminiscing about sex.

I was sore again, entirely focused on Penn every time I moved, and my body clenched from being used. He'd consumed me and utterly confused me.

Why chocolate?

Why *kiss* me with chocolate?

I hated that I now had two experiences with dessert and kissing.

The two memories did their best to mingle, to convince me that Penn was Nameless and Nameless was Penn.

I didn't have a picture of Penn, and Google had nothing on him—no company profile, no Facebook account. I wanted to stare into his face and force my brain to recall Nameless. To delete the scruffy beard and dark dreadlocks—to see if there was *any* chance (no matter how small) that the distinguished cocky businessman currently seducing me was that ragamuffin from my past.

* * * * *

By the afternoon, I was semi back to normal. There were no erotic texts from Penn, no pop-ins from Greg, and the back-to-back meetings with Japan wholesalers and a new supplier of handbags in Beijing meant I could remain focused on things I knew, rather than things I didn't.

Around noon, Dad brought me a chicken Caesar salad and kissed my forehead like I was still his twelve-year-old protégée. He stared at me as if he was awed and a little afraid. "Two things. If you still want me to hire a private investigator, I will—for your peace of mind."

"Thank you." I patted his hand, grateful but not as gung-ho as I thought I'd be about snooping into Penn's background.

"And two," Dad continued. "Greg cornered me this morning."

My heart picked up a sword while my voice remained nonchalant. "Oh?"

"He said you guys have agreed to go to dinner tonight."

I exhaled with frustration. "I did nothing of the sort." Deciding now would be a good time to tell him how wary I'd become of Greg, I added, "He's not as suave and sophisticated as you think, Dad." I fought my shiver. "He said some pretty nasty things to me yesterday. I wasn't comfortable."

Dad's eyes became snipers. "He did?" He rubbed his jaw. "I must admit I thought it was low of you to date Penn yet see Greg on the side. I should've known you'd never do such a thing."

"The male race could die out, and I *still* wouldn't entertain the idea of Greg being dateable."

He sighed. "I'm beginning to see that. I'm sorry I pushed you into something you're not happy about."

"It's fine. But would you do me a favor and have my back next time he tries to do anything?"

Dad nodded fiercely. "Absolutely. I'll have a word with Steve that you're with Penn now, and even if you weren't, you guys are old enough to set yourself up without meddling old matchmakers who don't have a clue what they're doing."

The heavy weight I'd been carrying for years slowly chipped off my shoulders, becoming manageable instead of mountainous. "Thank you."

"Don't mention it. I just want you to be happy. That's all I've ever wanted, Bell Button."

He stood and headed for the door. He smiled sadly. "I know you want answers about who Penn is before you give him a chance, but if I've learned anything, it's that love is the biggest truth there is." He shrugged. "All the rest—the questions and worries—it's all just noise."

He closed the door before I could reply, leaving me to my lunch.

* * * * *

By the time six p.m. rolled around, my back ached from spending the afternoon hunched over my laptop, and my eyes hurt even after wearing my glasses.

Fleur barged into my office with yet another dress wrapped in a clear protective bag. "Time to get ready, remember?"

I tugged my glasses down my nose, pinching the bridge. "Huh? I thought I was finished for the day."

"You are. You have that seven p.m. thing with your fiancé, remember?"

I groaned. "Ugh, don't call him my fiancé."

"He is, though, right?" Her face slipped with doubt. I wanted to be the one to fill her with truth, but I was tired and cranky, and I'd had enough for the day. I decided to take the more diplomatic approach and ignore her question.

Vague memories of Penn's invite—or command—about me joining him tonight came back. I'd stupidly mentioned it to Fleur when I'd arrived this morning.

I stood up, nerves joining my blood to stream around my heart. I didn't want to go. I was mentally exhausted.

Draping the dress over the couch, she placed a Belle Elle shopping bag beside it. "Inside are some heels, hair accessories, and a shawl. I also took the liberties of bringing up some lingerie for you too."

I rolled my eyes. "You know way too much about me. I don't know if I'm comfortable with you knowing my bra size."

She waved it away. "You know all your secrets are mine to keep." Marching to the door, she added, "Give me a call if you need help with your makeup and hair. I'm just finishing the spring catalog mock-up before heading home. Jack is taking me out to Mexican, and I can't be late."

It wasn't the first time she'd mentioned her boyfriend or life outside of Belle Elle, but for some reason, tonight it hit home. She had a life. She had someone to share it with. Was it so wrong of me to sample that? What made Penn Everett such a bad choice? And was he bad or was it all in my head? Why was I trying to twist him into another? Nameless was gone.

It's time I grew up and gave him a chance.

"Thank you for the dress."

"No problem." She smiled and disappeared.

Striding to the couch, I unzipped the bag, pulled out the softest silver gown I'd ever seen, and headed into my private bathroom to shower and prepare.

* * * * *

Penn (06:55 p.m.): *I'm downstairs. I won't come up because if I do, I'll fuck you in your office and then we'll be late. Come down.*

I slammed my phone down—partly because of the sudden shakes at seeing him again and partly because of his rudeness.

Staring at myself in the mirror, I second-guessed keeping my hair loose even though I'd secured it to the side with a clip in the shape of a crescent moon decorated with mirrored mosaics.

Fleur had once again chosen a stunning dress. The silver and white lingerie beneath the dress added secrecy to my outfit that I may or may not show Penn. The thick satin gown covered my body with sleeves draping like wings down my arms with the off-the-shoulder style. The length came to mid-calf with acres of material ready to flare out at the slightest movement.

I looked as if I'd stepped into the moon and come out wearing its metallic essence.

Penn (07:00 p.m.): *You're late.*

My teeth ground together as I scooped my phone into the little silver beaded bag and left my bathroom. Sage looked up from her spot on the couch, meowing softly. I padded over to her where my heels were. I kissed the top of her head. "I'm going to miss you, but you can't come."

She pouted as if to say there'd been multiple events she wasn't invited to these past few weeks.

Scratching her under the chin, I promised, "Dad will come and pick you up. You can spend the night at the brownstone and explore the garden rather than be stuck in the top floor apartment. How about that?"

She gently bit my finger in grudging agreement.

"See you later, kitty." Stepping from my office, I locked my door and double-checked I had what I needed. I'd done my own makeup and was pleased when one of the janitors did a double take at my smoky eyes and nude glossed lips.

I'm late, am I?

I'd show him I wouldn't simper and apologize. I was worth waiting for.

Taking the elevator down, I spotted the black limousine before I saw him.

Penn stood with his arms crossed and back reclining against the luxury vehicle. He didn't move as I swiped my keycard to exit the locked sliding doors, and my heels clipped elegantly across the sidewalk.

Belle Elle glittered behind me with window displays, rich red awnings, and the biggest sign on the block blazing our brand and promise.

Penn pressed his lips together the closer I got, his body stiffening. He didn't reach out and touch me. He merely stepped sideways, opened the car door, and inclined his head for me to hop in.

Keeping eye contact with him, I obeyed, ensuring I gathered up the dress and climbed in demurely. However, some inner minx decided to rise to his challenge and fight fire with fire.

I opened my legs a little, flashing him a quick glance of the white garter belt holding up sheer pantyhose and the silver lace hiding the place only he'd touched.

He slammed the door so hard the limousine rattled.

Nervousness climbed up my spine, waiting for him to walk to the other side and climb in. I jumped as he wrenched it open, claimed the seat beside me, then punched the intercom to the driver hidden behind a black wall. "To the Pemberly."

"Yes, sir," the driver said as the car moved into motion with a swan-like glide. Downtown moved past tinted windows while traffic noise and city smells invaded the interior through the open sky roof.

Still, Penn didn't look at me.

His hands fisted. His jaw clenched so tight, the muscles in his throat looked as if they'd shatter.

I didn't know what to do. Had he had a bad day? Was he that pissed at me for being late?

Not that I was late. *He* was early.

If he wanted to stew and not talk to me, then fine. I could do the same. Placing my handbag on the seat between us, I settled into the leather and glared out the window.

A second went past.

Barely a second.

Before my handbag went slamming to the floor as Penn swiped it away.

"What on earth—"

His lips bruised mine, his hands grabbing my waist, dragging me unceremoniously across the backseat and into his lap.

He attacked me in every sense of the word.

We were so close.

But it wasn't enough.

Pushing off his chest, I swiveled from damsel in distress in his arms to opening my legs, pushing my dress up my thighs, and straddling him.

His growl echoed so long and deep, I became instantly wet.

"Christ, Elle." He stole my mouth again, his hands coming

up to capture my face, his fingers tight against my nape, not giving me any room to run. "You're so fucking beautiful."

I let go and did what I'd wanted to do but pretended I didn't. I became a full participant. I'd let him take me the first night, allowing first-time jitters to subdue me. The second time, I'd been swept away by chocolate memories.

Not now.

Not again.

My hands mimicked his, cupping his five o'clock shadow, digging my fingernails into his cheeks.

He jolted in my hold, his lips tearing at mine as if he could eat me, bite me, consume me.

We gave up our humanness and turned ferocious.

I loved the way he kissed me. I loved the way I kissed him back. I loved the noises and hardness and rocking and touching and clawing. I adored how muggy the limo became. I relished in how my dress clung to sweat-beaded skin.

I sucked on his tongue, holding it tight as he groaned and thrust up, his hands slamming onto my hips to push me down onto him.

His body rocked as if he was already inside me, already punishing me for things I didn't understand.

His eagerness and viciousness fed the well inside me that had been empty until he'd barged into my life. This was true lust, and I wanted to drown in the sensation of having this powerful, secretive man come apart beneath me.

His hand slid off my hip and up my skirt.

I gasped as he found my soaked underwear. He shoved it to the side with a simple flick. The moment I was bare, he thrust a finger inside me, causing my back to bend until I was sure I'd topple off his lap if he didn't wrap a long, strong arm around my back and clutch me hard.

"Fuck you, Elle," he panted, inserting a second finger, stretching me, stimulating the slight soreness from last night.

"Fuck me?" I blinked hurt and turned on. "Now, what did I do?"

"You're screwing me up, that's what." His mouth stopped his confessions by once again seeking mine. My skin burned from his barely-there beard, stinging from fresh bruises. With my knees hugging his hips, I deepened the kiss, taking control, licking his tongue with mine.

His words turned on a carousel inside my mind: *'You're screwing me up. Screwing me up.'* I didn't know how, but I was glad. I was glad because I'd learned something terrible about myself thanks to him.

I might believe I was a woman with sinew, skeleton, and heartbeat, but in reality, my soul comprised of trust and my bones calcified with belief—I was a flimsy, trusting thing who could no longer tell if her instincts were true or masquerading as ridiculous desperation for hope.

Penn yanked away, digging his fingers into my hips. He shoved me back, teetering me on his knees, revealing his erection pushing up tight against the fly of his silver tuxedo.

I'd never seen a man dressed in silver before but, my God, it suited him.

It brought out the cinnamon in his eyes, the honey in his hair, the compassion hiding deep within.

"What the fuck are you doing to me?" His gaze couldn't hold mine, slipping over my body, locking onto my pushed aside panties and core. "It wasn't supposed to go on this long."

"What wasn't?"

"This." His groan was tortured as his thumb pressed into my wetness. "Whatever this is."

I quaked, fighting fluttering eyelids. "*You* chased *me*."

"Wrong." His teeth nipped my throat. "I hunted you."

Truth lay in that tiny paragraph, but I couldn't decipher it.

Finding courage in his undoing, I ran my hands down his chest, heading straight to his cock. He didn't stop me as I popped the fastener on his sleek trousers and undid the zipper.

I bit my lip as I inserted my hand into his tight boxer-briefs, never taking my eyes off his face. "I—I want you."

"Now?" His eyes narrowed then widened as I ran my

thumb over his crown.

"Now."

He rocked up, grabbing my hand with his own and
wrapping my fingers tighter, using me for his pleasure. "We do
this...we do it my way." He glanced at the silver watch on his
wrist—the same watch he'd noted when he'd told me my two
minutes were up with the almost blowjob.

I swallowed. "Fine."

"Do you trust me?"

The car kept coasting. But my heart slammed to a stop.
That question.

Another man, another time—same four words, identical
twelve letters.

My lips parted as I dove into his rich coffee eyes. I wanted
to demand why he'd asked that at this exact moment—the
same way another had asked before he kissed me.

But I couldn't. I couldn't shatter whatever existed in this
limousine.

I nodded ever so slowly, pretending hesitation while my
mind raced with possibility.
"Yes..."

"Good." He grunted, tearing my hands away and shoving
me off his lap. "Get on all fours."

"What?" My eyebrows rose. My hair clung to my back, no
doubt turning sweat-damp and curly.

"You heard me." Fisting his cock, he pulled a condom
from his pocket, and with jerky control, rolled it down his
length.

His throat contracted as every last bit of light disappeared
from his face. "Fucking turn around, Elle. You started this. I'll
finish it."

"I didn't start it. *You* kissed *me*."

"But then you straddled me and made me forget
something very important."

"What's important?"

His jaw hardened. "None of your concern. Now, turn

---

around." He slid off the seat, slamming to his knees. Shoving his trousers to mid-thigh, he twirled his finger in the air, waiting for me to obey and turn.

I didn't want to face away from him. I didn't feel safe not being able to see what he was about to do. But at the same time, the idea of being taken so rustic and pure made my breasts tingle and an orgasm already gather in my belly.

Without a word, I kneeled in the long runway of black carpeting with bench seats on either side. I had no support to hold onto as the limo turned corners. I had no way of preventing myself from soaring forward if we crashed.

I gave utter trust to Penn and his control of the situation.

My fingers dug into the rough carpet, already mourning the runs in my sheer pantyhose. No one in the outside world would know what we did even as we stopped at traffic lights and drove past pedestrians carrying their groceries.

I cried out as his hand clamped on my hip, tugging me backward. The tip of his cock found my entrance.

I tensed for him to take me. But he waited, tantalizingly close.

My body rocked back, forcing him inside a fraction.

He growled from behind me. "You have no idea, Elle. No idea."

Then he thrust.

One fast, all-consuming, unapologetic thrust.

I fell forward onto my elbows. My wrists weak from typing all day, I was unable to brace against his power. His hands latched around my waist, keeping my ass high and driving into me.

I breathed hard, inhaling scents of leather and car freshener, but most of all *him*. His dark aftershave, his arousal, the rich indescribable scent of Penn.

"I need you," he snarled, thrusting faster. "I need you so fucking much."

"So take me then." My head hung between my shoulders, forgetting everything but where we were joined.

There was no soreness or tenderness. Only the righteous feel of him inside, bruising me in all the right ways. My body fisted around him, already banding with the beginning of a release.

He smacked my thigh. "No, you don't get to come until I do." He was breathless, same as me. He was possessed, same as me.

I wouldn't need to drink tonight.

I was already drunk.

On him.

"Goddammit, Elle." He pushed forward, driving into me as hard as he could. His torso fell over my back with such a heavy groan it pained and excited me. Everything he did was erotic and wicked.

Reaching between my legs, I grabbed the base of him as he withdrew to thrust back inside me. He was hard as granite; so hot and slippery.

He grunted as I squeezed his balls, rolling them in my fingers until he batted my hand away and entered me with cracking brutality.

My breath caught as I trembled beneath him.

"Lust makes us do the most terrible things." His teeth latched onto my neck, biting hard, his hips pistoning quick. "I'm going to come so fucking bad."

I didn't know if I'd been the one to seduce him, but he'd utterly decimated me.

I whimpered and moaned, feeling too full, too empty, too used, too protected. Polar opposites all at once. My craving increased until I bared my teeth and focused every nerve ending where he penetrated me.

I let go of decorum and placed my hand between my legs, rubbing my clit as I backed up hard into his next thrust. I played his game. I met him fighting. Lust tinged the humid air. Temptation cloaked us with every breath.

And that was the end for both of us.

His hands flexed over my waist.

I dared look back.

He was exquisite, his gorgeous body straining against the binds of his tuxedo. He didn't look human, just a man intending to mate until death.

His head fell back, his lips tight against secrets he refused to share.

A flare of pain from inside set the unbearable pleasure into a free fall. I rippled and squeezed, my legs locking against my hand as I rubbed my clit in time to his thrusting cock. Nothing else mattered but the incessant want to give in to this ravaging hunger.

It was too good.

It was too much.

He grabbed the back of my neck, rising onto his knees as he drove into me with short, deep jerks. My orgasm evolved into elastic boomerangs, bouncing down the walls of my pussy, tightening and splintering until I gave up and fell cheek first against the carpet.

The tip of his cock hit me too hard, too high. I squirmed to get way, but he yanked me back and joined me in the golden blissful glow. He quaked and quivered, coming deep inside me.

Epic aftershocks shook us as we stayed exactly where we were—a heap of finery joined in place.

The outside world slowly made an appearance as the limousine slowed and the driver's intercom crackled. "We're here, sir."

Penn slapped the button. "Give us a minute. We'll get our own doors. Under no circumstances open them, got it?"

"Got it."

I had carpet burn on my cheek and looseness in joints I couldn't even name, but as Penn slid out of me and disposed of the condom into a tissue, he gently helped me up and pressed a stinging kiss to my delicate face.

"Christ, look what I did to you."

With infinitesimal kindness, he grabbed another tissue, positioned me onto the seat and knelt between my legs. When I tried to close them, he opened my knees and kept them wide with a stern look. Never glancing away, he wiped me clean, slid my panties back into position, and pulled my dress down.

"You got away easy, Elle. So fucking easy."

Doing up his fly, he ran both hands through his hair then opened the door and stepped out.

CHAPTER THIRTY-TWO

THOSE FIRST FEW steps into the night extravaganza were some of the hardest I'd ever walked.

Not only because I ached in places one should never ache in public but also because Penn shut down. He'd said things in the car I wanted to chase. He'd slipped, and I was anxious to encourage him to slip more.

All I wanted to do was find a quiet spot and demand him to open up to me, but he didn't give me a chance.

Grabbing my hand, he smiled and nodded at people milling around the entrance, tugging me inside the opulent hotel ballroom where the function took place.

Hundreds of people laughed and mingled, glittering like fallen stars all dressed in silver. The tables around the perimeter of the room looked like flying saucers adorned with lace and crystal candelabras.

"You have a choice, Elle," Penn murmured as he guided me through the thicket.

When he didn't give me the options to go with the choice, I frowned. "What options?"

"Two things are happening tonight that are non-negotiable."

My fingers tensed in his. "I don't agree to things I can't control."

He smirked. "Like you agreed to fuck me? That wasn't in

your control."

I swallowed, hating he had a point. Then again, he'd asked me if I trusted him. He'd sought permission, passing me the power to deny.

Which I didn't.

I nursed that little conclusion, giving him the limelight.

"Two things." He smiled roguishly. "The only thing you can control is the order in which they happen."

Pursing my lips, I accepted a glass of champagne he lifted off a silver platter carried by a white-uniformed waiter.

"Number one, you're going to drink. I want you tipsy—like you were that night you said yes. I want you loose and inhibited and open to doing whatever I want."

My swallow of champagne—already bitter and not wanted turned sour. "That was a one-time thing. I don't drink to excess."

"Tonight, you do." Unthreading his fingers from mine, he cupped my elbow, guiding me past a particularly big group of minglers. "I need you open."

"Why?"

"Because after this function, we're going to talk."

I tripped in my heels. "Talk?"

His forehead furrowed, his normally handsome face marked with frustration. "You want to know who I am, Elle?" He moved closer, whispering in my ear with seduction and chicanery. "I'll tell you. But for you to accept the truth, you have to have an open mind."

I took another sip of champagne—not because of his order but because my mouth shot dry with nerves. "Why do I need an open mind?" I pulled back, looking into his dark bronze eyes. "Who *are* you?"

"You'll find out soon enough." Rolling his shoulders, his voice clipped with tension. "You'll get your answers. But only if you do what you're told."

I bristled at the condescending remark.

"I'll tell you, Elle, but it won't change a thing." He

caressed my cheek with sudden devotion. "You've been mine since the moment we met, and you'll stay mine until I let you go. Anything else—all your arguments, denials, and refusals—mean nothing to me." He leaned forward until our noses brushed. "Remember that when I tell you. You've already lost. Why? Because you are *mine*."

I jerked back, breathing hard and slightly scared.

He either didn't notice or didn't care. Looking over the crowd—his vision easily a few inches taller than most—he murmured as if he hadn't just ransacked my world, "Your choice. Either drink now...or..."

"Or?"

"Or I'll permit you to keep your wits until after you've met Larry again."

"Larry?"

From the park?

Deciding to annoy him, I said, "Ah, your fictional husband slash benefactor."

"That's starting to get old."

My courage sprang from nowhere, bolstered by monster-sized curiosity. "Who is he to you? What exactly is a benefactor anyway?"

His face blocked all answers. "Why do you care?"

"I care because I hate being in the dark."

"It's better than other alternatives."

My heart squeezed. "What do you mean?"

He sighed, rubbing his face with his hand. "Fine. I'll answer the basics if it'll stop your damn questions. Larry is family. He's the only family I have. Stewie will be his adopted son soon. Which will make him my brother, for all intents and purposes."

He took a breath, bracing himself to continue. "I used to...work...for Larry, until I branched off into my own expertise. He helped me when I had no one else, and I'll forever have his back so if he gets sick again and needs to move to Zimbabwe for treatment, I'll take him. If he suddenly told me he couldn't adopt Stewie, I'd do it in a fucking heartbeat. Larry is the reason I still have a life—even if it is messed up."

I clutched each answer before he could steal them back. So many questions to tug out more truth, but I focused on the easiest…for now. "And what is your expertise?"

"Stock market."

I didn't picture him as Wall Street guy. A lawyer perhaps with his sharp tongue and argumentative desire to turn every conversation into a debate. But not boring stocks and impersonal trades.

"Where are your mom and dad?" I drank him in, doing my best to read his body language as he stiffened.

"Dead. Have been since I was eleven."

I flinched. "I'm sorry."

"You didn't do it." He looked over my head, his patience fraying. I doubted he'd permit any more questions, but I asked another. "You say Larry gave you back your life. How? Where did you guys meet?"

Penn chuckled darkly, shaking his head.

I tacked on another before he could revoke me asking anymore. "What about Stewie? Where did you meet him?"

He grinned, slipping back into the cultured shell that was utterly unreadable. "Enough." He cupped my chin with his finger and thumb, holding me tight. "Choose. Drink now or later. Your call."

I gulped as his gaze went to my lips. The room blurred with sexual tension. We'd just had sex but already the familiar ache began anew.

Deliberately placing the champagne on a table next to an identical empty flute, I straightened my back. "Later. I'd like to see what Larry will reveal before you scare me away and stop me from figuring out who you truly are."

He laughed softly. "He won't help with that, Elle. Only I can."

"Well, help me then. Tell me. I know nothing about you. Where did you go to school? What sort of stocks do you trade?

What's your favorite hobby, drink, color, time of day?" My voice ran into one endless request. "It's uncomfortable for me spending time with a man I don't know, basing everything I do know off whatever chemistry our bodies decide to share."

His lips tilted. "So you're saying sleeping with me, while knowing nothing about me, isn't exciting but terrifying?"

I nodded. "If you want to use extremes, yes."

He removed his hold, letting my face go. "Careful what you wish for, Elle. Sometimes, secrets make things better not worse." Dropping his eyes, they lingered on my naked throat, almost as if he traced an invisible necklace then he looked away, once again taking control by guiding me forward with an elbow touch.

Music fell gently from speakers, light classical with a thread of contemporary. It was meant to be relaxing, but I found a hint of macabre hidden in the notes. The laughing crowd didn't notice and I didn't dwell. Whatever happened tonight, I'd meet headfirst. If it meant this was the last time I'd see Penn because of some disastrous divulgence, then I would still wake tomorrow. I would still have my company, my father, my world.

Sure, it wouldn't be as spicy without him in it, but I didn't need him to make me whole.

Are you sure about that?

My heart had been a stupid thing. My ears had heard his lies, but my heart didn't buy them. It didn't judge or interrogate. It blindly followed where affection lay—making my feelings toward Penn woefully complicated.

I let him lead me—staying quiet and obedient out of respect that this was his night. His night to either reveal something I could accept or run away with horror. I was ready for either as long as he gave me answers.

Stewie found us first.

A small hand appeared from the crowd followed by an arm dressed in gray with navy pinstripes. He grinned as he planted himself in our trajectory, his attention on Penn.

"Whatcha think?"

Penn slammed to a halt, rubbing his chin with his fingers in mock-serious contemplation. "Hmm…"

Stewie bought into the pantomime while I watched as an outsider, witnessing once again how many facets Penn had. He was strict and unyielding, but with Stewie, he was a joker, friend, and protector all in one.

"Very nice." He looked at me. "What do you think, Elle? Your merchandise shrunk to Stew's size."

I reached forward, rubbing Stewie's lapel, playing into the role of judgment. "I think the tailors did an amazing job, but the suit wouldn't look good on just anyone." I smiled, standing upright. "You wear that suit, Stewie, the suit doesn't wear you."

Stewie's face scrunched up. "I don't get it."

Penn chuckled. "She likes it."

"Sweet!" Stewie spun in place. "Larry said I can wear it to my school interviews next month. Said it will help me open doors that may be locked thanks to my background."

Penn glanced at me quickly before nodding. "Wise man. But no doors will be locked; you have my word on that." His hands clenched before relaxing. "Now, speaking of Larry, mind showing us where he's hanging out?"

Stewie nodded, slipping into a quick jig-jog. "Sure, this way."

Penn raised his eyebrow at me, took my hand, and together, we navigated the room.

CHAPTER THIRTY-THREE

"I WAS WONDERING when you'd show up." Larry grinned, shaking Penn's hand as we popped from the crowd thanks to Stewie guiding us.

We'd traversed the ballroom to a quieter meeting room off to the side. Here, men and women huddled in their array of silver splendor, their voices hushed in discussion, soft with business and not for other people's ears.

"Fashionably late." Penn smirked. "Isn't that what you taught me?"

"Not to your own event."

Wait, his *event?*

I frowned. I died with impatience to ask what the evening supported. Why Penn would be the figurehead for something that deserved such a turn-out. But Penn waved at Larry then to me. "You remember Elle?"

"Of course, I do. I'm not blind, you idiot." The name-calling carried heavy affection as Larry leaned forward to kiss me on the cheek. "Hello, Elle. You look ravishing."

I accepted his greeting, doing my best not to blush. "Thank you. You look dashing yourself." Just like Penn dressed in a silver tuxedo, Larry wore a darker version. His salt and pepper hair matched the silver theme perfectly. Stewie was the only one to break the metallic code with his gray pinstripe.

Champagne was once again handed out. Penn plucked a

glass, handing it to me with another raised eyebrow. I accepted it but didn't take a sip—mainly in defiance.

Awkwardness fell.

I grasped for an appropriate subject. "So you said this was Penn's event?" I glanced at the men. "I must admit he hasn't given me any hints as to why I'm here or what the evening festivities are for."

Larry shot Penn a disapproving glare. "He didn't, did he?" He smiled. "Let me be the one to tell you then."

"Larry," Penn growled under his breath. "Remember our discussion."

Larry waved him off, taking my elbow and escorting me toward the bar and away from Penn. "This is a charity function. Every year Penn hosts it. He has since we started working together."

"Working together?"

Larry nodded as if it was perfect knowledge. "I'm a lawyer. My firm needed a helping hand, and Penn offered. He's smart with a quick tongue. He traveled with me to many cases—even helped provide the legwork on research when I got sick. However, while I was in recovery, he turned his hand to the stock market."

His eyes focused on a memory with pride. "He invested in a small penny stock. With his luck, it should've tanked. But it didn't. For the first time, he was rewarded for his risk and the stock took off overnight. He used the profits to inject into this charity and to day trade the same companies we took to court on behalf of some of its victims."

There were tangles and knots in his revelation that I couldn't work out. I needed a quiet room where I could write down what he'd revealed and mix them around on pieces of paper until I could rearrange them into comprehensible order.

"And what is the charity for?"

Larry beamed like any happy parent. "Homeless children, of course."

I slammed to a stop.

Homeless.

Nameless…

My strappy heels pinched my feet. "*What* did you just say?"

Larry noticed my sudden pallor. His face fell. "He hasn't told you yet. Has he?"

All I could manage was a shake of my head.

I felt sick.

I felt elated.

I felt *terrified*.

His face softened, looking over my shoulder as the electrical presence of the man I'd forever associate with heartache appeared. He'd lied and twisted my mind. He'd hidden honesty and made me crazy. He stopped me from learning anymore by interfering with our conversation.

Larry bent into me, murmuring, "I'll tell you this, then the rest is up to him. *He* was homeless himself. It's his way of giving back—to help other kids having a really hard time in life." Patting my arm, he said louder as Penn sidled close, "I need a refill. Anyone else?"

"No." Penn shook his head, wrapping his arm around my suddenly trembling body. "I think you've done more than enough."

Larry merely shrugged, unapologetic.

I glanced up, taking in Penn's profile. The way his jaw was sharp and strong and no longer covered in an unkempt beard. The way his eyes lightened and darkened depending on his mood but remained the same hue as the man in Central Park. How he'd asked me if I trusted him. How he had the same habit of jamming his hands into his pockets. How he'd kissed me with chocolate…

Oh, my God.

It's true.

My knees wobbled as Penn muttered under his breath, "We'll be right back."

I gave a weak smile to Larry, falling into Penn's fast stride as he guided me through the jostling ballroom.

I couldn't tear my eyes off him. Forcing my brain to overlap his appearance with that of Nameless. I started seeing things that weren't there. Or believing in things that had been there all along.

I couldn't decide.

Without facts or declarations or any confirmation at all, I tripped into the teenage crush I'd never escaped from. I was stupid. I was hopeful. I was blind.

A woman placed herself in our path, smiling coyly at Penn while ignoring me entirely. "Oh, Penn. Fancy seeing you here." She simpered. "Do you mind if I borrow you for a moment? I have a question about the Triple Segment Securities you recommended last week." She flicked her dark brown hair. "I want your *expert* opinion."

Rage and jealousy clawed me.

If Penn was Nameless, he was mine.

He'd been mine for three years.

I'd only just found him and now she wanted to take him away?

No.

She can't.

Disappointment and confusion followed as Penn sighed heavily and let me go.

Whispering in my ear, he commanded, "Leave the ballroom. Head to the first-floor restaurant. You'll see a family bathroom. Meet me there in five minutes. What I need to tell you should be done in private."

"But I'm not tipsy."

His gaze hardened then saddened. "It's too late. You need to know. I can't fucking lie anymore."

I shivered as he let me go.

He gave me one last eternally long stare then walked away with the woman, leaving me with fantasies and fears and a joy I never dared believe in.

CHAPTER THIRTY-FOUR

I MANAGED A few shaky steps toward the large archway that I assumed led toward the hotel foyer and a staircase or elevator.

I hated leaving him. But I wanted answers more. He'd promised he'd meet me. I had to trust he wouldn't forget or disappear without fulfilling that promise.

Hopefully tonight, I'll finally know.

The fear that he'd run and I'd never see him again escalated the further I traveled. I didn't see Larry or anyone else I recognized.

I reached the threshold of the ballroom.

A gray bullet collided into me.

My arms flew out for balance, steadying myself and the kamikaze who'd run into me. I blinked as recognition flowed. "Stewie. Are you okay?"

He smacked his lips, nodding distractedly. "Yeah, sorry for running into you."

"Don't worry about it. As long as you're good, it's fine."

He nodded, his face tight and not the usual happiness I'd grown used to. "Yep, all good." He pushed past me to join the throng but something sparkly fell from his pocket.

Something blue.

Something that didn't belong in a boy's possession.

He didn't notice, fighting his way past adults as I ducked

and plucked the silver necklace from the ballroom floor.

My heart stopped.

The world closed in.

I couldn't breathe.

In my hands sat the very thing I'd lost the night Nameless had saved me. The sapphire star glimmered under the bright strobes of the hotel, the white gold chain snapped in half where one of the muggers had yanked it off my neck.

I stumbled, crashing into a man who cursed as a splash of his orange cocktail tipped onto his silver tuxedo. "Hey!"

I vaguely remembered how to apologize while my mind was no longer here but *there.*

Back in the alley.

Back where it all began.

In an awful twist of fate, Stewie looked back, his gaze latching onto the necklace dripping through my shocked fingers. He slammed to a halt, looking around feverishly as if searching for Penn. Hoping to undo this minor, inconsequential action that'd ruined all Penn's lies. Destroyed his stories. Revealed every fact.

I'd believed in a fantasy.

And it'd just crumbled into dust.

I know the truth.

The awful, terrible, sickening truth.

Coming toward me, Stewie sheepishly held out his hand. "Can I have it back?"

My fist curled tightly around the chain. "This is mine."

"No, it's not." His forehead crinkled. "My brother gave it to me."

My heels were no longer stable or capable of holding me up. I swayed. "Your brother?"

Penn's voice entered my head, sounding far away. *"Larry is family. Stewie will be his adopted son soon. Which will make him my brother."*

No.

If Penn gave Stewie my necklace…that meant he couldn't

be my tragic hero.

He couldn't be my savior.

He couldn't be Nameless.

It's not possible.

This can't be happening.

Nameless had never retrieved my necklace.

I'd never asked for it back.

The last I'd seen it was in the alley, ripped off my neck, and pocketed by thugs.

My heart palpitated, threatening to faint.

Don't let it be true…

Only two scenarios existed as to who Penn could be.

The sapphire had shortlisted them.

My life had made a mockery of my heart.

The truth laughed in the face of my moronic trust.

My voice struggled to stay low so as not to attract attention when all I wanted to do was scream. "Why?"

"Why?" His face crunched.

I swallowed hard, pushing down my heart where it hyperventilated in my mouth. "*Why* did your brother give you this necklace? It's not something a boy would normally play with."

He scuffed his shoe on the ballroom floor. "I'm looking after it for him." His eyes blazed. "I would *never* play with it."

"You didn't answer me, Stewie." My panic made me sharp. "*Why* do you have this?"

His attitude prickled. He crossed his arms. "Because if he was caught with it, his sentence would've doubled."

My legs turned to liquid.

My knees to chocolate mousse.

"What sentence?"

His lips thinned. "I dunno if I should be telling you this."

"Yes, you should." I moved forward, towering over him, commanding my fingers to stay locked around my necklace and not reach for his throat to strangle the answers from him. "Tell me, Stewie. Tell me *right now.*"

He puffed out his cheeks, as if doing his best not to reply but unable to ignore the order from an elder. "His prison sentence, all right? He got done for robbery. He asked me to keep it, so they didn't have evidence." Fear turned his face red. "I know I should've hidden it somewhere, but I liked it, okay? I like blue, and I like stars." He kicked the floor. "I want to be an astronomer when I grow up. I know it's girly, but...I love stars." His hand came up. "Give it back."

My body obeyed before my mind caught up.

In a daze, my arm reached forward. My fingers opened, letting the sapphire slip from my grasp to his.

I was numb.

I was dead.

Two choices.

Two men I'd cursed their very existence.

Two men tried to rape me.

One man had succeeded.

But it wasn't rape.

It was consensual.

It was *wanted*.

He'd stolen more than just my necklace but my innocence and goodness too.

How could I move on from this?

How did I ever come to terms with what he'd done?

Who is he?

Which one?

Stewie clutched the evidence of Penn's heinous crime. He didn't wait for more questions. He didn't even thank me for returning what was rightfully mine.

Taking off, he vanished into the silver throng, leaving me destroyed and heartbroken.

Truth was a fickle thing. I'd believed I wanted it. I'd begged and cursed and demanded to receive it. And now that I had it...I wanted nothing more than for it to delete what it'd caused and choose a different ending to the one I'd been given.

I'd gone from euphoric joy believing Penn was Nameless

to finding out my worst nightmare.

Penn wasn't Nameless—the boy who'd protected and kissed me in the park.

He was one of the muggers who'd tried to rape me.

They'd known my name from my I.D badge.

One of them had come after me.

I'm going to throw up.

CHAPTER THIRTY-FIVE

I RAN.

How could I not?

I didn't know what was worse.

The fact he'd lied so effortlessly. Or the fact I'd believed—that despite being so dishonest—he was a good person underneath.

I couldn't have been more wrong.

He was a thief, a rapist, a scam artist.

And he'd successfully used me for whatever mind games he wanted to play.

He'd lied from the moment he'd coerced me into saying yes at the Palm Politics. Any truth I thought I saw in the split seconds of tenderness were rust-covered and full of counterfeit honesty.

Oh, my God.

How could I let this happen?

Tears gathered like vinegar in my eyes, stinging with disbelief.

The taxi bumped through the arteries of the city, carting me away from Penn and his empire of fibs. I hadn't called David because I didn't want anyone who knew me to see me like this. See how far I'd fallen.

My cheeks still glowed from limousine sex. My dress rumpled. My hair tangled. My lips red from throwing up in the hotel bathroom before bolting to the street and hailing the first cab I saw.

I didn't wait for Penn to confirm the hideousness of Stewie's revelation. I didn't meet him at our rendezvous for yet more lies. I could *never* have sex with him again.

I clamped a hand over my mouth, holding back another wash of nausea.

I slept with him.

I climaxed with him.

I have—had—feelings for him.

The vinegar in my tears pickled my insides, fermenting my heart, marinating my blood until my entire body turned acidic.

I just wanted to get home, shower away his touch, and sleep so I could forget what I'd done and who I'd done it with.

I couldn't think about who Penn was.

I couldn't let my mind poke at such appalling conclusions.

It's not real.

I can't let it be real.

The drive took forever, but finally, the taxi dropped me outside my building. Climbing unsteadily from the cab, I refused to think about what explanation I'd give for breaking off the engagement. Why I'd inform security that Penn was no longer permitted to step foot inside Belle Elle. Why I would get a damn restraining order if he pursued me.

How would I tell Dad that the man he believed was suitable—the successful entrepreneur who pretended to be an old-world romantic—was truly just a clever deceiver?

Thank God, I never told him what happened that night in the alley. Thank heavens, I kept the robbery and almost rape a secret because he would hunt Penn down and kill him for being one of those men who'd tried to take me.

A man who successfully got what he wanted in the end.

I swallowed a sob.

I only had myself to blame. I should've dug deeper into his past. I should never have trusted him.

Entering the exclusive foyer of my building, I swatted at a

tear that had the audacity to roll and marched to the elevators.

The doors opened immediately, and I climbed in. My heart plummeted, remembering Sage wouldn't be there to patch up my worries or lick away my hurts like normal. She was with Dad. Safe and secure.

Not like me whose world has just imploded.

My awaiting apartment was suddenly a cold, lifeless entity as the elevator zoomed me skyward. I wanted nothing more than to return home to the brownstone where Dad refused to decorate over Mom's last designs and constantly lived in the past with a broken heart.

Would that be me now? Had Penn ruined me for others? Had his lies destroyed whatever trust I had in men? How could I ever tell anyone I willingly slept with a man who'd tried to rape me three years prior in a dirty alley?

Stop.

Just stop.

I can't...I can't think about it anymore.

Unlocking my door, I kicked off my heels and headed straight for the sleek white kitchen. None of my lights were on, leaving the view to speak for itself as the skyscraper-filled horizon twinkled with bright orbs of light. The illuminated buildings seemed so happy, sheltering their chosen families. So sarcastic with their comforting glow.

I hated them.

Padding toward the pantry, I pulled out a bottle of wine I occasionally cooked with.

I never drank. But tonight was a night of firsts, and the liquor in my belly from a few champagne sips weren't enough.

I needed to drown every memory before they became long-term recollections. I needed to reset my life, so tomorrow I could be free.

Tipping the bottle, I swigged tart shiraz straight from the glass.

"Wow, I never thought I'd see the day."

The masculine voice terrified me.

Gulping my mouthful, I spun in the kitchen, facing the open plan living room. A figure sat on the leather couch.

He tutted, shaking his head. "Pity. I thought I'd be the one to drive you to drink." Greg chuckled then stood. His deliberate slowness reeked of mayhem and hazards.

He smiled coldly, his dark blond hair swiped back off his face. "Hello, Elle. Tough night?" He stalked toward me. "Should've gone out with me instead—like I said."

I froze; the wine bottle became more than just liquid friendship but a heavy weapon. "What are you doing in my apartment, Greg?"

This wasn't the first time. He'd been here for dinners and birthdays—even last Thanksgiving when I'd stupidly said I'd host it and burned the turkey. But he'd never been here alone, and he'd *definitely* never let himself in uninvited.

"How did you get in?"

He cocked his head. "The doorman. It's handy already having a relationship. It's allowed me to do things I wouldn't have been able to do if we were strangers."

What things?

My toes curled into the tiled floor, begging to run while I told them to stay put. I couldn't show weakness. This was my house. *Mine.*

"You're trespassing."

He sighed. "I was worried about you." He dragged a finger over the kitchen bench. "I wanted to make sure you got home safe and that prick didn't try something when he dropped you off." He grinned. "He doesn't deserve to fuck you, Elle." His face tightened. "I do."

I brandished the bottle. "You deserve to get your ass thrown out of my apartment or arrested. I'd prefer the latter. Now, get *out*."

He shook his head, smiling. "Yeah, see? That's where you're wrong, Elle. I deserve what I've worked so hard to get."

"You haven't worked hard your entire life. You've coasted by on your father's goodwill and mine." I narrowed my eyes.

"In fact, showing up here just gave me credible reason to fire you. Consider yourself unemployed."

I steeled myself for his retaliation.

I expected an outburst. A strike.

I shivered as he laughed, his eyes alight and face crinkled with mirth. "Aw, you're so cute when you're mad." He entered the kitchen, his gaze dropping to my legs as if judging how best to incapacitate me. "I'm not unemployed, Elle. I've just given myself a promotion."

I took a step back, trying to keep distance between us. Seconds turned to fractions, inching over a clock dial as his feet inched over my floor.

Closer.

Closer.

"Stop!" I cursed the wobble in my voice. "I don't want you here. It's time for you to go. Right now, Greg. I won't ask again." I fumbled for the silver bag I'd dumped by the pantry. My phone. The police.

Desperation for help pressurized inside me the closer Greg came.

He stopped, rubbing his jaw. "You're right, it *is* time to go."

I sighed in relief.

He's all talk.

He won't hurt me.

He's smarter than that.

He smiled a rapscallion smile. "But I'm not going alone."

CHAPTER THIRTY-SIX

I'D CARRIED THAT day in the alley with me for three years.

It was my dirty secret.

My one major screw-up.

And most of the time, I was able to ignore how it had made me feel.

How scared I'd been. How god-awful it'd been to be trapped. How petrified I'd been while being molested. How I hated being a prisoner even for a few terrible minutes.

But sometimes, when I was tired or stressed or sleep deprived, I couldn't fight off the shadows of that night.

Baseball Cap and Adidas were there, ready to touch me, hurt me—make me forget I was safe and they could never touch me.

I like the thought of you giving me a blowjob. Get her on her knees

Those times, I was able to shove aside awful memories by remembering Nameless. Believing the world was good and bad but most of the time right won over wrong. He was there, fighting off nightmares, giving me candy and kisses.

He was my safe place.

He made me believe things were fine.

Tonight had proven me wrong.

Twice.

If you scream, we'll beat you fucking bloody, and you'll wake up with nothing.

My mind was full of useless snippets and three-year-old voices from that night. They became louder and stronger as Greg switched his stalking for attack.

A silent cry fell from my lips as he charged.

"No!" I twisted on the spot, my bare feet sticking to the tiles as I forgot about standing up to him and chose running instead.

Only, I didn't get far.

First, we get what we want, and then you get what you want.

"Gotcha." Greg's arms lashed around my waist, pulling me to him.

My fingers gripped the wine bottle as I hoisted it over my head, wildly aiming, blinding hoping. Blood-red shiraz chugged from the tip, splashing me, Greg, my kitchen.

"Give me that." He held me trapped with one arm, grabbing my wrist with his free hand.

"Stop!" I squirmed and wiggled. I swung and pummeled. "Let me go!"

I tried to defend myself.

But it was no use.

You want to see my cock, bitch. Can't deny that shit.

He twisted the bottle from my fingers and placed it carefully on the bench. He didn't smash it or cause any noise.

He kept his abduction as silent as possible.

To keep it secret.

So make it un-secret.

I screamed as loud as I could. The back of my throat shredded, but I screamed and *screamed*—

He slapped a hand over my lips, silencing me. "Quit it." Breathing hard as I tried to kick his legs, he hissed, "Do you honestly think anyone will hear you? These apartments are triple walled. You're on the top floor. Save your breath."

Turning me in his embrace, he grabbed my wrists, trapped them behind my back, and kissed me quick and deep.

Let's see what your tits are like.

I tried to bite his tongue, but he was too fast. A swift claiming and then a retreat, knowing he'd won and I was his.

I fought harder, ignoring how strong he was and how weak he made me. "Stop this, Greg." My voice climbed a few octaves, making me beg even when I tried to command. "Let me go."

He merely laughed. "You're not the one in charge tonight." He strode over to the invisible drawer holding random pieces of junk. Unlike Penn, he knew how to press to open. Grabbing some twine I'd used to hold the turkey stuffing in place, he wrapped it around my wrists, tying tight.

Before we show you ours, you have to show us yours.

Once I was helpless, he marched me forward. "You and I are going for a little drive." Scooping up a pair of car keys I hadn't seen on my kitchen bench, he pushed me toward the door, opened it, and shoved me over the threshold.

Panic billowed faster.

I didn't want to leave with him.

Please!

"Where are we going?" My heart galloped as he punched the down button for the elevator and dragged me onto it.

He pressed the button for the garage below. "Somewhere no one will find us." He rocked his cock against my back as he kept me locked in front of him. "Somewhere we can get to know each other and finally agree that marriage between us is the best thing—for everyone."

I sneered. "I'm already engaged."

To a liar—just like you.

To a criminal—just like you.

I prodded the hurt inside that Penn had caused.

I asked the question I'd been avoiding.

Was Penn Baseball Cap or Adidas?

Was he the one who'd grabbed my breast or torn off my sapphire star?

Penn's promises echoed in my head.

Say yes, and you're mine. You'll answer to me. Sometimes, you'll hate me. Most of the time, you'll probably want to kill me.

He was right.

I *did* want to kill him.

Multiple times.

My chest ached as another of his truthless pledges rang in my ears.

I will lie to others about us. I will paint a picture that isn't true. I will curse and hurt and do whatever I damn well want, but you have my word on one thing. I won't lie to you. What you see from me will be the honest fucking truth.

Liar.

Liar.

Liar.

Greg chuckled. "That engagement is a sham." He kissed my throat, pushing aside my hair with his car keys, scraping me with the sharp-toothed metal. "I'm not a fucking idiot, Elle."

The elevator dinged, depositing us into the underground garage. He pressed his key fob, and a graphite Porsche beeped with welcome.

I'd seen his car before, hell, I'd been in his car when he drove me to a meeting across town when David suddenly came down with food poisoning. But I'd never been forced into his car or made to feel as if he would hurt me if I disobeyed.

I shot forward, taking him by surprise.

I managed a few steps before he looped his fingers around the twine on my wrists, slamming me to a stop.

"Where do you think you're going?"

My feet ached on the rough concrete thanks to mostly healed cuts and bruises from running barefoot a few nights ago.

If Penn was Adidas or Baseball Cap, why had he come to my rescue?

Why had he been my defender in my future when he'd been the offender in my past?

Nameless' voice was the third to enter my thoughts.

You don't need to hide. I won't let them hurt you. You're safe with me.

I fought harder, jumping in Greg's hold, kicking him as hard as I could.

He merely laughed, stripping me of strength with caustic ridicule.

Do you trust me?

Nameless and Penn had asked that.

I'd thought the link was enough to reveal his identity. Turned out, that question was common and far too flimsy to pin my hopes on.

Greg dragged me toward his Porsche, ignoring my attempts at fleeing.

I stopped fighting, choosing another alternative. "Greg…let's talk about this." I tried to appeal to the side of him I'd interacted with for years—the business side. The boy I'd grown up with surrounded by all things Belle Elle.

But that Greg was gone.

Compounded by jealousy and riddled with resentment, the man capturing me had a vendetta to earn what he believed was rightfully his, regardless if it was blasphemously wrong.

Opening the car door, he growled. "Get in."

"You don't have to do this."

He shoved his face in mine. "I know. I *want* to do this." He placed his hand on my skull, pushing me to duck so I could fit inside the Porsche. "Now, get in the fucking car."

I looked at the guard sitting in the distance by the exit ramp.

I made a stupid choice, one based on self-preservation.

I screamed. *"Heeeeeeelp!"*

He punched me.

The crack hit my cheekbone. The force threw me against the car. The garage vanished. The ground disappeared. I came to with my knees buckled and my body sprawled like a ragdoll in the passenger seat.

The slam of the door vibrated my teeth.

The guard hadn't heard me.

My pain was for nothing.

My vision fogged with candyfloss as Greg yanked open the driver's side, leaped in, and gunned the engine.

I groaned against sickness and agony. "Stop." My head lolled on my neck, too heavy, totally useless.

Larry's voice entered the medley in my skull, bringing thoughts of Central Park, airplanes, and kisses on a baseball field. *Thieves can become saints. Saints can become thieves. Most of us deserve a second chance.*

My heart boycotted his misunderstood wisdom.

He'd known all along that Penn was more than just a homeless man who'd been arrested on my nineteenth birthday. The entire time we'd spoken, he'd known I slept with an immoral crook.

He knows who Penn is.

And he didn't tell me.

He let me develop feelings. He believed whatever connection Penn managed to cultivate would be enough to get past the alley.

To get past the threat, the taunt, the trauma.

My face throbbed as I tried to figure it out.

I can never forgive him.

Baseball Cap's threat filled my ears. The last thing he'd said to me as Nameless shielded me and kept me safe.

You'll fucking pay. Both of you.

They'd made me pay.

They'd kept their oath to rob me of everything I had, including my body.

But what about Nameless?

What have they done?

The Porsche shot forward, pinning my head against the seat as Greg drove fast. He slowed as we approached the guard.

I blinked, forcing my eyesight to work past the bruising on my cheek.

We stopped, barricaded by the red and white ramp.

The guard was too high in his little booth. He couldn't see inside the car. I kicked the floor, hoping to make a noise.

It was pitifully non-existent.

Greg reached over with one hand, planting his sour palm over my lips. He whispered, "No screaming." With his other hand, he fished out his Belle Elle pass and smiled. "Evening."

The guard did his job. He checked the credentials. He opened the exit. "Have a good night."

"Oh, I will. Believe me." Greg threw his I.D card at me as he stomped on the accelerator.

We sped into the night.

He removed his hand. "That went well." His face gleamed black with triumph. "The hard parts are over now." He patted my thigh with unwanted fingers. "A little road trip then you and I get to have a private *chat*." His hand slid up my thigh, probing the silver dress.

The same dress Penn had hooked over my hips as he fucked me in the limousine.

The same dress I'd worn when I'd found my sapphire star and learned the terrible truth.

I yanked my legs away. "Don't touch me."

Greg clutched the steering wheel with a chuckle. "I plan on doing more than that, Noelle. Much more."

As New York blurred with speed, Dad filled my mind.

Would he come for me?

Would he save me?

I had no one else.

Nameless was gone.

Penn was banished.

I'm alone.

But it didn't matter.

Greg wanted what he couldn't have.

Belle Elle was my empire and my body was mine.

Penn had taught me how to lie.

I would don a crown of them.

I would lie and cheat and steal and beg.

I wouldn't back down.

I'll fight.

THRONE OF TRUTH

Crown of Lies concludes in ***Throne of Truth*** releasing
28th February 2017

*"My body blinded me while his lies destroyed me. Penn Everett swept me
from my world and into his, and when his lies fell apart, I finally opened
my eyes to the truth. The awful, terrible truth."*

Noelle Charlston had it all: her company, a love affair, power
and protection.
However, she didn't pay attention, and in one night, everything
she believed in, everyone she trusted turned out to be worse
than fake.
Now, she has no one to help her. No one to free her.
She's on her own and has to make the choice.
Who to believe?
Who to fight?
Who to trust?
Penn lied to her from the beginning. He taught her that words
could hurt and actions could steal, and now, it's her turn to
twist the truth. She doesn't have a choice. She'll fight for her
heart, her livelihood, her life.
Some lies will ruin her while others will set her free.
But the truth…the truth will change everything.

OTHER WORK BY PEPPER WINTERS

Pepper Winters is a multiple New York Times, Wall Street Journal, and USA Today International Bestseller.

DARK ROMANCE
New York Times Bestseller 'Monsters in the Dark' Trilogy
"Voted Best Dark Romance, Best Dark Hero, #1 Erotic Romance"
Start the Trilogy with
Tears of Tess (Monsters in the Dark #1)

Multiple New York Times Bestseller 'Indebted' Series
"Voted Vintagely Dark & Delicious. A true twist on Romeo & Juliet"
Start the Series **FREE** with
Debt Inheritance (Indebted #1)

GRAY ROMANCE
USA Today Bestseller 'Destroyed'
"Voted Best Tear-Jerker, #1 Romantic Suspense"

SURVIVAL CONTEMPORARY ROMANCE
USA Today Bestseller 'Unseen Messages' *"Voted Best Epic Survival Romance 2016, Castaway meets The Notebook"*

MOTORCYCLE CLUB ROMANCE

Multiple USA Today Bestseller 'Pure Corruption' Duology
"Sinful & Suspenseful, an Amnesia Tale full of Alphas and Heart"
Start the Duology with:
Ruin & Rule (Pure Corruption #1)

SINFUL ROMANCE
Multiple USA Today Bestseller 'Dollar' Series
"Elder Prest will steal your heart. A captive love-story with salvation at its core."
Start this series for only **99c** with
Pennies (Dollar Series #1)

EROTIC ROMANCE
Brand New Release 'Truth & Lies' Duet
Start this duet with
Crown of Lies (Truth & Lies #1)

ROMANTIC COMEDY written as TESS HUNTER
#1 Romantic Comedy Bestseller 'Can't Touch This'
"Voted Best Rom Com of 2016. Pets, love, and chemistry."

UPCOMING RELEASES
For 2017 and beyond titles please visit
www.pepperwinters.com

SOCIAL MEDIA & WEBSITE
Facebook: Peppers Books
Instagram: @pepperwinters
Facebook Group: Peppers Playgound
Website: www.pepperwinters.com

ABOUT THE AUTHOR

After chasing her dreams to become a full-time writer, Pepper has earned recognition with awards for best Dark Romance, best BDSM Series, and best Hero. She's an multiple #1 iBooks bestseller, along with #1 in Erotic Romance, Romantic Suspense, Contemporary, and Erotica Thriller. She's also honoured to wear the IndieReader Badge for being a Top 10 Indie Bestseller.

Pepper is a Hybrid Author of both Traditional and Self-published work. Her Pure Corruption Series was released by Grand Central, Hachette. She signed with Trident Media and her books have sold in multiple languages around the world.

On a personal note, Pepper has recently returned to horse riding after a sixteen year break and now owns a magnificent black gelding called Sonny. He's an ex-pacer standardbred who has been retrained into a happy hacking, dressage, and show jumping pony. If she's not writing, she's riding.

The other man in her life is her best-friend and hubby who she fell in love with at first sight. He never proposed and they ended up married as part of a bet, but after eleven years and countless adventures and fun, she's a sucker for romance as she lives the fairy-tale herself.

Printed in the USA
CPSIA information can be obtained
at www.ICGtesting.com
JSHW031707140824
68134JS00038B/3559